Found Wanting

Other Five Star Titles by Joyce Lamb:

Caught in the Act
Relative Strangers

Found Wanting

JOYCE LAMB

Five Star • Waterville, Maine

This novel is a work of fiction. Names, characters, places and incidents are either the product of the author's imagination, or, if real, used fictitiously.

First Edition
First Printing: September 2004

Published in 2004 in conjunction with Tekno Books and Ed Gorman.

Set in 11 pt. Plantin by Christina S. Huff.

Printed in the United States on permanent paper.

Library of Congress Cataloging-in-Publication Data

Lamb, Joyce, 1965–
Found wanting / by Joyce Lamb.—1st ed.
p. cm.
ISBN 1-59414-180-0 (hc : alk. paper)
1. Private investigators—Fiction. 2. Mothers and sons—Fiction. 3. Missing children—Fiction. 4. Single mothers—Fiction. 5. Millionaires—Fiction. 6. Birthfathers—Fiction. I. Title.
PS3612.A546F68 2004
813′.6—dc22 2004045114

For Mary,
whose incredible friendship has never been found wanting.

Acknowledgements

I am blessed with a very special family and many helpful friends:

My mother, Pat Lamb, is an amazing woman who has always been there for me.

My brother and his family—Glenn, Di, Danielle, Michael, Nikole and Zach—keep me young.

I have excellent writing and reading experts who tell me the truth (I think): Lisa Kiplinger, Lisa Hitt, Ann Brooking, Ruth Chamberlain, Karen Feldman, Chris and Mary Clay, Chantelle Mansfield, Susan Tollefson, Diane Amos and Joan Goodman.

Julie Snider and Cheryl Turnbull generously share their time and talent.

Patrick Olsen and Jennifer Mesenbrink provided some valuable information. Thanks!

Special thanks to Tim Loehrke, for so generously sharing his picture-taking skills, and Tracy Lucht and Mark Miller, for being such good sports about being handcuffed together only minutes after meeting for the first time.

My editor, Russell Davis, rocks!

And I'm eternally grateful to my agents, Kay Kidde and Kristen Fuhs.

Acknowledgements

Prologue

When the doorbell rang, Alaina stopped dusting, slightly annoyed at the interruption. She had only begun cleaning, and because it was one of her least favorite things to do, it had been hard to get motivated. Pausing at the stereo to turn down Bruce Springsteen's *Born to Run*, she mentally prepared the usual excuses as she went to the door.

"I bought from the kid down the street."

"My child is selling them, too."

"Have all the magazines I need, thanks."

"My higher power is chocolate."

But when she opened the door to the icy Colorado air, she wasn't prepared for the woman shivering on her porch. She had not seen her in nine years, had thought she would never see her again.

The woman, overcome by emotion, threw her arms around Alaina. Alaina didn't hug her back. Instead, she pulled her mother into the apartment and, after scanning the quiet apartment complex to see whether they had been observed, shut the door. Her hands on her mother's arms, Alaina gave her a slight shake. "How did you find me? Were you followed?"

"Followed? Why would I be followed?"

"Just answer me. How did you find me?" She checked her watch. Jonah was due home from school in half an hour.

"A private detective found you." Seeming to regain her

composure, Eve smiled through her tears and grasped Alaina's face in her palms. "Look at you. You're so grown-up, so beautiful." Tears welled again. "Your father's eyes."

Alaina noticed that the past nine years had ruthlessly aged her mother. She was only in her middle fifties, but she looked eighty, her face creased and sagging with exhaustion. Last time Alaina had seen her, her hair had been a chestnut brown, but now it was pure white. And bags underscored her sad, faded blue eyes.

"What private detective, Mother? Someone you hired?"

"Yes, of course. Someone I hired."

"Did you tell anyone you were coming to see me?"

"No. I told them I had a fund-raising conference." Eve was the wife of a corporate CEO, and she'd chosen charity as her career, using the power and influence of her husband to benefit the underprivileged.

"What about Addison?"

"No, I didn't tell your sister."

Alaina turned away, jammed a hand through her hair. Another look at the clock. Twenty-five minutes before Jonah was due. Ten minutes earlier, and she could have picked him up at school before he got on the bus.

It didn't matter that her mother said she had told no one. They would have to move—again. Resigned, she went into Jonah's bedroom, grabbed the suitcase out of his closet and started throwing in clothes. Her hands were shaking, her heart hammering. She didn't think, just plowed through the same routine she had plowed through only a year before in Madison, Wisconsin.

"What are you doing, Ali?" Eve asked from Jonah's bedroom door, then she seemed to notice the room, and her expression turned wistful. "Where is my grandson?"

Ali. She hadn't been called that in nine years. Because she

wasn't that person anymore. Alaina glanced at her mother, saw that her eyes had teared up, then went back to her furious packing. Eve had never understood and never would, so Alaina didn't bother trying to explain.

"It's time for you to come home, Ali," Eve said. "It's time for you to bring Jonah home."

Alaina stopped packing to stare at her mother. "And you think all will be forgotten the minute I walk in the door?"

Eve's lower lip trembled. "I miss you. Your father misses you."

Alaina snorted. "Yeah, right."

Eve stepped into the room. "We'll work it out. Your father—"

Alaina whirled on her. "I can never come home, Mother. I'm a fugitive. The minute I show up, I'll be arrested." She snapped the suitcase closed, dropped it by the door and went into her own bedroom to begin emptying drawers.

Eve, looking appalled, followed. "I don't understand why you would think that. Yes, you made mistakes, but there's no—"

"Hello, ladies."

Whirling from the closet, Alaina saw him blocking the door. She didn't waste time on surprise or fear. She just lunged for the bedside table, fumbled with the drawer and had the gun in her hand before he could grab her. Cocking it, she aimed it at his chest, praying he wouldn't call the bluff. There wasn't a bullet in the house.

Layton Keller raised his hands, palms out, a relaxed smile on his lips. Alaina's finger flexed on the trigger, and for a moment, she wished for bullets. She and Jonah would never have to run again.

Eve stared at her daughter in astonishment. "What on earth are you doing?"

"Don't come any closer," Alaina said to Layton. "I'll shoot."

Layton's smile spread. "Sure you will." He was as handsome as ever. Blond hair and blue eyes, square jaw and perfect, white teeth. He worked out regularly, not an ounce of fat on his hard, lean body. She remembered his strength, remembered how powerless she'd been beneath him. The gun started to shake, and she braced it with both hands.

"Would you mind leaving Alaina and me alone? There's something we need to talk about," he said to Eve, ever the gentleman. He had won over hundreds with his charm and good looks. He knew how to get what he wanted, and if he didn't get it, he took it. By brute force.

When Eve didn't move, Layton tossed car keys at her. "My car is parked out front. Why don't you go wait in it? We'll be out in just a few minutes."

Eve glanced at her daughter, clearly shocked by the weapon in Alaina's hands.

"Just go," Alaina said, not wanting her mother to get caught in any crossfire.

Eve backed out of the room, and Layton kicked the door shut behind her. "Alone at last," he said, grinning. "I've missed you, Ali. I've missed your fire, your passion." He positioned himself in front of the door, the only escape route. "When does he get home?" he asked.

She gauged she had fifteen minutes before her nine-year-old son charged through the door. "He's staying at a friend's house until tomorrow."

"You're a terrible liar. Pity that no one ever saw that but me." He stepped toward her, his grin broadening when she edged back. "No bullets, huh?"

She threw the gun at his head. He ducked, charged her. She had nowhere to go. He caught her around the middle, threw her onto the bed and, as she tried to scrabble away, straddled her. The air lodged in her chest, and Alaina fought the violent memory of him on top of her a decade ago. She clawed at his face and got only air. He backhanded her twice before she lay still, stunned and tasting blood.

Breathing heavily, he pinned her hands on either side of her head. "Ah, memories."

He nuzzled her neck, and panic choked her. Not again. God, not again.

"You changed your perfume," he said near her ear. "I like it much better than that cheap, lemony scent you used to wear."

Biting back the fear, she tried to focus on figuring out how to get him out of the house.

He smiled down at her, his eyes as empty and cold as ever. "What? You don't recall our night together as fondly as I do? Then perhaps a reenactment is in order." With one hand, he ripped her blouse open.

Alaina shrieked in rage, gnashed her teeth, snarled at him. Her fist glanced off his temple before he restrained it again. Rearing up, she slammed the top of her head into his chin and saw stars. He grunted once before toppling sideways off the bed. Alaina didn't comprehend what had happened until she saw her mother standing over him with a heavy, cast-iron skillet held high in one hand, ready to nail him again if he moved.

Rolling off the other side of the bed, Alaina gained her feet for only a moment before her knees buckled. She caught herself against the dresser. She was going to be sick. Dammit, no time, no time. Still, the room was spinning, turning gray.

Then Eve was beside her. "Put your head between your knees."

Alaina pushed her mother away.

Only when the strength drained out of Alaina's limbs was Eve able to shove her daughter's head down. As the blood flowed back into her brain, Alaina took several deep breaths. She saw Layton sprawled beside the bed. "Is he dead?"

"He's breathing," Eve said.

Alaina pushed to her feet. "Jonah will be here any minute." She looked down at her shredded blouse. Yanking it off, she replaced it with a T-shirt from the dresser. Her hands weren't steady. She couldn't think, didn't know what to do next.

Then the front door banged open, and his voice called out to her. "Mom!"

The moment snapped back into place. Alaina looked at her mother, saw tears on her face. "We have to go."

Eve nodded, her eyes sober. "I understand."

Alaina thought she really did. After so many years, so many lies. All it had taken was seeing her son-in-law in action. Her fear for Jonah propelled her toward the door, but she didn't know what to say to her mother.

Eve waved her on. "Hurry. Don't let him see this." She nodded at Layton. "I'll make sure he stays put."

Alaina intercepted Jonah in the hallway. He was grinning, his blond hair wind-tousled, his beautiful blue eyes bright with excitement. When he saw her, his grin faded. "What happened to your face?" he asked.

Alaina hugged him. "I'm okay, sweetie. I'm okay."

"Are we moving again?" he asked, his voice wavering.

She nodded, unable to speak. Already, he knew the routine. It broke her heart.

She sent him after the suitcase in his room and tried to plan. But there wasn't time. They would get in the car and go.

Where didn't matter. Just going mattered. They would start another new life in another new place where they would be safe again.

At least for a while.

Chapter 1

Five years later

"Looks like a doozy of a storm's rolling in," Rachel Boyd said as she cupped a hand around a lighter and touched flame to the tip of her Virginia Slim.

From their vantage point on the roof of the Tribune building, Alaina looked to the west, saw the rolling clouds that looked black because the sun still shone. Lightning flashed among them. The weather was unseasonably warm—in the upper sixties—for Chicago at the end of March, and WGN's chief meteorologist had announced the night before that a cold front was moving in, stirring up severe thunderstorms. The month was not going to go out like a lamb.

At the moment, Alaina and her co-worker were escaping the bustling newsroom so Rachel could take a smoke break. Alaina shielded her eyes against the sun as she glanced at her friend. Gorgeous. That's what she thought when she looked at Rachel. She had the presence of a movie star, a charisma that ingratiated her to others and intimidated them at the same time.

Alaina envied Rachel's curves, her short, naturally curly, blond hair, and her sky-blue eyes. Next to Rachel, Alaina felt like a boy. A dull one at that. Her own body was small and compact, athletic. Where Rachel looked soft and feminine, Alaina was firm and toned. She worked hard to stay in shape, believing that when it came time to run again—either from Layton or the feds—she had to be in tip-top physical condition. Her hair, so dark it was nearly black, was no-nonsense, falling straight to her shoulders without a wave in sight.

It was good, she had decided long ago, that she didn't look like Rachel, who could have never blended into a crowd.

The two women met five years ago on Alaina's first day as a copy editor. She'd had a new name, a new home, a new job and a resolve to keep her distance. Getting close to co-workers, neighbors or other parents at Jonah's school wasn't an option after she'd found out the hard way what could happen to people she cared about. She'd had no problem sticking to that rule in Colorado. But Rachel had been hungry for a buddy in a newsroom dominated by fortysomethings and married couples. She had pursued Alaina like a potential mate, inviting her to lunch, dinner and on breaks at every opportunity. Rachel was so engaging, so fun, and Alaina was so lonely, that eventually she was the one seeking out her new friend. She reasoned that the friendship would stay within the confines of work, that Rachel would not be at risk that way.

Then one night, after Alaina had dodged invitations to movies and other social activities for six months, Rachel had shown up at her apartment with takeout Thai and a video of Terminator. The instant Jonah had ambled into the living room, Rachel fell head over heels for him. She quickly became the aunt Jonah had never had, and Alaina hadn't been able to deny him, or herself. She still kept a certain distance. For instance, she'd turned down Rachel's offer to share a townhouse to cut down on expenses. While she had appreciated the suggestion, Alaina had worried that such proximity to her and Jonah would have been too great a risk for Rachel.

"Hey, Alex. Earth to Alex."

Alaina glanced up. Even after so many years of answering

to the different name, it still caught her off guard sometimes. "I'm sorry. What?"

"I asked what you and Jonah are doing for dinner," Rachel said as she blew out smoke. "Assuming you're not stuck here too much longer."

Alaina checked her watch. A computer network crash had thrown her schedule off by at least an hour. "I'm picking him up at Lucas's for our Wednesday night out. Want to go?"

"I think you should ask Lucas's dad to go," Rachel said, wiggling her eyebrows. "He's such a hottie."

Alaina rolled her eyes. "You're worse than Jonah. He keeps hinting at what a great dad Grant is to Lucas and how much I'd like him if I got to know him more."

Rachel beamed. "That's my Jonah. He's looking out for you."

"Maybe I don't need to be looked out for."

"I think you do. And you can't blame me for wanting my best friend to get laid. You're too uptight all the time."

"Please."

"Trust me," Rachel said, "sex is therapeutic. I would know. I've needed a lot of therapy in my thirty-two years. So what's the matter with him?"

Alaina laughed. "Nothing."

"Well, it can't be that dark wavy hair or those gorgeous green eyes. And there's no doubt he works out, judging by the way his ribbed shirts hug his pecs. Too much emotional baggage?"

Alaina shrugged. "Some. His wife died a couple years ago."

"What's he do again?"

"He's some kind of big executive at Boeing."

"Hmm," Rachel mused. "Rich, handsome and widowed. For God's sake, leap on him."

"I don't leap."

"Hell, when it comes to men, you don't even take baby steps." Rachel flicked away her cigarette. "Whoever the asshole was, I hope he rots in hell."

The venom in her friend's voice surprised Alaina. "Excuse me?"

"The chump who made you afraid of men. Jonah's father, I presume."

Uncomfortable, Alaina curled her fingers around the railing that edged the roof. This was shaky ground, and she was not sure how to navigate it. She had not shared her history with Rachel. She didn't see the point. "I'm not afraid—"

"Alex."

They both looked toward the co-worker who had stuck her head out the roof access door. "A couple guys in the lobby are asking to see you. They're flashing FBI badges."

Rachel shot Alaina a look of feigned shock. "You wanted by the law?" she asked.

Alaina didn't acknowledge the joke, her heart thundering as she started for the door. "I have to go." She paused, wanting to tell Rachel that she wouldn't be back, that they likely would never see each other again. "Take care."

As she walked away, she heard Rachel call her name—or rather, the name she had adopted half a decade ago—but didn't look back.

It surprised her that after all this time the FBI was still searching for her and Jonah. It surprised her more that it had taken them so long to track her down.

As she raced to gather up her purse and jacket, she wondered how much time she had. It would take her at least an hour to get to Mount Prospect, where Jonah was with Lucas. The knot in her stomach tightened as she wondered how long ago the feds had found her. If it had been days, they might already know where Jonah was. They might have already gotten to him.

As she hurried outside, fat raindrops began to splatter the pavement. The Metra train station was a twenty-minute walk from the newspaper. Pausing impatiently on the street corner, she figured she could run it in five. The "don't walk" sign blared red. Glancing up the street, she blinked against the driving rain, saw no traffic coming, and stepped off the curb.

Approaching the street corner, Mitch Kane hunched his shoulders against the torrential rain. He'd been downright toasty inside the coffee bar next to the Tribune building, only mildly curious about the break in her routine. Usually, she would be out with her son by now. That was the Wednesday routine: work early, pick up her son at the home of his friend, go out for dinner, then participate in some kind of activity together. Last week, they'd kicked a soccer ball around at a local park. The week before, the two had chowed down at a neighborhood pizza joint, then caught an early evening showing of the latest Tom Cruise action flick.

Today was different, though he didn't know what had made it different. All he knew was that she had just raced out of the newspaper, agitated and in such a hurry that he'd feared he would lose her before he got himself outside.

Pausing behind her, careful to keep his gaze away from her very attractive backside, he took the opportunity to regret leaving behind the coffee he'd been nursing.

And then she dashed into the street.

He saw the car coming and shouted a warning. But it was too late.

Her body hurtled almost gracefully across the hood of the

car and struck the windshield. Momentum arrested, her body reversed direction, tumbling off the hood and landing with a splash in the street.

Mitch, shouting at stricken bystanders to call 911, was the first to get to her. She was on her side, her dark hair streaming across her face, blood from a scrape on her forehead mixing with the rain.

He expected her to be unconscious, but as he knelt beside her, she rolled onto her back. Seeing her eyes open—a striking light gray-green—startled him, and for a heart-stopping instant, he thought she was dead. But then she blinked and focused on his face.

"Don't approach her. Don't talk to her. Just tell me when you find her."

He'd been paid well to follow those guidelines, but under the circumstances he couldn't turn away.

He heard her draw in a wheezing breath, then another, as raindrops struck her face and ran in rivulets over her cheeks. She gave no indication of pain, her eyes glazed with shock. Her fingers sank into his jacket and gripped. "Help me . . ."

He patted her hand. "Just take it easy. It'll be okay."

Sirens began to shriek in the distance, but the day suddenly seemed preternaturally quiet as Mitch gazed down at her face and felt her fingers clasp his. Her lips moved. He leaned close, and rain dripped from his hair and face and onto hers. Drops that clung to her eyelashes splattered when she blinked in slow motion. She was trying to tell him something.

He lowered his ear to her lips to hear better.

"Help . . . me . . . up."

"You need to stay still," he said, stripping off his jacket and spreading it over her. Giving her what he hoped was a reassuring smile, he stroked his hand over her wet hair. "Hang on. Help is coming."

The driver of the car dropped to his knees on the other side of her. "Is she okay? Oh, Jesus, I didn't even see her. She ran right out in front of me."

"Alex!"

Mitch glanced up to see a blond woman wedging her way through the crowd of onlookers. "Alex!" She fell to her knees next to Mitch, her hands shaking as she started to touch her fallen friend, seemed to think better of it and instead covered her mouth with both hands. "Oh God, oh God."

The driver of the car began to babble. "I couldn't stop. I didn't see her. She ran out in front of me."

"Jonah."

The name snapped the woman out of her hysteria, and she leaned over her, oblivious to the muddy water soaking her linen slacks. "What? Talk to me, Alex. What can I do?"

"Get Jonah." Her teeth started to chatter.

The blond woman nodded. "Yes, of course. I'll get him. Don't worry."

"Now. Get him . . . now."

"Step aside, people, let us through."

Paramedics had arrived. Rising, Mitch stepped back, drawing the blond woman up with him. She started to protest, but he said, "Let them do their jobs."

She wouldn't back away more than a few steps, her gaze glued to the paramedics as they set their equipment down, removed Mitch's shielding jacket from Alaina and went to work.

Mitch bent to retrieve his jacket, and between the medical workers, he could see Alaina staring intently at her friend. Her lips moved, formed a word that made his stomach muscles clench, and then her eyes rolled back.

Please.

Chapter 2

"We were too late."

Addison Keller sank onto the black leather chair by the phone. Her hand that gripped the receiver was damp with sweat. "What do you mean, too late?" she asked.

"Your sister bolted before we could get to her, but we'll have her in protective custody before the day is done."

"I told you this was delicate, that she'd run."

"Yes, I know. But something spooked her before we got to her, and she took off."

"And my nephew? Where is he?"

"We're also checking into that."

Her stomach did a flip. "You don't know?"

"We'll find out."

"You assured me that this wouldn't happen."

"We're doing the best we can, Mrs. Keller."

"I don't want you to do your best. I want you to do whatever it takes to protect them. That was the deal."

She punched the off button on the phone but didn't put it down. This was what powerlessness felt like, she thought. She was dependent on others to handle something very important to her, and if they screwed it up, there wasn't a damn thing she could do about it. She couldn't reprimand anyone or fire them. She was at the mercy of their incompetence.

Looking around at her dream house, with its sleek black furnishings, white marble floors and walls, glass and chrome tables and lamps, she took no pleasure in it. At one time, it had mattered to her that the house was perched on a hill in an exclusive Alexandria, Virginia, community that overlooked the Potomac River and Washington, D.C. A high, black, iron gate and fence kept unsavory characters off two acres of the most expensive land in the area. Unfortunately, she had discovered—quite by accident—that one of the most unsavory characters of all shared her bed.

She was still sitting there, nervous and fuming, when Layton walked in, a bounce in his step that had not been there that morning. He smiled as he paused before her, a drink in his hand that might have been alcohol or water.

"What's the trouble?" he asked.

She set the cordless phone back on its charger, concentrating on keeping her hand steady. "No trouble."

"You look stressed, dear. I don't like it when you look stressed."

She forced herself to smile as she helped herself to the glass in his hand. A sip told her it was water. She had hoped for alcohol. "You, on the other hand, look happier than you have in days," she said. "Weeks, actually."

Six weeks, to be exact. That was how long it had been since her father had died at the hands of a mugger while out for a morning jog. His will had changed Layton, who apparently had expected that he and Addison would inherit the entire estate, not the least of which was a software company worth several million dollars. It wasn't an unreasonable expectation. PCware would never have grown into the company it was if Layton had not devoted himself to it—and his father-in-law—years before.

But Paul Chancellor, for all his hard-ass, hell-bent ways, apparently had a soft spot that no one had suspected. He'd left one-third of everything to his youngest daughter and the grandson he had not seen since he was a newborn.

Reclaiming his water from Addison, Layton drained it with a clink of ice cubes. "You're right," he said. "I am happier."

"Care to share?"

He cocked his head, blond hair falling across his forehead. "Not yet. Celebrating too early could jinx my plan."

"A plan," she said, her tone casual even as her nerves tightened. "That sounds promising."

"Oh, yes. Promising, it is."

She pushed her lower lip out in a pout. "And you're going to make me wait? That hardly seems fair."

"This is too good to spoil, my dear. I prefer to knock your socks off when the time is right." He kissed her on the cheek before heading for the door. "I have some work to do."

Addison watched him go, resisting the urge to throw something at his back. Alone, she crossed to the black-lacquered bar, poured herself a goblet of red wine and swallowed most of it in one gulp. The mirrored wall behind the bar reflected her image back at her, and she narrowed her eyes in disdain.

In a year, she would be forty. And she looked it. Gray was seeping into black hair that sported an artificial sheen. Lines creased the skin around gray eyes that bore just a hint of green. Magazine articles had described her chin as sharp, her nose as pointed and her body as too thin. But her eyes were intelligent, her cheekbones the envy of models everywhere. She'd taken the good with the bad and smiled her way through the endless stream of philanthropic breakfasts, lunches, dinners, auctions and benefits. That was part of being the wife of a corporate CEO, just like her mother had been.

On the surface, she and Layton had it all—money, prestige, influence—thanks to the powerhouse that was PCware.

But there was something else that Layton wanted, something she—and all the money and power they had—couldn't give him.

A son.

Several doctors and every fertility drug available had made no difference. She'd endured procedure after procedure, treatment after treatment, with no results.

Compounding the pain and frustration for them both was that another woman had given Layton a son. And not only had she taken his son away, but she and her child had inherited a third of everything that Layton had worked so hard to build.

But none of that justified the phone conversation Addison had overheard less than a month ago.

"Kill the bitch and bring the kid to me."

She'd approached Layton's study door to check on him. He'd been at work far longer than was usual, and she'd gotten worried. Plus, she'd wanted to talk to him again about adopting. He'd shot down the idea before, but she wasn't willing to give up so easily.

But those words—"Kill the bitch and bring the kid to me"—spoken in a tone that she'd never heard her husband use, changed her world.

Kill the bitch.

She wanted desperately to have heard wrong.

But she knew in her gut that she hadn't. She had prayed for fifteen years that she was right about Layton, that he was everything she thought he was, everything that he seemed to be.

"Kill the bitch and bring the kid to me."

Now she knew she was wrong.

"Can you hear me, Alex?"

Pain rolled over her in pulsing, white torrents. Alaina

struggled to stay above it even as darkness threatened to close over her head.

A young man's face swam into view. He had the greenest eyes she'd ever seen. "I'm Dr. Marks, Alex," he said. "Do you know where you are?"

She couldn't move. Panic tumbled with the pain, like tennis shoes in a dryer. Both the panic and the pain were blinding.

"I need you to relax, Alex," Dr. Marks said, his voice soothing. "The paramedics put you in a neck brace and strapped you to a backboard as a precaution."

He asked her questions, poking her with a pin in various spots, while nurses in gauzy yellow protective clothing buzzed around her, like bees without the black stripes and stingers.

Alaina tried to concentrate on the doctor's voice, but the pain was so intense, she couldn't think over it, couldn't breathe. The blood roared in her ears as black spots splattered her vision and grew. She fought them off, clinging to consciousness. She didn't have time for this. She had to get to Jonah before the feds did.

Someone shined a light into her eyes as Dr. Marks, leaning over her, released her from the backboard. "Looks like the worst of it is a dislocated shoulder, Alex. We're going to give you something for the pain, get you out of the neck brace, then slip the joint back into place."

Out of the corner of her eye, Alaina saw a nurse with a syringe. Alarm sank its teeth in.

"Something for the pain."

She couldn't get herself and Jonah out of town if she was drugged.

She grabbed the nurse's wrist, aware of how pathetically weak her grip was. "No."

Startled, the woman recoiled. Dr. Marks put a hand on Alaina's arm, his brow creased with concern. "It's morphine, Alex. It'll make you feel better."

She forced herself to be calm, to appear reasonable, even as agony sliced reason to shreds. "I don't want it."

"You need it," the doctor said.

"I don't want it," she repeated, her voice thin and hoarse.

"Put it away," he said to the nurse, then placed a gentle hand on Alaina's forehead, his fingers warm through a latex glove. "This is going to hurt like hell. You'll probably pass out."

But when she resurfaced, she thought, her head would be clear.

He searched her eyes, his gaze kind and concerned. "Are you sure about this?"

"Do it."

"On the count of three."

He put pressure on her arm, and she writhed, trying to get away from him, escape the torment. Nausea rolled through her in undulating waves.

"One. Two." He jerked, and the joint snapped back into place as Alaina slid down into a black hole.

"She's coming back."

Alaina blinked up at the two faces above her, pain now a steady but tolerable throb in her shoulder. The cacophony that had filled her ears was gone. So were her clothes. A sheet and blanket were tucked around her.

"Alex?"

She focused on the doctor with the green eyes. He had a sweet face, the kind that would make it easy to confide in him. "Do you remember what happened to you?" he asked.

"Car got in my way."

He smiled. "That shoulder's going to be a pain, especially if you don't let me give you something to help you out."

"No, thanks."

"Do you have a history of drug abuse?"

"No."

Baffled, he made a note on a chart. "I don't get too many patients who turn down a good dose of morphine."

"Sorry." Feeling groggy, she wondered if they'd slipped her something anyway. They'd certainly managed to strip her fast enough. "How long was I out?"

"About ten minutes. Your clothes were wet, and we needed to get a good look at you to make sure we didn't miss anything."

Slotting the chart at the end of the gurney, he patted her uninjured arm. "We'll have to stabilize that shoulder, but the good news is there's no evidence you hit your head. You might have a couple cracked ribs, so we're going to get some X-rays. All in all, though, I'd say you were a very lucky woman today, Alex."

Chapter 3

Sitting at a stoplight in rush-hour traffic, Mitch rubbed his hands together in an effort to get them warm. He wasn't sure what to do. Technically, he needed to call his boss and tell him what had happened and where she was. But something about it all made him uneasy.

He'd worked for Layton Keller for two years, doing background checks on potential PCware executives. He liked Keller. The man didn't treat him like an employee. He talked to Mitch as one man to another. When Keller had asked him to track down the son who had been kidnapped fourteen years before by his mother, Mitch had been floored.

Keller had chuckled at his look of shock. "Not what you expected, huh?"

"I didn't know . . ." Mitch trailed off, unsure how to respond. He felt a sudden affinity with the man. He hadn't seen his own son in three years, and while his ex-wife had not kidnapped the boy, she had made it very difficult to see him. Tyler was four the last time Mitch saw him, just before his ex-wife moved to another state with him. Mitch acknowledged that it was mostly his own fault that he had not seen Tyler in so long. But Shirley had made every visit so arduous, so painful, that Mitch had given up trying. It wasn't something he was proud of.

"I made a mistake," Keller said. "I was young and stupid and easily manipulated. The mother . . . this is difficult to say . . . but the mother of my son is my wife's sister."

That surprised Mitch, too, and for a moment, his image of Keller shifted. What kind of man slept with two sisters, got one pregnant and still managed to be married to the other? The scenario was incongruous with the man Mitch thought he knew.

Seeming to sense the waver in Mitch's opinion, Keller said quickly, "It happened while Addy and I were engaged. Quite a bit of alcohol was involved." He gave a rueful smile. "We've all had moments like that, haven't we?"

"I suppose," Mitch said, relaxing some. As a young man, he'd had his own alcohol-related bouts of stupidity. For some people, some bouts were worse than others.

"After much apologizing and groveling," Keller went on, "I was damn lucky Addy forgave me. Unfortunately, once the child was born, things got . . . ugly. There was a custody fight. I won't go into the details except to say that I won. But my sister-in-law kidnapped him, and I haven't seen my son since."

"I'm sorry, Mr. Keller."

"Please, call me Layton. I feel we've become friends. I trust you, Mitch."

"All right."

"I've kept this business low-key over the years, mainly because . . . well, not only would the press have a field day, but it's painful." He paused, sipping from a glass of fizzy water on his desk. "I'd like to continue to keep all of this as low-key as possible."

"I understand."

"The truth is, I've had several private investigators searching over the years." He slid a folder across the glossy surface of the desk toward Mitch. "These are their reports, paltry as they are. My sister-in-law is a shrewd, ruthless woman. The only man who managed to track her down earned a knife in the gut. He's dead."

Mitch grimaced.

"Right," Keller said. "Not the kind of woman around whom you'd want to let down your guard."

"What about the FBI? I assume they've been looking for her, too?"

Keller shifted, just slightly, as if the question made him uneasy. "Actually, no. It's probably difficult for you to understand, given the circumstances, but my father-in-law was an intensely private man."

Mitch nodded. He'd met the late Paul Chancellor once. The exchange hadn't been significant enough for him to get a sense of the man, but he'd heard he was a strict boss with a penchant for micromanaging. Word was that while his passing at the hands of a mugger had been tragic, few PCware employees would miss his overbearing ways.

"When Alaina took off with my son," Keller went on, "my father-in-law insisted that the situation be handled within the family. He didn't want Alaina to be arrested and charged with kidnapping if she was found. Yes, she's a troubled woman, but she's not a danger to society and he couldn't bear for her to go to jail."

Mitch interpreted that to mean Chancellor was such a prig that he hadn't wanted unsavory publicity, and a felon in the family would have been highly objectionable. "You said she killed one of your detectives. In my eyes, that makes her plenty dangerous. Aren't the feds looking for her for that?"

"Well, to be honest, that case is unsolved. Alaina had assumed another identity when it happened, and because her fingerprints had never been on file before then, she was never connected to that."

Mitch nodded, understanding. "And to avoid connecting her, you didn't 'fess up to employing the man she killed."

"To protect Alaina, yes."

"To protect Alaina," Mitch repeated, one eyebrow arched.

"To protect the family," Keller conceded. "Look, I'm not proud of any of this. It's a scandal of epic proportions if the media ever get wind of it. I'm taking a huge risk sharing this information with you, Mitch." He paused, sipped more water, as if giving Mitch time to think. After putting the glass down, Keller leaned back in his chair and steepled his fingers under his chin. "Are you interested in the job?"

Mitch didn't hesitate. He was always up for a challenge, and this one sounded especially enticing. "Sure, I'm interested."

Keller gestured at the folder on the desk. "There's a picture of her in there. It was taken about a year before she took off, so I don't know how much it will help."

As Mitch flipped open the folder, he hoped his boss couldn't read his shock. The girl in the professionally taken photo looked like she couldn't have been more than seventeen, her cheeks rosy, her eyes bright with laughter. She was striking, to be sure, with almost-black hair that fell past her shoulders and eerie gray-green eyes that conveyed a mischievous glint.

"She looks young," Keller said.

Mitch glanced up to find the man watching him carefully, as if gauging his response.

Keller smirked. "Don't let her looks fool you. She's not innocent. If you find her, you'll understand how, as a naïve young man, I could be so weak." He waved a well-manicured hand before Mitch could respond. "I'm not making excuses, of course. I admit it takes two to screw up as royally as Alaina and I did. But the truth is, I want to put all that behind us and move on. I want to give my son the life he deserves, build a relationship with him and be his role model. It's very important to me to have an heir." He paused for a moment, studying Mitch. "I'm a thorough man," he went on. "I don't hire people without checking them out. I know we have something in common."

"My son wasn't kidnapped, Mr. Keller."

"No, but I'm sure you understand my desire to connect with my child, the helplessness I feel because he's been kept from me. That feeling has been heightened since my father-in-law passed away."

"I understand."

Keller nodded. "This is why I want you working for me, Mitch. You get it. And you're damn good at what you do. I respect that."

Mitch knew when he was being stroked and figured that meant Keller had said all he planned to. Rising, he extended his hand. "I'll do what I can to find your heir, Mr. Keller. It might take some time, though."

But it didn't take nearly as much time as Mitch had expected.

Alaina Chancellor had done a fine job of disappearing. An amateur detective might have struggled tracking her down. But she hadn't done anything spectacularly clever. At least, not anything that a professional couldn't have figured out.

Which was why, while observing mother and son from a distance, Mitch began to carefully study the reports from the other detectives. They were pedestrian, some of them not even making sense. It quickly became obvious that none of the investigators had tried very hard to locate Alaina and Jonah. In fact, they'd barely made any effort at all. He couldn't even tell which reports came from the PI she'd supposedly killed—he'd hoped for some clues in that one, seeing as how that man had been the only one to actually find her. But all the reports were the same. Dead ends everywhere.

He could understand how one or two might have milked the job. But four? It made no sense. Especially considering the level of Layton Keller's influence. He no doubt would have handsomely rewarded the detective who delivered his son to him. The man would have been a hero, a media sensation.

Increasingly uneasy, Mitch kept the news to himself that he'd found the mother and son, preferring to think the situation through before making a move. In the meantime, he noted that the boy appeared well-adjusted and happy, lacking the usual sullenness of a teenager. The interaction between mother and son was easy, comfortable, even playful. It was clear that they respected each other, loved each other. The thought of shattering the teen's life nagged at Mitch.

As did Alaina's frantic dash just before the accident. What had she been running from? Or perhaps to? Her adamance that her friend go get Jonah right away had been desperate. Mitch understood a mother being protective—he felt protective of the kid himself—but there was another level to it, a fear that seemed almost irrational. And Mitch wasn't about to let anything happen to Jonah on his watch.

It was dark, and rain was still falling by the time he steered his car onto the street where Grant Maxwell lived with his teenage son, Lucas, who seemed to be Jonah's closest friend. Mitch had followed Alaina to the Maxwells' home several times in the past weeks as she had picked up her son or dropped him off. The past two Wednesdays, she had picked him up after her early shift at work. Mitch figured it was a good bet that she had intended for this Wednesday to be no different than the two before it.

Seeing flashing red lights, Mitch parked a block up and took in the two squad cars parked in front of the Maxwells' home. An ambulance, lights blazing, siren screaming, sped by him, away from the house.

Mitch began to sweat.

Chapter 4

Alaina sat on the gurney in a hospital-issue gown, her bare legs dangling, one hand tightly gripping the edge of the mattress, the other cradled gingerly in her lap.

About ten minutes ago, the ER staff had determined her injuries were not life-threatening and moved her to a tiny room by herself to await her turn after the more critical patients.

Alaina, much of her body feeling bruised, was beginning to regret her refusal of the pain medication. But she would have regretted a fuzzy head more. All in all, she didn't feel as bad as she would have expected after being hit by a car. The vehicle had been stopping, so it hadn't struck her that hard. The worst injury, as far as she could tell, was the dislocated shoulder, which, the doctor had told her, would probably be susceptible to dislocation in the future if she wasn't careful, at least until it had healed. Her ribs had taken some abuse, as well, but none felt broken.

She knew she was lucky. Very lucky. And with Rachel picking up Jonah—

"Hey." Rachel peered around the edge of the door. "You decent?"

Alaina's spirits soared, all pain forgotten. She hadn't expected her friend to return so quickly with Jonah. "Yes, come in." Now, all she had to do was get out of here, and they could get home, collect some belongings and the documentation for the identities she'd been building for the past several years for just such an occasion, and hit the road. Where would they go next?

Stepping into the room, Rachel dropped her brown leather bag on the floor near a sterile-looking metal stool on wheels, then looked Alaina over. "Nice jams."

Alaina glanced at the door, which Rachel had left open a crack. Was he behind it, feeling shy or worried about how she might look? "Jonah?"

"Oh," Rachel said, waving a dismissive hand. "I wanted to make sure you're okay before I go get him."

For a moment, Alaina couldn't breathe. Her heart felt like a balloon that someone had thoughtlessly pricked with a pin. "He's not with you?"

"I didn't want him to be scared." Bending, Rachel slipped her cell phone out of her purse on the floor. "What's his cell phone number? We'll call him right now."

The room began to whirl, and Alaina fought the dizziness. "I asked you to pick him up."

"Yeah, and then you were unconscious," Rachel said. "What was I supposed to tell the poor kid? That you'd been hit by a car and I didn't know what kind of shape you were in? He would have freaked. And, frankly, I wasn't in any shape to drive after seeing you lying there like that . . ." Her voice cracked, and she trailed off. "I guess I needed a little time to freak myself." She grasped Alaina's hand, squeezed. "You scared—"

Rachel broke off as a nurse opened the door. "Alex Myers?"

Alaina looked at the woman, her brain unable to process anything other than how to get to Jonah as quickly as possible, then out of town before the FBI showed up and arrested her. The feds could be on their way right this second.

"Alex?"

She forced herself to focus on Rachel, who was eyeing her with concern. "I'm sorry?" Alaina asked.

Rachel gestured at the nurse. "She said there are two FBI agents asking to see you. Do you feel up to talking to them?"

"No," Alaina said quickly. "I, uh, . . . no."

Rachel's brow creased. "Are you all right?"

Alaina shook her head. Think. Think. "In a few minutes," she told the nurse. "Tell them I'll see them in a few minutes."

Once the nurse was gone, Rachel said, "Those feds are pretty adamant about talking to you. What's the deal?"

Instead of answering—because she didn't know what to say or where to begin—Alaina slid off the gurney, grateful that, when she wobbled, Rachel braced her.

"Uh, what are you doing?" her friend asked.

Alaina had no idea. Now that she was standing, however unsteady, she realized she couldn't just walk out. She wore nothing but a hospital gown. Her purse was nowhere to be seen. She had no money, no ID. All she had was Rachel, who was staring at her as if Alaina had just ripped off her human face to reveal an alien one underneath.

She took a shallow breath, bruised ribs preventing anything deeper. "I need to get out of here. Now."

Rachel stepped back, hands raised, cell phone still grasped in one. "Okay, you're officially wigging me out."

"I'm not kidding, Ray. I need to get to Jonah."

"I'm sorry, but you're going to wig him out, too."

"Ray—"

"How about this?" Rachel cut in. "I'll get Jonah. You stay here and get X-rayed."

"No. I need to go."

"Well, I'm not helping you. You just got hit by a car, and you're shaky on your feet."

"I'm not asking your permission."

"Then I'll get a doctor in here to talk some sense into you."

"Yes," Alaina said, seizing on the opportunity to get Rachel out of her way. "Let's consult a doctor."

Rachel hesitated, thrown. "You'll sit tight if a doctor tells you to?"

Alaina nodded vigorously. "Yes."

But Rachel, her eyes suddenly wary, folded her arms and stayed put. "You're just trying to get me out of here so you can take off."

Alaina almost screamed in frustration. "Ray, dammit—"

"Just tell me what the hell's—" The cell phone in her hand rang, cutting her off. She checked the display.

"Who is it?" Alaina asked. It was a long shot, but if Jonah had gotten no answer on her cell phone or work phone, he might have tried Rachel.

"It's work," Rachel said.

Leaning against the gurney, Alaina stared at the floor while her friend turned her back to take the call. That was when she spotted Rachel's purse propped against the casters of the metal stool. The edge of her key ring peaked out of the side pocket.

Keeping an eye on Rachel's turned back, Alaina bent and snagged the keys, careful to clamp them against her palm to prevent them from jangling.

"I'm here with her now," Rachel was saying. "She's fine. I think. . . . I don't know how long I'll be. I'll call you later, okay? . . . Great, thanks for calling."

Lowering the cell phone, Rachel turned. "People at work are worried about you," she said, her smile strained.

Alaina shrugged, knowing the gesture was far too casual, considering the conversation they'd been having. But she didn't know how else to behave now that she was moments away from betraying her best friend. "I'm fine. Don't I look fine?"

"Actually, you look like hell."

"Hey, I'd like to see you look this good after being hit by a car."

Rachel laughed softly, her eyes searching Alaina's. "You'd tell me if you were in some kind of trouble, wouldn't you?"

Alaina sank down onto the stool. Everything ached. Her body. Her heart. Her soul. She hated her life, hated being afraid, suspicious. And it would never end. Never. She clamped her jaw against the emotion that tightened her throat. "I panicked," she said. "I can't explain it." Glancing up, she tried to look contrite. "You win, okay? I'll stay here while you go get Jonah. I'll probably be ready to go by the time you get back."

Rachel scooped her purse off the floor. "No problem. I'm sorry I didn't go before, like you asked."

"I understand, Ray. I do." *Just go, Rachel. Go.*

"It'll take me about forty minutes to get to Grant's and back," Rachel said. "Do you want me to call once I've got him?"

Alaina let her shoulders drop, as if in relief. "That'd be excellent. Thanks."

Rachel gave her a quick, gentle hug. "Don't freak out any more, okay? You were scaring the crap out of me."

"Sorry."

"I'll be back in a jiff."

As soon as Rachel was gone, Alaina ducked out of the room and edged around the nurses' station. She needed clothes, a jacket . . . something to replace the gown, which would draw attention. Luckily, there was so much activity in the ER that no one paid attention to her.

Finding a cabinet that held fresh scrubs for the nurses and

doctors, she snagged a pair, along with some of the booties that surgeons wore. Back in the room, she doffed the gown as quickly as her throbbing shoulder and ribs would allow and slipped into the pale green scrubs. Afterward, she rested, bracing her hand on the gurney as her head grew light and took a lazy spin. *Hang on. Jonah needs you to hang on.*

Feeling relatively disguised and about as steady as she figured she was going to get under the circumstances, she strolled as casually as possible into the ER waiting room. A bank of pay phones occupied a section of wall adjacent to the ER's automatic sliding glass doors. She took up position at one of the phones, where she could watch people come and go without being noticed herself. With a phone pressed to her ear, she waited only about a minute before Rachel hurried into the ER, looking stressed. She didn't even glance in Alaina's direction.

As soon as Rachel was out of sight, Alaina exited through the same doors, Rachel's keys dangling from her fingers. The cold wind struck her body a soft blow—obviously, the forecasted cold front had arrived. She ducked her head against the steady rain, walking as fast as she could, every step sending jarring pain through her shoulder and side.

She found Rachel's silver Toyota RAV4 without trouble and told herself she had no choice as she climbed in. Her hands shaking as if she had Parkinson's, she turned the key to start the small SUV.

Protecting Jonah from his father took precedence over everything and everyone. She'd made that promise to herself long ago, and she would never break it.

She would die first.

Chapter 5

Mitch stepped out of his car and approached the Maxwells' front door, which stood open, the lights inside casting buttery light on the walls. Darkness had fallen early and quickly, thanks to the relentless rain that still fell. Hunching his shoulders against the cold, Mitch strode onto the porch like he belonged there and peered inside.

Overturned furniture and a large bloodstain on beige carpet told of a violent encounter in the living room. One man was busily collecting evidence while police officers hovered around the perimeter.

"Can I help you, sir?"

Mitch pulled out his investigator license and flashed it at the police officer. "Mitch Kane. I got a tip that someone I'm looking for might be here. What happened?"

"Guy got shot, and his kid was pistol-whipped."

"Jesus. They going to be okay?"

"The father's in bad shape but nothing life-threatening. The kid's probably got a concussion."

"Robbery?"

"Don't think so," the cop said. "Fancy TV and stereo equipment haven't been touched."

"Only the father and son were here? Nobody else?"

"Not that we know of."

"Witnesses?"

"Nope."

"And you're sure the kid was the guy's son?" Mitch asked.

"Yeah. He was asking about his dad when he regained consciousness." The officer narrowed his eyes. "What'd you say your name is again?"

Raising his hands, Mitch backed off. "Looks like my tip was wrong. Sorry."

In the driveway, he paused, wondering what the hell was going on. It couldn't be a mere coincidence. Alaina Chancellor makes a frantic run for the train, and now the place where her kid was supposed to be is a crime scene, with Grant Maxwell shot and Lucas knocked around. Had she known that something had happened?

"Get Jonah."

That's what she'd said. Not "check on Jonah" or "help Jonah."

"Get Jonah."

She'd been concerned about him, maybe even frightened for him. But Mitch's gut told him that she hadn't thought her son was in grave danger. That would have been accompanied by a whole other level of desperation.

Flipping open his cell phone, he hit the speed-dial button assigned to his partner. Julia Rafferty sounded rushed when she answered the call.

"It's Mitch."

"Hey, how's it going out in the Windy City?"

"Everything's gone to hell." He gave her the update, then said, "What I need is a more thorough background check on Maxwell. Was what happened here the result of his entanglements or Alaina Chancellor's?"

"I was thorough the first time. He's an upstanding citizen. No rap sheet. No warrants. Not even any outstanding parking tickets. The guy's a catch."

"Humor me."

She blew out a breath. "All right."

"Check out his kid, too. Maybe there was some gang activity—"

"Now you're reaching. That family is as squeaky clean as Alaina Chancellor and her kid."

"Yeah, well, she's only clean on the surface, isn't she?"

"Mitch, I hate to keep repeating myself, but this job is bad news. I think you should walk away."

"It's too late now. I was hired to find the kid, and now the cops are all over the place where he was supposed to be and isn't. To me, that means he's at risk."

After a long moment, as if she could wait out his resolve, she sighed. "I'll get back to you as soon as I know something new."

"Thanks."

As he slipped the phone back in the leather holder on his belt, headlights slashed across the front of the house. Squinting, he shielded his eyes. The driver of the small SUV didn't kill the lights, and Mitch heard a door open and close.

When the driver came into view, shock froze him.

She staggered and would have fallen if he had not moved quickly to catch her by the elbows. He felt the tremors shuddering through her, saw she was pale and perspiring, the green scrubs she wore damp and clinging. Her eyes didn't look right. They were wild with fear—the kind he would have expected earlier if she'd thought Jonah's life were in danger.

"Let me go," she gasped, pushing him away with surprising strength and stumbling toward the house.

Mitch chased after her, grabbed her arm. "He's not in there."

Alaina wrenched away from him, her strength manic. At the front door, she dodged a cop, barely seeing him.

Instead, she saw a mess. Overturned chair. Coffee table on its side. A busted lamp.

A large bloodstain on the light carpet.

Oh, God, no.

She swayed as her heart thumped in her ears, slammed against her ribs. Ignoring the dizziness that came in waves, she searched for Jonah, didn't find him. Maybe he was upstairs.

Ordering her jelly legs to obey, she lurched toward the staircase. "Jonah!"

The man from the driveway blocked her way. She saw his lips moving but couldn't hear his voice over the ringing in her ears. All she could smell was blood, metallic and sweet.

Her knees threatened to buckle, and she sank her fingers into his damp shirt to keep from falling. She felt his arm go around her and fought the black spots. But she was losing the battle. Dammit, dammit, dammit.

There was no time for this. She had to find Jonah.

But her body had other plans.

She fainted.

"I'm sorry to have kept you waiting."

Addison Keller turned to face FBI Assistant Director Norm Potter as he walked into the office and shut the door. He was a tall, lanky man with thick red hair and a face full of freckles. She'd been skeptical the first time she met him three weeks ago, the day she had sat across from him at a Dupont Circle coffee bar and told him that the revered and respected Layton Keller was plotting the murder of her sister.

Potter hadn't shown one twitch of surprise. Without hesitation, he'd told her the FBI would be more than happy to find and protect her sister and nephew. He'd followed that up with a smooth request for her help in return.

It had stunned her that the FBI was already investigating Layton. For what, Potter refused to say. And while he didn't tell her that the feds would protect Alaina and Jonah in return for Addison's assistance in the investigation, he implied it, and Addison was frightened enough for her sister and nephew to agree to help. So far, though, Potter had asked for nothing, and she'd begun to think that maybe he didn't need her help after all. Until he'd called today and asked her to meet him. He'd given her the name of a dentist and told her to make an appointment. He would meet her at the dentist's office.

She had arrived for her "appointment" five minutes before, and the receptionist had led her down a long hallway to a sparse room at the back of the office. The room held a gunmetal gray desk, a chair behind it and in front of it, and a lamp. It was as stark as her life had become.

Potter's somber expression didn't help. A chill passed through her, and she clasped the edges of her coat together. "What's going on?"

Potter gestured at the chair facing the desk. "Why don't you sit down, Mrs. Keller?"

"I don't want to sit down. I want you to tell me what's happening. It's dangerous for me to be sneaking around like this. You know that."

"Yes, and I'm sorry about that, but I felt it was important for us to have this conversation in person."

She felt a little dizzy as the implications of that statement whirled through her head. Alaina dead. Jonah lost and alone. The Chancellor-Keller empire wiped out by the one man who had nearly single-handedly built it.

Potter touched her elbow. "Can I get you something to drink?"

Addison shook her head, swallowing. "I'm fine. Please, let's . . ." She trailed off, searching for the right word. Talk?

Negotiate? But hadn't they already done that? Hadn't she already traded her husband's future freedom for the safety of the sister she had spent nearly two decades detesting?

Potter leaned back against the front of the desk, his brow furrowed as he crossed his arms. "I'm not going to lie to you."

Addison grasped the back of the visitor's chair for support. "Please, just tell me what's happened."

"Your sister and nephew are missing."

"They're together?"

"We don't know. Your nephew was last seen at a private home in Mount Prospect, a Chicago suburb. A father was shot, and his son was knocked around at the home."

Addison decided to sit after all.

Potter moved behind the desk and lowered himself to the chair, folding his hands on his desktop. "Your sister was last seen at a Chicago hospital after being struck by a car running away from the two agents I sent to take her into protective custody."

"Is she okay?" Addison asked.

"She walked out of the ER, so her injuries weren't that bad."

"So what you're telling me is that everything went wrong."

He cleared his throat. "The Bureau is committed to fulfilling its end of the deal, Mrs. Keller. I've got agents working night and day to find your loved ones."

Loved ones. She didn't know whether to laugh or dissolve into tears. "You didn't bring me here to tell me this. You could have told me over the phone."

Instead of responding, Potter took a cell phone out of an inner jacket pocket and punched some buttons. "We're ready for you," he said into it.

After stashing the phone, he said, "A gentleman is going to be here shortly to show you how to distribute listening devices throughout your home and your husband's cars and offices."

Addison felt exhaustion and defeat settle over her like a heavy, black cloud. "We made a deal."

"Yes, we did. And the Bureau has made, and continues to make, a good faith effort to fulfill its part. Now, it's your turn."

Chapter 6

Alaina opened her eyes. The ceiling above her was unfamiliar. So were the scents—mint, stale cigarettes and the faint odor of bleach. A frantic glance around told her she was in a hotel room. And apparently alone.

Ignoring the slashes of pain from various bumps and bruises, she tried to sit up. That's when she discovered her left wrist was handcuffed to the wooden slatted headboard of the bed.

Her heart jackhammering in alarm, she scanned the room for clues. It was standard Best Western—two double beds, a TV on top of the dresser, a desk and chair, flowered décor in teal and wine, and heavy curtains that blocked whatever light might have come through the single window. Someone's belongings littered the room—loose change scattered on the desk, a denim shirt draped over the back of the desk chair, a suitcase open on the other bed. In it, she could see balled socks, folded T-shirts and polos, a couple pairs of rolled blue jeans, a black leather belt. Man things.

Her shoulder throbbed, and she massaged it, realizing that the hospital scrubs she wore were wet and cold, clinging uncomfortably to her skin.

And then she remembered the blood on Grant Maxwell's carpet. It hadn't been from an accident. Furniture wouldn't have been overturned from an accident. Police cars, lights flashing, wouldn't have been there because of an accident. Something horrible had happened. And Jonah had to have been there when it did. That was the Wednesday routine. He took the bus with Lucas after school to Lucas's home and waited for her to pick him up after work. So whatever had happened at the Maxwell home might have happened to Jonah. The blood might have been his.

Panic spilled through her, filling her head with a deafening roar. She fought it down, inch by nauseous inch. Jonah knew what to do. She had trained him, painstakingly drilled into him the details of what to do and when to do it. Ever since he'd been old enough to read. The teen was as prepared as any adult to do what he needed to do to survive. Alaina had made sure of it.

She flashed again on the blood on Grant's carpet, and her brain stuttered.

Guns. She had not prepared Jonah to handle people with guns. She hadn't known how to without scaring him, hadn't known where to begin. Now she realized what a mistake that was.

Panic welled again, like blood from a pinprick, and she shoved it away. Getting hysterical wasn't an option. She had to focus on how to free herself so she could find her son.

The bedside clock told her it was 5:32. Judging from the dampness of the scrubs, it had been only an hour since she had swiped Rachel's keys. That meant the hotel couldn't be far from Mount Prospect.

Turning her attention to her restraints, she tried to slide the handcuff over her hand. When that didn't work, she tried to snap the wooden slats encircled by the opposite cuff, managing only to bruise her captured wrist and send throbbing pain shooting through her injured shoulder. She accomplished more of the same trying to snag the phone that sat on the other bed, its cord just a finger's length beyond her reach. She couldn't reach it with her foot, either.

Finally, she searched the drawer in the bedside table for anything she could use to pick the lock, but it held only hotel stationery and a Bible.

A subtle click brought her head around as the electronic key on the room door tripped. She could do nothing but hold her breath.

The man who walked in wore faded blue jeans, a white polo shirt and a black leather jacket, a backpack over one shoulder and a navy sports bag dangling from one hand. He had dark brown eyes, razor stubble and short, dark hair salted with gray. He reminded her of George Clooney, and under ordinary circumstances, she would have considered him very attractive. Except, unlike the actor, this man didn't look the least bit affable. In fact, he looked pissed off.

As the door closed behind him, he paused, his dark gaze flicking over her, unreadable as he dropped the bags at his feet.

Alaina sensed that remaining calm was imperative, even as her muscles twitched to bolt. She would have tried already if not for the manacle encircling her wrist.

"Who are you?" she asked, conversational, even a little casual.

"Mitch Kane." His voice was deep and rough, his tone matching hers.

The name meant nothing, but he didn't offer any more information, as she'd hoped. She raised her handcuffed wrist. "What's this for?"

"I didn't want you bailing on me."

She might have assumed he was a stupid henchman hired to do a job, but his eyes were sharp, his stance tense, ready to react if she made an unexpected move. "It's a strange way of asking me to stick around," she said, still casual.

"From what I've heard, you're slippery."

Her pulse started to sprint. "Who would you have heard that from?"

"Your son's father."

Nausea began to churn. "You know Layton?"

He gave a curt nod. "I work for him, yes."

Jesus, oh, Jesus. "Where's Jonah?"

His gaze flickered ever so slightly. "I don't know."

So he had escaped. She could have wept in relief. "What did you do? I saw the blood."

Surprise arched his dark eyebrows. "I didn't have anything to do with that."

"But you were there."

"I was looking for your son."

"How did you know where to go?"

"I'm a detective. I've been following you for three weeks. I know your routine."

For a long moment, she couldn't think. Then it began to sink in: A stranger had been watching their every move. He had watched her drop Jonah off at school, pick him up, take him to the dentist, to soccer practice, to the movies to meet his friends. This man had witnessed the heated discussion they'd had in the parking lot of their apartment complex after she refused to let her son buy a dirt bike with the money he'd been saving. This man knew when Jonah was home alone. He probably even knew that after Jonah turned off his bedroom light at night, he usually huddled under the covers with his Game Boy, determined to win one more level of the latest James Bond video game before calling it a night.

She imagined all the snippets of their life that this man had watched, uninvited, plotting whatever Layton had in mind. The sense of violation and dread rolled over her in a hot wave. "I'm going to be sick."

Mitch moved fast, whipping the key to the cuffs out of his

pocket and springing the lock without hesitation. She stumbled getting off the bed, and he caught her around the middle and helped her to the bathroom.

She dropped to her knees in front of the toilet and lost the contents of her stomach.

Mitch stood in the bathroom doorway as she sat back on her heels, a hand pressed to her right side. Her breathing was ragged, her face pale. The scrubs were too big for her, the material slipping off one smooth shoulder. Myriad bruises marred that shoulder, spreading across her collarbone. His stomach clenched.

Slipping the handcuffs into his back pocket, he reminded himself that she had stolen a man's son, had robbed that man of fourteen years of knowing his child. She had killed a fellow detective. Feeling sorry for her wasn't allowed. People who shattered lives and broke hearts like she had, deserved whatever they got. And if he got to be on the giving end of that, well, then, he was more than happy to take care of business.

His main concern at the moment was for Jonah. Wherever he was, he was no doubt frightened and confused. His mother had done that to him, and that angered Mitch.

"Do you have a plan?" he asked.

She pushed damp hair back from her face. "What do you mean?"

"In case you get separated."

She closed her eyes, swallowed hard. "No."

Kneeling beside her, he waited until she turned her head to look at him. Her eyes were rimmed in red, making them look more green than gray. She had started to shiver. "If you lie to me, I can't help you," he said.

"Help me do what?" Her voice was low, hoarse.

"Find your son."

"So you can take him away from me."

"That's not my job. My job is to find him."

She tightened her lips as if fighting off another surge of sickness. "I won't take you to him."

He straightened and, tired of seeing her shiver, reached down to help her up. She recoiled as if he were a striking snake, scrabbling back until her back hit the wall. The impact made her gasp, but her gaze, wide and fearful, never left his face.

Startled by her reaction, Mitch backed off. Panic poured off of her in waves that seemed to shimmer like heat. *Don't let her get to you.* He hardened his jaw. "This is how it's going to be. You're going to get dressed, and we're going to go meet Jonah at your rendezvous point."

She glared up at him, some of the panic shifting into defiance. "You can't force me."

"No, but the longer you leave him out there by himself, the harder it's going to be to find him. Don't you think?"

"He knows how to take care of himself. He's a survivor."

He stared her down for several moments, but her gaze stayed level on his, and he couldn't help but admire her resolve. He also couldn't help but notice that the wet scrubs clung to her body, and that she wore nothing beneath them.

Turning on his heel, he left the bathroom to retrieve the sports bag he'd bought while she'd been out of it. Dropping it at her feet, he said, "I picked up some clothes and other necessities for you. Get dressed, and we'll talk some more."

Chapter 7

While Mitch waited for Alaina to change, he thought about Layton Keller. He couldn't imagine him and Alaina together. The man was a corporate maverick, an icon in his field, known as a ruthless perfectionist who didn't hesitate to fire an underperformer. His peers respected him, his managers worshiped him and his underlings feared him. In essence, Mitch surmised, Keller was a mirror image of the late Paul Chancellor.

Keller also loved money. Loved making it and loved showing off how much he had, with fancy parties, fast cars and a rich social life filled with theater, five-star restaurants, bottles of expensive wine and luxury boxes at major sports arenas.

From what Mitch had observed of Alaina and Jonah, and what his partner, Julia Rafferty, had turned up on them, they lived simple lives. Their apartment was small—barely large enough for two. Alaina took brown-bag lunches to work and drove a late-model Honda that had seen better days. The wardrobes of both mother and son didn't appear shabby, but they weren't new or sporting designer tags, either. The kid, he noticed, needed new athletic shoes, though Mitch figured the holes in his jeans made them fashionable rather than worn.

Mitch wondered what Alaina had gained by keeping Jonah from his father. Considering the child was conceived out of wedlock, he was sure Keller, who obviously prized his pristine public image as much as his late father-in-law had, would have shelled out handsomely to keep it that way. She could have reaped thousands a month in support payments simply to keep quiet, and it would have been chump change compared with Keller's fortune. It certainly would have topped the piddly salary she pulled down as a journalist.

Instead, mother and son survived paycheck to paycheck, eschewing full-price movies and fancy restaurants for macaroni and cheese, matinees and videos, hiking and biking, usually just the two of them. Jonah didn't seem to mind hanging out so much with his mother. She was certainly able to keep up with him athletically. Last week, when the weather had been unseasonably warm, Mitch had watched Alaina and Jonah engage in a competitive one-on-one basketball game at a local park. It had been evident from the game that Jonah adored his mother. When she scored, he high-fived her like a good buddy.

Mitch wondered what Alaina had told Jonah about his father. He wondered how she justified keeping the boy from the man who so badly wanted to know him. He wondered how she slept at night knowing what she had denied Jonah by taking him from his father, where he would have had anything he wanted, the best of everything, not to mention a good male role model.

The bathroom door opened, snapping him out of his thoughts.

Alaina walked out in the jeans and T-shirt he'd picked up for her. The jeans hugged her slim curves a little too well, and the white T-shirt, with its short sleeves, showed off the toned muscles in her arms. She looked too young to be the mother of a teenager, too vulnerable to be a scheming bitch.

Who was he kidding? Looks had nothing to do with a person's capacity for deception. He gestured toward the chair that went with the desk. "Sit."

She didn't move. Instead, she folded her arms across her chest, a renewed determination in her eyes. "Let's cut the civilized bullshit. You look like the kind of man who has a hard time with it. What did Layton hire you to do?"

Mitch wanted to tell her that it'd take more than a tough attitude to convince him that she wasn't quaking on the inside. Her eyes were far too readable. "I think you've forgotten who's in charge here," he said.

"You got a gun in your pocket you're going to aim at my head until I beg for mercy?"

Deliberately, he slid his hand back to his hip, shifting his jacket enough for her to see the holster under his arm. Her gaze settled on the gun. Then, as those haunting eyes slowly lifted to meet his, he realized that she'd played him. She hadn't known whether he was armed, and now she did. Annoyed that she had manipulated him so easily, he snapped, "Don't worry, I don't point guns at unarmed women."

She smirked. "I bet you don't kick puppies, either."

He jerked the chair out from the desk. "I prefer kittens. Sit."

She stayed put. "You're wasting your time. Jonah knows what to do. In fact, he's probably already long gone."

"Unless the people who shot your friend have him." He tried to enjoy the way the color drained out of her face, but he couldn't.

"Grant was shot?"

He nodded.

"How bad?"

He could see she held her breath in dread. "He's expected to recover," he said. "His kid got roughed up, too. Pistol-whipped."

"Oh, God," she said, closing her eyes.

He waited until she opened them again, ignored the sick horror in them. "It wasn't a robbery," he said. "What was it?"

"I don't know."

"I think you do. You were in an awfully big hurry when you left work. You obviously thought something bad had happened at the Maxwells' even before you saw all the blood."

"The police cars—"

"And when you flew out of work?"

She squared her shoulders, lifted her chin. "I don't have to explain anything to you."

"Maybe you'd prefer to explain it to the cops or the feds. Because we can go see them at any time."

She pressed her lips together, as if suppressing a frustrated scream. "Layton found out where we are, and he sent someone to collect Jonah. Grant probably resisted—" She broke off, swallowed hard.

"I'm afraid there's a gaping hole in that theory." Mitch savored how still she went, enjoyed that moment of power, enjoyed knowing he could so easily turn her world upside down. Enjoyed it even as he wondered why it should matter. She was nothing to him. A job. "Layton Keller doesn't know where you are," he said.

"Of course, he does. You said he hired you to find us, and you did."

He didn't respond, watching all the possibilities flit through her eyes, impressed by how quickly she drew the right conclusion.

Confusion created a crease between her brows. "I don't understand," she said. "Why haven't you told him where we are?"

He didn't say that the situation had made him uneasy, that

he'd been trying to work out some inconsistencies before calling Keller. Instead, he shrugged. "Maybe I'm milking the job."

When she just stared at him as if she thought he was nuts, he said, "My point is that he couldn't have been involved with your friends getting hurt because he doesn't even know about them. Someone else did that job."

"Well, the FBI knows where I am. He probably has a source among the feds."

"Wait a minute," he said. "The FBI?"

"You wanted to know why I bailed out of work so fast. That's why. Two agents were there asking for me."

"Why?"

"What do you mean why? They found me. Just like you did."

He was silent a moment, puzzling it through. Keller had told him the feds weren't after Alaina. So why were they asking for her at the newspaper? It had to have been about something unrelated. Yet, the coincidence seemed too much.

"Let me guess," Alaina said, impatient. "Now you're thinking Layton can't possibly have a mole in the FBI. Do you think he got where he is today without having connections in high places like the federal government? Without having multiple backup plans? It's highly unlikely that you're his only hired thug."

Irritation at the job description flared, but he shoved it down. "It doesn't matter. What's going to happen here—"

She charged him. Her body hit him hard, and he dropped back against the dresser, shocked by the attack. She may have been small, but she was fast and strong and already her hand was inside his jacket, groping for the gun. Grabbing her wrist before she could jerk the weapon out, he twisted until, gasping, she went down on her knees in front of him.

Thinking he had her subdued, he loosened his grip. She instantly surged up, knocking the top of her head under his chin. As his head snapped back, lights bursting before his eyes, she nailed him in the gut with her elbow. His breath left him in a pained whoosh, and before he could drag in air, she whirled and brought the heel of her hand down on the bridge of his nose.

The pain was red. As was the blood that spurted out of his nose. His rage was black.

She was only halfway to the door when he mowed her down. On her stomach under him, she immediately started to squirm. He put an end to that by planting his weight on the middle of her back, tangling his legs with hers and pinning her shoulders to the floor. Immobilized, she went limp under him, her breath sawing in and out.

"No more Mr. Nice Guy," he growled, shifting so he could jerk her arms back to snap the cuffs on her.

She cried out at the rough treatment, but he ignored her as he pushed himself to his feet and swiped his hand under his bleeding nose. He couldn't tell if it was broken, but it throbbed in time with the frantic race of his pulse. She'd almost had him. He outweighed her by an easy seventy pounds. He'd had extensive FBI training, had held his own in many a bar fight in his younger days, and this slight woman had very nearly bested him.

He glared down at her. "Be glad I'm a reasonable man, because anyone else would be kicking your ass right now."

She rolled onto her side, still out of breath. "You're not his only detective."

Turning his back, he stalked into the bathroom for a towel. His head was pounding now, too. His head, and his pride. He told himself that he'd held back because she was a woman. A man he would have dropped with one punch. But the truth was, he hadn't really held back. And that made him feel like an asshole. She'd almost made him lose control. When she'd hit him, he'd wanted to hit back. He'd wanted to hurt her, to make her pay. Where had that come from?

Bracing his hands on the edge of the sink, he met his own eyes in the mirror. *She's a job. None of this is personal. Do your job and go home.*

He heard her voice but not what she said. "I don't want to hear it," he replied, splashing water on his face.

He was drying his face on a white towel, streaking it with blood, when he walked out of the bathroom. She was as he'd left her, on her side, her hands chained behind her back. Her flushed face was damp with sweat, her dark hair falling into her eyes. He could see why Layton Keller had gone for her. She was easily the most striking woman he had ever seen.

He knew, too, that she was far stronger than she looked.

She still hadn't completely caught her breath, and the cords in her neck stood out in sharp relief. With a hitch in his stomach, he remembered her bruised shoulder. The pain around that damaged joint must have been blinding when he'd cuffed her so roughly.

There was no choice, he told himself. She'd given him no choice.

Resting the side of her head on the floor, Alaina wet her lips, her gaze never leaving his face. "He probably had someone follow you while you were following me."

Mitch leaned against the dresser, draping the towel around his neck. "And why would he do that?"

"If he suspected you were milking the job—"

"I wasn't."

"Then why haven't you told him you found me?"

He let the question hang as he crossed his ankles and tried to puzzle a way to get her to tell him where to find Jonah. It occurred to him that she might be a kidnapper and a liar—even a killer—but she was also a mother desperate to ensure that her only child was safe.

"Jonah is out there," he said. "Alone and scared. You're just going to leave him like that?"

Some of the tension left her body, like hope draining away. "He knows what to do."

"It's abandonment."

"You obviously don't have any children."

He stiffened. "My status as a father has nothing to do with this."

"If you had a child, you would know that I will do anything to keep my son safe."

He knelt beside her. He didn't know whether he should feel satisfaction at the way her eyes widened and she pressed back, or shame. "Explain to me how stealing that boy from his father kept him safe," he said.

She looked away from him, up at the ceiling. "I don't have to explain it to you."

"No, but I suppose eventually you'll have to explain it to a judge, won't you?"

Her gaze shifted to him, and her eyes shimmered. "I didn't have a choice. Layton convinced a judge that I would be an unfit mother. You watched Jonah and me for three weeks. Do I look like an unfit mother to you?"

He straightened, his knees cracking. "I have no way of knowing what kind of mother you were fourteen years ago, so that's not an issue."

"They took my child away. I was going to be allowed supervised visits every two weeks. They weren't even going to let me be alone with my son. He was my life. My everything. What would you have done?"

"This isn't about me." He strode into the bathroom,

where he rinsed the towel and applied its cold wetness to his throbbing nose.

"It's at least partially about you," she said from the other room. "Layton is using you to do his dirty work. He's smooth and charming on the surface, but underneath, he's mean and cunning. You may think you know him, but you don't. Not like I do."

Leaving the bathroom, he stared down at her. "And I suppose you're the only one who knows the true Layton Keller."

"One other person knows."

That surprised him, and he lowered the towel. "Who?"

"My mother."

His surprise turned to irritation. "How convenient that the only person who can corroborate your claims is dead."

Her lips parted in shock, the angry color in her cheeks fading. "What?"

It struck him that she hadn't known, and he regretted his insensitive tone. Before he could say anything, she asked, "When?"

He rubbed the back of his neck, trying to remember the notes Julia had given him. "Five years ago. Car accident in Grand Junction, Colorado."

"Oh my God," she said, her lips barely moving as her eyes slid closed. "He killed her."

His annoyance returned, along with the conviction that she would stop at nothing to try to turn him against Layton Keller. "Not quite. Her car slid off the road and down an embankment."

She didn't seem to hear him as tears rolled back into her hair. "She found me, and he showed up. She saw him . . . oh, God. He killed her to keep her quiet."

Unnerved by the emotion, and even more by the allegation, he said, "We don't have time for this. Tell me where to find Jonah."

She looked at him, the grief unmistakable in her gaze. "Forget it."

"All right," he said. "Get up."

He reached down to pull her up, bracing her shoulders when she stumbled against him. A small moan escaped through her clenched teeth as he eased her onto the edge of the nearest bed. She sat gingerly, her hair hiding her face. She was obviously hurting. Inside and out.

Guilt at how he might have further injured her slithered through him. Taking out the key, he released the cuffs and waited patiently while she rubbed her wrists and rotated her sore shoulder, her gaze quizzical on his. Pointing at the chair in front of the desk, he held up the cuffs. "One end goes around your wrist, the other attaches to the furniture."

"You don't have to—"

"It's not up for debate. Park it here." He pointed at the chair. "Now."

Surprisingly, she obeyed, sitting silently as he secured her left wrist to the leg of the desk. "I'm going out," he said. "I'll be gone for fifteen minutes, maybe less. That means that if you start to scream for help, I'll be back before the cops or anyone else gets here. Got it?"

She nodded.

Chapter 8

As soon as Mitch slammed the door behind him, Alaina reached down, stifling the groan that threatened as her abused shoulder and ribs protested. Lifting the corner of the desk so that the leg she was handcuffed to was suspended an inch off the floor, she shook her cuffed wrist until the manacle dropped free of the leg.

She didn't waste time marveling at how easy it had been. She was too busy thinking about what to do next. She assumed that Jonah had escaped the people who had shot Grant. Mitch Kane considered him missing, which meant that Layton's people couldn't have him, otherwise Mitch would know. So that had to mean that Jonah had indeed gotten away. All she had to do was find him before Mitch or any of Layton's other henchmen did.

Seizing the phone, she dialed Jonah's cell phone number. An automated voice said, "The party you are trying to reach is unavailable at this time."

Breaking the connection, she tried their home phone. By the fifth ring, the answering machine hadn't picked up, and she couldn't get a response to the numbers she punched in to check for messages. That meant the device had been turned off or wasn't working.

She had to make a decision, and she forced herself to be calm, rational. Unemotional.

If Jonah were in crisis mode, like he should be, he wouldn't be at their apartment waiting for her. But if by some fluke he didn't know that all hell had broken loose, he could be there, wondering where she was. It was possible, too, that seeing his friends get hurt had frightened him so much that he had gone into hiding rather than proceeding with the plans they had made over the years. In fact, the past few years, he hadn't really taken the plans seriously anymore. She couldn't even be sure that he had listened the last time she had gone over them with him.

Going to their apartment could waste precious time. But it was also the most likely place Mitch would go upon finding her missing. And if Jonah were there, Mitch would get to him first, and that absolutely could not happen.

Alaina grabbed the denim shirt hanging on the back of the desk chair and shrugged into it, tucking the dangling handcuff into the sleeve. Whipping open a desk drawer, she dug out the hotel information to decipher where she was and where to find the closest bus stop or train station.

Finally, luck was on her side: A bus stop was only two blocks away.

On her way out the door, she spotted the loose change on the desk and stopped. Her predicament hammered home. She'd dropped her purse when she'd been hit by the car and had not seen it since. She had no ID. No money. No credit cards. No checkbook.

Even if she hadn't decided to try to catch Jonah at home first, she had to go there anyway to retrieve the locked fireproof box stashed at the back of her closet for exactly this instance. That box held the new identities that she'd bought for them just after they'd arrived in Chicago, when she'd made preparations for the next time they'd have to run. She'd expected it to be sooner than this.

Scooping the change into her cupped hand, she pocketed it. She'd need it to pay for the bus and train ride to her car.

Luckily, she had had to double-park her Honda for work that morning and had left her keys with a garage attendant. She didn't anticipate having any problem getting them back without the ticket because she parked there every day, and the attendants knew her.

Outside in the cold drizzle, she walked as fast as she could for the first block, constantly scanning for Mitch and praying that wherever he had gone hadn't taken him in the direction she was headed. The wind was sharp, and she huddled against it, ignoring the throb in her shoulder, the ache in her chest.

She prayed that Jonah was okay, that he hadn't seen what had been done to Grant and Lucas or hadn't been injured himself. Remembering the blood that Mitch said had been Lucas's made her head spin. It so easily could have been Jonah's blood. She shoved the memory away, turning her face into the rain to clear her head.

Even so, guilt was a balled fist in her stomach. The Maxwells had gotten hurt because of her. She had tried to cut herself off from others, to isolate herself and, with the exception of Rachel, she had succeeded. But she couldn't have asked the same of Jonah. The boy had to have friends. How could she have possibly denied him friends?

And, really, she hadn't thought any of them, even Rachel, were in direct danger from Layton. He had never indicated that he wanted to harm anyone close to her. One of his people had found her once, and that had had a tragic outcome, but not because of any orders that came from Layton. Yes, it was true that she feared him. She had good reason to fear him. But her main objective the past fourteen years had not been to run for her life. It had been to keep from being found, because if she was found, she would lose Jonah.

But now her mother was dead, and the only reasonable explanation was that Layton had killed her to keep her quiet. Her death was simply too much of a coincidence. Eve had seen him for who he was. He couldn't have let her live, knowing what she knew.

The fist of guilt clenched tighter as Alaina remembered how she had taken Jonah and run, leaving her mother behind with the unconscious Layton. She had thought about nothing but escaping, saving herself and keeping Jonah from his father. But she hadn't known, she told herself. She hadn't known he would kill.

And now both her parents were gone. Just six weeks ago, she'd seen in the news that her father had died. She'd felt bad, even grieved for him, but the sadness had been nothing compared with what she felt now. Her mother was dead because of her, because she had run away.

Tears mixed with the rain that dripped down her cheeks. Inevitably, she remembered another woman whom she had loved like a mother. That woman had also become a casualty of Layton's, however indirectly.

Alaina kept the memories at bay until she had boarded the bus and was staring out at the rain-drenched Chicago streets. Madison, Wisconsin, was little more than a hundred miles away, and her life there felt like it had happened a hundred years ago.

The first two years had been a struggle, but she and Jonah had survived.

But then chronic ear infections and bronchitis had besieged Jonah, and she began to lose waitressing job after waitressing job because she couldn't afford a baby-sitter to stay with him alone, and the day-care center that catered to working, single mothers wouldn't take a sick child. She was at the end of her rope, broke, scared and starving, having spent almost the last of her cash feeding Jonah and paying for his medicine. She hadn't paid utility bills in three months, and the phone had been cut off the day before. The rent was due, and the landlord had been about as understanding as he was going to be.

She remembered standing on a street corner downtown, Jonah perched on her hip as she waited for the "walk" sign to flash. The dome of the capitol building loomed several blocks up, massive and white against the bright blue sky. Glittering Lake Mendota stretched to the horizon on her right. The air was cool and crisp, fresh with the promise of spring. She had five dollars in her pocket and was heading to a diner the next street over to apply for a waitressing job. If she didn't get it, she didn't know what she would do.

They would have to go back.

She shuddered just thinking about it, but let the scenario unfold in her head. She would go to jail for kidnapping. And Layton Keller would raise her son to be just like him. Stone-cold dead inside. She imagined she would never see Jonah again, not even for a supervised visit.

But at least he wouldn't starve.

"Want down," the toddler said, squirming in her arms.

She smiled as she lowered him to the ground, glad for the reprieve. The muscles in her arms were screaming from carrying him, and she felt weak and shaky from lack of food. "Okay, but you have to hold Mommy's hand."

He gripped her fingers obediently, his blue eyes wide as he looked around at the tall buildings and rushing pedestrians.

The light turned, and they crossed the street, Jonah's little legs pumping to keep up. They were halfway down the next block when Alaina began to feel dizzy, and she paused to brace a hand on the wall of a building. Pedestrians streamed by, oblivious as Jonah tugged her fingers.

"Let's go," he said, mimicking the commanding voice she used to get him into the bathtub at night. "Let's go. Let's go."

She wondered vaguely if, when she said that to him at night, her tone was as annoyed. But then the sunny day turned white, and her knees buckled.

When she opened her eyes, she started up. "Jonah!"

A firm hand pressed her back. "Just take it easy, missy. He's right here. Look."

She turned her head to see him plopped on the floor only a few feet away, surrounded by books and toys. His brow was furrowed as he concentrated on trying to fit a red plastic square into a triangular hole, not a care in his two-year-old world.

A glance around told her they were in a bookstore. Shelves reached to the ceiling, packed with old and new books alike. Overstuffed sofas and chairs provided comfy perches for customers while they read. Soft piano music set the mood for the store: soothing, unhurried.

Alaina realized she was stretched out on one of those overstuffed sofas, and that the older woman kneeling beside her was watching her intently. The woman was at least seventy, her hair white, her face lined in a way that reminded Alaina of a comfortable, well-worn leather coat. Her eyes, a brilliant blue that time had not managed to fade, were kind. And concerned.

Alaina tried to smile as she sat up. "I'm so sorry I—"

The woman put a cool hand on her arm. "I think you should stay put a little longer, dear."

"I'm fine, really."

"It won't hurt you to sit here a minute," the woman replied, gentle but firm. "Cliff will be back any minute now with some water."

Still shaky, Alaina let the sofa's cushions support her back, too weak to even sit up fully. She hoped water would help. Checking her watch, she saw with dismay that she was going to be late for her job interview. Again, she started to get up. "I really need to go. I'm late."

The woman gripped her arm, her strength surprising. "Whatever it is can wait," she said.

Alaina relented because she didn't think her legs would support her anyway. "Where—"

She broke off as a teenager with floppy blond bangs and wire-rimmed glasses—he reminded her of cousin Oliver from *The Brady Bunch*—returned with a glass of water. "Here you go, Miss Whitfield."

The older woman accepted the water. "Thank you, Cliff. Now, I need you to fetch something else for me, dear. Run next door and bring me back a peanut butter and jelly sandwich and one of those turkey clubs that Gus has on special today. Tell him to pile on the chips and add a couple of his famous oatmeal cookies. Oh, and grab one of those little cartons of milk he has in the fridge by the door."

As Cliff scampered away, the woman smiled at Alaina and offered the water. "You're drooling, dear."

Alaina's hand flew to her mouth, but then she saw the teasing sparkle in the woman's eyes.

"Ah, yes. It's good to see some color in your cheeks," the woman said, smiling, then patted the bottom of the glass. "Drink up now."

Alaina swallowed the cool water, her gaze shifting to Jonah, who had conquered the red square and now had a jack-in-the-box upside down on his lap. He inspected it from every angle, trying to figure out what it did or how it worked.

"I'm Emma Whitfield," the woman said.

Alaina looked at her. "Thank you. You're being very kind."

Emma waved a dismissive hand. "You fainted in front of

my door. I couldn't leave you there. It would have been bad for business."

Alaina laughed softly. "I suppose so."

Emma waited a beat, apparently expecting Alaina to introduce herself. When she didn't, Emma said, "You're not one of those anorexic girls, are you? Maybe some kind of model?"

Alaina shook her head, but Emma appeared unconvinced as she gripped Alaina's chin and turned her head this way and that to inspect her features. "You've got the bone structure of a model, that's for sure. You sure you're not starving yourself for your art?"

"I'm sure."

"Then why are you?"

Hunger apparently had made Alaina's brain sluggish. "Why am I what?"

"Starving."

"I'm not—"

Emma stood, cutting her off as she moved to balance on the end of the sofa where she could see Jonah better. Her warm gaze turned quizzical when it returned to Alaina. "Is it drugs?"

Alaina stiffened her back, alarmed. "Of course not."

Emma's smile was slight. "Relax."

But Alaina pushed to her feet. She didn't need this, some meddling woman deciding she was a terrible mother and getting social services involved. "We really have to go. I'm—"

"Late. You mentioned that earlier. What are you late for?"

Alaina faltered, annoyed at the third degree but intimidated enough by the woman's commanding tone to answer. "A meeting." Seeing Emma's brow arch, she added, "A job interview." She didn't know why it mattered that this woman not think she was a deadbeat.

"Ah. Do you read?"

Puzzled and a bit insulted, Alaina said, "I can read, yes."

Emma's blue eyes sparkled with amusement. "What was the last book you read?"

"*If You Give a Mouse a Cookie.* It's Jonah's favorite."

"Jonah." The older woman glanced at the little boy, and her expression turned wistful. "He's a beautiful child."

"I take good care of him."

"I can see that." Emma pursed her lips as she looked Alaina over. "It would appear that you're not as good at taking care of yourself."

Cliff returned, laden with bags of food, and Emma rose to meet him. "Thank you, dear."

Alaina started to call Jonah over, but Emma said, "You eat first. He's busy right now."

Alaina didn't have to be persuaded. She'd lived with the gnawing hunger for too many days now, and she had fed Jonah the last of their cheese and crackers only an hour before. As she tore into the turkey club, she felt Emma watching, assessing. She sensed the woman's disapproval but refused to worry about it. She'd endured worse, and she and Jonah would be on their way soon enough.

"You haven't told me your name," Emma said.

"Anna," Alaina said, feeling an unexpected twinge at the lie. "Anna King."

"Anna King," Emma repeated, as if testing the name for authenticity. "Anna, I happen to have a job opening."

Alaina lowered her sandwich, shocked.

"It doesn't pay much," Emma went on. "But if it works out—"

"I'll take it." Alaina didn't care how desperate she sounded. She *was* desperate. She'd do anything to avoid going back to her family, defeated.

Emma smiled. "Well, then. Finish your lunch, and we'll start getting you trained."

And so began the first truly nurturing relationship Alaina had ever had. Emma was a godsend in every way. She seemed to sense that Alaina had no interest in discussing where she and Jonah had come from, and she didn't ask.

After the first month, she persuaded Alaina to move into the extra bedroom in her apartment above the bookstore. Alaina didn't hesitate. She had come to adore Emma, and so had Jonah. The feelings were mutual. Emma doted on them both as if Alaina were her daughter and Jonah her grandson. The three of them lived in Emma's tiny apartment for a year before Emma talked Alaina into applying to the university whose campus was practically next door to the store.

With the aid of scholarships, student loans and supplemental help from Emma, Alaina entered the University of Wisconsin as a freshman the same day that Jonah started preschool.

Alaina began to marvel at her good fortune. She finally felt safe. She finally felt secure, sure that a college education would guarantee her ability to provide her son a good life. What was more, she finally knew unconditional love.

That was when she started having the nightmare. It was always the same: Layton attacked her while Jonah lay nearby, bleeding. She knew her son was slowly dying, but no matter how hard she fought, she couldn't get away from Layton to help Jonah. Each time, she woke up screaming and sobbing.

Emma didn't pry. She simply, very gently, persuaded Alaina to see a counselor. Alaina surprised herself by agreeing. She surprised herself further by telling the counselor what Layton had done to her, though she edited out any details that might have given away his, or her, identity.

The diagnosis: post-traumatic stress. "You've begun to let

your guard down," the counselor said, "and that's when it's most likely to sneak up on you."

By the time Alaina concluded her junior year of college and her third year of therapy, she felt healthier mentally and physically than she ever had. Life was damn good.

She should have known that that would be when it was most likely to fall apart.

Chapter 9

Alaina's hands shook as she dug in the flower bed outside her apartment door. Last fall, after Jonah lost his key and was locked out, she had buried a spare in a fake rock. But the maintenance crew had since planted new flowers, adding mulch and fresh soil. If the rock had been found, it might have been tossed out. She was already working in her head how to get in if she couldn't find the key.

The sliding door on the deck didn't have the most reliable lock, but she didn't think she was strong enough to force it. The windows were securely locked—she made sure every night before turning in, no matter how unlikely it was that one had been opened without her knowledge.

Sitting back on her heels, keyless, she studied the front door. Kicking it or otherwise forcing it was not an option. She wasn't strong enough, and besides, the force it would take would probably drive her to her knees. Maintenance was no longer on the clock by now, so it would take too long for someone to come open it for her.

Frustration welled up inside her until she had to concentrate to keep from screaming. She didn't have time for this. Jonah needed her. She'd already determined he wasn't here. That meant he had to be at the airport, waiting and worrying.

Hang on, baby, I'm coming.

Brushing the dirt from her hands, Alaina pushed to her feet and raced around the building to the back. The sliding door on the cement slab that served as a deck seemed to be the best option. But when she examined it, she discovered that someone else had reached the same conclusion. The door, half off its track, slid jerkily open, and Alaina stepped into the kitchen and hit the light switch.

The devastation stole her breath. Dishes that had been in the cupboards had been smashed to bits on the floor. The microwave looked like it had been hammered by a brick, the cart that had held it reduced to sticks. The ficus tree that had thrived near the sliding door had been ripped apart, the dirt from its pot thrown around by the handfuls.

The rubble crunched under her feet as she picked her way through it. When all was said and done, it didn't matter. She'd planned to leave it all behind anyway. But the destruction of what was hers and Jonah's was another violation. Whoever had done this hadn't been looking to steal. If they had, the screen of the television wouldn't have been shattered. No, whoever did this did it to violate, to punish. She imagined that the people who shredded the cushions of her sofa had also shot Grant and hurt Lucas.

In the bedroom, her stomach pitched as if she stood on the deck of a boat tossed by three-foot waves. She braced a hand on the wall, her heart stuttering. The closet had been emptied, all of its contents torn to pieces and scattered. A burnt smell permeated the air, and she glanced inside the metal waste can near the door to see blackened sides and a pile of ashes.

What did they burn?

The answer struck her like a fist to the temple. "No," she whispered, tearing through the debris for the locked fireproof box she used to store the paperwork she had accumulated over the years to maintain the identities she and Jonah would assume next. Along with the passports, birth certificates and credit cards she had bought through underground channels years ago, she kept more than a thousand dollars in it.

She found the beige metal box and sat back on her heels, almost giving in to despair. The lock had been broken. The box was empty. Its contents—or probably everything except the cash—had been reduced to ashes. She hurled the box against the wall. "Dammit!"

Now what would she do? She and Jonah would have to start from scratch again. No money. No credit. No job. No friends. The thought of it made her head spin, and she fisted her hands in her hair, struggling to get a grip.

When she had the despair under control, she realized that none of this mattered if she didn't find Jonah. If she lost him, then she truly would have nothing. He was her life, her reason for breathing. Everything she had done for the past fourteen years had been for him. She would die for him. She would die without him.

Shoving to her feet, she surveyed the damage in her room and Jonah's and determined that nothing was salvageable. Not even a pair of underwear. The thoroughness of the destruction was staggering, and it struck her that she had seriously underestimated the depth of Layton's rage. Apparently, he had nurtured his hatred for her for fourteen years, and now he was venting it. Though, knowing him, rather than getting his own hands dirty, he had instructed his henchmen to do this. Not as a warning, but as a promise.

The message: First, I'm going to make it very difficult for you to run, and then I'm going to destroy you.

Alaina walked out of the wreckage that had been the home she had shared with Jonah for the past five years and didn't look back.

* * * * *

"What is that?" Addison asked.

"PlayStation 2." Layton grinned over his shoulder at her from where he sat in front of the television, a game controller gripped in both hands. "Want to play? I'll show you how."

"Since when do you play video games?"

He shrugged, grimacing in frustration as the colorful character on the TV let out a wounded sound and, wearing a pair of angel wings, drifted toward the top of the screen. "That damn turtle thing with the saw blades on its back kills me every time."

Addison sauntered over to the coffee table and examined the CDs piled on it. The titles ranged from ominous-sounding, like *Tomb Raider* and *Resident Evil*, to themes like basketball, hockey and car racing. She imagined the games would appeal to a teenage boy.

Her pulse took off at a clip as she studied her husband, who was intent on maneuvering the character on the TV to smash boxes to collect points. His blond hair was damp from a recent shower, and she thought he looked tired, though he seemed to have more energy at the moment than he had had in weeks. "Are you expecting a guest?" she asked.

He didn't respond, or even glance at her.

"Layton."

The video game character issued another yelp, and Layton sat back, the controller in his lap. He glanced up at her, looking boyishly exasperated. "This thing is addictive."

She was struck by how handsome he was, reminded of why she had fallen for him so many years before. The first time she'd met him—on a visit to her father's office—she'd wanted him. He was everything: charming, good-looking, smart. When they'd begun dating, he'd lavished flowers and gifts and compliments on her, always seeming interested in what she had to say, always fascinated by stories of her childhood. He'd shared little information about his own, but what he had said suggested that his past was desperately unhappy. His wounded soul had made him all the more attractive to her, and she'd vowed to give him a life so full, so joyful that he would forget his wretched past. Now, full and joyful were not words she would use to describe their lives together. And she was pretty sure she wasn't the only one to blame.

Clearing her throat, conscious of the way he watched her with an expectant look on his face, she asked, "Who's the game for?"

His expression gave away nothing. "Why can't it be for me?"

"You don't have time for games. You rarely even have time to dine with me."

"Maybe I'm trying to change."

"Why now?" she asked.

"Why not?"

She sat beside him on the sofa. "You'd tell me if something was wrong, wouldn't you?"

"Nothing's wrong, Addy. Everything's just great."

She looked into his eyes and saw that he meant it. There was a light in them that hadn't been there for a long time. She wondered again why the FBI was investigating him, wondered for the millionth time what he had done with her father's company when no one had been looking.

She took a breath. "It's been six weeks, Layton. I think we should talk about it."

"Talk about what?"

She sighed. "I know Daddy's will upset you."

Getting up, he began disconnecting the game and packing it in its box. "I'm over it, Addy."

"Are you?"

He kept his head down, shook it. "I worked my ass off for him for sixteen years. I made PCware what it is. He didn't have vision. I did."

She reached inside herself for sympathy and came up empty. A year ago . . . hell, a week ago, she would have been on her knees beside him, commiserating her heart out. *Yes, Daddy screwed you out of what you deserved. Alaina and her brat did nothing to earn a third of PCware. We'll fight it, my darling. We'll fight for every penny that should be ours.* Not because she wanted it. As far as Addison was concerned, they had more than they could ever know what to do with. But because it was important to him.

But now . . . now . . . she kept hearing his words: "Kill the bitch and bring the kid to me."

What he'd said was menacing enough, but his tone had been downright chilling. At that moment, her husband had become a stranger to her. Now all she could do was comb her memory for all the things he'd done over the years, searching for clues to the man her husband really was. The search wasn't that extensive. The clues had been there all along, some of them so alarming and distasteful, so unbelievable, that she had long ago pushed them far from her consciousness.

Her chest constricted with the memory of Alaina in tears, so distraught she couldn't speak. Curling her hand into a fist in her lap, Addison hoped the rage didn't show in her body language. Rage at Layton, for what he had done to her sister, the assault and the character assassination afterward, and rage at herself for letting him get away with it.

"We'll work it out, Layton," she said, proud that her voice sounded so even. Maybe after this was over, she would head to Hollywood for a new career.

Layton raised his head to look at her, and his blue eyes were bright. "Yes. We will."

Chapter 10

At seven-thirty at night, Chicago O'Hare Airport was busy. Now that she was in the United Airlines terminal and so close, Alaina started to run, her hand pressed to the ache in her side. Breathing hurt, but she ignored the pain, consumed by the fear that was lunging against the leash she had put it on.

She hadn't been here in three years. The last time, Jonah had been eleven and irritated that he had had to pass on a pickup basketball game with some friends. Alaina promised him then that she wouldn't put him through the drill again.

Now, hoping to God that his memory had retained something from that day, she followed the signs to baggage claim. The airport had always seemed like the most logical place to meet. It never closed for the night, and there were only a few hours a day when flights weren't taking off.

It also offered the most avenues of escape. From the baggage claim area, they had nearly instant access to several modes of transportation. Cabs and buses waited right outside the automated doors. Rental car counters were a few paces away, along with access to the Metra train. If their identities were intact, they had only to go upstairs to buy plane tickets.

She'd taught Jonah to carry a couple of twenties and change to pay for subway tokens and cab fare, and he was well-versed on how to use public transportation.

Carousel number two was to the left, and, winded, Alaina slowed to a fast walk. She remembered Jonah at eleven, standing with her beside carousel number two, bored and probably thinking his mother was a nut job as she asked him, "Why carousel number two?"

"Because it's just the two of us," he'd said. "I'm not a baby anymore, Mom. I got it, okay?"

She could see carousel two now. It was still, surrounded by people awaiting the delivery of their luggage from a newly arrived flight. She scanned the crowd, scanned the faces. Some were animated as they told their family and friends about their flight, asked about the local weather, exchanged the latest news. Others were tense, impatient for the luggage to arrive so they could be on their way. Jonah was not among them.

She spotted an information desk nearby, occupied by a man peering at a computer screen.

He looked up when she approached. "May I help you?"

"I'm late picking up a boy, a teenager," she said, trying to sound calm. "Blond hair, blue eyes, White Sox jacket." She raised her hand, palm down, three inches above her head. "About this tall."

"Doesn't sound familiar."

"He might have been here, waiting in this area, hours ago."

"I'm nearing the end of my shift, ma'am, and I haven't seen any kids that look like that. Want me to page him?"

She hesitated. Would that be safe? But then she thought, if Jonah were here, he would be where she had told him to wait. He might have been annoyed at her compulsive planning and quizzing, but he had understood that it was important. When they had fled Wisconsin and then Colorado, he'd been old enough to grasp that someone bad was after them, and they had to hide.

Shaking her head, she turned away and scanned for him again.

"What do I do if you're not there?"

The question, offered after they'd settled in Chicago, when he was nine, had startled her.

"I'll be there, Jonah. Don't worry."

"But what if? What should I do?"

"I promise I'll do everything in my power to be there. But if I'm not, find a police officer and ask for help."

She'd never stopped to consider what she would dc if *he* didn't show up.

Despair began to wind its tentacles around her heart. Now what? Now what?

She told herself to calm down, to wait until the travelers cleared out. Maybe he had gone to the bathroom. Or to get something to eat. Maybe he hadn't even arrived yet.

But of course he should have. If he had escaped Grant's and Lucas's unharmed, Jonah should have been here hours ago. She couldn't imagine what might be going through his head, what he might be feeling. Worry. Fear. Anger.

All the things she was feeling. Except he had no idea who he was running from. Because she had not told him.

So many mistakes.

She sank onto a chair, her vision blurring with tears. She'd made so many mistakes. She should have told him everything so he could have been completely prepared, so he could know what he was dealing with. But how could she have told him they were running from his father? How could she have told him *why?*

On the verge of losing her composure, Alaina pushed to her feet and went to a pay phone. She tried Jonah's cell phone again, got the same infuriating automated message.

There was one last option. It was the one she had warned him against over and over: If something bad happens, don't turn to anyone we know for help. She hadn't explained, too concerned about his emotional health and sense of security to tell him that involving people they cared about could get them hurt.

Maybe, because she had never told him the rationale, he had ignored the directive. On the face of it, the instruction was ludicrous and counterintuitive. Why not turn to people you trust during a time of need?

Alaina plugged her last coins into the phone and dialed. Rachel answered on the first ring, sounding anxious.

"It's me," Alaina said.

"Where are you? Are you all right?"

Hearing her friend's voice, Alaina almost lost her grip. "I'm fine. I just need to—"

"You don't sound fine. And what the hell did you think you were doing ditching the hospital like that? All you had to do is say you needed to go, and I would have taken you to Grant's. You didn't have to trick me like that."

"I'm sorry about that, but I don't have time to explain. I really need—"

"Grant was shot, and someone knocked Lucas around. I assume you know that seeing as how my car was found in their driveway."

"How are they?"

"They're going to be fine, though Grant is going to be in the hospital a while. Is Jonah with you? Lucas said he ran away after Grant was shot."

Alaina felt both relief and dismay. Relief that Jonah had indeed run away, and dismay that he had seen Grant get shot. And he wasn't with Rachel. Closing her eyes, she rubbed at her temple with chilled fingers. A headache was raging. Along with a finely honed knife blade of panic. If he wasn't with Rachel, then where the hell was he?

"Jonah's fine, Ray. He's with me." She hated to lie, but

Rachel couldn't help. And the truth, and fear for Jonah, would devastate her.

Rachel heaved a relieved sigh. "Thank God. I've been worried to death. Those feds questioned me for an hour after you took off. And when they were done, the cops cornered me—"

"I have to go," Alaina cut in.

"Wait. Where are you guys?"

"I'll call you later, Ray." Another lie. It struck her that her entire life was built on lie after lie after lie, like a tiny house made of Popsicle sticks that hadn't been glued together. One jolt, and her existence, and Jonah's, was reduced to a pile of worthless splinters.

"Alex, wait. I have your purse. An ER nurse gave me a bag with your stuff in it after you took off. Tell me where you are, and I'll bring it to you."

The desperation in her friend's voice nearly undid Alaina, and she clenched her back teeth so hard an ache shot through her jaw. "I'll get it later. Thank you, Rachel. For everything."

"Alex, dammit, please. I know you're in trouble. Tell me what it is. I'll help you. Whatever it takes to—"

Alaina hung up on her best friend.

Standing near the Hertz car rental counter beside baggage claim number two, Mitch Kane watched Alaina lower herself to a chair. He recognized the denim shirt that hung to her knees as his own. It looked damp, as did her dark hair, shoved behind her ears. The energy that had gotten her to the airport appeared gone as she bent forward in the seat, one arm curled around her middle.

He almost felt sorry for her, but then he reminded himself that she was the one who'd kicked the rock that had started this avalanche. She was lucky that Layton Keller was a reasonable man. A malevolent one with his kind of power and money might simply have had her killed and taken his son back.

Sauntering over to where Alaina sat, he paused beside her chair, fighting the urge to drape his coat around her trembling shoulders. "Is there a contingency plan?"

When she looked up at him, the desolation in her eyes jolted him. She also didn't seem the least bit surprised to see him. "You let me escape," she said.

"You didn't think I'm really that stupid, did you?" he asked.

"I wanted to."

The handcuff had fallen free of her sleeve, but she didn't seem to notice. Casually, he lowered himself to the chair beside her.

"I screwed up," she said, her voice cracking. "I screwed up, and he's gone."

"Saying you screwed up is putting it a bit lightly, don't you think? Keeping a child from his father for fourteen years is more than a screwup. It's a felony." In one smooth motion, he grasped the free end of the cuffs and snapped it around his own wrist.

She stared down at their linked wrists, not reacting. "I did what was best for my son, Mr. Kane. If I go to jail for that, then so be it."

"Whatever." He stood, hauling her up by the arm.

Her breath hissed out between her clenched teeth, and the little color that had been in her face drained away. Annoyed at the tug in his gut, Mitch steadied her, then dropped his hand, reminding himself that he couldn't show her an ounce of sympathy. If he did, she'd know she was getting to him and use it against him. "If you pass out on me, I'll just haul you over my shoulder."

Her jaw tightened, and she stayed on her feet. "Fine. Turn me over to the police and get it over with."

He froze, surprised. That made no sense. She should have wanted to avoid law enforcement at all costs. Was she trying to trick him? Did she think he was so easily manipulated? "I'm turning you over all right," he said. "But it isn't to the police. We're going to D.C., where your ex gets to decide what to do with you."

With her free hand, she grabbed the links between the cuffs to stop him. "Wait. The police have to start looking for Jonah."

"Now you want to go to the cops?"

"Look, whatever you think of me, don't make him pay for it. If he's hurt or he's been kidnapped—"

His sharp bark of laughter cut her off. "*If* he's been kidnapped? You're the one who kidnapped him."

"I'm begging you—"

"Save the begging for your former lover."

She flinched as if he'd struck her, and he turned away quickly, not wanting to see her eyes.

"You think you know him, but you don't," she said.

"I don't need to know him, or you, to understand what's happened. You two had a kid, and you stole him. That pisses me off. That pisses off a lot of people. You're going to pay for that, lady, and I'm happily going to help." He dropped his jacket over their linked hands to hide the cuffs from passersby. "Come on."

He walked fast, and Alaina struggled to keep up, the handcuff biting into her wrist. Her breath sawed through her aching chest, but it was the least of her worries.

Where are you, Jonah? Where the hell are you?

In the parking garage, Mitch picked up his pace until

Alaina stumbled and went down on her knees. Agony sliced through her shoulder as he inadvertently dragged her forward by the wrist before he could stop. Biting back a cry of pain, she braced her free hand on the gritty pavement and fought to breathe.

Mitch made no move to help her up. He probably thought she was trying to slow him down. Tears of pain and frustration burned behind her eyes, but she fought them. He would see them as a ploy.

"Whenever you're ready," he said, his tone dispassionate.

Alaina looked up at him through hair that had fallen into her eyes. "If there's a decent bone in your body, you're going to regret this."

His eyes, curiously veiled, narrowed. "I regret it already."

"Did he tell you I seduced him?"

"He didn't tell me anything about how you two hooked up, except that it was a mistake."

Her laugh was bitter, hollow. "Hooked up. That's an interesting way of putting it."

Mitch bent forward so their noses nearly touched. "I'm going to give you some advice. Don't try to convince me that Layton Keller is the bad guy here. I've watched him in action for two years. You, I've only just met, and so far you haven't done a whole lot that impresses me. All you've done is put your child's welfare at frightening risk. And, now, instead of asking for help from the man who can and will do everything in his power to find your son, you're disparaging his good name. You know what that tells me? You're a selfish woman. You think the rules don't apply to you. Well, sooner or later, what goes around comes around, and it just came around on you. So get over it and get up."

There was no reasoning with him. If she told him now that Layton probably planned to kill her for revenge and to protect his pristine image, Mitch wouldn't believe her for an instant. And besides, it didn't matter what this man thought. Nothing mattered but finding Jonah. Gritting her teeth, she pushed to her feet.

At a black Mustang, Mitch opened the driver's door and motioned for her to crawl across the emergency brake and console to the passenger seat. The awkward maneuvering left her breathless and hurting.

Mitch started the car. "Fasten your seat belt."

She started to reach for it but dropped back on an involuntary moan.

Stretching across her, he grabbed the buckle and fastened it for her. Still close, smelling of soap and pine, he paused and searched her eyes. He had the darkest eyes she had ever seen, and their intensity unnerved her. "What?" she asked.

"Is something broken?"

"I don't know. I didn't wait for X-rays."

"Great." Sitting back, he shifted the car into gear, her hand dangling from his wrist.

She decided she had nothing to lose to try again to reason with him. Jonah's well-being depended on it. He wasn't with Layton or Mitch would have known. That meant he was still out there somewhere. "Please, we have to go to the police. They need to be searching for him," she said.

"They could have been searching for him hours ago if you hadn't wasted precious time."

"I didn't plan to get hit by a car."

"No, but there was nothing stopping you from asking for help when you were in the ER."

"I didn't know what I was dealing with then. I thought it was just the FBI. I was going to pick up Jonah at the Maxwells' and get out of town. I didn't know what had happened there." Her voice broke on a surge of emotion, and she pressed the back of her free hand to her mouth to help hold it in. *Hang on. Hang on. Just a little bit longer.*

Mitch glanced over, but instead of snapping at her, he looked away as he downshifted for a turn. "And what did happen there?"

"We already went over this. Layton sent his men to get Jonah. Grant's a good man." She paused, swallowing as she imagined what it had been like for him to face a gun with two teenagers counting on him to protect them. "He wouldn't have stood by and let someone take my son."

"I told you before that Keller doesn't know where you are."

"You think all this is just a big fat coincidence?" she asked.

"If he knew, he would have contacted me to let me know Jonah was accounted for. He's not a man who lets people waste their time, or his."

"You saw that my home was trashed, didn't you? Not just ransacked, but destroyed."

"And what would be the point?"

"Revenge would be the point," she said, trying hard to keep her patience under control. She didn't mention the paperwork that had been burned, making it extremely difficult for her and Jonah to run away easily.

"I find it hard to believe that a man like Layton Keller would—"

"Are you his friend?" she cut in.

He glanced at her as he braked at a stoplight. "He's my employer."

She saw it, the glimmer of doubt, and hope flared. "Then you really don't know what he would or wouldn't do."

"I'm a good judge of—why am I defending myself or anyone to you?"

"Because you're a reasonable man, and you want to do the right thing."

The light turned green, and the car leapt forward. "I'm done with this conversation."

"When Jonah was nine, Layton tracked me down—"

Swerving onto the shoulder of the road, Mitch slammed on the brakes. Turning in his seat, he sank his fingers into the front of her shirt and yanked her forward. Her handcuffed hand dangled from his, trapped between them, and in the darkness of the car, his eyes were black holes. "You act like you think you have a shot at turning me on him," he said, his voice low. "You don't. I've already chosen a side, and if I'm anything, it's loyal. Got it?"

She let her held breath out slowly. His anger vibrated through his arm against her, and she realized that Layton must have wanted her alive so he could kill her himself. Otherwise, this man would have murdered her long ago. And he probably would have enjoyed it.

He gave her a shake. "Got it?"

She managed not to wince. "Yes."

After releasing her, he steered the car back into traffic.

Deflated, Alaina looked out at the passing night. Perhaps she could signal to another driver that she needed help. Maybe they would pass a police officer.

She let three cars go by without making an effort to get their drivers' attention.

The truth was, Mitch was right. If Layton really did want to find Jonah, he would spare no expense. She, on the other hand, had nothing. She couldn't afford to hire a detective. If she went to the FBI or the police, they would find out that she was the one wanted for kidnapping him in the first place. Worse, they might connect her to the man she had been forced to kill in self-defense many years ago, if they hadn't already. Awful as it was, Layton was probably the only one capable of locating Jonah quickly and efficiently.

And then what?

Jonah would be found. He'd be safe.

He'd no longer be hers. The pain that squeezed her heart took her breath away.

He would know how she had lied.

Chapter 11

On the highway, with nothing but the hum of the engine to fill the silence, Mitch fished his cell phone out of the leather holder strapped to his belt. After thumbing the button to get to the phone's directory, he pushed the speed-dial number for Layton Keller. Beside him, his passenger remained quiet, but he sensed the sharpness of her attention.

His boss answered. "Keller."

"It's Mitch."

"Ah, Mitch. How are you?"

"I've got her."

There was silence on the other end of the line, and Mitch began to wonder if the phone had lost its signal. Then Keller said, "She's there with you now?"

"Yes. But I'm afraid your son is unaccounted—"

"Tell her I've got him."

Mitch hesitated, uncomfortable, and a bit surprised at the glee he heard in his employer's voice. He glanced sideways at Alaina, found her watching him intently. He didn't know what to say to either of them.

"Are you there, Mitch?" Keller asked.

"Yes. I, uh, that's good news. I trust he's unharmed?"

"I haven't seen him yet. Some of my associates put him on the corporate jet this afternoon. It was delayed a couple of hours because of weather, but he's due in in the next hour."

"How, if you don't mind my asking, did that happen?"

"It's a long story," Keller said. "One I'll tell you when you get here. The PCware jet will be in use in the morning, but I'll send it to Chicago in the afternoon to pick her up."

"We can take a commercial flight tonight—"

"No, no, that's not necessary."

"It's no problem," Mitch said.

"The thing is, I'd like some time with my son. Do you understand?"

Mitch felt Alaina's gaze boring into the side of his face, felt her holding her breath, hanging on his every word. "I understand."

"Good. I knew you, of all people, would. I'll call you tomorrow to let you know when to bring her to the airport. No need for you to accompany her back here. I'll have the feds meet her at Dulles. Once you drop her off, your job is done."

Mitch disconnected the call and slipped the phone back into its slim pocket. "Jonah's okay. He's flying into D.C. on the PCware jet."

The tension that held Alaina rigid drained away, and she sagged back in the seat, covering her face with her free hand. Several minutes ticked by, and Mitch wondered whether she was crying. He should have felt triumph. The kid wasn't missing after all, and the good guys had won. Layton Keller was going to be reunited with his son within the hour.

But the knot in his stomach didn't loosen. The tension that tightened his shoulders stayed stubbornly put.

"He's never flown before."

The sound of her voice jolted him. Dead. As if someone had just punched a fist through her chest and ripped out her still-beating heart. She sat with her head bowed, her eyes closed. Her face was so still she might have been a corpse.

It took all of his will to turn his gaze back to the road. It didn't matter, he told himself. It didn't matter what she was feeling. She had made her bed . . .

"You'll see him tomorrow," he said, his voice gruff. "Focus on that."

She raised her head. "Tomorrow?"

"Keller is arranging to fly you to D.C. tomorrow afternoon."

"Why not tonight?"

"Because tomorrow is the soonest—"

"No. I need to go tonight." Some of the strength returned to her voice. "Now."

It surprised him that she was so eager to get to Washington, where she faced the likelihood of being arrested and charged with kidnapping and maybe even murder. In fact, the feds must be on to her. Otherwise, why would they have showed up at her workplace? Instead of heading right into trouble, she should have been trying to figure out a way to get away from him, so she could go into hiding and save her own butt. "Why the hurry?" he asked.

"Jonah is going to be scared. Confused."

"What's to be confused about? He's finally meeting the father he never knew . . ." He trailed off as the real reason for her anxiety hit him. "You never told him Keller is his dad."

She didn't respond, and he took her lack of an answer as affirmation. The knot in his gut drew taut as he imagined what it would be like to meet your son for the first time and know, that to him, you would be nothing more than a stranger. Because someone else—his mother—had denied you ever existed. "Son of a bitch," he said under his breath.

"I had good reasons," she replied, no more emotion in her voice than if she'd said that it looked like rain.

He snorted in irritation. "Of course you did."

"You have no idea what happened then. You don't know what that—"

"You're right," he cut in. "I don't know, and I don't need

to. All I know is that you never told his kid who his father is. When Jonah finds out . . . he's not going to be too happy with you. All the lies you've told him—"

"I never—" She broke off, fisting her hand on her knee. "I protected my son."

"You lied to him. Every damn day of his life."

"I don't have to justify anything to you."

"No," he said, shaking his head. "No, you don't. But your son will want an explanation, and I hope it's a good one, because what you've done is going to leave some deep wounds."

"Can we focus on getting to D.C. tonight?"

"We're not going to D.C. tonight. We're staying put like my boss told me."

"So that's it? You're just Layton's lackey? You do whatever he tells you and don't ask questions?"

"I ask questions when the situation warrants it."

"Then why aren't you asking yourself how it is that Jonah is on a jet to D.C. when you supposedly never told Layton where to find us?"

Ignoring her, he took the exit that would lead them to the hotel room he'd kept for the past three weeks. "I'm done with the Q&A session."

"Because you can't answer that."

"It doesn't matter. The drama is over. Your son is safe, and tomorrow, you'll face the music."

At the hotel, Mitch was relieved that no one was in sight, because he didn't doubt that, given the chance, Alaina would have screamed her head off. Luckily, no opportunity presented itself. In the room, he told her to sit on the bed as he worked the key to the cuffs out of his pocket.

She obeyed, completely docile, her head down, dark hair falling forward.

He figured the fight had finally gone out of her. He couldn't blame her. She'd had a tough day. On the other hand, it left him a little disappointed. He hadn't expected she would ever give in. Not when it came to her son. He realized his mistake when he unlocked the cuff from his wrist and moved to secure it to the headboard.

Her body leapt to life and, jerking away from him, she made a break for freedom.

Even caught off guard, he was able to get to her before she had her hand on the doorknob. Grabbing her shoulder, he whirled her around and levered her against the wall next to the door.

She fired a fist at his head, and he caught and pinned it to the wall. Ditto the other hand. Next, she tried to fight with her knees, and he trapped them, too, until he was pressed against her from head to toe. His every hard angle dug into her every soft curve. He had to be hurting her, but he couldn't back off. She would nail him the instant he did.

Panting, she leaned her head against the wall, her eyes flashing with frustration. He dragged his gaze from her mouth, conscious that, as she moistened her lips, the drumming beat of his heart tripled. An alarm went off in his head. What the hell?

Oblivious, she strained against him, still determined to break his hold. Lifting his hips back, he immobilized her at the shoulders and firmly planted one of his thighs between hers to keep her knees from attempting any damage. The change in position did nothing to calm his sudden, raging awareness of her as a woman. Her scent—lavender and vanilla—filled his head.

She must have felt the shift in him, because she suddenly went deathly still. Breathing hard, he wondered what had chased the flush out of her face.

Wary now, and clearly frightened, she asked, "What are you doing?"

"I'm trying to keep you from knocking my balls up into my throat," he growled.

Closing her eyes, she swallowed, every inch of her rigid, as if she expected him to rip into her throat with his teeth. "You can let go," she said.

"Are you going to behave?"

"Yes."

But he hesitated to release her. She'd fooled him with compliance only a few moments before, and then she'd struck. He didn't trust her.

"Let go," she said, giving her wrist an impatient jerk.

Instead, he lifted her off her feet and hauled her toward the bed. She writhed so violently in his arms that he almost dropped her. "Dammit, knock it off," he snapped. Then, annoyed at her and himself, he tossed her onto the bed.

She barely bounced before she twisted and tried to scramble away. Seizing her by the ankle, he dragged her back and straddled her, trying to subdue her long enough to get the handcuff attached to the headboard. Under him, her eyes went blind with terror. "No! No! Get off!"

He reared back to dodge a flailing fist, caught her wrist and flattened it to the bed next to her head. She bucked frantically, the cords in her neck standing out. "Don't! Don't!"

The frenzied desperation of her struggles, as if she were suddenly certain he was going to kill her, shocked him. He couldn't hold her still long enough to snap the handcuff around her wrist. Afraid she would hurt herself, though she gave no indication of pain, he leaned over her and said her name: "Alaina."

She didn't seem to hear as she thrashed. Then she started to beg. "Please, no. Please, no."

His stomach wrenching, Mitch made one last effort to secure the cuff and nailed it. Relieved, he rolled away from her and to his feet.

Alaina curled into a protective ball on her side, shuddering as she covered her face with her free hand. Her breathing was harsh and uneven.

He watched her, a sick feeling in his gut. Getting the hell out of that hotel room suddenly became imperative. "There's something I have to do," he said, then cleared the shakiness from his throat. "I'll bring back food."

She made no sound, her eyes tightly closed.

Before he left, he crossed to the phone and ripped the cord out of the wall. Though he doubted she was in any shape to try to make a call, he couldn't take the chance.

When the cool air outside struck his face, he stopped and drew it into his lungs, seeking its calming effect.

She'd thought he was going to assault her.

The knowledge made his head whirl, and he tried to process it. Had she glimpsed the flare of lust in his eyes? Because he acknowledged that, for a moment, his thoughts had veered in that direction. How could they not? She was an attractive, spirited woman with enormous appeal. Had their gazes met across a crowded room, on neutral ground, he would have been drawn to her in an instant. In the past few weeks, while watching her with her son, he had noted her attractiveness, but it had been of no consequence. She'd been an assignment, a job. How striking she was didn't change his objective.

Perhaps that was why the physicality of the moment against the door had caught him so off guard. He hadn't expected to have those feelings for her. He wasn't even sure now why he had.

One thing he did know for sure: The wild fear in those

gray-green eyes of hers would haunt him for the rest of his life. And his heart ached with the knowledge that he had terrorized her.

Standing near the door for several moments, he listened for weeping, but if she made any noise, he didn't hear it.

Finally, he pocketed his hands and walked away.

Alaina lay with her eyes closed, one hand fisted against her chest, the other cuffed to the headboard. Her muscles were so taut, they ached, but she couldn't get her body to relax. She focused on breathing, telling herself that she was okay, that he had not hurt her, that he'd had no intention of hurting her. Still, memories pummeled her. Layton tearing at her clothes, shoving himself into her. The terror was fresh, as if it had happened yesterday rather than fifteen years ago. She had worked hard over the years to keep the memories at bay. Counseling had been a tremendous help. But perhaps more effective: There had been more important things to do, a child to take care of, someone whose very survival depended on her maintaining her grip.

But now Jonah might be lost to her. And there was nothing . . . nothing she could do to stop the inevitable. Soon, he would know. Soon, he would meet his charming father, a man who could sell a side of beef to a vegetarian. That man would tell the vulnerable fourteen-year-old boy that his heartless mother had stolen him away, denying him a life beyond his wildest imaginings.

Despair was a live thing, writhing inside her, and she fought to control it.

As her raging heartbeat slowed and her breathing calmed, she turned her attention to the cuffs securing her wrist to the headboard. Jerking against them, she found them to be steadfast. The movement also sent a surge of pain into her injured shoulder. She rubbed the soreness absently, considering her options.

They were beyond limited. In fact, there was only one: Go to D.C. and face the past.

Chapter 12

Addison Keller stood at the sink, staring at herself in the dark window as she sipped her third glass of pinot noir and wondered what the hell she would do with her life when the feds hauled Layton away in cuffs. Imagining the sight, she smirked at her reflection, even giggled a little. Take that, you lying son of a bitch.

Realizing that she'd had too much wine, she set the glass aside. She could have finished the bottle for all that it mattered. Layton had slipped out an hour ago without telling her where he was going or when he would be back. Not that she cared. The longer he was away, the less she had to pretend she still cared.

Sixteen years. Wasted. She was almost forty years old. She had devoted her life to being a corporate wife. She sat on all the appropriate community boards. The YWCA. The public library. The women's club. The community college. Schools for mentally handicapped children. She organized fundraising events for single moms. Chaired a drive to collect toys for underprivileged kids during the holidays. Headed a literacy program for families on welfare. Her days were packed with activities that kept her in the public eye and polished to a golden sheen the images of her husband and family. Just like her mother had.

"Addy? Where are you?"

She turned from the window, surprised at the excitement in her husband's voice. Smoothing the wrinkles in the front of her blouse, she walked through the dining room and into the living room, where she stopped in mid-step and stared.

Standing beside Layton was a disheveled, exhausted teenager with messy blond hair in need of a haircut, piercing blue eyes and the same angle-cut features that age had softened on her husband. He was on his way to being as tall as Layton and wore grungy-looking blue jeans with holes in the knees, black athletic shoes that had seen better days, and an incongruous "Welcome to Washington" T-shirt sporting an artist's rendition of the nation's Capitol. One wrist bore a sports watch, the other a loose bracelet woven out of black and red material. One ear was pierced, a diamond stud winking in the light.

Her sister's son took her breath away.

Layton, beaming, gave Jonah a nudge toward Addison. "Addy, this is Jonah. Jonah, your Aunt Addy."

Speechless, Addison tried to smile, feeling as if a stranger had control of her facial muscles. Dammit, too much wine. "How do you do, Jonah?"

He met her gaze briefly before his blue eyes—so like his father's—darted away.

"He's tired," Layton said. "He needs a good night's sleep." He slapped the boy on the shoulder, pal-like. "Don't you, kiddo?"

Jonah cast his gaze down at the floor, clearly shell-shocked. Addison looked at Layton. "How did—"

"I'll explain everything once Jonah here is settled. He's had a long day."

She studied her husband's face, alarm growing at his triumphant glow. Oh God, what had he done? Her stomach churning, she turned her attention to her nephew. "I'll show you to a guest room, Jonah—"

"His room," Layton interrupted. "It'll be his room."

Addison forced a smile. "Right." She led the teen up the stairs. "We have several guest rooms, but you can have the biggest one," she said, unable to stop herself from babbling. That damn wine. "In the morning, you'll see that it has a fantastic view of the Potomac."

She flicked on the bedroom light. The décor was all wrong for a teenage boy—from the white down comforter to the gauzy black sheers that fell to the floor. She indicated a closed door along one wall. "There's a full bathroom with clean towels and a selection of toiletries. Use whatever you want." Facing him, she clasped her trembling hands before her and tried to think of something to say. "Is that a new shirt?"

He sank onto the bed, his gaze fastened on her face. "You look like my mother."

Her chest tightened with dread. "How is she?"

He looked down at the hands tangled in his lap. "I don't know. She'll be worried."

If he thought that, then perhaps Alaina was okay. She clung to that. Considering anything else was too distressing. "When did you see her last?"

"This morning before school," he said, rubbing at his right eye as if it itched.

She sat beside him, careful not to crowd him. "Can you tell me what happened?"

He turned his head to look at her. Even though his eyes were Layton's blue, she saw in them what she remembered most from Alaina's. Mistrust. Dejection. Anger.

"I want to help," she said softly, gripping his forearm. "I'm going to help you."

"He says he's my father."

She nodded, giving him a sympathetic smile. "He's very happy to finally meet you." She squeezed his arm. "So am I. The last time we saw you, you were a tiny baby."

"She told me she didn't know my father, that he was a one-night stand."

Addison's heart twisted. Alaina couldn't have told him the truth, but how it must have tormented her to present her son such an unsavory image of herself. "She was protecting you."

Rage leapt like fire into his eyes. "From what?"

"It's very complicated—"

"No kidding." Pushing himself up, he crossed to the window and peered at the darkness outside. There was nothing to see, but he concentrated as if he could see every blade of grass.

Addison stayed on the bed, allowing him the space he sought. "Jonah," she said. "Tell me what happened today."

His shoulders squared, then sagged, the weight of the day too heavy for bravado. He leaned his forehead against the window as if the contact would cool a raging fever. "I was at Lucas's." He stopped, and when he spoke again, his voice shook. "They shot his dad."

Addison flinched, as much at his words as at the pitiful catch in his voice. "Who shot him?" she asked.

"Two guys. They busted in, and when he tried to fight them, they shot him." Turning, he dug his fingers into the front of his shirt and pulled it away from his skin as if the feel of it chafed. "His blood splattered on my shirt."

He rubbed at his eyes again, and this time when he lowered his hand, they were bloodshot and watery. "I ran," he said. "I just took off, but one of the guys came after me." He swallowed hard, his gaze turning inward. "I hope they didn't hurt Lucas. He's my best friend."

"He's fine, Jonah. I promise."

"How do you know?"

"I just do." She paused. "Can you tell me what happened after the man caught you?"

Jonah focused on her. "He tied my hands. Made me get into the trunk of their car. They drove for a long time, and I could hear them talking, but they were doing it too quiet and I couldn't hear what they said. Then one of them called someone, and the connection must have been bad, because the guy on the phone started talking really loud. Said they had something that person wanted. I thought they called Mom. I started to yell, to tell her I was okay, but I didn't want to, you know, scare her. The guy asked for money. Fifty thousand dollars."

As he talked, the words began to spill out faster.

"They set up a meeting," he went on. "Said they'd turn me over, no harm done, for the money in small bills. I kept thinking there was no way Mom could pay them. We don't have that kind of money. And then I started thinking that they grabbed the wrong kid, that they'd meant to get Lucas. He's got rich grandparents down in Florida." He lowered himself to the other side of the bed. "After a while, they parked and opened the trunk, and I was trying to figure out if I should tell them they got the wrong kid, but I was afraid." His voice lost volume, and he paused, seemed to take a moment to regroup. "I was afraid they'd kill me if they realized I wasn't who they wanted. I saw we were in one of those big buildings at the airport where they park airplanes. A hangar. The car was parked next to one of those corporate planes. White. With a dolphin nose."

Addison recognized his description of what could have been the PCware Gulfstream.

"I started yelling for help, and the guys laughed at me. They told me no one was around to help me. This other guy walked up in a suit and tie. He had a bag that I guess had the money in it, because he handed it to one of the guys and told them to beat it. They took off, and the new guy . . . he untied my hands, told me not to worry. He asked if I was okay. Maybe because he saw all the blood on my shirt. I told him he had the wrong kid. He looked at my face really hard and said, 'You Jonah?' When I said, 'Yeah,' he pushed me toward the steps that led up into the plane. Told me to get in, we were going on a trip. He closed the door to the cockpit, so I couldn't talk to him. We stayed on the runway a long time, I guess because it was storming. Then we finally took off. I was scared. I'd never flown before. But it was also kind of cool. I was beginning to think I was going to be okay." He gave a small shrug. "He could have left me tied up and all."

She tried for an encouraging smile. "What happened when you landed?"

"We taxied a long time, to a hangar like the one in Chicago. When the door was opened . . . he was there."

Addison understood who "he" was. Layton. She waited.

"He gave me a clean shirt." Jonah looked at her. "Is he really my father?"

She nodded. "Yes."

"He told me you're my mom's sister. She's never mentioned you."

That stung, even though Addison knew she had no right to feel hurt. Straightening off the bed, she moved toward the door. "You're tired. Why don't we talk more tomorrow, after you've gotten some sleep?"

"I want to call Mom. She's going to be worried."

"I'll call her, okay?"

He hesitated, not happy with that suggestion but apparently unable to figure out how to insist. "Tell her I'm fine. They didn't hurt me."

"I will. Sleep well."

In the hallway outside the closed door, she met her husband's veiled gaze. He was leaning a shoulder against the wall, the tail of his white shirt out of his slacks, hands in his pockets. He offered no apology for eavesdropping, not that she expected him to.

"That's quite a story, isn't it?" he said.

She walked by him to their bedroom at the other end of the hall, conscious of him following, hands still in his pockets, that damn bounce in his step. Once in the bedroom, she shut the door and whirled on him. "What the hell happened, Layton?"

He spread his hands before him. "Why are you angry at me, Addy? What did I do?"

"That boy was kidnapped and delivered right to you. Forgive me for being a little suspicious about how that came about. Jesus, a man got shot."

Layton dragged a hand through his blond curls, and some of the happiness in his face fell away. "You're right, honey. It's terrible. I feel terrible."

She refused to believe that he felt anywhere near as contrite as he suddenly looked, and she had to fight the urge to throw something heavy and lethal at his head. "Tell me what happened."

He crossed to her, put his hands on her shoulders and gently squeezed. "Don't get so upset. All's well that end's well."

"How has this ended well? A man was shot. He could have been killed." She stopped, hitched in a breath, told herself to get a grip before she blew it. "Where is Alaina?"

His eyes hardened. "That's not our problem, Addison."

"She's his mother. The hell it's not our problem."

"Hey, if she can't keep track of the kid—"

"Layton, I'm begging you." She curled her fingers into his shirtfront. "Tell me what happened."

Releasing her, he turned away, one hand going back into

his pants pocket, the other massaging the back of his neck. She could see his features in the reflection of the full-length mirror in the corner. He looked genuinely distressed, and she wondered whether he knew she could see his face.

"All right," he said. "You know I've had detectives looking for them all along. Well, a couple weeks ago, I hired a new guy, and it paid off. He found them. But instead of telling me where they were, the son of a bitch hatched a plan to take me for an extra fifty grand. He kidnapped the kid and told me he'd kill him if I didn't pay the ransom. Of course, I paid. I wasn't about to take any chances with my son's life."

He was lying. She was sure of it. But damned if she could see the deception in his expression. Even with his back to her, he kept his game face firmly in place.

"We have to let Alaina know he's okay," she said.

He faced her, indignation artfully replacing his distress. "Why? We haven't heard from her in fourteen years. She hasn't once let us know a damn thing about my son, and she never bothered to tell him a fucking thing about me. Can you believe that?" He shook his head. "It's our turn now, Addy. She lost him, and now he's ours. Like he was supposed to be all along. Remember? That judge gave him to us, not to her."

She couldn't argue with him. Not without making him suspicious. Forcing herself to relax her shoulders, she said, "You're right." She turned her back as unexpected tears flooded her eyes. Her chest ached for her sister, for the father who'd been shot in his own home by her husband's thugs. Guilt mixed with the sorrow. Maybe if she hadn't been a blind idiot so long ago . . .

Layton's fingers settled on her shoulders again, kneaded. "Don't cry, honey. It'll be okay. I know it's messed up right now, but we'll make a good home for him." He chuckled.

"Did you see his holey jeans? That earring? What kind of mother was she to let him dress like that?"

Her heart seized up at his use of past tense. "Was?"

"Yes, was. You're his mother now, Addy. And I'm his dad. He's the luckiest kid on the planet."

Chapter 13

Alaina woke, knowing instantly where she was and why. What she didn't know was how long she had been asleep or what had awakened her. Had Mitch returned? She lay still and listened, hearing only the hum of the room's heater and the traffic of a busy street.

The clock beside the bed told her she'd slept for half an hour, yet it seemed hours had passed. Would Mitch come back tonight or wait until morning?

Sitting up, she gingerly rotated her shoulder as much as the cuffs allowed, trying to work some of the soreness out. It probably should have been iced and stabilized in some way to prevent further injury, but she didn't know how to accomplish that, especially while shackled to a bed.

Her stomach growled, and she realized that, having skipped lunch at work, she had not eaten since breakfast, some twelve hours before. No wonder her arms felt leaden.

She worked the cuffs anyway, alternately trying to slip the manacle over her hand, then checking each and every chain link for a weak one. When that didn't work, she inspected the contents of the drawer in the bedside table for the second time that night, hoping against hope she'd find a stray paper clip to try to pick the lock.

She was sitting there, propped against pillows and staring at the steel encircling her bruised wrist when the door slammed inward and a man she didn't recognize sauntered in.

He had a gun in his hand and a grin on his face.

* * * * *

Mitch sat in his car in the hotel parking lot, tapping the heel of his hand against the steering wheel. A paper bag of burgers and fries sat on the seat next to him. The greasy smell turned his stomach, even though it had been more than eight hours since his last meal. He wished like hell it were the next day and that his captive was on the PCware corporate jet, en route to the feds. His job would be done, just as Keller had said.

The good guy would win. Just as it should be.

Then why did it all feel so wrong?

He rubbed at his temples, where a headache was taking root. He considered calling Julia. He needed someone objective to talk to. But, he reminded himself, his partner wasn't objective. She had given Alaina the benefit of the doubt from the start, advising him against taking this job. Julia had warned him that it would become personal, and, dammit, she'd been right. He didn't think hearing her gloat would help, so he nixed the urge to call. Instead, he tried to sort it out, despite the ache in his head.

It bothered him that Keller had obviously had him followed. It bothered him more that Keller may have sent henchmen with guns to the Maxwell home to collect Jonah. Mitch kept seeing that bloodstain, evidence that an innocent man had been shot. His teenage son had been hurt, too. It didn't make sense. If the thugs had guns, why harm innocent people? Why didn't they just take what they came for—Jonah—and move on? Unless Grant Maxwell had indeed tried to protect Jonah and got shot in the process.

There certainly seemed to be no doubt in Alaina's mind that people who worked for Keller were responsible.

She's paranoid, Mitch told himself.

But he'd dealt with his share of paranoid people, and she didn't fit the bill. He'd also dealt with terrified people. That bill she fit. Which begged the question: Why, now that Jonah was on his way to his father, hadn't she bargained with Mitch to let her go? She'd done just the opposite, adamant that they go to D.C. right then, apparently giving no thought to the consequences to herself. She faced being imprisoned. Yet her only thought was her son.

Mitch remembered leaning over her after she'd been hit by the car. She hadn't just begged him to help her. She'd begged him to help her up, determined to get to Jonah, no matter the cost to her own health. That determination had carried her out of the hospital and to the Maxwells' when she'd been barely able to walk, had sustained her on her mad dash from the hotel to her home and to the airport, had compelled her to try more than once to overpower him, a man nearly twice her size and God knew how many times stronger.

Dammit, he respected her for that. She wasn't giving up, even when she didn't stand a Popsicle's chance in Florida. He wished he'd had her fortitude when Shirley had taken their son and moved out of the state. But he'd been too busy being angry at the world for dealing him a pair of twos when he desperately needed a full house. Maybe if he'd fought harder . . . hell, at all . . . ah, what was the use? It was done. He'd folded and walked away a sore loser years ago, and now another man was raising his son. There wasn't a damn thing he could do about it now.

Grabbing the bag of fast food, Mitch got out of the car. He lectured himself as he walked through the parking lot to the room: Do the job, collect the check, move on. So simple it was absurd. From here on in, it was the easiest money ever.

He slipped the key card into its slot, heard the latch slide open—

"Gun!"

"Bitch!"

Mitch, dropping back against the outside wall, heard the sharp crack of flesh against flesh. The fast-food bag fell to the floor as he seized his gun from the holster under his arm. He strained to hear over the blood roaring in his ears. Silence.

"Alaina?"

"Get in here or the bitch buys it. I'm not shitting you, man."

The voice was male and low, coming from somewhere in the middle of the room. Mitch imagined the guy crouching between the two double beds, using the one closest to the door as a shield. His gut lurched as he recalled that that was the bed he'd handcuffed Alaina to. Not only was she helpless in there, unable to defend herself because he'd shackled her, but she also was between him and the intruder, making it impossible for Mitch to get off a clean shot without the risk of hitting her.

"All right," Mitch said, slipping his gun into the waistband at the small of his back. "All right. I'm not armed."

"Yeah, right. Toss your piece in here before you wander in, tough guy."

Well, it had been worth a shot, Mitch thought, as he pitched his gun through the open door.

"The piece strapped to your ankle, too. Make it quick."

Swearing under his breath, Mitch slid the smaller handgun out of its sheath and chucked it into the room.

"Good. Now, keep your hands up," the guy said. "And no fast moves. I'm pointing my gun right at her face. Anything stupid from you, and she's a freak show."

Mitch eased around the door, hands raised, keeping his gaze steady on the intruder.

The man was huge, easily six inches taller than him and probably a hundred pounds heavier. His bulk was clad entirely in black. Even his eyes looked black. His square head was shaved, his neck as thick as a football player's. He held the gun on Alaina with authority, his free hand bracing the forearm of his gun hand, his feet set wide. A professional.

"Close the door."

Mitch kicked it shut, keeping his gaze above Alaina's head. But he heard her uneven breathing, sensed fear in her stillness.

The hit man relaxed a little. "That's better."

"Who're you looking for?" Mitch asked.

"Who does it look like?"

"I'd hate for you to make a mistake."

The guy chuckled. "Do I look like the kind of guy who makes mistakes?"

Mitch tried another angle. "Who do you work for?"

"I hate to cut you off, buddy, but small talk ain't my—"

The pillow hit the thug square in the face. Mitch leaped across the bed, slamming into the man's middle and landing on top of him on the other bed. The hit man shoved him away, taking a swing at him and missing. Mitch rolled off the end of the bed, grabbed the heavy wooden desk chair and swung it up like a golf club, catching the guy under the chin.

The man's head snapped back and, for a moment, he seemed unaffected. Then he toppled over backward, unconscious.

"Nice shot," Alaina said.

Bending over, Mitch braced his hands on his knees to catch his breath. He'd thought they were both dead. "What the hell was that?" he demanded. "The pillow defense? It was stupid."

"Maybe you hadn't noticed, but he was going to shoot us. Somebody had to do something."

He looked at her finally, angry that she hadn't just let him handle it. "I don't suppose you noticed that he's bigger than I am. He could have snapped me in two—" He broke off, narrowing his eyes. "What the hell?"

She blinked, raising a hand to her face at the same time that he moved closer. As he remembered the sharp report of flesh on flesh, it registered that the dark smear across her jaw was blood. He caught her wrist before she could touch it, his fury drowning in a flood of guilt. "Don't," he said under his breath.

Without another word, he went into the bathroom and wet a towel. She'd paid for the warning she'd shouted before he could walk, unsuspecting, into the room and a loaded gun. She could have just let him come, let the beefcake kill him, then try to strike a deal with the bad guy. But she had warned him, the man who had cuffed her to a bed, the one who'd terrorized her. The one who worked for her mortal enemy.

And what had he done? He'd just stood there waiting for the goon to make the next move. If Alaina hadn't taken matters into her own hands, they'd both probably be dead by now.

As he wrung out the towel, he avoided looking at himself in the mirror.

Returning to the bed, where she watched him with puzzled eyes, he sat beside her and gently wiped away the blood, relieved to see only a shallow cut along her jawline. Glancing at the unconscious brute, he noted the onyx ring on his left ring finger. The bastard had backhanded her. Mitch fought the urge to pummel the guy.

"There are probably others like him," she said.

He focused on her eyes, so sad, so determined. Life had trained her to act, not wait to see how events might play out. Too often, circumstances hadn't turned in her favor, and she had stopped expecting them to a long time ago. He couldn't imagine what it was like to live like that.

Forcing his brain to engage, he asked, "Who is he?"

"He's got to be one of Layton's."

"That doesn't make sense."

"What doesn't make sense?" she asked, exasperated. "Layton sent the son of a bitch to kill me. And you, apparently."

Mitch shook his head, unable to wrap his brain around the rationale. Keller had what he wanted. His son. In less than twenty-four hours, the boy's kidnapper would be in FBI custody. Why kill her, or them, and risk the inevitable scrutiny? The investigation and accompanying suspicion would undo even the most spotless public image.

But who else knew where to find them?

Impatient, Alaina took the towel from him and pressed it to the darkening bruise on her jaw. "While you're trying to figure out Layton's twisted logic, would you mind unlocking the cuffs? I'd prefer not to be chained to the bed when the next hit man walks through the door."

Mitch couldn't argue with that. After unlocking them, he tossed them onto the desk.

She immediately scooted off the bed and headed for the bathroom. "Where are you going?" he asked, then felt like an idiot. His brain obviously wasn't operating at full steam yet.

"I think I've earned a visit to the bathroom, don't you?"

"Hey," he said.

She paused but didn't turn.

"Thanks for the warning."

She resumed her stride. "Don't mention it."

When she left the bathroom, her face washed and her hands steady, she found Mitch throwing his belongings into his suitcase. The gunman was on the floor, his wrists secured behind him with a length of belt.

"I just talked to my partner," Mitch said. "She's arranging for us to fly tonight to D.C. There's no point in hanging around here waiting for another hit man to find us."

Leaning against the doorjamb and folding her arms, Alaina couldn't resist needling him. "Don't you want to call Layton and clear it with him?"

He paused in his packing to glare at her. "I'd say that gloating is highly inappropriate right now and not your style."

"I think I have a reason to gloat. I've been telling you all along that Layton isn't who you think he is."

"And what makes you think I believe for a second that your ex hired that guy?"

She straightened, dropping her arms to her sides where her hands formed fists. "He's not my ex." As soon as she said it, she knew it was beside the point. "Of course he was hired by Layton. Who else would he be working for?"

"Hell if I know. But chances are good that Keller wasn't the only poor bastard you've screwed over."

"You are unbelievable," she snapped. Crossing to the fallen intruder, she knelt beside him and worked her hand into one of his back pockets.

"I'm also out of patience," Mitch said. "So let's make a deal: We'll fly to D.C. tonight, like you wanted, and then I'll give you a choice. I'll turn you over to the FBI, who can offer you protection. Or I'll take you to your dastardly former lover, who can reunite you with your kid. You can make the call."

She ignored him, checking each of the goon's pockets, hoping for something, anything, that would help her prove to her thickheaded captor that she spoke the truth.

Mitch sighed. "He's a professional. Professionals don't carry ID or little pieces of paper that say, 'I work for Layton Keller.' "

"It can't hurt to check, can it?"

"I already did. There's nothing."

Sitting back on her heels, she rubbed at her temples. Frustration made her head ache and her chest burn. She wanted to scream, cry, throw something. She wanted Jonah.

"How about that deal?" Mitch asked.

She shifted her gaze to him. "There's a problem with it."

"What?"

"I can't get a boarding pass without picture ID."

"Where's your ID?"

"It's in my purse, which the ER people gave to Rachel."

"Willowy blond knockout?"

She started to ask him how he knew, but then she remembered he had followed her around for three weeks, and Rachel was a staple in her life. Or had been. She shoved aside the encroaching despair. "Yes."

Retrieving the cuffs from the desk, Mitch crossed to her and held out his hand.

Alaina recoiled. The memory of being trapped while a man pointed a gun at her nose made her shake her head. "You don't need those."

"Get used to them. I'm not chancing you giving me the slip."

When she held back, he reached forward and snagged her wrist. She tried to jerk away, accomplishing nothing more than sending a jolt into her sore shoulder. Tears of pain and frustration stung her eyes.

His head down as if he couldn't bring himself to look her in the face, Mitch zipped the steel around her wrist, then his own. "Let's go."

Chapter 14

Alaina stared out the passenger window at streets that looked like shiny black metal, trying to figure out how to explain Mitch to Rachel. Her friend wouldn't accept some pithy explanation. She would want answers, and she would be bullheaded about getting them. She'd be protective and demanding and unyielding, the big sister Alaina had never had.

Beside her, Mitch was silent, as he had been while he had circled several blocks to make sure they weren't being followed. Then he had spoken only curtly to ask for directions to Rachel's and to ask what she wanted to eat when he'd pulled into a McDonald's drive-through. The cheeseburger she'd wolfed down felt like a thick ball of lead in her stomach now.

"That's Rachel's on the right," she said.

Pulling into the drive, Mitch killed the engine, then sat with his fingers wrapped around the gearshift, Alaina's hand dangling inches away. He stared at the front of Rachel's home, as if searching the newly shorn bushes for assailants.

Alaina also studied the small slate-blue house with black shutters, hoping that Rachel wouldn't be home. They could break in, swipe Alaina's purse, and be gone before her friend returned. But, no, the light that glowed beyond the large picture window wasn't from the hall light that Rachel left on when she wasn't home.

"I'm going to have a tough time explaining the cuffs," Alaina said.

Without a word, Mitch worked his hand into his jeans pocket and drew out the key. As he unlocked them, he said, "Make one wrong move in there, and I'm cuffing your hands behind your back until we get to D.C."

The manacle sprang open, and Alaina gingerly massaged the bracelet of bruises that marred her skin. "And how would you explain cuffs to the flight crew?" she asked, irritated. It was as if he thought he could get away with anything. Shades of Layton.

He met her eyes, and the look in his was deadly. "Don't fuck with me, lady. I've had a bad day."

"Really? Because my day has been stellar."

"I'd say both our days are going to improve tremendously as soon as we have what we came for. All you have to do is follow a few rules. No signals, no going to the bathroom, no secret messages."

"Rachel isn't stupid. She'll know something is up."

"Then it's up to you to put her mind at ease. You don't want her ending up like your friend Grant Maxwell, do you?"

Alarm widened her eyes, sent her pulse tripping. "Are you threatening her?"

"I'm telling you to protect her. Get the ID, get out. You don't want her involved in any way. Got it?"

"You don't have to tell me that. I know better than to get her involved."

"Right," he said. "That's why you've been best buddies for, what, five years? You're lucky that whoever's after you hasn't already tried to get at you through her."

"He doesn't need to get at me through her," she said. "He's got my kid."

"So what was Maxwell then? A bonus?"

She gaped at him. "You son of a bitch."

"I'm just telling you to keep it light, keep it quick." He checked his watch. "We don't have much time before our flight. Let's go."

From behind Alaina and three steps down, Mitch watched the emotions that flitted across Rachel Boyd's face when she opened the door to her friend's knock. Shock. Worry. Then rampant relief. Whipping open the heavy storm door, she hugged Alaina hard. "I've been worried to death," she said.

Alaina stiffened visibly, and Rachel drew back, her forehead creasing in concern. "Jesus, you look like shit." She grasped Alaina's hand to draw her inside. "Come in and sit down."

But Alaina shook her head, bringing Rachel up short. "I just came for my purse."

Rachel focused on Mitch as he stepped onto the porch. He made it a point to stand close enough to Alaina that their shoulders touched, a subtle warning.

Rachel's eyes darkened with suspicion. "Who are you?"

"Please, Ray, I just need my purse, okay?" Alaina said. "I'll explain everything later."

Rachel held on to Alaina's hand as if to keep her from bolting. "I recognize you," she said to Mitch. "You were there when she got hit by the car."

"Rachel, please," Alaina said.

"No," Rachel said, her tone firm as her attention swung back to her friend. "I'm not handing it over until you tell me what the hell's going on."

Alaina groaned in frustration. "I really don't have time for this—"

"Then make time," Rachel cut in. "I deserve an explanation, especially after the questioning that I endured. The FBI couldn't be bothered to tell me what was going on, either. And you stole my car today, remember? You owe me."

"I'm sorry, Rachel. I really can't—"

"Where's Jonah?" Rachel peered past them at Mitch's car in the driveway. "You said he was with you."

Alaina was silent, and through his shoulder, Mitch felt the shudder that went through her. Rachel must have seen it, because the anger faded, and her expression softened. "Oh God, Alex. How can you expect me to pretend that nothing is wrong? Why don't you trust me to help you?"

When Alaina covered her face with her hands, Mitch tensed. She was losing it, and he couldn't afford to wait for her to get it back together in time for them to make their flight. "Look," he said to Rachel. "We're in a hurry. She'll explain everything in a few days."

But Rachel wasn't listening to him. Her hand shook as she reached for Alaina's left wrist. Even in the porch light, the bruises that ringed it were stark. "Have you been tied up?" Horror made Rachel's voice faint. "And your face—"

The glass in the storm door shattered.

Rachel dropped back with a shriek, and Mitch shoved Alaina into the house and slammed the door behind them.

"What the hell was that?" Rachel demanded.

"Gunshot," Mitch said. "We need to kill the lights."

But Alaina was already hitting the switch near the door. The room went only semidark as light seeped from a room down the hall. "Get down, Ray," Alaina said.

Rachel, frozen in fear, gawked at her. "Someone shot at us?"

The bay window exploded inward, and Alaina dove for Rachel as glass rained over all three of them. As the women tumbled to the carpet out of harm's way, Mitch dropped to a squat, grabbing the gun from the holster under his arm. With the wall supporting his back, he kept an eye on the front door. "Is there a back way out?"

"Oh shit."

He turned his head to see Rachel leaning over Alaina, who was curled on her side, a hand clutched to her shoulder. Her head was back, the tendons in her neck taut, her lips white. His heart stuttered. "Is she hit?"

Rachel shook her head. "There's no blood."

Pocketing the gun, he crawled to them, keeping his head down. No more shots had been fired, which probably meant the gunman, or men, were trying to find a way into the house. "Is there a room without windows?"

"The bathroom," Rachel said. "Down the hall, second door on the right."

Seizing the gun strapped to his ankle, Mitch shoved it into her trembling hands. "Do you know how to use it?"

Rachel, her breathing labored, her face pale, nodded.

"Shoot anyone who comes through any of these doors," he said, sweeping the room with a hand to indicate the three passages into the living room. "I'm not kidding."

"Who's shooting at us?"

Ignoring the question, he bent and lifted Alaina into his arms. She released a ragged moan and stiffened. "Don't fight me," he growled. To Rachel, he said, "Come with me."

He carried Alaina down the hall and into the bathroom. After lowering her to the floor so that she could lean back against the tub, he faced Rachel. "Lock the door and don't open it for anyone but me. If anyone who isn't the police or the feds kicks in the door, shoot them. Got it?"

Rachel hesitated, her face glistening with perspiration.

Mitch grasped her shoulders. "Rachel, I swear to you, I'm the good guy."

With that, he slammed the door behind him and waited to

hear the lock engage. Then, gun in hand, he eased down the hallway toward the living room, praying there was only one gunman.

Alaina couldn't think, couldn't breathe. The agony slicing through her shoulder told her it was dislocated again, and she had to force herself not to writhe from the pain.

Rachel knelt beside her. "What can I do?"

Alaina tried to school her breathing, tried to think beyond the pain and nausea. "Nothing."

"Who is he, Alex? Is he the good guy?"

Alaina couldn't answer as a dull roar filled her ears, and the bathroom started to gray.

Rachel grasped her cheeks. "Dammit, don't pass out on me. I don't know what the hell I'm dealing with."

The desperation and terror in her friend's voice snapped her back. And Alaina knew she had to tell her friend the truth. She deserved to know what was happening, now that she might die because of it. "I kidnapped Jonah," she whispered, her voice ragged. "Fourteen years ago."

Rachel sat back on her heels as if she'd been slapped. "You what?"

A thump outside the bathroom door made them both jerk, and Rachel twisted around, holding the gun with both hands, her back braced against the tub beside Alaina. Running feet pounded down the hall away from the door, followed by silence.

"Jesus," Rachel breathed. "Oh, Jesus. There's more than one."

"I'm sorry," Alaina whispered. "I'm sorry I brought them here."

"Who are they?"

Alaina leaned her head against the porcelain rim behind

her, unable to answer as she fought to keep her head above the waves of pain. Black spots did a merry dance in front of her eyes.

"Alex," Rachel said, her tone sharp.

Alaina blinked several times, trying to focus. "My name's not Alex."

Rachel was obviously struggling to absorb it all. "Who's the guy with you? A cop?"

"Detective." She swallowed around the lump in her throat, determined not to be sick. "I'm so sorry. I should have told you—"

A gunshot cut her off. Rachel yanked the gun toward the door.

A minute passed, and nothing outside the door moved. Rachel's hand began to shake. "I can't believe this," she said. "I can't believe people are shooting each other in my house." She pierced Alaina with a furious gaze. "I can't believe my best friend is a kidnapper. Where is Jonah now?"

"I did the best thing for him."

"Where is he? Did you hide him somewhere? Does he even know what you did?"

"I'm his mother," Alaina said, her voice faint.

Rachel didn't appear to hear her. "How could you?" she asked, and tears ran down her cheeks. "That poor kid. He has no idea. How could he love you like he does if he knew?"

"You don't know—"

"You're right. I don't." Rachel pushed to her feet, awkward with the gun in her hand. "I don't know you at all."

At a knock on the door, Rachel whirled, jerking the gun up.

"It's Mitch."

The relief that surged through her surprised Alaina. Battling to stay conscious, she watched Rachel let him in and scanned him up and down for any sign of blood. He appeared unharmed, but his face seemed whiter than usual as he knelt before her, placing a gentle hand on her ankle.

The way he touched her, the way he looked at her, seemed different. But the pain apparently had warped her sense of reality.

"How're you doing?" he asked. His voice, his gaze . . . both gentle, concerned.

"Think I dislocated my shoulder. Oops." She smiled but didn't know why. She was just very glad to see him in one piece. He was, after all, her only link to Layton, and therefore Jonah.

Mitch pressed two fingers to the inside of her wrist. "Think you can stand up?"

"I'd rather just stay here like this for a minute," she said, and wet her dry lips with the tip of her tongue. The fuzzy gray around the edges of her vision was encroaching on wider territory.

Rachel eased toward the door. "I heard something. Is someone still here?"

"Feds," Mitch said. "They're securing the area."

"Feds were shooting at us?" Rachel asked, astonished.

"No, the feds were watching the house. The gunman got away."

"Feds were watching my house?"

He didn't respond as he slid his palm, warm and slightly damp, against Alaina's cheek. "Dammit," he said softly, pulling out his cell phone. "Rachel, can you get me a blanket?"

She stepped up behind him, his gun still dangling from her hand. "What is it?"

"She's going into shock."

Turning on her heel, Rachel dashed from the room.

"No, I'm not," Alaina said, and grasped his sleeve when the bathroom started to whirl.

Mitch gave her a tolerant smile. "Yes, you are." He pressed 911 with his thumb.

"Who are you calling?"

"Ambulance."

She stiffened, and instantly regretted it as fresh pain sliced through her. In spite of it, she swiped at his phone hand. "No, we'll miss our flight."

Mitch edged back. "You're not getting on a plane with a dislocated shoulder."

"You can fix it."

"Like hell. You need a doctor."

She grabbed at his arm as he raised the phone to his ear. "No, dammit."

He gently disengaged her grip as the floor tilted under her. She braced a hand on it, the gray sliding smoothly toward black. She only dimly heard Mitch saying Rachel's address as she clung desperately to consciousness.

No! She screamed it inside her head. *I need to go to Jonah now.*

That was her last thought.

When she slumped over, Mitch's heart started to jackhammer. He fumbled for the pulse in her wrist and couldn't find it. He located it in her throat—fast and erratic—just as Rachel appeared in the doorway. "Oh my God," Rachel said. "Is she—"

"She fainted," he said, getting up. Pocketing his phone, he swung Alaina up in his arms, careful of her shoulder. She was dead weight, her head lolling back over his arm. "Bedroom?"

Rachel pointed down the hall, then followed him. "What can I do?" she asked.

He put Alaina on the bed, then took the blanket from Rachel and spread it over her. "Let the paramedics in," he said.

Sirens sounded in the distance as Rachel hurried away and Mitch slid pillows under Alaina's feet to elevate them. Sitting on the edge of the bed, he grasped her limp hand in his. It was cold, and he pressed it between his palms, trying to warm it. Unconscious, she looked achingly vulnerable, and his stomach gave an ominous flutter.

"You keep surprising me," he whispered.

Chapter 15

In the ER waiting room, Rachel paced while Mitch sat stiffly in a chair, checking his watch every three seconds. An hour had passed since the ambulance had brought Alaina in. The nurse at the front desk had said someone would come talk to them as soon as she had been stabilized. How long could it take to fix a dislocated shoulder, for God's sake?

In the meantime, he puzzled over why the feds had yet to grill him or Rachel about what had happened at her home. Two federal agents—he'd nicknamed them Itchy and Scratchy—hovered around the ER exit, apparently keeping watch on him and Rachel, lest they decide to make a run for it. They were obvious rookies, young and inexperienced, assigned merely to observe, then call in the big guns when something actually needed to be done.

Mitch got the sense they were waiting for someone, a supervisor probably.

Rachel stopped in front of him, hands on her hips. "I didn't catch your name earlier."

He looked up at her. She was more beautiful up close than she'd been from a distance, even with no makeup, messy blond hair and blue eyes dark with fury. He couldn't blame her for being angry. Her home had been invaded, her personal space and sense of security violated. "Mitch Kane," he said. "I'm a private detective."

"Do you know why the feds were watching my house?"

"I'm guessing they were hoping Alaina would show up."

Her brow creased. "Alaina. So that's her real name."

Mitch nodded.

"And the feds at the newspaper were there to arrest her for kidnapping Jonah?"

"I'm not sure what they were doing there, but that's a possibility, yes."

"Do you know where Jonah is?"

"By now, he's with his father."

Her shoulders relaxed some, and she chewed her bottom lip. "Good. That's good."

Her reaction baffled him. Shouldn't she be on Alaina's side? He cleared his throat. "What has she told you about Jonah's father?"

Rachel pursed her lips, her eyes flooding but not overflowing. "Not a damn thing. I thought I knew her. I thought . . ." She trailed off, dragging a trembling hand through her short curls. "Jonah adores her. That poor kid."

"Is it possible she told you about his father without you realizing it?"

"In what way?"

"Maybe she talked about a past relationship that didn't—"

"Relationship?" Shock raised her eyebrows. "She said she kidnapped Jonah. I assumed she meant from strangers."

"Jonah is her son. She ran away with him fourteen years ago. His father hired me to find them."

Rachel sank onto the chair next to him. "Son of a bitch." Fisting a hand, she knocked it against her knee. "Five years we've been friends, and she never said a fucking word. How's that for friendship?"

Irritation tightened his throat. "I'm guessing you missed the part tonight where she saved your life."

Rachel met his gaze, her expression quizzical. "What are you talking about?"

"The second shot, the one that blew out the front window? She threw herself on top of you. That's how she dislocated her shoulder again."

Rachel seemed to think about that for a long moment, then dropped her head into her hands and moaned. "Oh God, I'm such a shit. What the hell was I thinking?"

"Rachel, she said she took Jonah from his father to protect him. Do you have any idea what that might have been about?"

Raising her head, she pierced him with a stare that streaked from stricken to suspicious. "You said you work for him."

"Yes."

"Then why are you asking me questions about him? Don't you know who you work for?"

"I'm trying to figure out who was shooting at us."

She pushed up from the chair, as if unable to sit still. "Jesus," she breathed. "Someone was shooting at us. I still can't believe it." She faced him suddenly, horror growing in her eyes. "Grant and Lucas. What happened to them is related to this, isn't it?"

"I think so, yes." He paused, but when she didn't respond, he asked, "Do you know who might have a grudge against Alaina?"

"Who would have a grudge against her?" she replied, as if the idea were absurd. "She never pisses anybody off. She won't even blow her horn when some asshole cuts her off in traffic." She rubbed her hands over her face. "God, I'm such an idiot. The Alex I know wouldn't hurt anybody. She couldn't have taken Jonah without a damn good reason." She turned her burning gaze on him, and he could see she was reaching a conclusion he wasn't going to like. "I don't think I should be talking to you," she said slowly.

"Rachel, I want to help—"

"How did she get that bruise on her face?"

"I didn't—"

"And the bruises around her wrist?" She looked like she might be sick. "You tied her up."

"You're wrong. That wasn't how it—"

He broke off, surprised to see a former colleague striding toward them.

Norm Potter wore an FBI power suit—navy with a white shirt and red tie—under a black trench coat. Gripping a cell phone in one hand, he looked the same—red hair and freckles—as he had the last time Mitch had seen him. Mitch realized that the two newbie agents had been waiting for his former co-worker.

"Norm, hello," Mitch said, shaking the man's hand.

"Mitch Kane," Norm said. "I'll be damned. It's been, what, five years?"

Mitch nodded, conscious of Rachel closely watching the exchange. "About that, yes. You here on official business?"

The grin on Norm's face faded. "Yes, my two agents over there," he jerked a thumb over his shoulder toward the rookies at the door, "tell me you had some excitement tonight involving someone we've been looking for."

Rachel said, "I'm going to check on Al . . . Alaina."

Norm's blue gaze landed on Rachel, and he pointed his cell phone at her. "Rachel Boyd, right?" he said.

She nodded, wary.

He thrust out a hand. "Assistant Director Norm Potter, FBI. I'm going to want to talk to you, too."

"Fine," she said. "I'll be only a few minutes."

Norm watched her walk away, then said to Mitch, "Why don't we take this somewhere private?"

★ ★ ★ ★ ★

Alaina was flying. She had been since regaining consciousness, her shoulder and the rest of her body blessedly pain-free. She didn't even care that someone had once again replaced her clothes with a hospital gown that gaped open in the back.

She remembered Mitch saying something about the feds watching Rachel's. They'd been waiting for her to show up.

So it was over. Fourteen years of running, of hiding, of living in constant fear that she would come home one day and Layton would be waiting, flanked by the sheriff, the county police, the state police, the FBI . . . whoever it would take to claim the child she had taken from him.

She'd known it would happen someday. She had expected it long ago. Now that it had . . . she was curiously numb. Maybe it was the drugs. Or maybe the despair was so overwhelming, so blinding, that her mind had shut down in defense.

Next stop: Prison. Or perhaps death at the hands of one of Layton's hit men.

After all was said and done, maybe that was what she deserved. She'd lied to her son for fourteen years. Sins of omission could be just as damaging as outright deception. Layton probably hadn't even had to reach that much to paint a heartless, cold portrait of her for Jonah.

She had stolen Jonah from his bed in his home.

She had denied him the comfort and benefits of a wealthy upbringing.

She had deprived him of knowing his father, a public icon of goodness and strength, a man who on the surface was charming and kind, intelligent and warm.

Looking back, she realized that she should have told Jonah the truth. Then he would have been prepared. He would have had a frame of reference. But how could she have told him the truth about how he came to be? It would have broken his heart, perhaps even his spirit.

She closed her eyes against the hot tears that welled, swallowed against the fissure of grief that splintered the numbness. What would she do without him? How could she live?

"Hey."

Alaina opened her eyes to see Rachel standing by the bed, looking stressed, a pair of scrubs tucked under her arm. "We have to get you out of here," she whispered. "The feds are here for you." She lowered the metal bar that ran along the edge of the bed. "Can you sit up?"

Alaina didn't move, staring at her friend in confusion. *"I don't know you at all."* That was what Rachel had said to her in the bathroom. She'd been disappointed in her, angry.

Now, Rachel leaned over her, her gaze sharp and urgent as she studied Alaina's face. "Great, you're high as a kite."

Alaina smiled, letting herself float a little higher, where the despair couldn't touch her. "Good drugs."

Tossing the scrubs onto the bed, Rachel stripped back the blanket covering her. "Let's get you dressed."

Wanting to please her friend, to make up for how she had let her down, Alaina tried to sit up. Dizziness instantly spun the room, and she would have sunk back to the pillow if Rachel hadn't caught her arm and kept her upright.

"No, you don't," she said, taking Alaina's hand and curling her fingers around the metal railing that remained up. "Hold on to that."

Alaina's chin wanted to loll onto her chest. "Why are you doing this?"

Rachel didn't respond as she untied Alaina's hospital gown and pulled it away. "Damn."

Startled, Alaina followed her friend's horrified gaze.

"Look at that," she said in wonder. Purple bruises smeared across her collarbone and left shoulder. More bruises marred the right side of her rib cage. None of them looked real, probably because she didn't feel them at the moment.

Her face pale, Rachel began unbuttoning her own blouse. "It'll be easier for you to put this on," she said, shedding her top and holding it up. "Let's start with your sore arm."

Alaina, too high to care that she was naked from the waist up, let Rachel slip the blouse on her and button it. "There, that wasn't that tough," Rachel said as she pulled the scrubs top over her own head. "Now the pants." Shaking out the bottoms, she leaned toward Alaina. "Hold on to me."

But Alaina stayed put as it occurred to her again that Rachel had been angry, really angry, with her. Now she was helping her escape? "You're aiding and abetting."

Rachel smiled, her eyes brightening with amusement. "I am, aren't I?"

"It's not funny," Alaina said, wishing the fog in her head would lift. "You could go to jail."

"Then we'll share a cell. Now get up. We don't have much time."

"I don't think this is a good idea."

"Now is not the time to debate this," Rachel said.

"Yes, it is. You haven't done anything wrong yet."

"I'll take my chances."

"Rachel, no. I won't let you put yourself in jeopardy for me."

Rachel looked into her eyes. "Listen to me, Al—" She faltered, then plunged ahead, "Did you have a good reason to take Jonah from his father?"

"Yes, but—"

"You knew when you did it that it was the absolutely right thing to do, didn't you?"

Alaina rubbed her eyes, trying to keep up. "Yes."

"Then you know exactly where I'm coming from. Now put your arm around my neck and hold on to me."

Once they were in Rachel's car and turning out of the ER parking lot, Alaina leaned her head back and closed her eyes. And thought about what happened the last time someone she cared about walked into Layton's crosshairs.

Jonah's eighth birthday was in a week, and Alaina couldn't wait to see the look on his face when he unwrapped his gift. He'd been begging for a Nintendo video game console for months. All the kids at school had one, he said. It was important for his social development, or so he said in his third-grade language.

She'd been reluctant to buy the game. It was pricey, and while Emma paid her significantly more than minimum wage at the bookstore, she still had to be frugal. In ten years, she'd have to be able to start paying for his college education, and she knew firsthand that that would be expensive.

Emma was the one who persuaded her to get the Nintendo. Dear old Emma, not the least bit tottering despite turning seventy-five only a month before, professed to be hip to what made kids happy these days. "Besides," she'd said in her smooth-as-porcelain voice, "video games build excellent hand-eye coordination."

Jonah had used the same argument, and Alaina grinned as she realized he had, in all his resourcefulness, enlisted Emma's help. He made her proud.

"But don't you think that implant he'd have to get in the back of his head is a bit overboard?" Alaina asked.

Emma's white eyebrows shot up. "Implant?"

Alaina burst out laughing and hugged her friend. "I love you, Em."

But the older woman wasn't impressed. She set Alaina back from her and strode out of the room, calling Jonah's name. "I want to talk to you, young man."

Now, two days later, Alaina hummed as she climbed the steps to the apartment above the bookstore, carrying a bag that held the game, already wrapped in vibrant birthday paper with a big red bow. After the day's classes, she had borrowed Emma's car to drive to Toys "R" Us before Jonah arrived home from school. She planned to stash the bag in the back of her closet before reporting for work downstairs.

Pushing through the door, she breathed in the scent of fresh-baked bread and garlic. She loved Emma's kitchen, which smelled exactly as Alaina thought a grandmother's kitchen should.

Checking her watch, she saw she had about ten minutes to spare. Plenty of time to dive into the chocolate chip cookies Emma had loaded into the cookie jar just that morning.

"Hello, Alaina."

She stopped dead.

The man leaning casually in the dining room doorway on the other side of the kitchen was a stranger. Serial killer, was her first thought. He was unusually pale, with pockmarked cheeks and watery blue eyes, his light brown hair thin and graying. He wore an old maroon Members Only jacket, faded jeans and black Chuck Taylor sneakers.

He'd called her Alaina.

"What do you want?" she asked, her voice firm in spite of the fear that threatened to clamp around her throat.

He ambled toward her, hands in his back pockets, his sneakers silent on the tile floor. "Relax," he said softly, smiling. His teeth were surprisingly straight and white, a toothpick clenched between them. "I'm not here to hurt you."

She didn't believe him for an instant, and she ticked off in her head the locations of everyone she cared about. Jonah had at least an hour left of school. And moments before, Emma had been in the bookstore discussing the latest Stephen King novel with a male college student who'd seemed surprised that such a senior citizen was familiar with the horror writer's work. There would be no reason for Emma to leave the store unattended to come upstairs.

"Tell me what you want," Alaina said, infusing her voice with strength.

The intruder continued to smile, the toothpick wiggling as he repositioned it with his tongue. "I got a proposition for you, Ms. Chancellor. You know who I work for?"

"Yes, I've figured that out." She clenched her teeth against the impatience. She was due in the bookstore in a few minutes. If she were late, Emma might come looking for her.

"Mr. Keller wants you bad. You and the kid."

"You said you have a proposition."

His grin broadened, and retrieving the toothpick, he pointed it at her. "Five grand, and I report back to Mr. Keller that I hit another dead end."

Alaina's knees began to tremble. Five thousand dollars? She didn't have even one thousand. How would she get five? "I don't have that kind of money."

"Yeah, but you're smart. I bet you can figure out how to get it."

"I can't."

His gaze hardened. "You're not even going to think about it?"

"I don't have to think about it. I don't have access to that kind of money."

He glanced around the tiny kitchen as if regrouping.

Clearly, he wasn't the sharpest knife in the drawer. He hadn't been able to tell by observing her life that excessive cash was not a part of it. His expression brightened. "The old lady downstairs," he said. "What's her name?"

Alaina's muscles tensed so hard they began to ache. "She doesn't know."

"I don't give a shit. This her place?"

"Yes."

"Geezer like her's probably got cash stashed between her mattresses, stuffed in stupid places in the kitchen." He grabbed the cookie jar shaped like the Pillsbury Dough Boy, ripped off the lid and tipped it upside down. Fresh chocolate chip cookies tumbled onto the counter.

Alaina eased away from him, until her back encountered the edge of the doorway. A slight turn to the right, and she could be down the stairs and into the stockroom of the bookstore in just a few seconds. But then what? He would chase her right into the store. He might be armed. She looked him up and down, searching for a gun, a knife.

Catching her seeking look, he dropped the cookie jar, which shattered at his feet. The greed in his eyes shifted to something far more terrifying. "Were you just checking me out?"

Her heart seized into a tight fist. "No." The word nearly strangled her.

His grin returned, accompanied by a leer. "Yes, you were. You were checking me out."

She raised her hands, palms out. "Look, I'm sorry. But I don't have any money. I can't pay you."

His tongue flicked out over his bottom lip as his gaze slithered down her body and back up, mentally stripping away her jeans and bulky sweater. Her skin crawled as if he had touched her with a clammy hand.

He swallowed, and his pale cheeks pinkened. "You know what? I'm thinking we can work something out."

She pressed against the doorjamb. A quarter-turn. The steps were right there. But that would put Emma and her customers at risk . . . Alaina still didn't know if he had a weapon.

Then her dangling fingers brushed against smooth, cool wood, and she remembered the baseball bat propped in the corner. She'd fussed at Jonah that morning to put it away, but he had either ignored her or forgotten.

Dropping the shopping bag, she swung the bat up at the same moment that the intruder rushed her. Almost by accident, the bat caught him in the crotch, more of a glancing blow than a dead-on home run. He folded nonetheless, going down on one knee, his hands cupped over his groin. "You bitch," he wheezed. "Fucking bitch."

He was down, but his body blocked her escape route. She pivoted, intending to bolt through the dining room. Despite his pain, he moved like lightning, grabbing the back of her sweater and swinging her into the kitchen counter. The edge caught her hard in the hip, the impact knocking the bat from her fingers. As it clattered to the floor and rolled, she threw a hand out to keep from falling, her fingers crushing through cookies. She hurled crumbs in his face.

He stumbled back, sputtering in surprise, and she tried to dodge by him. But he snatched her around the middle and slammed her back against the refrigerator. Pain zinged down her spine, and her knees almost buckled. Locking them, she aimed for his eyes.

He screamed as her nails scratched his scarred face, and enraged, he jerked her away from the refrigerator by the collar and ruthlessly hammered her back against it. Her legs turned to jelly, and as he backed off and let go, she slid down the fridge, gasping.

He glared down at her, one hand pressed to his bloody cheek. "Now I'm really pissed off." Reaching down, he grasped the collar of her sweater and yanked her to her feet. Levering her against the counter, he snarled, "I'm going to take what I want. Then I'm going to kill you real slow."

She groped behind her for a weapon, a pan to hit him with, a glass, anything.

His breath was hot on her cheeks, his face mottled red with rage. "And when you're good and dead, I'm going to wait for your kid to come home and I'm going to start on him—"

The Chicago Cutlery slipped easily between his ribs, and blood warm and thick gushed over her hand, spilling a sweet, coppery scent into the kitchen.

For a stunned instant, his forehead creased as if he'd felt a pain but didn't know what it was. Then he released her and staggered back, staring down at the handle of the knife sticking out of his gut.

Gagging, Alaina sank to her knees, her vision graying. Perspiration dripped into her eyes, and she fought to keep from blacking out. She had to get out, had to get out.

The intruder wobbled, sweat making his face appear greasy as it faded from red to gray. "Oh, shit," he mumbled as his legs gave out and he pitched forward.

Alaina couldn't move, her breath sawing in and out of her chest.

He was lying facedown in front of her, and she concentrated hard on his back. A pool of dark red blood seeped from under him, oozing toward the bloody hand she braced on the tile floor. He wasn't breathing.

She'd killed him. A roar began in her ears, became deafening.

"Anna?"

Alaina raised her spinning head and saw Emma standing

in the kitchen doorway. As the older woman digested the scene before her, her stunned disbelief gave way to horror. "Oh my God, Anna!"

Emma lurched forward, reaching toward Alaina, as if to help her up or comfort her. But before she got there, she froze and clutched at her chest. Her soft pink complexion turned white, and she grasped the back of a chair for support. She made a strange sound, a gurgle or maybe it was a gasp, and then she crumpled to the floor, dragging the chair down with her.

Her brilliant blue eyes stared up at the ceiling, unseeing.

Alaina's eyes snapped open. It took a moment to orient herself. She was in the car with Rachel. It was dark outside. "Where are we?"

"Just crossed the Wisconsin border. You didn't sleep long." Rachel glanced at her in concern. "You okay?"

A fine sheen of perspiration coated her face, and Alaina wiped the back of her hand across her damp forehead. A bump in the road sent a jolt through her shoulder, and she winced. The drugs were wearing off already. Even so, her head was still woozy. But not so woozy that she couldn't curse herself for letting Rachel talk her into this insanity. If Rachel were to get hurt, or worse, Alaina would never forgive herself.

"Alex?"

"I'm fine."

Rachel suppressed a smile. "Of course you are. Like you would admit it if your hair was on fire."

Alaina didn't laugh. "You're checking to make sure we're not being followed?"

"So far, so good. If anyone does start to tail us, this puppy'll outrun them, no problem." She stroked the dash of the Thunderbird.

Before hitting the back roads heading north, Rachel had called on her on-again, off-again relationship for help. Tom Peters, who worked in accounting at the *Trib* and had been smitten with Rachel for years, met them in a Target parking lot and agreed to trade his late-model red Thunderbird for Rachel's RAV4. Alaina still couldn't believe he had been so agreeable, asking only a few questions that Rachel had deftly deflected, promising to return his car in a few days.

"You really shouldn't be doing this, Ray," Alaina said.

"Just shut up and let me help you. Can you do that?"

"Those men who shot up your house—"

"There was only one, and he got away." Rachel paused, as if letting that sink in. "Which is another reason you couldn't stay in the ER. You were a sitting duck."

"There are probably others besides him."

"Then we'll deal with them," Rachel said lightly. "They won't know what hit them."

The false bravado brought tears to Alaina's eyes. She couldn't have asked for a better friend.

Rachel cleared her throat. "So . . . what should I call you? Alex? Alaina?"

Alaina couldn't help but laugh at the absurdity of the quandary, considering the circumstances. "You can call me Al."

Rachel grinned at her. "You're not going to sing, are you? Because if you do, I'm turning around."

Alaina considered breaking into a showstopper. Anything to protect her friend. But it would never be that easy. Rachel wouldn't let it. "You're sure the house is safe?" Alaina asked.

Rachel nodded. "It's been vacant since Aunt Rita died a couple months ago. It's not too much farther. It's in Middleton, just outside Madison."

Alaina longed for Emma, for the life she and Jonah had had with her in Madison.

"My name isn't attached to it in any way," Rachel said. "She left it to my Uncle John, but he's been living abroad for the past two years."

Alaina gingerly massaged the ache in her shoulder. "In Rome."

"So you were listening to me all those times I rambled about my dysfunctional family."

Yes, she had listened, and envied Rachel her quirky but loving relatives. "I've got you hands down on the dysfunctional family," she said.

"Oh, you think so? My cousin Bobby literally ran away to the circus, to be a lion tamer. Last I heard, he's missing a few fingers and the tip of his nose. And my Uncle Louie? Well, he's a she now. Aunt Louise. I'm still not used to it."

"My sister is married to Jonah's father." Alaina instantly regretted the words. That's what happens when you let your guard down, she thought, as she glanced over to see Rachel staring at her. "I said that out loud, didn't I?"

"How did that happen?" Rachel asked.

"I opened my mouth, and out it came." She smiled, even though she knew Rachel wouldn't let her joke her way out of this one.

"You know what I mean," Rachel replied, impatient. "If he's such a jerk that you went on the run to keep him away from your kid, how'd he get both you and your sister into bed? I mean, I've never known you to even want to be touched—"

She broke off, and Alaina imagined she could hear the gears grinding in her friend's head. She didn't say anything, not sure she could. Other than a counselor ten years ago—who had maintained a cool and professional distance—she had not told anyone who wasn't her family, not even Emma, that Layton had raped her.

Rachel gripped the steering wheel harder. "That prick," she said, her voice soft and strained.

That was all she said. As it became apparent that a barrage of sensitive questions was not coming, Alaina slowly relaxed, grateful that for once Rachel wasn't eager to dissect her feelings.

Alaina let her eyes close. Almost immediately, an image of Mitch—kneeling at her feet, his hand gentle on her ankle—popped into her head. She may have been out of it with pain at the time, but she'd seen the unmistakable change in his dark eyes. Warm, worried. No anger. As if his opinion of her had shifted somehow.

Puzzling over what could have caused the transformation, she sank into sleep.

Chapter 16

Layton Keller had put out a contract on Alaina's life.

Norm Potter, Mitch's former FBI colleague, had just confirmed it as he'd handed Mitch a cup of coffee.

They had left the hospital little more than an hour before to go to the FBI's Chicago office, where Norm had led Mitch to a glass-walled meeting room that was serving as Norm's makeshift work space. Between them on the conference table, Norm's briefcase was open, folders and papers strewn across the surface of the blond wood.

"Odds aren't good my agents are going to find them quick," Norm said, taking a seat on the other side of the table. "They got too much of a head start."

Mitch scrubbed his hands over his face. Keller had duped him, and he felt like a grade-A, extra large jerk. Except the egg wasn't just on his face, it was dripping all over his entire head. "If that son of a bitch gets his hands on her, I'll never forgive myself."

"How'd you end up working for Keller anyway?" Norm asked.

Mitch sipped coffee and grimaced. "Why is Bureau coffee always shit?"

Norm shrugged. "Far as I know, it's the law."

Mitch drank it anyway, needing the caffeine. He itched to be out in the field, helping to track the women, but Norm had insisted Mitch accompany him to the office to answer more questions. He suspected that Norm would have arrested him if he'd refused.

Mitch set down the cup. "I've been doing employee background checks for two years. He asked me more than a month ago to find his kid and the kid's mother."

"Background checks?" Norm asked. "He's awfully high up in the company to be dealing with the person who does background checks."

"We went over this two hours ago."

"Humor me."

"The security checks were on his top lieutenants, something he wanted handled discreetly," Mitch said. "It wasn't a full-time job."

"So you don't work inside PCware."

"I went to his home a few times, but mostly we talked on the phone."

Norm pursed his lips. "Why'd he send you and not one of his goombahs after Alaina and Jonah?"

"Apparently, I *am* one of his goombahs," Mitch said with disgust.

"But he didn't ask you to take her out."

"Jesus, no."

"So he just hired you to find them, then sent someone else in to grab the kid and try to kill the mother."

Nodding, Mitch swallowed hard against the guilt. "He played me. He knew exactly which buttons to push."

"How do you mean?"

"Shirley took my kid away from me. Alaina took his kid away from him. He wanted me to equate the two women, and I did." He drew a finger down his sore nose, remembering his rage when Alaina had hit him. "I wanted to hurt her, like I could never have hurt Shirley, because I was too civilized. But with Alaina, there were no repercussions. I didn't have to be civilized." He felt sick as he recalled how rough he'd been when he'd tackled her and how much he'd frightened her when he'd handcuffed her to the bed the last time. Jesus, he thought, nausea churning in his knot-filled belly. He'd *handcuffed* her to a bed. "Keller wanted someone who would find her and wouldn't sympathize, someone who he wouldn't have to worry about trying to be a Good Samaritan."

Norm waved a dismissive hand. "You're overanalyzing. Keller needed a damn good investigator, and he got one. It took four of my best agents to track her down in the time it took you to find her on your own."

"I had help," Mitch said under his breath, thinking that Julia was going to want to throttle him when she found out what was going on. Dammit, he should have listened to her. His partner had good instincts, and he'd brushed her off. Another instance in this case where he'd let his idiotic ego dictate his actions rather than common sense. He was listening to those instincts now, and he hoped to hell Norm would be able to provide some answers without copping the usual FBI "I can't tell you that" bullshit.

Mitch cleared his throat. "Don't you think it's odd that we were able to find Alaina and her son in weeks when Keller's had detectives looking for fourteen years? Only one of his men was able to track her down."

A look of confusion crossed Norm's features. "When?"

"I don't know anything about it except Keller told me she killed the guy."

Norm's bafflement seemed to deepen. "That doesn't make any sense."

"Then your people haven't linked her to anything like that? She would have had a different identity then, one I'm not familiar with."

Norm shook his head. "Once we get her prints, we can run them through the system to see if we get any hits. As Alaina

Chancellor, she was never arrested and fingerprinted, so her prints aren't on file. But they'd be in the system unidentified if she left them at the crime scene." Snagging a legal pad, he jotted a note, then stared down at it as if he'd just written in a foreign language.

"What is it?" Mitch asked.

"Before now, Keller didn't want Alaina found, so I don't get why one of his people would actually track her down."

Stunned, Mitch stared at his former colleague. "I think I need you to elaborate."

Norm's chair gave a squawk as he leaned back. "When Alaina took off with Jonah, Keller convinced his in-laws that the matter needed to be handled within the family. No law enforcement, no glaring media attention, no embarrassment. He knew how much Paul Chancellor hated bad publicity. Keller said he'd take care of everything and hired a couple private eyes to file bogus reports about their progress, keeping the feds out of it and ensuring that Alaina and her son would never be found."

"But why?" Mitch asked.

"Mainly, the kid would have been some major league competition."

At the dubious arch of Mitch's brow, Norm said, "Paul Chancellor was an old-fashioned guy. He had two daughters, but he wanted a son, bad. Layton Keller comes along, and he's everything a man like Chancellor could possibly want in a son. He's smart, he's handsome, he's interested in the family business." Norm smirked a little. "He likes golf. Chancellor loved his golf. At any rate, a grandson would have compromised Keller's 'only son' status. Plus, consider the fact that the kid's mother is Keller's sister-in-law, and it all gets very messy. He didn't want the kid around to remind anyone of his indiscretion with the sister, and he didn't want to share

Chancellor." He stroked his jaw, as if checking for razor stubble. "It's tough to wrap your brain around it, but we did some background on Keller and turned up some interesting stuff."

"Such as?"

The FBI agent shuffled through the piles of papers spread across the table and came up with a manila folder, which he flipped open. "Never knew his father. Raised by his mother until he was ten. She was a real piece of work. Not physically abusive, as far as we can tell, but she messed with his head, constantly telling him what a pain in the ass he was, how he didn't deserve anything she gave him, which wasn't much to begin with. Filled his head with all kinds of crap about how kids are nothing but a drain on a parent's resources." Flipping through the folder, he stopped at a page and read from it. " 'All they do is suck you dry and give you nothing in return. They're worthless parasites.' "

"Damn. Where'd you get this stuff?"

"He spent eight years in the system after his mother abandoned him when he was ten. Just took off one day and didn't come back. He was shuffled from one foster home to another. Apparently, he never clicked with any of the families, and eventually, they stopped trying to place him. Lived in a home for kids until he was eighteen. Got tons of counseling, though it's doubtful it did him any good. That quote I just read came from his last session before he was released from the orphanage."

"Jesus."

"He did incredibly well, regardless. Straight-A student. Earned a scholarship to MIT and worked his way through. After graduation, he spent some time at a couple different companies before landing on PCware's doorstep at twenty-eight. Worked his way into the boss's good graces, and next thing you know, he's meeting the big guy's oldest daughter and supposedly falling head over heels."

"He found the family he always wanted," Mitch said.

"More likely, he found the father he'd always wanted."

"He must have been devastated when the old guy was killed."

"Well, that's where there's a glitch and, we're assuming, the trigger for what's going on now," Norm said. "When Chancellor died, it looked like Keller stood to inherit the entire company, or at least a majority of it. But Chancellor left a third of everything, including PCware, to Alaina and Jonah. We think that's why Keller wants them found now. Not to hand over their inheritance, of course, but to make sure they don't get it."

"But they were missing for years," Mitch said. "It was highly unlikely that Alaina was going to come out of hiding with Jonah and try to claim their third of the company. Couldn't Keller have had them declared legally dead?"

"You'd think that would have worked, yes."

Something else puzzling occurred to Mitch. "Why's the Bureau on a case that would normally be handled by authorities at the local level? It's not a kidnap case because Keller never reported his son missing. And the death threat against Alaina—that's a police matter."

Norm met his gaze steadily, as if trying to decide whether Mitch could be trusted.

"Does Alaina have information on Keller?" Mitch asked, impatient.

"Not that we're aware of," Norm said.

"So you're going to a lot of trouble to track down someone who doesn't have something you need. What's the deal?"

"I've already told you too much."

"Yes, you have. And you obviously don't think I'm a

threat or you wouldn't have been sharing all along." Mitch had already surmised that would come at a price later. "So tell me the rest of it."

Norm sighed, rubbed the back of his neck. "The Bureau is assisting the Justice Department in an investigation of Keller."

"Justice," Mitch repeated, surprised.

"I'm not going to give you the details."

"But Alaina's not a witness."

"No," Norm said.

"And neither is Jonah."

"No."

"Then why go to the trouble to find them if they're irrelevant to the case? You could just have the cops handle it so you can concentrate on the Justice—" He broke off as it began to click. "How'd you find out Keller wanted Alaina dead?"

Norm shifted, as if uneasy. "We got a tip."

"From someone close to Keller."

"I'm not at liberty to say."

"His wife?" Mitch asked.

"Dammit, Mitch."

"Come on, Norm. You've already told me way too much."

Stalling, Norm took his time sipping coffee.

"Come on," Mitch prompted.

Norm scratched his head, rubbed his chin, then finally sighed. "All right. Yes, Mrs. Keller tipped us off. We're helping each other out. We agreed to find her sister and nephew and protect them from Keller in exchange for her help on the Justice investigation."

Mitch sat back. Finally, something that made sense. "She must be majorly pissed right now."

"How do you mean?"

"Well, you found her sister and nephew all right, but now

one of them is on the run and the other is in enemy hands. Not to mention the guy who got shot and the kid who got roughed up. I'd say you dropped the ball on the protection part."

"No one expected Alaina to make a run for it."

Mitch thumped a finger on the table, unable to squelch his growing irritation. "She thought she was wanted for kidnapping. As far as she knows, she's been on the run for fourteen years. What did you think she would do when you walked into her workplace flashing badges?"

"We didn't think she would run."

"What about the kid?"

Norm's brow wrinkled. "What about him?"

"What are you doing to get him away from Keller?"

"For now, Jonah stays put. We have no reason to believe he's in any danger."

"His father wants his mother dead," Mitch said, his jaw clenched.

"Yes, but Keller has shown no such inclination toward the boy. If we make any move to interfere, it would compromise the larger investigation."

That didn't surprise Mitch, but it did nothing to cool his rising fury. "Where does that leave Alaina?"

"In what way?"

"Assuming the feds find her before Keller's hit men do, she's going to want her kid back. If there are no kidnapping charges, she's in the clear. If Keller wants custody of Jonah now, he'd have to file—"

"I'm afraid that will have to wait," Norm cut in. "We can't have anything distracting Keller right now."

"So she's just left out in the cold without her kid."

Norm's face flushed with annoyance. "She's not innocent, Mitch. She did indeed kidnap him, and there's no statute of limitations on kidnapping. Plus, if she killed a man, like you told me, she's undoubtedly wanted for questioning in that case. The simple fact that she fled the scene of a crime is enough to put her in jail. If we have to, we'll go after her to keep her out of the way. The simple fact is: I can't afford distractions on this investigation. It's too big."

"So you'll protect her and her kid as long as it buys you help from Keller's wife, but if they get in the way, you'll mow them down without a second thought. Does Mrs. Keller know how this deal works?"

Norm tossed up his hands. "What do you want from me, Mitch? I've got a job to do."

Mitch rose, went to the door. "I think I've heard enough."

"Mitch."

He turned, his hand on the knob. "What?"

"I've shared quite a bit of information with you. I have a request in return."

Mitch gave his former colleague a humorless smile. "I know what you want, Norm. You wouldn't have been so loose-lipped without a plan. And you can forget it. I don't work for the son of a bitch anymore."

"Mrs. Keller is shaky at best. The Bureau needs someone inside who Keller trusts."

"Yeah, well, good luck on that." Mitch left, slamming the glass door behind him.

Alaina woke to a hand on her arm.

"We're there," Rachel said.

While Rachel hopped out of the car and unlocked the front door, Alaina eased out slowly, her body protesting every move. She supposed she should be happy she could move at all.

The house smelled faintly musty inside and was chilly.

"No heat," Rachel said with an apologetic shrug. "But there's electricity, go figure. Aunt Rita's kids aren't the most organized when it comes to taking care of utilities. But I can start a fire in the fireplace and close off the rest of the house."

While Rachel threw some wood into the brick fireplace, Alaina lowered herself to the sofa in front of it. The clock on the mantel said it was after one in the morning.

"Are you hungry?" Rachel asked over her shoulder. "When was the last time you ate?"

Alaina remembered the burger she had choked down in Mitch's car. That had been about four hours ago, and it seemed like days. In fact, it felt as if an entire week had passed since that moment when federal agents had asked for her at the newspaper.

"Alaina?"

She blinked up at her friend standing before her. It was so strange to hear Rachel say her given name. "I'm sorry?"

"Are you hungry? I can fix you something. I'm sure there's soup in the cupboard."

Alaina shook her head. The thought of food turned her stomach. The thought of living turned her stomach. How could she go on without Jonah? There was no point.

Rachel sat beside her, groping for her hand. Her fingers grasped Alaina's, squeezed, and her chin trembled as she tried to smile. "It's going to be okay."

Alaina lowered her head, fighting the emotion that crowded into her aching throat. How many times had she peered into Jonah's sweet face and said the same thing?

"Aunt Emma had an accident, so we have to move. But it's going to be okay, honey."

"The bad people found us, so we have to go somewhere new and start over again. But it's going to be okay."

"What can I do?" Rachel asked. "Please tell me what I can do."

Hearing the tears in her friend's voice, Alaina didn't dare look at her. She needed to hang on. Letting go now would be a mistake, and she couldn't afford any more mistakes. "I'm tired," she said. "I need to . . . I need . . ."

Rachel held her hand another moment, then rose. "I'll get you a pillow and blankets."

Mitch took several deep breaths, trying hard to get the helpless anger under control. He was surprised Norm had let him walk away, but he had. Now, Mitch was in a cab on his way back to the hospital where he'd left his car to go with Norm to the Bureau offices. He had to do something to help her, he thought. Something to make things right.

His hands shook when he called his partner. "I lost track of Alaina," he said without preamble.

"How'd you manage that?" Julia asked.

"Long story. I need you to work your online mojo to find her. I'm on a tight schedule."

"What kind of stuff should I be looking for?"

"Credit card transactions, E-mail, cell phone calls, whatever you can tap into."

She sighed as if he were hopelessly stupid. "She's too smart to be using any of the stuff under Alex Myers's name. She's probably already moved on to her next identity."

"Not Alaina. Track Rachel Boyd."

Addison gripped the phone in her clammy hand, scanning her surroundings for potential witnesses to her call. She was at a pay phone outside the Macy's at Fair Oaks Mall in Fairfax, Virginia, at least fifteen miles from Alexandria and her home with Layton. She'd told her husband that she was going shopping, that she needed some new clothes to celebrate her new role as Jonah's mother. Layton had found that amusing and had still been laughing when she'd walked out into the garage and got into her Mercedes SUV.

That giddy laugh haunted her as she dialed Norm Potter's cell phone number.

"Potter."

"It's Addison Keller. We've got Jonah."

"Yes, I know."

That made her pause, until she realized the feds had heard everything Jonah had told her because of the listening devices she had planted. "Have you found Alaina?"

"I'm afraid not, but we will. I promise you that."

"When you find her, I want to see her." Silence answered her, and she began to think they'd been disconnected. "Are you there?"

"I don't think that's a good idea," he said.

"I'm not asking you to think it's a good idea, Mr. Potter. I want to see my sister." She didn't know what had compelled her to want this, but the need had come on strong. Maybe it was meeting Jonah. He was so much like Alaina it made Addison's chest ache. And suddenly there were a million things she wanted, and needed, to say to her sister.

"I'll see what I can arrange," Norm said. "But—"

"I know where all the bugs are, Mr. Potter," she said. "I placed them, remember? I can just as easily go back and collect them all."

Silence again. She imagined his face turning a shade that matched his hair.

"I'm assuming your lack of response is confirmation that you're agreeing to my new terms," she said.

Norm cleared his throat. "Once your sister is found, she'll need to be transported immediately to a safe house. That's what we agreed to, remember? Your cooperation in return for her safety."

"I can tell Layton the feds are investigating him," Addison said. "That would damage your investigation, wouldn't it?"

"Mrs. Keller, I can have you taken into custody as a witness—"

"To what? A death threat? That won't help you in the big investigation, will it?" She paused, giving him time to digest that. "All I want is to see my sister for a couple of hours." She paused, listening to him breathe. "Arrange it, or I'll tell him." She hung up.

Chapter 17

Alaina woke to a dead fire and sun streaming across her face. She sensed right away that she was alone in the house. And there was heat. Sitting up, she groaned as aches and pains blared reminders of the abuse her body had taken the day before. She sagged back, tempted to stay put, but then she scented coffee in the air.

Pushing aside the multiple layers of blankets piled on top of her, Alaina set her feet on the floor, surprised that her shoes were off. She didn't remember removing them.

Gingerly, she rose, gritting her teeth and wishing she had some of that heavy-duty pain medication they'd pumped into her at the ER the night before.

"Ray?"

Alaina wandered into the tiny kitchen and found a note on the counter next to a full coffeepot, a new bottle of Advil, a pile of fresh bagels and a gun. The note was written in Rachel's doctor-like scrawl:

> Ran out to get a few things earlier and called the gas company—there's hot water! Put new clothes and clean towels in the bathroom for you. You were still snoozing, so I went for a run. Save me some coffee.
>
> Ray
>
> P.S. Found the gun between Aunt Rita's mattresses. She used to call it her watchdog Brutus. Just in case. R.

Ignoring the gun, Alaina poured a cup of coffee and sipped. It was easily the best thing she'd tasted in two days. After she downed three Advil and half a bagel, the fog in her head dissipated some.

She yearned for Jonah. Prayed he was okay. She imagined his eyes, wide and blue and clear. She hadn't seen fear in them in years. Since they'd moved to Chicago from Colorado, he'd grown to be so brave and stoic that she hadn't even seen him cry since Emma died.

Swallowing back the rush of emotion, Alaina began to wander the house, as much to distract herself as to loosen aching muscles.

The home was small, but it was also warm and cozy, from the yellow sheers in the kitchen to the old-fashioned blue-and-yellow plaid sofa she'd spent the night on. A matching loveseat and curtains made the country appeal complete.

Aunt Rita apparently had been a voracious reader, because books were stacked everywhere there was space. The dusty old books reminded Alaina of Emma, and she turned her back on them to survey a curio cabinet of Precious Moments figurines. Emma, she recalled, had collected owls and displayed them in a similar manner.

"Why owls?" Alaina had asked her once.

"Because they're wise."

Alaina and Jonah had both burst out laughing at the way she'd said it, as if Alaina's skull were the thickest Emma had ever encountered. Emma had ended up laughing, too, and it was at that moment that Alaina had realized how truly happy she was. The fact had amazed her, and left her feeling a bit smug. She'd beaten Layton, she thought. She'd beaten him, and she was happy. In her head, she'd done a victory dance.

A week later, Layton's detective had shown up in Emma's kitchen.

Alaina turned from the curio cabinet. She supposed she'd begun to feel a bit smug in Chicago, too. Five years had passed, and no thugs had appeared. She'd had a good job, a good friend and a solid, adoring relationship with her son. Now, a good man had been shot and his son hurt because of her, because she had tried to beat Layton again. Now, Jonah might be forever lost to her.

She found herself in the doorway to the bathroom, not sure how long she'd been standing there. If she didn't get busy, she was going to fold. Setting aside the coffee cup, she stripped out of Rachel's blouse and the scrubs bottoms that Rachel had helped her don the night before.

Under the steady stream of almost too-hot water, Alaina kept her mind carefully blank. Not thinking, not feeling—that was how she would get through this.

By the time she shut off the water, she felt somewhat human again, if not tip-top, then at least clean. Wearing nothing but the brand-new underwear Rachel had picked up for her, she was combing out her hair when a noise outside the door made her pause.

"Ray?"

No answer.

"Rachel?"

Still no answer. Heart thundering, she grabbed the blouse Rachel had left for her and jabbed her arms into it. Before she could thread one button through its hole, the bathroom door crashed inward.

Alaina gasped, stumbling back. The backs of her legs hit the side of the bathtub, and she made a grab for the shower curtain to break her fall. It popped free of its rings, one by one, as she tumbled back into the tub.

A hulk of a man stepped into the room and pointed a gun at her chest.

She recognized him in an instant.

Mitch cruised through the Middleton, Wisconsin, neighborhood, his shoulder scrunched up to hold the cell phone to his ear as he braked at a stop sign. He was exhausted, having been up all night waiting for Julia to call. Less than two hours ago she had, and he'd hit the interstate in a mad dash to Wisconsin.

"I'm at Appleton Lane and Daugherty. Which way?"

He heard the tap-tap of Julia's fingers on her computer keyboard. "Hang a left. It's three blocks up on the right. Five-eight-one-four."

"You're sure about this, Jules?"

"Are you not trusting me after everything we've been through together?"

"I just don't have time for you to be wrong."

"I'm not wrong. Rachel Boyd sent an E-mail from this phone number about two hours ago. Chances are, I'm not the only one who traced it."

"Don't move. Don't scream. Don't breathe."

The last time Alaina had seen the black-clad, thick-necked man, he'd been trussed up on the hotel room floor after Mitch had nailed him with the desk chair. That altercation had left its mark: Bruises underscored his eyes, and stitches laced up an inch-long laceration across his chin.

The look in his black gaze was murderous.

"Are you alone in the house?" he asked.

She didn't hesitate to respond, knowing he would hit her with only the slightest provocation. "Yes."

Reaching down, he grasped her right arm and hauled her

up out of the tub, not giving her a second glance when she clasped the edges of her shirt closed over her bare breasts. He nudged her toward the door with the gun. "Out."

She left the bathroom ahead of him, praying that Rachel was far away on her run. At the same time, she wondered why the guy hadn't just killed her. When he'd busted into the hotel room, he'd cocked his gun right away. He'd been ready to blow her head off when Mitch had arrived. Now, there was nothing distracting him.

In the blue-and-yellow plaid living room, he said, "Hold it. Hands behind your back."

The unmistakable sound of duct tape stripping off a roll had her turning. She glimpsed the gun stuffed into the waistband of his black jeans before he dropped a meaty hand on her shoulder to stop her. "Don't."

He wasn't going to kill her. Why would he secure her hands for that?

He had other plans.

Her terror shifted into high gear, and she pivoted, thrusting her good shoulder into his chest, trying to off-balance him so she could grab his gun. But his torso was solid muscle. Unaffected, he easily grabbed her wrist and wrenched it behind her and up between her shoulder blades. Alaina cried out, going down on one knee as stars burst in her head.

"Don't make this more difficult than it has to be," he growled near her ear.

She rammed her elbow back into his crotch.

Releasing her, he fell back a step on a sharp wheeze of breath. Alaina scrambled up and sprinted for the kitchen. It didn't take long for him to come after her. "Bitch!" Crashing into a table, he shoved it aside. "You're dead!"

In the kitchen, Alaina dove for the counter and Aunt

Rita's gun. She had it in her hand, was fumbling with the safety, when the goon plowed into her from behind. His weight slammed her forward against the counter, but she didn't feel any pain. There was only white noise in her head as she slid to the floor. He flipped her over and straddled her, grappling for the gun. His hands closed over hers, his grip crushing.

She couldn't breathe under him, the gun trapped between their bodies, its butt jammed against her sore ribs, its barrel pressing into his chest. She was losing her grip. If he got the gun, she was dead. For an instant, she was back in Emma's kitchen, fighting for her life. She remembered the gush of warm blood over her hand, the sweet copper smell, the sick realization that she'd killed a man.

She couldn't pull the trigger.

Mitch dropped to a squat near the back door of the tiny house. Glass crunched under his feet, and he glanced up at the shattered window.

"Fuck," he said under his breath.

Pulling out his gun, he cocked it and went in through the back door. He paused inside the mudroom, his back against the wall, and listened. He heard scuffling sounds.

Peering around the edge of the door into the kitchen, he saw the top of Alaina's dark head, the rest of her body obscured by the bulk of the man on top of her. As the man reared back, Mitch recognized him as the hit man they'd overpowered in the hotel room. He also saw that Alaina had a gun pressed to the guy's chest. All she had to do was pull the trigger—

The goon went still for a heartbeat. When nothing happened, confusion wrinkled his forehead. Then he clamped his gloved fingers around her throat.

Mitch heard her make a choking sound, saw the gun in her hand waver. Still, her finger didn't squeeze the trigger.

Mitch shot him.

Blood spurted from the hit man's chest, and he toppled backward off Alaina.

Mitch jerked back behind the cover of the door, acutely aware that she still had the gun and probably wouldn't consider him the conquering hero. "Alaina?"

Nothing.

He tried again. "Alaina, it's Mitch Kane. I'm here to help you."

It sounded ridiculous, but he didn't know what else to say.

She didn't respond, and he listened hard for activity. Had she already slipped out of the kitchen? Looking around the edge of the door, he saw her leaning against the kitchen cabinet beneath the sink, her knees drawn up to her chest, her forehead on her bare knees. The gun, clasped in her hand, rested on the floor.

As if sensing him there, she jerked her head up. Her dazed eyes widened in recognition, and she pointed the gun at him, her hand shaking. "You." Her pale face was damp with sweat, her breath coming fast and hard.

Mitch dropped his weapon and raised his hands, having no doubt she would shoot him. "I'm not going to hurt you, Alaina. I came to help."

She braced a hand on the floor, keeping the gun trained on him, and shifted to her knees. Mitch could tell that moving was painful for her. Only when she straightened did he see the blood that covered her. Her blouse looked like it had been ripped open, and all she wore was it and underwear.

"Jesus," he breathed, feeling sick as he moved toward her.

She steadied the gun with both hands. "Don't."

He stopped, his heart hammering, not because he feared

she would shoot him, but because he feared what had been done to her. "You're bleeding."

She glanced down at herself, wavering. "It's not mine." Her gaze moved to the man on the floor, and the gun in her hand shook violently. "I don't remember pulling the trigger."

"You didn't. I did."

She looked at him, confused. "But why?"

"I came to help you." He stepped toward her, reaching for her weapon, his hand as unsteady as hers. "Give me the gun, Alaina."

But she firmed her grip. "No," she said. "You work for Layton. He wants me dead."

Before he could dispute that, he heard shouts in the front room. "Federal agents!"

Mitch lunged forward, grabbing Alaina's gun hand and thrusting it up. He had the pistol away from her and tossed aside before the first fed burst through the door, gun drawn.

"Hold it!" the agent cried.

Mitch shielded Alaina with his body. "We're unarmed!"

The fed kept his weapon trained on them as more agents poured into the kitchen.

Mitch felt Alaina trembling against him, smelled the blood that covered her, and his heart twisted. Shrugging out of his jacket, he folded it around her. "It's okay. You're going to be okay."

Chapter 18

Mitch sat in his car in the parking lot of a Mobil station, glaring at the cell phone in his hand as the conversation he'd had with Norm only an hour before ran through his head.

"That hit man got to them too fast," Mitch had said. "The Bureau could be compromised."

Norm's eyes were flat, mistrustful. "Keller's people probably tracked them the same way we did. What I'm curious about, Mitch, is how you did it."

"I didn't get my info from Keller, if that's what you're getting at."

"Yeah, that is what I'm getting at."

"If Keller sent me here, why'd he send a hit man, too?"

But Norm hadn't been interested in arguing. He said he had more important things to do, such as ensure that Rachel and Alaina got to safe houses.

Which meant Mitch was shut out.

Which meant that if the FBI did have a leak, no one was doing anything about it.

Which meant that even if the feds sent Alaina to a safe house, she wouldn't be safe.

He kept seeing her, covered with blood, her eyes dazed as she stared down at the dead man at her feet. The image sent chills the length of his spine.

He shouldn't feel this way, he told himself. He shouldn't feel so frustrated and worried. She was a stranger to him. He didn't know her, hadn't had time to even care about her.

But he did. Somehow, he did.

And it made him feel desperate.

He had only one option to find her. He hit the speed-dial button on the cell phone and waited for an answer. When he got it, he said, "I lost her."

"I gathered that, Mr. Kane." Keller sounded so smooth, so unconcerned.

Mitch wrapped one hand around the steering wheel and gripped hard. *Son of a bitch. If you hurt her, I'll rip your heart out.* "I had her, and some half-wit intervened. Was he yours?"

"Hmm, why would I send a half-wit to find my son's mother when I hired you to do that?"

"That's what I'd like to know. Is there something you wanted the half-wit to do that you think you can't ask of me?"

"I can't have this conversation at this time, Mr. Kane. You're on a cell phone."

"I'll call you back on a land line."

"You do that."

Mitch pocketed his cell phone, got out of the car and walked to a pay phone only ten feet away. Keller answered on the first ring, and Mitch said, "The FBI has her, and your half-wit is dead. That means you have an opening, and I'm interested."

Keller was silent a moment. "I see."

"Maybe you do, maybe you don't." Closing his eyes, he leaned his forehead against the phone. "Because of that bitch, I've been chasing my tail for two days. She almost broke my fucking nose, and she's been a major pain in the ass."

Keller was silent, and Mitch worried he'd laid it on too thick. Finally, Keller said, "Perhaps I underestimated you, Mr. Kane."

"I'd say you did. You hired two people when you could have had one do the same job. All you had to do was ask."

"I had the impression that you didn't do that sort of work," Keller said.

"I had the impression that wasn't the sort of work you wanted done."

"Fair enough."

Mitch almost breathed a sigh of relief. "I'll expect a larger fee, of course."

"That won't be necessary, Mr. Kane. I'll send you what I owe you."

Mitch's relief faded. "I don't understand."

"I no longer need your services."

"Fine, I'll take her out for free."

"I warned you about her, didn't I? She gets under your skin." Keller chuckled, and Mitch imagined him tossing back a shot of expensive whiskey. "Well, I appreciate the offer," Keller said. "But I've got it covered."

"The only way you could is if you've got someone inside the FBI."

"It would be unwise of me to divulge that information, don't you think?"

"All right. Let me put it to you this way: Your former girlfriend and I have some unfinished business that I'd like to take care of before your guy takes her out."

"Tell you what: If you get to her before my man does, you're welcome to have at her. All I ask is that when you're done, she's still breathing."

Mitch faltered, surprised. "I thought you wanted her dead."

"Yes, well, that was the ideal situation. But it turns out that Alaina and I have some unfinished business of our own. You see, she never bothered to tell our son about me. He has no idea who I am, which is going to make it very difficult for me to win him over. That angers me, and I'd like to discuss the matter with her."

His skin crawling, Mitch said, "Fine, when I'm done, she's still breathing."

"If you want to get to her before I do, you might want to hurry. My man promises me delivery tomorrow afternoon. Good luck." Keller disconnected the call.

Mitch pressed the receiver to his forehead, resisting the urge to pound it against the phone's metal shell. "Fuck," he said under his breath. "Fuck fuck fuck."

If Keller expected his newest goon to deliver Alaina to him by tomorrow afternoon, he had to have someone in the FBI. How else would he be able to locate the safe house so quickly? And if that were the case, it couldn't be all that tough for him to eventually find out his wife had turned on him. Which could sink the feds' entire case, further putting Alaina and Jonah at risk, not to mention Alaina's sister.

Back in his car, Mitch called Norm's cell phone and got the agent's voice mail. "Yeah, it's Mitch. I need to talk to you ASAP. Keller has someone in the FBI."

After he disconnected the call, helplessness snaked through him. Until Norm got back to him, there wasn't a thing he could do.

Starting the car, he pulled out of the gas station and headed for the airport. The least he could do was be in a position to react when Norm called him back.

Steering onto the highway, he called Julia. "I need you to book me on the first flight back to the District."

"Hello to you, too," she said, but he heard her fingers already at work on her keyboard.

"What are the odds that you could track down an FBI safe house?" he asked.

"Uh, how about none?"

"I'm serious, Jules."

"So am I. There's a reason they call it a safe house, Mitch. What's up?"

"Keller has someone inside, and I can't reach Norm to warn him."

"What about you? Surely you have contacts. What about your former partner? Isn't he a director of some sort now?"

"My former partner had an affair with my former wife, remember?"

"And that means you can't talk to him ever again? Not even to save a woman's life?"

God, she was right. What was wrong with him? "Get the number."

"It wouldn't hurt you to say 'please' every so often."

"Please. And please make it fast."

"Okay. Here's your flight number. Delta 839. Leaves in an hour." She told him the confirmation number.

"One more thing," he said.

"Shoot."

"I need you to start staking out Keller's home. Figure out what his security is like. I've been there, but I didn't pay particular attention to his setup. It'd be great, too, if you could get your hands on blueprints."

"Why?"

"If I can't get to Alaina before he does, I'm going to need to know how to get in there to get her out."

Alaina felt the scratchiness of the new T-shirt and jeans that Rachel had picked up for her in Middleton. It had been more than four hours since the hit man had attacked, and she still wasn't entirely certain what had transpired in Aunt Rita's kitchen. How had Mitch Kane gotten there? And why had he saved her from Keller's henchman? Weren't they on the same side?

Whatever the answers, what was happening now was just as confusing. The FBI agent prowling the hotel room—red hair, freckles, black trench coat—hadn't left her side since he'd arrived at Aunt Rita's. He'd introduced himself as Assistant Director Norman Potter of the FBI. From there, he'd escorted her in a dark sedan with tinted windows to the Madison airport, where they'd boarded a small jet that flew only them to Washington Dulles International Airport. During the flight, Alaina had drilled Potter with questions, few of which he had answered.

She knew only that Rachel had been transported to an FBI safe house and would remain there until it was determined that she was in no danger.

Potter asked his share of questions as well, some of them about the man she had killed in self-defense in Emma's kitchen. She'd told him the truth, and he'd listened intently, taking notes. When she asked whether she would be arrested, Potter had said, "Not at this time."

Now, to her bewilderment, they were in a D.C. hotel. It wasn't a cheap one, either. It had a king-size bed with a thick, green comforter and multiple pillows in gold and wine. The entertainment center, armoire, dresser and desk were constructed of heavy, expensive oak. From the one large window, framed by wine-colored curtains, Alaina took in the Kennedy Center and the Jefferson and Lincoln memorials. Cherry blossoms were in bloom all around the Tidal Basin, making the trees look like they were covered with soft pink snowballs.

Behind her, Potter roamed the room. Clearly, there was something else he wanted to be doing, or perhaps being there, waiting for whomever they were waiting for, had him agitated.

Alaina turned from the window. "Please tell me why we're here."

Picking up a room service menu, he studied it. "You'll see soon enough, Ms. Chancellor." His cell phone chirped, and he turned his back to answer it.

"Fine," he said. "Room 916." Flipping the phone closed, he slipped it back into his inside jacket pocket.

"Who's coming up?" Alaina asked.

"Just sit tight."

A few minutes later, a knock came at the door. Potter went to it and, gun drawn, checked the peephole. When he eased the door open, and Alaina saw who stood there, she couldn't breathe.

Addison stepped into the hotel room, ignoring Norm Potter and seeking her sister. Alaina stood with the window at her back, the afternoon light behind her casting her face in shadow. But Addison saw her stiffen, and her pulse took off at a trot. She'd known this would be hard, but she hadn't anticipated how unsteady she'd feel.

"Hello, Alaina."

Alaina took a step toward her. "Is Jonah with you?"

The quaver in her voice broke Addison's heart. "No."

Her shoulders sagging, Alaina strode past her to where Norm hovered near the door. Addison watched her, noting that in new blue jeans and a white long-sleeved T-shirt, Alaina looked trim, with the same graceful curves that Addison had envied when they were younger.

"I didn't agree to this," Alaina said to Norm.

"I requested it," Addison said. The light hit her sister full in the face now, and Addison registered Alaina's thinner, more mature features. Even so, she still looked far too young to have a teenage child. Her dark hair was longer than it had been the last time Addison had seen her, its color rich with subtle auburn tones that no hair dye could imitate. Her gray-green eyes, still her most striking feature, seemed to have aged thirty years in fourteen.

Those haunting eyes brimmed with mistrust. "You requested this meeting?" Alaina asked. "Why would you do that?"

Norm said, "I'll wait in the hall."

But Alaina grasped his arm a little too desperately. "No."

When Norm cast a glance at Addison, she nodded for him to leave them alone.

Alaina watched him go, her back to Addison. After a long moment, she faced her sister, her gaze veiled. "So I take it you're in charge here."

Addison clasped her hands, at a loss. This wasn't going well, and yet she hadn't expected it to. It was just something she had to do. "Mr. Potter is humoring me, yes."

"Humoring you. That's an interesting way of putting it. He's humoring your desire to look me in the eye and tell me you and Layton have finally won?"

Her sister's animosity was a little too much for Addison, and she glanced away, her gaze catching on the minibar. She crossed to it, set her purse aside and helped herself to a single-serve bottle of merlot. "Drink?"

Alaina laughed, and the sound carried no humor. "Are you kidding me?"

Addison didn't respond, willing her hand to steady as she poured the wine into a glass. She drank without tasting it, then lowered the glass. "Don't you want to know how he is?"

Silence answered her, and Addison turned to see Alaina grasping the back of a wing-backed chair so hard the tips of her fingers had turned white. "Don't taunt me."

Addison's heart squeezed, and she gulped down a generous amount of merlot. She was realizing how severely unprepared she was for this. It would take more than one impromptu meeting to heal more than a decade of damage. "He saw a man get shot," she said.

"Oh, God." Alaina edged around the chair and sank onto it. Rocking forward, she wrapped an arm around her midsection as if she might be sick. "No."

The sorrow in that one word tore at Addison, and she grappled for something to say. "He wanted you to know that he's fine."

Alaina raised her head, and tears streamed down her cheeks. "He can't possibly be fine. Are you still so blind?"

Addison drained the wine and immediately wished for more. Resisting, she moved to sit in the chair across from her sister. "I made a deal with the FBI."

Alaina's reddened eyes narrowed. "To do what?"

"To spare you this." Spreading her hands, Addison gave a bitter laugh. "Like everything else in my life, it's fallen well short of my expectations."

"I don't understand. What kind of deal?"

"I asked the feds to protect you and Jonah and, in exchange, I'm helping them gather evidence for a case against Layton."

"Why would you do that?"

Addison yearned for more anesthetizing wine. Instead of satisfying that longing, she said, "I was wrong, Alaina."

Alaina stared at her sister, uncomprehending. "You were wrong?"

Addison's gray-streaked black hair fell into eyes that were gray and lifeless, and she smoothed it back with a hand that trembled. "Yes."

Alaina pushed out of the chair. She didn't know where she

was going, but she couldn't sit across from her sister any longer without lunging at her. At the window, she gazed out at the blossom-filled spring day. Fluffy white clouds crowded the sky, momentarily blocking the sun.

Bracing her hands on the windowsill, she focused on taking deep, calming breaths. Confronting her sister had been the central theme in many a daydream over the years. Alaina had imagined telling Addison how stupid she was for being so easily tricked by a man, which led to Addison in a puddle of tears at her feet, sobbing and begging for forgiveness. But now that the opportunity to let it all out was here, words failed her.

She heard Addison get up, heard her twist the cap off a glass bottle and splash liquid into a glass. "I know there's nothing I can say . . ." Addison trailed off. "God, this is tough."

Alaina turned. "Innocent people have been hurt because you were wrong."

Addison pressed a glass half-filled with red wine against her pale cheek, as if it offered a comforting chill. "I know."

The softly whispered words only infuriated Alaina more. Remorse was there, but it wasn't nearly enough. "Our mother is dead because you were wrong."

Addison lowered the glass, confused. "What are you talking about?"

"Your husband killed her."

"Her car slid off a road in Colorado—"

"Where she had come to see me. Layton followed her. She finally saw him for what he is, and he had to keep her quiet."

Addison, her face growing paler by the minute, shook her head in disbelief. "No, it's not possible. She went to Colorado for a fund-raising conference. She had a car accident."

The sharp edge of memory sliced through Alaina. She'd

heard that line—"it's not possible"—before. Right after she'd told her sister that Layton had raped her. And again after she'd told her father. It astonished her how much it still hurt. After all this time. Frustration and betrayal raged anew, but Alaina blocked them out. There was no point revisiting what was said and done. It wouldn't help her get Jonah back.

She squared her shoulders. "Why are you here?"

Addison didn't respond for a long time, and Alaina watched myriad emotions flicker over her face—anger, resentment, hurt and, finally, shame. Addison's chin quivered, and she pivoted away, draining the wine in one furious gulp. At the minibar, she slammed the glass down. When she spoke, her voice was low, controlled. "I'm here because he wants you dead, Alaina. Believe it or not, I want you to stay alive. You and Jonah are all the family I have left."

Alaina focused on her sister, noticing that lines in her face—especially those etched like parentheses on either side of her too-generous mouth—made her look years older than thirty-nine. She had the face and demeanor of a desperately unhappy woman.

Alaina realized that the recent death of their father had to have been especially hard on Addison. He and Addison had adored each other. On top of that, she'd also recently discovered the ugly truth about her husband. Moments before, she'd gotten the shock that her mother had fallen victim to her husband, too.

Alaina massaged her temples, where the roots of a headache were burrowing in. She didn't want to feel sorry for her sister. She didn't want to feel anything for her.

Ice clinked against glass, and a moment later, Addison stood beside her, offering a tumbler of amber liquid. Alaina's stomach turned at the thought of alcohol, and she shook her head. "It'll make you feel better," Addison said. "Trust me."

Alaina glanced up at her. "What does he want with my son, Addison?"

Addison chewed her bottom lip. "I think Layton has changed his mind about Jonah."

"In what way?"

"He never wanted him before, and now he does."

"What?" Alaina was sure she had heard her wrong.

Addison set the glass on the table beside Alaina and took the chair across from her. "After you took off with Jonah, Layton hired private detectives, but it was a ruse to make Daddy think people were looking for you. Layton paid the detectives to file fake reports about all the ways they tried to find you and couldn't."

Alaina absorbed that, tried to make sense of it. "But one of them did find me. He wanted me to pay him not to tell Layton where we were."

"He wasn't paid to find you, Alaina. He was paid to pretend to search."

Which meant the man she'd killed in Emma's kitchen probably had had no intention of telling Layton where she and Jonah were. And if he had, it wouldn't have mattered anyway because Layton hadn't wanted to know. Nausea twisted through her as she saw Emma on the floor, her eyes open and staring. She forced her brain away from the memory. "Have you known this all along?"

"No. I gave the detective reports to the feds, and they determined they were bogus."

"But the feds have been looking for me."

"Before now, the feds weren't involved." The alcohol apparently was working on her system, because the disgust Addison surely would have hidden showed clearly on her face. "Daddy and Layton wanted to keep the problem in the family."

"So all the time I spent running, terrified we'd be found and Jonah would be taken away from me . . ." Alaina's voice faded, her head spinning with the implications. Their lives could have been so different. Jonah's life could have been so different.

"No one was even looking for you."

"Mom was," Alaina said. "She told me she'd hired a private detective herself." Lowering her head, she rubbed the middle of her throbbing forehead. "She was so happy to see me, and all I could think was that Layton couldn't be far behind. I was so angry with her." Tears burned in her throat. "She died because of me."

Addison sat forward, grasping Alaina's hand. "I'm sorry. I'm so sorry for so many things."

Drawing away, Alaina got up and retreated to the window, where the sun was breaking through the clouds. Her emotions swirled as if caught in a twister, jerked from disbelief to anger to grief back to disbelief. All the time she'd spent looking over her shoulder . . .

"The FBI agents who came to the newspaper yesterday . . ." She trailed off, almost choking on the words.

"They were there to take you and Jonah into protective custody."

Despair dropped Alaina's shoulders. "And I ran." Which set off a chain reaction that led to Grant Maxwell being shot and Jonah being taken by Layton's people.

But who was to say whether Grant would have been shot if she had shown up at his home before Layton's men? Perhaps she would have been shot, too. In fact, she realized, it was probably their intent to kill her at the same time that they grabbed Jonah. A computer glitch at work had thrown off her routine yesterday. Otherwise, she would have been at Grant's picking up Jonah when the hit men stormed in.

She faced Addison, wanting more answers. "If Layton never wanted Jonah to begin with, why did he file for custody?"

"Daddy wanted him to. I remember them fighting about it. Daddy was adamant that you weren't ready to be a mother, and he said that if Layton didn't file for custody, then Daddy would. Remember how eager Layton was to please Daddy? Daddy'd say jump, and Layton would ask which bridge." Grimacing, Addison picked up the drink she'd made for Alaina and drained it. Her eyes were glazed from the alcohol, her smile sad. "Would it help to know that Daddy might have felt guilty about what happened?"

Ridiculously, it mattered. "Did he tell you that?"

"No, but when he died, he left you and Jonah a third of everything."

For a moment, shock held Alaina rigid. "He what?"

Addison laughed, waving the glass. "Layton was crushed. He thought he'd get it all. PCware is worth millions, you know."

Alaina pushed away from the windowsill. "If Jonah owns a third of PCware, and Layton wants it all . . . it seems pretty obvious he wants Jonah to sign over his third."

But Addison shook her head. "You both own the third, and Jonah can't sign over his part of it until he turns twenty-one. That's a stipulation in Daddy's will. The only way Layton would get it now is if you and Jonah were dead, and he could have done that with some paperwork without having to actually kill you. I checked."

"Then what does he want with Jonah?"

"I've gotten the impression that Layton wants to make a go of it as Jonah's father. You, on the other hand . . . you, he wants dead. I heard him tell someone on the phone to kill you."

Alaina shuddered, wondering whether that someone had been Mitch Kane. But when he'd found her, he hadn't tried to hurt her, let alone murder her. In fact, he'd protected her from a hit man, had even killed him. Which didn't make any sense. Weren't Mitch and the hit man on the same team? And why the hell did Layton suddenly want to be a father to Jonah when he'd never even wanted him in the first place?

The questions made Alaina's head hurt all the more.

"I'm sorry," Addison whispered. "For everything."

Alaina met her sister's liquor-glazed eyes. She didn't know what to say, how to react. The apology, after so many years, seemed too easy. But what else did she want? That answer was easy: "I want my son."

Tears spilled down Addison's cheeks, and she sniffled as she swiped them away. "That's Mr. Potter's domain."

"Then let's get him back in here." Purposefully, Alaina strode to the room door.

"Ali."

She paused but didn't turn, her hand on the knob. She didn't know why hearing the old nickname should cause such a surge of emotion, but it did. "What?"

"Do you think you'll ever be able to forgive me?"

Alaina closed her eyes. What could she say? "I don't know, Addison." She looked at her sister, dug deep for some feeling other than bitter anger and found nothing. "I don't know."

"I understand," Addison said, and her voice had gone flat, hopeless.

Chapter 19

Mitch was standing at the gate, the only passenger to have not boarded Delta Air Lines Flight 839. A gate agent had informed him that if he didn't get on the plane in the next five minutes, he wouldn't be allowed to. The woman was beginning to glare when his cell phone rang. He gave her a winning smile, then turned his back to answer it.

"Talk to me, Jules."

"It's Chuck."

Mitch told himself to get over the renewed surge of betrayal. A woman's life was at stake. "Chuck. Hello."

"Your secretary told me it's urgent."

"She's not my secretary—" He broke off, took a breath. "I need a favor."

"Of course you do."

Mitch ignored the sarcasm in his former partner's voice. "I don't have time to give you details, but the feds took a woman to a safe house in the D.C. area. I need to know where."

"You know I can't—"

"She's dead, Chuck, if you don't help me with this. You know I wouldn't have called you for help unless I was desperate."

"I haven't talked to you or seen you in years. I don't know who you are anymore."

"We used to be partners," Mitch said. "You know who I am."

"I know who you were."

"I took a bullet for you. You still owe me for that."

After a brief silence, Chuck said, "I'm not promising anything."

"I need the address in two hours."

"That'll be tight."

"That's all the time I have," Mitch said.

"What's the woman's name?"

"Alaina Chancellor. They might have her under the name Alex Myers."

"I'll get back to you."

"Chuck, I probably don't have to tell you to keep it under the radar. I'll explain later, but I think there might be an information leak in the Bureau."

"Maybe you'd better explain that now."

"I don't have time. Just trust me." Snapping the phone closed, Mitch handed the impatient airline worker his boarding pass.

"I'm not going to a safe house. I want to see my son."

FBI Assistant Director Norm Potter, having just arranged for a car to pick them up in the alley behind the hotel, pocketed his cell phone and gave Alaina an unperturbed look. "I'm sorry, Ms. Chancellor, but that's not possible at this time. But rest assured, Mrs. Keller has promised us that your son will be fine."

Alaina wanted to strangle him. "My sister isn't the best judge of what her husband is capable of."

"No, but Layton Keller has given no indication that he plans to hurt the boy in any way."

"I don't care. I'm his mother, and I want him out of there. I don't give a shit about your investigation."

Potter's cheeks flushed. "I'm afraid your rights are limited, Ms. Chancellor. A judge granted Layton Keller custody of Jonah."

"That was fourteen years ago. That's no longer enforceable—"

"That would have to be decided in a court of law. Which would take time. Which means your son probably would either stay where he is or go into foster care until a decision is made. Which option would you prefer? Your sister or the unknown of foster care?"

Desperate frustration made Alaina's ears ring. Suddenly, she was eighteen again. Layton had stripped her of innocence, her sense of security and control. Now, he was taking all she had left. Jonah. "Then let me go to him," she said.

Surprise arched Potter's brows. "There's a contract on your life. The risks—"

"I need to see my son." Her voice cracked.

Potter's face softened. "You need to stay alive. Which is what you'll do at a safe house."

"You can't force me to go."

"I'm afraid I can."

"Then I'm under arrest?"

"I'd prefer to call it what it is: protective custody," he said.

"Don't I have to be a witness for that?"

Potter sighed heavily. "Let's try this: Five years ago, you killed a man and fled the scene of the crime. I can arrest you for that, if you'd like."

"Why haven't you?"

"Because I'm a decent guy and I believed you when you said it was self-defense. Now, if the safe house just won't do, I'd be happy to get on the phone and let the Madison cops know where to come pick you up." He arched an eyebrow at her. "Those are your options: You can sit in jail in Wisconsin or you can shut up and go to a safe house here, where you'll at least be in the same vicinity as your kid. What's it going to be?"

Mitch's phone rang as he was handing over his credit card at the Avis rental car counter.

"It's Chuck."

"Have you got an address?" Mitch asked.

"I'm not giving it to you."

Mitch scrawled his signature on the form the woman behind the counter slid before him. "I take it you've been briefed on the case," Mitch said.

"Yes, and I don't think you should get involved."

"It's too late for that."

"Your friend needs to stay put, and she'll be fine."

The clerk handed Mitch keys, and he nodded his thanks as he stepped away from the counter. "If she stays put, she'll be dead," he said into the phone, his tone low and urgent.

"There are some high-powered people involved, Mitch. I don't think you realize—"

"I don't care about any of that, okay? I just want this woman to be safe."

"What is she to you?"

"No one."

"Yet you're getting tangled in some serious shit."

"Look, I made a mistake." He sighed, dragging a hand through his hair. "I made a mistake, Chuck, and I need to make it right. Tell me where I can find her."

A pause stretched over several seconds as Mitch walked out of the airport terminal and onto the walk where shuttles picked up rental car patrons to take them to their vehicles.

Rain fell in sheets in the areas that weren't covered, thunder rumbling faintly in the distance.

Finally, Chuck said, "It's not safe to give the address on a cell phone."

"Then give me a hint," Mitch said, shouldering the phone and digging in his pocket for a pen.

Another pause, but shorter this time. "Remember that place we used to go that had the really fine steaks?"

"Yeah." Mitch scribbled "Alice's" on the back of his rental car agreement. "Drive? Street?"

"Lane. The house number is 856. It's in Manassas."

Mitch checked his watch. Manassas was at least twenty-five miles from National Airport. He was looking at about an hour drive at the tail end of rush hour. His sense of urgency told him to hurry. "Thanks, Chuck. I mean it."

Chuck responded, but Mitch didn't hear what he said as he snapped the cell phone closed and boarded a shuttle.

"It's not much, but it's got heat and running water," Potter said, flipping on a light.

Alaina looked around at the bare furnishings. She didn't care that the linoleum was worn, the wallpaper was peeling or the kitchen chairs looked like cats had sharpened their claws on them. She didn't care that the air was stale or that the neighborhood they had just driven through had seen better days. None of it mattered. Only one thing mattered.

"I want proof that Jonah is okay," she said.

He glanced at her, clearly irritated that she'd been hammering at him about Jonah all day. But as he considered her, his demeanor softened. She didn't care that he felt sorry for her. The more pitiful she appeared to him, the better. Then perhaps he would give her what she wanted.

"I'll see what I can do," he said. "In the meantime, you

should eat." He opened the avocado green refrigerator. "I guess there wasn't time to stock the fridge. I'll have someone bring some food in tomorrow." Moving to the pantry, he said, "Looks like there's peanut butter and crackers. That's something."

Alaina was certain her stomach wouldn't take kindly to food, even though the last thing she had eaten had been half a bagel at Aunt Rita's. "I'd prefer to sleep."

Norm closed the pantry. "I'll show you around."

He led her into the living room, which was as worn and stale as the kitchen. A TV set with rabbit ears looked older than she was. A short hallway led to a bathroom and two bedrooms. Norm said, "Take your pick."

She stepped into the nearest bedroom and started to close the door, but Potter put his hand on it to stop her. "Another agent will be here in an hour to take over for me. I probably won't see you again for a while."

"Fine."

"The windows have been reinforced. They don't open, and the glass doesn't break."

Alaina didn't care if her disappointment showed. "May I sleep now or do you want to tie me up first?"

He gave her a grim smile. "This is for your protection, Ms. Chancellor."

"Funny, it feels like it's for the FBI's protection. I'm just in the way of the big collar."

"It'll be over soon enough."

"And what happens if my son gets caught in the crossfire?"

"We're doing everything we can to ensure that doesn't happen."

"Do you have any children?"

"I don't see—"

"Do you?" she prodded.

"Yes. A daughter. She's three."

"Tell me how you would feel if someone took her away from you and handed her over to your worst enemy. And then tell me you wouldn't do anything, *anything* to get her back."

"If Jonah were my son, I would trust the FBI to protect him."

"And that's where you'd screw up. Because when you've been through what I've been through, you don't trust anyone with what's precious to you."

Chapter 20

Mitch steered the rental car down Alice Lane in Manassas, Virginia. It was after seven and already dark, forcing him to squint to try to read house numbers. It wasn't the nicest neighborhood, the small homes older and shabby. Many of the cars parked along the curbs were just as run-down. Landscaping hadn't been a priority as bushes had been left to grow wild and weeds trimmed most lawns. Ramshackle fences surrounded some yards, and an occasional dog let out a raucous bark.

In the 600 block, Mitch parked and got out of the car. The rain had tapered off to a steady sprinkle, and he flipped up the hood of the sweatshirt under his leather jacket to afford some sort of a disguise as much as protection from the rain. Who knew whether Keller's man was already watching the house or if Keller had warned him about Mitch?

A few houses before 856, hoping there were no mangy mutts nearby to give him away, he slipped between two houses, planning to approach from behind. But as he rounded the side of the house next door, he glimpsed a shadow and dropped back. The shadow moved stealthily, dressed head to toe in dark clothing. This was no neighbor walking his dog. And he was much closer to 856 than Mitch was.

Mitch considered his options. Because that guy was taking the back way, that left Mitch with the front. He backtracked at a trot, mud squishing underfoot. But on the sidewalk out front, he froze. Another shadowy figure was crouching before the front door of 856 Alice Lane. As Mitch watched from behind a tree, the front door eased open, and the man slipped inside.

Something in his hand reflected light from a streetlamp.

A gun.

In her dream, Alaina crept slowly up the stairs to her bedroom, careful to avoid the places in the steps that creaked. She had become a pro at this, sneaking into the house well into the wee hours of the morning. No one ever knew, or even suspected, that she'd been out. It was a liberating feeling that lasted until her alarm went off, thrusting her back into the chains of life as the teen daughter of Paul Chancellor, community icon and high-profile entrepreneur.

Easing open her bedroom door, she slipped into the room, silently shutting it behind her. She leaned back against it and breathed a sigh of relief. Yet another late-night mission accomplished. A smile tugged at the corners of her mouth, pleased that the buzz from the wine still remained, remembering how it had felt to have Michael's hands on her skin. If he'd asked, she might have let him go further. They'd been a couple for six months now, and being with him had felt that good—

"Good morning, Alaina."

Her breath caught as the light beside her bed winked on. Her sister's fiancé sat on the edge of her bed, grinning at her look of shock. She relaxed, smiled. "Hey. What are you doing here?" She felt awkward with him on her bed, a little surprised that he was there without Addy, but pleased, too. Layton was the only one who seemed to care what she thought about stuff. He'd been her ally in several arguments with her father, reminding him that she was a teenager after all, and teenagers tended to get into trouble sometimes.

His grin broadened. "Waiting for you."

She dropped her purse on the floor and plopped onto the desk chair across from the bed. "Where's Addy?"

Layton gave a negligent shrug. "At her place, I guess. Where have you been?"

She smiled. "Out with Michael celebrating."

Layton waggled his eyebrows. "Eighteen today. Was it a good birthday?"

Her shrug mirrored his. "It was okay."

"Come on, you've been looking forward to being eighteen a long time."

"It'd be cooler if I were going away to college like all my friends."

"You're going to college," Layton said.

"Community college."

"That's just until you prove to the old curmudgeon that you can handle going off to college by yourself."

She giggled. "Old curmudgeon."

His blue eyes began to sparkle. "Have you been drinking?"

She held up her thumb and index finger about an inch apart. "Maybe a little."

"Your dad's going to be mad."

She giggled again. "Who's going to tell him?"

His wink was conspiratorial. "I could be persuaded not to."

"Yeah? What would it cost me?" She enjoyed their banter, enjoyed how he flirted. How could she not? He was a hunk. She envied the hell out of her sister.

Rising, he crossed to her, one hand held out as if inviting her to dance. Puzzled but amused, she took his hand and stood. His size was overwhelming, his chest broad, his arms muscled and strong. He smelled of gin and aftershave.

"What are you willing to pay?" he asked, his voice dropping as he feathered his fingers through the hair that rested against the side of her neck.

The way he touched her startled her, and she stepped back, raising her palms to his chest to hold him off when he leaned forward. "What are you doing?"

His grin turned wolfish, and he let his weight rest against her hands, forcing her back against the desk. Angling his head, he inhaled as if drawing in her scent. "You smell amazing, Ali. Did you know that you've been driving me crazy?"

"I want you to go."

He pulled back, his fingers in her hair curving around to the back of her neck and tightening. "I'm not going just yet."

She tried to jerk away from him, but his hand was strong and held her immobile. She tried to push him back, to slap at him. He easily swung her around and gave her a shove, hooking his hand in the collar of her blouse and swiping down. Buttons popped and flew.

Gasping, she gathered the tattered edges of her shirt together, staring at him in disbelief. This couldn't be happening. He was her friend, her ally, her sister's *fiancé*. He was Layton.

"If you scream," he said, "your father will come running. And you know what I'll tell him? You came on to me."

"You're in my bedroom," she said, her voice shaking. "How will you explain that?"

He scratched his chin as if thinking through his story. "I ran into you at the Lazy Flamingo, where you'd had a little too much to drink. Rather than let you leave with friends who'd been drinking and planned to drive, I persuaded you to accept a ride from me." Grinning, he advanced on her. "Unfortunately, you weren't in any shape to walk up the stairs, so I helped you. When we got into your bedroom, you started trying to undress me. And, well, I'd had a little to drink, too, and I wasn't quite myself, so I responded. What red-blooded man wouldn't? I mean, look at you. You're hot, Ali. The kind of woman a man can lose himself in."

She backed away, shaking her head. "Stay away from me."

"I've stayed away for months, and it's killing me."

He lunged, hitting her like a linebacker and knocking her back onto the bed. Before she could get her breath to scream, he smashed his palm over her mouth, his other hand fumbling with the button and zipper on her jeans. She struggled furiously, trying to buck him off, but he outweighed her by a hundred pounds or more and had managed to trap her right arm under his elbow. She flailed at his head with her free fist, but he didn't seem to notice.

She felt his erection as he ground it against her hip, and panic choked her. And then his hand was inside her jeans, rough and groping, shredding her underwear.

His breathing went ragged as he fought to free himself from his pants. "This is going to be good, Ali, so just enjoy it. You're about to find out that your boyfriend's a loser in bed because I'm going to show you what it's like with a real man."

She screamed against the hand smashed so tight over her mouth that she couldn't even bite it. Tears ran back into her hair as he—

Alaina jerked awake, her heart thundering. She couldn't breathe, couldn't see.

A hand was clamped over her mouth.

She struggled, caught between the nightmare and reality, panic so ripe she could taste it. She felt hot breath near her ear, tried to twist her head to see.

"Relax, it's Mitch."

Fear morphed into confusion, and she strained against the strength of his hand.

"There are two men in the house," he whispered. "They've both got to be Keller's."

She sank her teeth into his palm.

"Dammit!" Mitch hissed, yanking away from her.

Sitting up, she shoved him back and swung her legs off the bed, glad that she'd been too exhausted earlier to shed her clothes. But before she could stand on her own, Mitch grabbed her by the front of the shirt, levered her against the nearest wall and pinned her there with his superior weight. His nose nearly touched hers. "Listen to me, you idiot, I'm here to help you," he whispered urgently. "Keller wants you dead, and I'm trying to keep that from happening."

"Why would you do that?"

He grimaced, shaking the hand that bore her teeth marks. "At the moment, I have no freaking idea."

He went still as something thumped somewhere else in the house. "Ah, shit."

"What was that?" she asked.

"If I had to guess, I'd say the bad guys just took out your FBI guard."

Before Mitch could do much more than meet Alaina's frightened gaze, the lights blazed on. A man twice Mitch's size ambled through the door, a gun looking like a toy in his meaty hand. If he had been green, he might have passed for the Incredible Hulk.

Mitch, positioning himself between Alaina and the goon, raised his gun, cocked it. "Stop."

The Hulk kept coming, calmly batted the gun out of his hand and rammed him hard against the wall as Alaina scrambled to get out of the way. Mitch had only an instant to register that the impact had knocked the weapon from his hand before he saw the fist coming at his face. Stars exploded in his head, and he felt himself sliding down the wall.

But the Hulk didn't let him fall. Grasping Mitch by the front of his jacket, he jerked him up, lifting him nearly a foot off the floor and slamming him against the wall hard enough to rattle teeth. "You're not giving up already, are you, hero?"

"Let him go."

Over the hit man's shoulder, Mitch saw Alaina, his dropped gun braced in both hands. Thrusting Mitch away from him, the Hulk focused his attention on her while Mitch stumbled against the door, grappling for balance, frantically searching for another weapon. A floor lamp stood ten feet away. He lunged for it, but the cord tethering the lamp to the wall thwarted him.

Frantic and fumbling with the cord, which was trapped under the wide heavy foot of an armoire, he glanced up to see the Hulk cornering Alaina against a dresser. She aimed the gun at the guy's chest, and Mitch flashed on the scene in the kitchen, when she'd clearly had the advantage but hadn't pulled the trigger.

"Shoot him!" Mitch shouted. "Shoot him!"

The Hulk tugged the gun from Alaina's hands and backhanded her. As she crashed into the dresser and slipped to the floor, Mitch heaved the armoire off the cord and yanked it out of the wall. Enraged, he swung the floor lamp like a bat at the bastard's head. The Hulk twisted, blocking the blow with an arm as big as Mitch's thigh. Seizing the long neck of the lamp, the Hulk jerked it out of Mitch's hands. He raised it, and Mitch thought, Oh shit, I'm dead.

But then the Hulk staggered and collapsed at his feet. Mitch gaped down at him.

"You okay, Kane?"

He glanced up to see his former partner in the doorway,

feet braced, his Glock 9mm pointed at the man on the floor.
"Excellent timing, Chuck," Mitch said, releasing a faint, humorless laugh that echoed through the ache in his jaw. His gaze skipped from the goon to Alaina, who lay unmoving. His heart jackhammering, he knelt beside her.

"She okay?" Chuck asked, holstering his gun. He bent to check for a pulse on the hit man. "This one's breathing."

Pressing his palm to Alaina's cheek, Mitch watched her lashes flutter. Recognition skittered through her eyes, and she stiffened. "You're safe," he said gently, wondering if he should be concerned by the ominous flutter in his belly when he looked into her eyes.

From behind him, Chuck said, "Actually, she's not."

Chapter 21

Layton finished off his salmon with gusto and dabbed his mouth with his linen napkin. Picking up his wineglass, he directed a questioning gaze at Jonah. "Don't like salmon, Joe?"

Addison winced at the nickname, but the teen didn't react as he set down his fork. "I'm not hungry."

"He's probably not used to having dinner this late in the day," Addison said.

Layton made a big show of checking his watch. "It's seven-thirty. Still the dinner hour." He gestured at Jonah's full plate. "Salmon's good for you," Layton said. "Lots of vitamin C. Or something." He glanced at Addison. "What's your excuse?"

She had to force herself not to glare at him. "I'm not hungry, either."

He drained his chardonnay. "Tell me, what did you do today, Addy?"

The question startled her. He rarely, if ever, asked about her day. Did he know something? "I ran errands."

"Such as?"

She returned his gaze without blinking. "Why?"

"Why what?"

"Why do you want to know? You've never been interested before."

He sat back, a smile tugging at the corners of his mouth. "Perhaps I was attempting to make polite conversation in front of our guest."

Jonah scooted his chair back. "May I be excused?"

"Not yet." Layton let his smile bloom wide to soften the sharpness of the words. "I'd like to have a conversation with my son, if you don't mind."

Jonah returned his chair to the table.

"Why the long face, boy?" Layton asked, an edge to his voice that let Addison know he was annoyed. "Are you not pleased with your room?"

"It's fine," Jonah said.

"Have you tried the PlayStation 2?"

The teen nodded, but Addison could see his heart wasn't in it. "Jonah seems tired to me," she said.

Layton snorted. "A teen like you should be brimming with energy at this time of night."

Jonah shrugged.

"Okay," Layton said. "I'm going to spell it out for you. Maybe your mother tolerated moody behavior, but that's not how we do things around here."

"Layton," Addison said, as gently as possible. "Give Jonah a break. It's been a day, for God's sake."

"And I'm saying he needs to get over it," Layton snapped.

Raising his head, Jonah looked Layton in the face. Fire burned in his blue eyes. "Fuck you."

Addison gasped, expecting Layton to surge up out of his chair and strike the boy, but her husband just gave her a smug smile. "Hear that mouth, Addy? Where do you think he got that?" He shifted his gaze to Jonah. "You sound just like your mother, kid. She has a foul mouth on her, too."

Twin circles of color rose on Jonah's cheeks. "Don't talk about my mother."

Tossing his napkin on the table, Layton sat back. "I think we should. We're going to have to eventually. Why not get it all out early on?" Leaning forward, he aimed a finger at Jonah's nose. "She lied to you, Joe. For fourteen years."

"My name's not Joe."

"You could have had all of this." Layton made a sweeping gesture. "All of it. She didn't give a damn what you would want or need. That's selfish, Joe. It's damn selfish."

"Layton—"

"Do you mind, Addy? I'm talking to my son." He looked at Jonah. "You didn't even know I existed. What do you think about that, Joe?"

"I think you should stop calling me Joe," Jonah said, and his voice was soft.

"What are you going to do about it?" Layton asked, amused. "Hit me? Did she teach you to hit when you're angry?"

"Stop baiting him," Addison snapped.

Shaking his head in disgust, Layton waved a dismissing hand. "You're excused. Go to your room."

Jonah was up and out of the room in a flash.

"What are you doing, Layton?" Addison asked. "Bullying him isn't going to win him over."

He rubbed his hands over his face. "I know, I know. But it irritates me seeing him moping around like he's lost his best friend."

"He's lost his mother."

"But shouldn't he be happy to be here? Shouldn't he be excited to finally get to know his dad?" Then his shoulders sagged, and his anger drained away, replaced by remorse. The change was so swift, and looked so genuine, that it caught her by surprise.

"Jesus, Addy, I'm so desperate to win him over that I've acted like an asshole," Layton said. "I'd better go apologize."

"I think you should just leave him alone for the night."

"You're probably right." He sighed, drumming his fingers on the table. "She did a number on him, didn't she?"

"How do you mean?"

"He doesn't trust. She made him like that."

No, he just doesn't trust you. The kid has good instincts. She said, "You'll have plenty of time to turn him around."

Chapter 22

"Pull over."

Mitch glanced at Alaina, surprised that she had spoken. It had been more than an hour since he had awoken her, since his former partner had returned a long-ago favor by saving his life. They had left Chuck at the safe house to deal with the aftermath, which included intensive questioning of the hit man—whose wounds appeared non-life-threatening—and the FBI agent in charge of securing the safe house throughout the night. The man had staggered into the bedroom after the shooting was over. The simple bump on the head from a man hired by Keller to kill at all costs had raised suspicions—especially considering the fear that Keller had somehow infiltrated the FBI.

Chuck, who as deputy director had taken over the investigation from Assistant Director Norm Potter, and Mitch had quickly decided that Alaina would be safest if Mitch took her to a location that he didn't share even with Chuck. At the time, Alaina, still stunned by the hit man's attack, hadn't argued. But now she apparently had snapped out of it.

"Pull over," she repeated, more vehemently.

Thinking she was going to be sick, Mitch steered the car onto the highway's shoulder and stopped. She bailed out fast, slamming the door. But instead of being ill, she ducked her head against the rain and began to stride in the direction they had come.

Mitch fell in step beside her, hunching his shoulders. An

occasional car whizzed by only a few feet away, tires hissing on the wet pavement. "What are you doing?" he asked.

Her hair, already drenched, hung in curling tendrils, and she swept them out of her face. "I'm not going anywhere with you."

"So, what, you're going to walk back to the city?" He looked around at their surroundings in an exaggerated manner, his hands spread. "We're sixty miles out already. There isn't even a streetlight out here."

Whirling toward him, she planted her hands on his chest and shoved, knocking him back a few steps. "Get back in your car and get the hell away from me."

He had to run to catch up to her again. "Alaina, come on. It's cold and it's raining and, in case you haven't noticed, there's a big target on your back."

"Would that be the same target you've been aiming at?"

"I told you I don't work for him anymore."

"And I'm supposed to just take your word for it."

"I don't think you have much choice."

She responded by picking up her pace.

Staying with her, he tried another angle. "I defied the federal government for you. The feds could toss me in jail for interfering in their investigation."

"Good. Maybe then you'll leave me alone."

He grabbed her arm, hauling her to a stop. "This is nonsense. Just listen—"

She swung around and slapped him. And it was as if the violent action released a torrent of rage and emotion. "How dare you! How dare you say this is nonsense!" The next time she hit him, it was with her fist.

Catching her wrist before she struck him again, he twisted her around, wrapped one arm around her waist and pulled her tightly against him, trapping both her arms against her body. He didn't know how else to subdue her without getting a knee in the groin or an elbow in the gut. At the same time, he was all too aware of how they must have looked on the shoulder of the highway. All he needed was for some Good Samaritan to pull over and try to help the damsel in distress. Luckily, no cars had passed them since he had grabbed her.

Against him, Alaina squirmed, groaning her frustration through gritted teeth. He felt her muscles coil and strain, as if she were trying to get leverage to flip him over her shoulder. He was surprised he was able to hold her so easily. In their earlier skirmishes, she'd proved a worthy and strong opponent. But she was weak now, exhausted both mentally and physically. And that seemed to frustrate her all the more.

"Let me go."

The emotion in her voice nearly broke his resolve, but he steeled himself and held on, conscious of her racing pulse in the wrist clamped in his hand. It beat against his palm like a frantic bird trying to escape a glass cage. Her already weakening struggles and sobbing breath made his throat ache. "You're safe with me, Alaina. I promise. You can trust me."

"Let me go, damn you!"

He held fast. "Listen to me. I'm going to help you get Jonah back. That's what you want, isn't it?"

She continued to strain against his grip, but he sensed her attention had focused.

"Think about where you'll be if you walk away from me," he went on. "You have no way of getting to Keller. If you contact him, he'll just send another hired thug after you. You're not safe with the FBI. That's obvious after tonight. But I know where Keller lives."

Her body tensed again, but it was the tension of someone who was listening intently.

"We're going to go somewhere safe," he said. "Where

Keller's hired killers can't find you. Because if you end up dead, Jonah's out of luck. Right?"

She relaxed some, her breath hitching.

He took that to mean he had gotten through to her. "I know you have no reason to believe I'm on your side," he said. "But I'm willing to prove it to you if you give me a chance."

She didn't respond for a long moment, but she also didn't try to fight him anymore. Finally, she whispered, "Please let me go."

He released her. Facing him, she studied him while rain ran down her face in rivulets. It reminded him of the first time he'd looked into her eyes, when she'd been flat on her back in the street after being hit by the cab. The jolt he felt was stronger now, and made it difficult to draw a deep breath.

Without speaking, she walked past him toward the car. He followed, relieved that he had gotten through to her. She might not have trusted him, but he could give her what she wanted most. He knew her well enough to know that she would risk everything to get it.

In the car, he shucked his leather jacket and handed it over to her. "You need to get warm," he said, and cranked up the car's heater.

He pulled back into traffic while she burrowed under his jacket. "When was the last time you ate?" he asked.

"I don't remember."

Reaching into the back seat, he hauled forward a backpack that he plopped into her lap. "There're PowerBars in there. Eat one."

She bristled at the command, but he headed off her protest. "Yesterday, you nearly kicked my ass twice. Tonight, you couldn't best a kitten. You're going to need your strength to take on that son of a bitch."

Zipping open the canvas pack, she plucked out a PowerBar and ripped open the packaging. He let her swallow three bites before he glanced sideways at her. She was staring out the side window, her jaw working as she slowly chewed. He figured he didn't have to wonder what she was thinking. Her thoughts were focused entirely on Jonah. He couldn't relate to such single-minded determination, and it made him feel inadequate as a father and as a man. If he'd had half her resolve, he never would have allowed his ex to shut him out of his son's life.

He cleared his throat. "So tell me why you have no problem slapping the crap out of me, but you can't seem to pull a trigger to save your own life."

Finishing off the PowerBar, she crumpled the wrapper in her hand. "How did you know where to find me?"

He let her change the subject for now. "Chuck—the guy who took down Keller's man—he's a deputy director in the Bureau. He gave me a hint."

"How did the hit man find me?"

"We think Keller's got someone in the Bureau," he said, glancing sideways in time to see her fist clench around the PowerBar packaging.

At least half a minute passed before she said, "My sister could be at risk."

It was the response he'd been hoping for, an indication that she cared about the woman who'd put her own life on the line to protect her and Jonah despite the circumstances of Jonah's birth, whatever they were. He didn't know why that seemed important, but it was. It reassured him that he'd chosen the right side. "Chuck said the Bureau has gone to great lengths to shield her identity," he said. "She's been dealing only with A.D. Potter and his office. If Keller hasn't found out about her by now, it's likely he won't."

"You trust them?"

"I used to be one of them."

"That's not an answer." Her voice sounded stronger now.

"I trust Chuck," he said. At least in times like these, he thought.

"But you wouldn't tell him where we're going."

"It was safer not to."

"Where are we going?" she asked.

"Cabin in the Shenandoahs I've rented a couple times. Very secluded," he said. "Of course, it's about a three-mile hike, so it's a good thing you ate something. You're going to need it." He paused, hitting the high beams as the road curved, trees growing dense on either side. "Now it's your turn. Why didn't you shoot that guy when you had the chance?"

Looking out the side window, Alaina drew his jacket up to her chin and burrowed farther under it as if seeking shelter. He thought she was going to avoid the question again, and he was prepared to let her. But then she spoke, and her voice was so quiet he had to strain to hear it. "I killed a man once. It was an experience I don't ever want to repeat."

"You defended yourself," he said, unsure why he knew now that there was only one way Keller's hired hand could have ended up dead. He just knew.

She seemed surprised by the conclusion he'd reached, and regret arrowed into him. He wanted to apologize for every harsh thing he'd said to her, but had no idea where to start or even what to say. Instead, he said, "You'll learn to live with it eventually."

With her gaze intent on his profile, he focused on the shiny wet asphalt that stretched ahead of the car. "Five years ago—I was a fed then—I worked a kidnap case in which a woman took off with her neighbor's toddler. A sad story. She and her husband had lost their three-year-old in a hit-and-run accident. A year later, the husband walked out on her. She just went berserk. Grabbed the neighbor kid off the lawn and ended up in North Carolina before we caught up with her. My partner—Chuck—and I cornered her at a beach house she'd holed up in, tried to talk her out while we waited for backup. By then, she was holding the kid and threatening to shoot him if we didn't back off. We were all ready to do it, too. You know, wait for a psychiatrist to show up. But for some reason, she started shooting at us." He paused, taking a moment to draw in a calming breath. "She was waving that gun around, holding that helpless little boy so tight he couldn't breathe. He started to scream, and that just seemed to send her all the way over the edge. First chance I got, I shot her."

Only the hum of the engine and the hiss of tires on rain-drenched pavement filled the car. Alaina was still, and he sensed her attention, sharp and searching. He wondered what she saw, how she felt. And then he wondered at what point what she saw and how she felt had become so important to him.

After what seemed an eternity, he heard her swallow. "I'm sorry," she murmured. "That must have been terrible for you."

Her face was wet, but he couldn't tell whether it was tears or the rain still dripping from her hair. She'd never been more appealing. He moistened his lips. "You do what you have to do," he said. "And then you deal with it."

"How did you deal with it?"

He gave her a sardonic smile. "Quit my job, drank a lot, alienated my friends and family. What did you do?"

"Drove for two days with Jonah to Grand Junction, Colorado, and started over."

His insides did a slow roll. She hadn't had the luxury of

falling apart. She'd had a child depending on her for his next meal. No time for wallowing in self-pity. "I don't know how you did it, how you survived," he said.

"You do what you have to do," she said, repeating his own words back to him.

And she had, he thought. She'd run away with her child. She'd made a decent life for them against the odds. She'd killed for him, survived for him. When a normal person would have crumbled, she had persevered. And he sensed she had done it for one reason only. He prayed they wouldn't have to find out what would happen to her if that reason was taken away.

"We'll get Jonah back," he said in a low voice. "I promise."

"You shouldn't do that," she said.

"Do what?"

"Make promises you can't keep."

"I don't."

Chapter 23

"This is it," Mitch said as he shone the flashlight on the front porch of the cabin.

It was dark, tiny and desolate, and Alaina didn't care. Her legs felt rubbery from the two-hour hike over slippery, rough terrain, and she was desperate to get warm. The rain had stopped a half-hour ago, but she'd been soaked when they'd started out, and Mitch's jacket had afforded little protection against cold and wet that was on the inside. The night was frigid and windy, and while the grueling hike had kept her blood circulating, it had done little to warm her.

Apparently, he was chilled, too, because he was having a hard time picking the lock.

She hunched her shoulders against the icy wind, shivering almost uncontrollably. Heat. She would have done anything for heat.

Finally, finally, the cabin door swung open. "It's been closed up all winter, so the air's probably a bit stale," he said, arcing the beam of his flashlight around a large, rustic room with a vaulted ceiling, knotty pine walls and furniture that looked well-lived-in.

Dust hung in the air and layered everything in sight, which wasn't much: a big, overstuffed sofa, matching easy chair and a dining room table with four slatted chairs. A short hallway led into darkness, and she figured a bedroom or two lay at the end of it.

"We'll have to do without electricity until I can get fuel

for the generator," Mitch said.

Alaina's gaze settled on the stone fireplace before the sofa. "A fire would be nice," she said.

"It sure would. Once everything outside dries out."

Her hope bottomed. "You're kidding."

"It's too wet. Sorry." Shutting the door, he started off down a short hallway, almost instantly leaving her in darkness. She caught up with him in a kitchen that held only the basics: a small refrigerator, a smaller stove with two burners, a couple of cabinets and a sink.

Opening a cupboard, Mitch peered inside. "Thank you, God," he murmured, drawing out a lantern. Liquid sloshed in its base. A drawer near the sink yielded matches and a fresh wick.

"Hold this, please?" he asked, handing her the flashlight.

She did her best to train it on the lantern while he threaded the wick, but she was so cold, her hand jiggled the beam. "Sorry," she said.

Striking a match, he held it to the new wick until it flared, and a warm glow filled the tiny room. "Let there be light," he said.

His grin was so disarming that she gave him an answering smile, but it felt weak as she hugged her arms around herself, fighting the desire to let her body fold.

Mitch's amusement faded. "Your teeth are chattering."

She shrugged. "It's kind of reassuring, actually. Means I'm not dead."

He gave her a critical once-over. "You need to get out of those wet clothes."

"And into what?"

She followed him into the other room, where he held the lantern aloft to cast its glow into the far corners of the room. "Usually, linens are provided, but since we've arrived uninvited and out of season, we'll have to improvise until I can go get supplies." Spotting a Mexican blanket draped over the back of the sofa, he dragged it up, sending dust dancing into the air. "For tonight, we can share," he said.

Alaina swallowed the sudden constriction in her throat. She imagined what it would be like to be that close to him, sharing his body heat. She had to admit that in the lantern light, he looked damn good, his dark hair spikey across his forehead, his cheeks pink from the wind. He hadn't shaved in a day or two, and his beard had filled in nicely, tempering the angles of his jaw and making his eyes look like melted chocolate. She imagined what it would be like to kiss him, to feel that rough beard scraping against her cheeks . . . and other places.

Her pulse began to skitter. Which was startling enough because no man had made her pulse scramble like this, but also because this man had seemed to hate her guts only yesterday and now he was being warm and kind and helpful. Plus, she hadn't paid much heed to how attractive he was, because she had considered him the enemy. Now, he seemed to be on her side, and as she assessed him, she conceded that he was immensely appealing.

Seeming oblivious to what she was thinking, he held out the blanket. "Get undressed and wrap this around you. I'm going to try to find some dry wood."

She stood for a moment after he was gone, wondering at the foreign feelings bouncing around inside her, until a shudder racked her from the inside out. Feeling like a palsy victim, she began to undress. Chills were racing through her so violently that it took her several moments just to undo her jeans. Shimmying out of the soaked denim was even more of a challenge.

By the time she wrapped the rough blanket around her

bare shoulders, her muscles felt as insubstantial as water. Leaving her drenched clothes in a heap on the dusty floor, she burrowed into the corner of the sofa with her legs up under her and her hands clasping the edges of the blanket closed under her chin.

Mitch returned from outside, empty-handed and dripping anew. "Everything's too damn wet," he said. Crossing to the sofa, he peered down at her. "You're still shaking."

She buried her chin under the blanket's edge. "It's c-cold in here."

"There's no way to heat the place without dry wood." He toed off his shoes at the same time that he began to unbutton his shirt. "The sun should be up in a few hours and start drying things," he said, shrugging out of the shirt and draping it over a chair back.

Alaina sleepily took in the smooth, sculpted muscles of his chest. If she hadn't been so cold, she was sure heat would have been working its way through her system. She remembered feeling those muscles bunch and flex under her hands when she'd tried to escape the hotel room in Chicago. She remembered the restrained power that she'd sensed in him. Then, it seemed menacing and scary. Now, incredibly, she felt safe.

She let her head loll against the sofa's cushions. Safe. That was a new feeling for her. She hadn't felt safe in fifteen years. But she was safe now, with Mitch.

She stopped caring that she was so cold.

Watching her eyes slip closed, Mitch took in the paleness of her cheeks, the blue tinge to her lips. "Alaina?"

"Hmm?"

"You okay?"

"Sure."

He was standing over her in the next instant, pressing a palm against her forehead. As he feared, her skin was cold and clammy. Symptoms of hypothermia.

Quickly, he shed his wet jeans and underwear, nudged her fingers away from the edges of the blanket and slid the length of his body against hers on the sofa.

Shivering, she instinctively pressed against his warmth, and he put his arms around her, flattening his hands against her bare back. He moved his palms over her skin, creating friction that generated heat. "Alaina?"

She kept her eyes closed.

"Alaina."

His urgent tone roused her. "What?"

"Don't sleep just yet."

"So tired," she said.

"I know you are, but sleeping isn't an option, okay?"

"Why?"

"Just humor me, okay?" He groped for something to get her talking. "Tell me about the day Jonah was born."

Feeling her lips curve into a smile against his chest, he tried to force his brain away from the aching awareness that the woman he held in his arms was naked. Yes, she was still shivering, covered with goose bumps, and her feet, captured between his calves, were like ice. But her breasts were compressed against his chest, her head tucked up under his chin, her cold nose pressed to his throat. It hadn't escaped him that they seemed to fit together without the usual maneuvering for comfort. "Alaina?" he prodded. "Tell me."

She sighed softly, the moist heat of her breath caressing his throat. "I went into labor at home. My mother took me to the hospital, and I had a baby."

Mitch chuckled, his plan to keep her talking backfiring. "It can't have been that easy."

"Uh-huh. Very easy. Three hours of labor and out he came."

He felt her goose bumps subsiding, until her skin was silken smooth against his. His pulse kicked up to the next level. "Why did you name him Jonah?"

"You'll laugh."

"Try me."

"I felt like a whale when I was pregnant."

His laugh broke off when she snuggled into him, her thigh coming dangerously close to venturing into intimate territory. "You feel so good," she murmured. "So warm."

He closed his eyes, trying to regulate his breathing. It had been entirely too long since he'd held a naked woman. He wondered whether his body would have reacted differently if it had not been this particular woman pressed to him. Yes, she was beautiful. He'd noticed that from the very beginning. But his growing attraction to her, while certainly physical on many levels, had much more to do with the kind of woman she was. Strong. Smart. Determined. Resilient. A fighter.

As Alaina's shivering abated, her muscles relaxed, and her body went lax against his. He let her sleep, certain the threat of hypothermia had passed. He probably could have eased away from her, but holding her felt good, and he didn't want to interrupt sleep she so desperately needed. After a while, he drifted off, too.

Chapter 24

Alaina woke slowly, content to lie with her eyes closed and her brain fuzzy. She tried to remember where she was. One thing was for sure: She was so warm and toasty she could have purred. Eventually, she also noticed that she was naked.

And that hairy legs tangled with hers.

Her eyes flew open, and she found herself face to chest with a softly snoring Mitch Kane. Her instinct was to stiffen, but she had become an expert at fighting panic and thinking clearly. She did that now, holding still, taking stock.

She was naked.

Mitch was holding her.

And it wasn't unpleasant, didn't feel threatening.

The expanse of his chest, his skin smooth over hard, well-defined muscles, was a hair's breadth from her lips. When her breath caught in admiration, she quickly raised her gaze, seeking less-perfect territory.

His nose was slightly crooked. Had she done that when she'd smashed the heel of her hand against it in the hotel room in Chicago? But, no, it didn't even look bruised.

His beard had thickened overnight, darkening the angles of his jaw, the slope of his throat. He had a nice neck, she noticed. His skin was tanned and flawless except for a small pucker of flesh on his left shoulder that might have been the memory of a bullet wound. She wondered at the pinch of concern she felt as she studied it. He had been shot. Years ago, from the look of the scar. But shot nonetheless.

"Good morning."

Alaina glanced up. His dark gaze, not the least bit sleepy, was locked on her face. She saw the desire in his eyes at about the same time that she felt it against her thigh.

Startled, she bolted up but was stopped by the blanket, which was trapped under his arm, and the pain that shot through her battered body. She fell back, a groan slipping through her clenched teeth.

"Hold on," he said, shifting to release the blanket. "There."

Eyes watering, she sat up gingerly, drawing the blanket with her for coverage as Mitch rolled to his feet. Her discomfort was forgotten as she noticed what a fine butt he had as he hurried across the wooden floor, snagged the jeans draped over the back of a chair and stepped into them. His muscles flexed as he drew them up. Oh, yes, a fine butt, indeed.

"Good thing it's cold in here," he said as he zipped and faced her. His grin was sheepish, his cheeks faintly red. "Sorry about that."

He'd left the button of his fly undone, and she had to force herself not to look at it or his washboard abs. Her thigh burned where his heat had scorched her, and she wished she hadn't flinched away from him. The regret shocked her, and her cheeks heated.

Snagging his backpack off the floor as if he needed something to do, he rummaged through it. "You must be sore as hell," he said, coming up with Advil and bottled water. After tapping two orange pills into his palm, he brought them to her and unscrewed the water.

She washed down the pills. The water tasted fantastic, and she swallowed more before handing it back to him. "Thanks."

He gulped some down, his Adam's apple bobbing. "How'd you sleep?"

Rolling her shoulder to test its mobility, she tried not to wince. "Apparently without moving."

Setting aside the water, he sat down beside her on the sofa. "Want me to try to rub some of the stiffness out?"

She hesitated, imagining how it would feel to have his hands on her. Her breath grew shallow with anticipation, and she clasped the edges of the blanket under her chin. This . . . attraction . . . had to be related to fatigue, she thought. Her defenses were weak, and he was being so kind . . . and looking so good.

Mitch smiled. "You're not shy, are you?"

She heard the subtle challenge, sensed he issued it because he knew it would goad her into submission. It worked. She shifted so that he was behind her, and she felt his warm breath against her skin as he edged aside the blanket, baring her shoulders to the nippy air.

But instead of putting those big, warm hands on her, he sucked in a sharp breath.

"What?" she asked, glancing back to see the faint blush from a few minutes ago gone.

"You've got some major league bruises," he said, his voice soft but tense. "I'd better not . . ." He trailed off, cleared his throat. "I don't want to hurt you."

Rising abruptly, he went to the table, where the clothing she had dumped on the floor in a sodden heap the night before was draped over various chairs. He must have gotten up after she'd slept to spread them out to dry. Now, he gathered her belongings and brought them to her.

"Thank you," she said, holding them on her lap, watching him curiously.

"I'm going to run out and see if I can find some dry wood this time. You can get dressed while I'm gone. Everything's still a bit damp, I'm afraid." He gestured toward the hallway that the night before had led into darkness. "There's a bathroom that way. I got the toilet working last night—it's one of those pull-chain kinds. Shower works, too, but it'd be cold."

And he was gone.

Alaina gazed at the closed door for a moment, wondering at his odd behavior. And her own lingering disappointment.

Several yards from the cabin, Mitch braced a shaking hand against a tree and took deep breaths. He thought about the hike through the woods the night before in the cold rain. She had to have been in screaming pain and hadn't said a word. She'd been hit by a car, had her shoulder dislocated twice and had been knocked around by two brutes. Three, if he counted himself. All the abuse had left a rainbow of marks on her back, around her shoulder and across her ribs.

Closing his eyes, he berated himself for not being more sympathetic. The woman had been through hell, physically and emotionally, and he had forced her to keep pace with him over rough, slick terrain, all the while freezing her ass off. She'd nearly slipped into shock from hypothermia afterward.

Hell, if it hadn't been for him, maybe none of this would have happened to her. If he hadn't tracked her down, leading Keller's henchmen right to her, she and Jonah this minute could have been enjoying a lazy Sunday morning breakfast of pancakes smothered in syrup.

Instead, Alaina looked like she'd been beaten and faced being holed up with him in this godforsaken cabin in the middle of the Shenandoahs for who knew how many days without her son, the light of her life. Because of Mitch. Because he'd been stupid and naïve and easily manipulated. Because he'd led with his anger instead of his common sense.

Guilt, he was discovering, sucked.

★ ★ ★ ★ ★

Alaina was dressed when Mitch returned, his arms laden with newly chopped wood. Kneeling, he stacked a few logs in the fireplace and began breaking up pieces for kindling.

"Isn't it kind of a waste to start a fire now?" she asked.

"What do you mean?" He gestured at the backpack. "Could you grab the matches out of there?"

She dug around inside it until she found them in a Ziploc bag. As she handed them over, she said, "We're not going to be here long enough to enjoy it."

His brow creased. "Where else are we going to go?"

She felt a sinking in her chest. "You said you were going to help me get Jonah back."

"I am. But it's not going to happen today."

Straightening, she folded her arms as a chill passed through her. The fire cast heat into the room, but her body and slightly damp clothing seemed unable to absorb it. "You said you have access to Layton."

He rose, pocketing his hands, his expression sober. "We're going to need a plan, which is going to take at least a few weeks—"

"Weeks?" She barely managed not to yell it.

"You know what it takes to plan, Alaina. You did it very well for fourteen years. You can't rush it."

"No, but a sense of urgency—"

"It's not just Keller we have to worry about. It's the feds. If they get a whiff of something, they'll do whatever they have to to stop us. I guarantee that."

She forced herself to be reasonable. But it was difficult when every instinct screamed at her to run to Jonah and shield him from Layton's twisted world. How could she stand to be away from him for weeks? He was her anchor.

Something in her chest shifted as she realized that she was

as desperate to get to Jonah for her sake as for his, probably more.

"You don't have to worry about him," Mitch said. "Chuck's a good agent. He'll look out for Jonah. If he's anything like you, he can handle himself."

"You don't know that. You don't even know him."

"I know you. You've prepared him."

"Not nearly enough," she said, turning away.

He grasped her arm, drawing her around to face him. His dark gaze searched her eyes, and she tensed, as much unnerved by the scrutiny as the way her pulse tripped and raced. "What?" she asked, irritated at the rasp in her voice.

"You have no reason to trust me," he said. "I understand that. But I'm asking you to do it anyway. I'll get your son back, but it will take a little while. Can you trust me to do that?"

She wanted to pull away, alarmed by her body's response to his touch. He emanated heat in waves, and her skin absorbed it until she was almost uncomfortably warm. It heated the air around them, too, making it seem too thick, too heavy. Breathing took effort.

And what he wanted . . . trust . . . it was too much to ask. She didn't know him. All she knew for sure was that at one time he had hunted her on Layton's behalf. He might well be playing her right now, stalling her while Layton accomplished whatever the hell he was trying to accomplish with Jonah. But what choice did she have? She was at his mercy here, in this cabin in the woods in the middle of nowhere. If he'd wanted to harm her, he'd had ample opportunity. More simply, he could have let the hit man kill her the night before.

Yet, if she trusted him, she risked everything. Her life. Jonah's. Swallowing the lump in her throat, she lifted her arm out of his grasp. "I don't think I can."

If he was hurt, he didn't show it. "But you understand that it's going to take time," he said. "My partner will need to do surveillance, get a sense of Keller's security, his schedule. If we had help from someone on the inside . . ." He trailed off, waiting expectantly.

"You're the only insider I know."

"What about your sister?"

That surprised her. "Addison?"

"If she could give us information about the security system—"

"No. She'd tip off Layton."

"She's working with the FBI."

"So?" Alaina asked.

"Whatever happened between you two is the past. She's on your side now."

"She's on her side. That's the only side she's ever been on. I don't trust her."

"Yeah, well, you might have to trust someone before this is over, Alaina."

"Maybe it's easy for you, but it's not for me."

"It's not easy for anyone." Going to the door, he lifted his jacket from one of the hooks arranged in a row on the wall. "I'm going for supplies. There's enough wood for the afternoon."

She followed him. "I want to go with you."

"I don't think that's a good idea."

"Well, I don't think it's a good idea for you to leave me in the middle of nowhere. What if something happens to you? I'd be screwed."

"Nothing's going to happen to me," he said.

"But aren't you a target, too? Does Layton know you're helping me?"

"As far as he knows, I'm still itching to get my hands on

you." His lips quirked as if he'd just said something amusing, but then he shook his head. "He thinks I want to exact my own revenge. I doubt it would occur to him that I've switched sides."

"Have you?"

His face was expressionless as he zipped the jacket. "What do you think is going on here, Alaina?"

"For all I know, you're still working for Layton."

"Doing what?"

"Keeping me a prisoner here until he's done with whatever it is he's trying to do."

"He wants you dead. That's what he's trying to do."

She raised her chin a notch. "So you say."

"So say two hit men. So far."

"Both of whom could have been setups."

His jaw hardened, and a muscle flexed near his temple. "Setups for what?"

"Setups to make you look like the good guy."

"I *am* the good guy."

"And the day before yesterday you were working, quite wholeheartedly, for the bad guy."

"That employer was found wanting."

She wanted to believe him. It surprised her how much. "Who's employing you now?"

"I am."

"That makes no sense to me. What are you getting out of this if there's no paycheck?"

"Not everyone's motives revolve around money, Alaina."

"If that's the case here, then you're the exception."

"You're damn right I am."

His vehemence set her back a step, even as she realized he had made no move toward her. She couldn't form a response, not when his eyes burned with such intensity.

After a long moment, he gave her an easy smile. “Now that that’s settled,” he said. Digging a cell phone out of his backpack, he set it on the table. On a business card, he jotted a number. “You want a backup plan in case I don’t come back, I’ll give you one. This is my partner Julia’s number. She knows how to get here.” He gestured at his holster, which he had hung on the back of a chair, the gun strapped in. “And I’ll leave that for you.”

“This is silly when I can just go with you. I’ll help carry stuff back.”

“You’d only slow me down. And, frankly, you need to rest and regain your strength. I’ll be back by dark. Any requests?”

She hesitated, wanting to argue more but knowing she wouldn’t win. So the next logical step was to wait for him to leave, then try to find her own way out. She cleared her throat. “Can you find out how Rachel is?”

“I can tell you that now. Chuck had her moved after your position in Manassas was compromised. She’s at a safe house in the area. Chuck took her there himself.” At the door, he put his hand on the knob. “There’s water and more PowerBars in the pack. I promise to come back with something a bit more gourmet.”

“Don’t go spoiling me.”

His chuckle followed him out.

She let two minutes go by before, grabbing his gun and backpack, she eased out the door into the chill morning air.

Chapter 25

Mitch plugged quarters into the pay phone outside Wal-Mart in Front Royal, Virginia, hunching his shoulders against the cold wind. Luckily, it didn't take long for Julia to answer.

"Hey, it's me."

Her chair creaked in the background, and he imagined her sitting down fast. "Where are you? I've been worried."

"I'm fine. Can't say where I am. Your line might be tapped."

"Great. And I just made a 900 call to the pool boys line."

He laughed. "I told you to seek help for that obsession of yours."

"So you're sounding much less stressed than you were last time I talked to you."

"I am. Can you get to our secure phone?"

"I'm on my way."

"Thanks." He hung up and checked his watch. He had two hours to shop for supplies before calling Julia at the pay phone they had chosen to use in case of emergency, back when they'd first teamed up. This would be the first time they put it to use. It was only fifteen minutes from the office, but he'd used the code word "secure," which meant "people might be watching." They had decided on two hours to give either of them plenty of time to shake whoever might be watching.

Mitch doubted that anyone was. Keller would have no reason to have men still tracking him. And it was unlikely the feds would be watching with Chuck in charge now.

But Mitch wasn't about to take any chances.

"Have you heard from my mother?"

Addison looked up from the salad she was pretending to eat and gazed at her nephew. The circles under his eyes indicated that he had not slept well, if at all, in two nights, and his eyes—so blue like Layton's—betrayed his growing unhappiness. She also saw worry for his mother. "I talked to her yesterday," she said. "She's doing just fine."

He scowled down at his plate. "Why hasn't she called me?"

"I'm sure she wants to give you time to adjust to your new situation."

"I'm fourteen, you know. A friend of mine at school said that when he turned fourteen, he got to pick who he lived with, his mom or his dad. Is that some kind of law or something?"

She returned to her salad, wishing more for a soothing glass of wine. "I don't know."

"I'm going to find out," he said.

He was so much like Alaina. "Your father really wants this to work out, Jonah."

"Is that why he made me go to the doctor?"

She focused her full attention on him. "What did you say?"

"This morning," he said, slouching back in his chair. "They took blood." He pointed at the tiny bruise in the crook of his arm.

"Why did they do that?" Addison asked.

Jonah straightened in his chair, and his face brightened.

"Maybe he doesn't think I'm really his kid. If I'm not, I can go back to my mom, right?"

The hopeful note in his voice made her chest ache. "I don't think there's any doubt about who your father is, Jonah." All she had to do was look at his eyes.

Slouching again, Jonah pushed aside his unfinished tuna salad.

Addison set down her fork. "Do you not like your sandwich? I can put something else together for you."

"Not hungry."

"You haven't eaten much in three days," she said, noting that he looked like he might have dropped some weight already.

"I'm not hungry," he repeated. "You don't have to mother me. I'm a big kid."

A big kid with a breaking heart. "Hang in there, Jonah. I know it's hard right now, but it'll get better—"

"What do you know about it?" he interrupted, his voice rising. "Did your mother dump you on strangers without bothering to explain or say good-bye?"

"She didn't dump you—"

"No, but she sure hasn't shown up to get me, has she? She hasn't even called to talk to me. You'd think she'd be worried about me. But she's too chicken to face me now that I know about my father, isn't she?"

"She's been very brave—"

"Brave is facing your problems and dealing with them. That's what she told me. But I guess those rules don't apply to her." Shoving back his chair so fast it almost tipped backward, he jumped up. "Maybe she decided after I was gone that she didn't want me anymore."

"You know that's not what happened."

"No, I don't. I have no clue what happened. For all I

know, you and . . . him have been lying. Maybe you kidnapped me. How would I know the difference?"

"Let's get something straight, Joe."

Addison flinched as Jonah whirled toward the door where Layton leaned, his hands pocketed. It was impossible to tell how much he had heard. As usual, his expression, his stance were pleasant, giving nothing away.

"Your mother's the one who did the kidnapping," Layton said, his tone level, even conversational. "Did you know that, Joe? She took you away from me when you were a helpless baby. A court of law decided she was unfit to be a mother, so she stole you. If she tries to come see you now, she'll be arrested and sent to jail. Do you know what that means? It means she's not coming. Ever. And you need to get used to the fact that your mother is more interested in saving her own ass than coming for you."

Jonah looked so stricken, his face so pale, Addison felt tears prickle behind her eyes. But she made no move toward him, fearing a show of sympathy would undo him in front of Layton, who would use any sign of emotion against the teen.

Crossing to the boy, smiling warmly, Layton squeezed his shoulder. "You don't have to worry about her, son. You're safe here, where you belong. This home—the home you should have had all along—is stable. You don't have to worry about anything."

"I don't want her to go to jail," Jonah said, his voice shaking. "I didn't get hurt. She took good care of me. I'm a good kid. I don't ask for much. I don't get into trouble. Doesn't any of that count?"

Addison thought her chest would burst at how much Jonah loved his mother.

"But you did get hurt," Layton said. "Just the fact that

we're standing here having this conversation is proof that she hurt you. She can't be allowed to get away with that."

"But if I forgive her—"

"It's not up to you, Joe."

"Jonah," Addison said. "Why don't you go out back and shoot some hoops?"

Jonah hesitated, clearly not interested in basketball or anything else that didn't involve keeping his mother from being incarcerated. Addison both admired him and envied her sister. She couldn't imagine what it would be like to have someone be so fiercely protective of her.

Layton clapped him on the back. "Yes, shoot some hoops. I'll take you on in a few minutes in a little one-on-one."

After Jonah slogged out the door, Addison turned on Layton. "Why did you take him to the doctor?"

Layton shrugged. "He seemed under the weather."

"He's depressed."

"Yes, and I wanted a doctor to check him out. Who knows how long it's been since the kid had a physical?"

"He's the picture of health, Layton."

"And sometimes kids who are the picture of health drop dead for no apparent reason. Forgive me for wanting to make sure that won't happen to my son. It'd be a cruel irony after being kept apart for so long, wouldn't it?"

"He thinks you're checking to make sure he's yours."

Layton shrugged. "Maybe I am."

"Of course, he is. Alaina was a virgin when you—" She broke off as his eyebrows arched sharply.

"When I what?" he asked.

She swallowed, looked away. *Watch it.*

He moved to her, lifting her chin with his forefinger and looking into her eyes. "I told you a long time ago what happened that night, Addy. Don't tell me you're doubting my word after all this time."

She kept her gaze steady on his, marveling at how he could lie so convincingly and hoping that she was as talented. "I don't doubt you," she said.

"She seduced me."

Bastard. You lying bastard. She gave him what she hoped looked like an apologetic smile. "Of course. I remember."

"I was weak then, and I admitted it. I'd had too much to drink that night, and that screwed up my judgment."

She nodded, even as her throat ached for what he had done to her sister. The ache grew with the knowledge of what she herself had done to Alaina afterward, the awful things she'd said, the accusations and condemnation. Oh, how it must have hurt.

Layton brushed his lips against her cheek. "Didn't I make it up to you, Addy? Didn't I spend the past fifteen years making it up to you?"

"Yes." She closed her eyes, swallowing the revulsion that rose in her throat at his touch. It had been months since he had come anywhere near her, and she hoped he planned to go no farther at the moment. She wouldn't be able to stomach having his hands on her ever again.

Drawing back, he was still smiling, and his gaze locked on hers as he gave her a sweet smile. "And just so we're clear, Addy: Your sister was no virgin when she fucked my brains out. Believe me, she could have taught you a thing or two."

When he walked out, Addison stood, paralyzed by disbelief.

Alaina lowered herself to a fallen tree, dejected. She'd lost track of Mitch almost immediately after picking up his trail through the woods. His strides had been too fast and long for her to match without giving away her presence. Now, she'd wandered around for at least three hours, searching for something, anything, that looked familiar. Nothing did, of course, because she'd never seen any of it before.

Frustration swelled in her chest, and she wanted to scream, to pound the ground with her fists. She was at Mitch's mercy, just like she'd been at her father's mercy so many years before.

Suddenly, she was seventeen again, six months shy of high school graduation, and her dream had come true in the form of a letter from Juilliard inviting her to audition for admission. She'd been sitting on her bed, her violin resting on her lap, the invitation on the bed beside her.

The thought of an audition at the prestigious school scared her to death . . . and gave her chills of anticipation. If she was accepted, certainly her father would have to acknowledge that playing the violin, being a musician, was what she was born to do.

She was reaching for the phone to call her boyfriend, Michael, to tell him the good news when her father walked into her bedroom. It irked her that he never knocked, but then she saw the look on his face, and braced herself.

He didn't speak for a long time, just stared down at her with his dark, dark eyes, as if daring her to squirm. Everything about him screamed authority. His suit was expensive and tailored, its fit on his trim body perfect. His short hair, dark brown and only recently salted with gray at the temples, was combed the same way every day, very neatly to one side. She had never seen him run a hand through it. His teeth, straight and white, rarely showed in a smile.

"Your mother told me your news," he said in a deep baritone that resembled a rumble when he was angry.

She nodded, holding her breath, praying he wouldn't react the way she expected him to.

"You should have consulted with me before applying to that school."

Hopes dashed, she squared her shoulders and set her beloved violin aside. "I really want to do this, Dad."

"You don't deserve to do it, Alaina. Your grades aren't good. You're in trouble every time I turn around. What makes you think I'm going to let you go to school away from home?"

"You make it sound like I'm a delinquent, and I'm not."

Pocketing his hands, he rocked back on his heels. "How many girls your age do you know who've spent a night in juvenile detention?"

Her temper stretched taut, and she fought for control. "I spent the night because you left me there."

"You needed to learn a lesson."

"My friends and I got caught toilet papering someone's house. It's not like we set it on fire. The cops didn't even arrest us."

"No, but perhaps that's next. Considering the kids you hang out with—"

"My friends aren't—"

She broke off as he held up a hand. "We've already had this discussion, Alaina. The bottom line is: I don't trust you to go away for college. You'll go to community college and live here at home." He turned to go, then paused. "I want you to think about something, Alaina. I want you to consider what kind of contribution violinists make to society."

She raised her chin. "I can answer that right now. Music is a—"

"I'll be blunt. Music is not a career choice. Not today. Not tomorrow. Your mother was wrong to encourage you. I'm going to make an appointment with your guidance counselor next week, and we're all going to sit down and decide what's an appropriate career for you."

"I'm a good violin player, Dad. Have you ever listened to me practice? I got an audition at Juilliard based on a tape that I sent them."

He waved a dismissive hand. "It doesn't matter. I don't care if you can dance a jig and recite Shakespeare at the same time. The arts are a waste of time. You might as well accept that now and get over it."

She clenched her jaw against the stinging behind her eyes. Tears, a sign of weakness, wouldn't be tolerated. "You can't stop me from pursuing my dreams. I'm not like Addison."

He smiled, and there was no humor in it. "You could learn a lot from your sister, Alaina. She's got a good man. She's an excellent role model."

"She does whatever you tell her. That doesn't make a good role model. That just makes a pretty little robot for you to order around. Just like Mom. When are you going to understand that I'm not like them?"

Blood suffused his face and, for a moment, she thought he might strike her. She almost hoped he would. A nice black eye to show her guidance counselor might work in her favor. As it was, no one would ever believe that her father was a merciless tyrant.

Instead, he stepped by her and picked up the violin off her bed, where she'd foolishly left it unprotected. "You can't take that away," she said quickly. "I need it for class tomorrow."

He broke it in two over his knee and tossed the pieces to the floor at her feet.

Alaina stared in disbelief at the destroyed instrument, the scent of split wood filling her senses.

"You're dropping that class," her father said. "And I don't

want to hear another word about music school." He stalked out, slamming her bedroom door behind him.

No matter how hard she tried, a few tears squeezed free. She vowed that he wouldn't break her spirit. She wouldn't let him. In four months, she would be eighteen. She would finish high school, and then she would run away. Her father wouldn't be able to control her anymore, and she would be free to pursue her dream of becoming the best damn violin player in the world.

Now, more than fifteen years later, Alaina sat shivering on the trunk of a fallen tree, hopelessly lost.

"I guess I showed you, Dad, didn't I?"

Wearily, she pushed herself up and turned in a circle, trying to figure out which way would take her back to the shelter of the cabin.

Chapter 26

Mitch, warm now from loading up the rental car with supplies to last at least a week, plugged his last quarters into the Wal-Mart pay phone. Julia picked up on the first ring.

"Were you followed?" he asked.

"Don't think so."

"Excellent. Alaina and I have taken refuge at one of those cabins we stayed at last year."

"How's she holding up?"

"She's doing as well as can be expected."

"Where is she now?"

"I left her at the cabin."

"And you think she's staying put?" Julia asked.

"I imagine she's exploring her options."

"Jesus, Mitch, if she takes off, she could end up lost on that mountain."

"I left her my cell phone and your number," he said. "She'll call if she gets desperate."

"Yeah, or she might freeze to death before asking for help from us."

"She's stubborn, but she's not stupid."

"You like her," Julia said, a smile in her voice.

"I do. But she doesn't trust me."

"Gee, that's a shock."

"I told her I'd help her get Jonah back."

"Of course, you did."

He smiled into the phone. “You don’t have to sound so smug.”

She laughed. “But I *am* smug.”

“I’m going to need you to do a few things.”

“Shoot.”

He paused, struck suddenly by how lucky he was to have her. “Thank you, Julia.”

“I haven’t done anything yet.”

“You’ve done tons. I owe you, big time.”

“Yeah, well, I won’t let you forget it. So tell me what you need.”

“You’ve been keeping an eye on Keller’s place like I asked?”

“Yep. When I’m not there, I’ve got Steve on it.” Steve Larson was a freelancer they used to help on bigger cases.

“Great,” Mitch said. “I need a sense of Jonah’s schedule. I realize that it’s too soon for him to have developed a routine, but there might be certain times of the day when he’s outside by himself, maybe hanging out by a pool or something.”

Silence answered him.

“You there?” he asked.

“You’re going to try to kidnap him back?” Julia asked slowly.

“If we have to.”

“Wouldn’t it be safer and more practical for Alaina to file for custody? I mean, a judge is going to do what’s best for Jonah, and what Jonah has to say is going to carry a lot of weight,” she said. “Plus, Keller didn’t file a complaint after she took off with him, so it’s unlikely that she’d be charged with kidnapping fourteen years later.”

“They might not have a case against her, but that doesn’t mean they won’t try.”

“What are you saying?”

"The feds have threatened to go after her if she does anything that hampers their investigation of Keller," he said. "They don't want him distracted by a custody battle."

"So you think they might arrest her to get her out of the way, even if they have no grounds to charge her?"

"Right. She kidnapped him. There's no question about that. What the feds can or can't do about it now could get messy. A judge would have to sort it out, and the feds might be able to delay the process for months."

"How long is this investigation into Keller supposed to take?"

"I don't know. Chuck wouldn't tell me what it's about."

"Typical fed bullshit."

"He's just doing his job."

"Wait a minute. Are you defending him?"

"Yeah, I guess I am. He's a damn good agent. Alaina would probably be dead by now if he hadn't helped me out. Can we get back to Jonah's schedule?"

"Keller isn't letting him off by himself at all. He probably expects Jonah to try to make a run for it, so he's watching him like a hawk. And his security is pretty standard for a paranoid millionaire who's built himself a fortress to keep the riffraff out."

"Any progress on getting blueprints?"

"The guy hasn't shared his fabulous home with *Better Homes & Gardens* or *Architectural Digest*. I might be able to cozy up to someone at the architectural firm that designed the place, but that'll take some time."

"That's fine."

"Uh, is that the best approach? I mean, knowing the layout of the place would make it easier to get the kid out of there, but if time is of the essence, someone on the inside and some security codes would serve us better."

Mitch gripped the phone tighter. “Time is not of the essence right now.”

“I was thinking you’d want to move quickly on this.”

“I do, but not too quickly. If by some chance the feds manage to wrap up their case in the next few weeks, none of this will be necessary. Alaina, hopefully, would get Jonah back without having to commit another crime to do it.”

“A few weeks is a long time to stall.”

“I know.”

“She’s going to be antsy as hell,” Julia said. “And ticked off if she figures it out.”

“Then I’ll have to make sure she doesn’t.”

“He’s different,” Addison said.

“Different how?” asked FBI Deputy Director Chuck Reiser as he jotted a note in a small spiral notebook.

Addison shifted in the rattan chair across the small wicker table from him. She had come to the Dupont Circle coffee bar to meet Assistant Director Norm Potter, who had introduced her to Chuck before slipping out. This man—in his perfectly creased navy suit, impeccable dark blue shirt and artsy yellow tie designed by Jerry Garcia—made her nervous. He didn’t necessarily look FBI. His thick, light brown hair was slightly too long in the back, its waves swept back from his brow as if he constantly ran his hand through it. She imagined his blue eyes—not piercing, but alert, watchful—didn’t miss a detail. All in all, he made her uncomfortable, and she longed for the familiarity that she had with Potter.

“Why did Agent Potter leave?” she asked.

“He’s being reassigned.”

“Why?”

“Your husband’s investigation has become a high priority, Mrs. Keller.”

She couldn't stand it, the not knowing. "What is he doing?"

"I'm not at liberty to say."

"Don't feed me that bullshit—" She broke off, sliding her hand to the back of her neck and rubbing as she glanced around to see whether anyone was watching them. "I'm sorry. I'm under a great deal of pressure."

"I understand. Can you tell me how your husband has been different?"

"It's like he thinks he doesn't have to be polite anymore. He's starting to do and say things that he never would have. He's been sarcastic. Taunting. Even mean."

"Has he tried to harm the boy?"

"No, of course not. I wouldn't let him."

"What about you?"

She stared at him, aghast. "Have I tried to harm Jonah?"

Chuck gave her a patient smile. "Has your husband tried to harm you?"

Addison had to laugh, and her eyes watered as she looked around for a waiter or waitress. "Do they have anything stronger than coffee here?"

"Mrs. Keller, has your husband mentioned a business trip to Belize?"

She refocused on him. "In a couple weeks, yes. He has a meeting with a software company there. Why?"

"Are you going with him?"

"No. I haven't gone on a business trip with him in several years. If I want to go to Belize or wherever, I go. Why?"

Chuck slid a photo out of his briefcase and onto the table. "Do you know this woman?"

Addison gazed down at the photograph of Layton and a pretty redhead, facing each other in a park, their heads close together as if they were speaking intimately. It took a few moments for what she was seeing to sink in. Then suddenly it made sense why her husband hadn't touched her in months. And she felt a stab of jealous fury. "Who is she?"

"Do you recognize her?"

"Give me an answer, damn you," she snapped. "Who is she?"

"Winnifred Ellison. She's a doctor at Johns Hopkins in Baltimore. She and Mr. Keller have been meeting regularly for several weeks now."

"And you're just now sharing this information? Is this another instance of 'need to know'? The FBI didn't think I needed to know before now that my husband appears to be having an affair?" More pieces fell into place in her head. The taunting, the sarcasm, as if he no longer cared whether he hurt her. Layton was planning to leave. The mask was starting to slip, not because he was getting less adept at keeping it in place, but because very soon he wouldn't have to wear it anymore and he just plain didn't care.

Chuck cleared his throat. "Your husband has made travel arrangements for three to Belize the week after next. One-way."

Huffing and puffing from the hundred pounds of supplies strapped to his back, Mitch mounted the steps to the cabin's porch. Sweat poured down his face, and he swiped his forearm across his eyes. Unbuckling the pack, he eased it to the floor, then rotated his shoulders and twisted at the waist to stretch fatigued muscles. The sun had set an hour before, and a brisk wind was picking up, hinting at the spring thunderstorm that had been forecast.

Walking into the cabin, he was relieved to find Alaina on the sofa, curled in a ball under the Mexican blanket. He knelt before her, gently brushing dark hair back from her forehead.

Her cheeks looked flushed, as if she'd spent a significant amount of time outside in the cold or had a fever. Her skin was warm and dry, though, her breathing even and deep.

Trailing his fingers lightly over the bruise that spread purple along her jaw, he experienced anew the rage that a man had struck her. It didn't make him any less angry that he himself had shot that man dead. He'd been Layton Keller's hired killer, and that made Keller the man behind the fist. Keller, he vowed, would pay for that.

Marveling at this fierce protectiveness toward a woman he had met only days ago, he tucked the blanket more securely around her, then rose to tend to the fire.

When he had that going, he started to return to the porch to unpack the supplies but paused at the door. Something about Alaina's shoes—he picked one up, turning it over. The mud caked on the sole was fresh.

She had made a run for it and returned.

Glancing over at her, he wondered what had brought her back: trust or necessity. He figured he knew the answer.

Chapter 27

Seven days later

Mitch rinsed the shampoo from his hair, his muscles seeming to hum from chopping wood to last a few days. It had been an invigorating workout, and now he was hungry. He was thinking about what to throw together for dinner when a piercing shriek startled him. Whipping the shower curtain aside, he fumbled for his gun, in its holster hanging from the doorknob, and sprinted, dripping wet, toward the front room. Instead of an intruder threatening Alaina, he found her thrashing on the sofa, caught in the grip of a nightmare. Setting aside the gun, he dropped down beside her.

"Alaina."

She reared up and, surprised, he grabbed her arms to restrain her. "Alaina."

Her struggles grew desperate. "Let go!"

He gave her a hard shake. "Alaina! Wake up!"

She came out of it, choking off in mid-scream. Instantly recoiling, she shoved at his hands on her arms. "Let go. Let go."

He released her, something twisting in his gut when she retreated to the corner of the sofa farthest away from him. Holding his hands up in supplication, he backed off the couch to give her space. She'd been plagued by nightmares since they had holed up at the cabin a week ago, and he'd learned the routine quickly. No touching. "It's okay. It was a dream. You're okay."

Gasping for air, she stared at him, pale and shaking, hair falling into her eyes.

"It was a dream," he repeated. "You're safe."

Finally, her eyes cleared, and her breathing slowed. Then her cheeks flooded with color, and she pushed the sweat-damp hair off her face with trembling hands. "I'm sorry," she said, her voice hoarse. "I'm sorry."

He stayed where he was, hands up, heart still racing. Thunder shook the walls, and she flinched, but he made no move to go to her.

Wiping her eyes, she gazed into the fire for several seconds, as if trying to get her bearings or perhaps get raging emotions under control. When she looked at him, her eyes looked more green than gray. "You're naked."

Glancing down at himself in surprise, he laughed as he edged forward, grasped the corner of the blanket and drew it around his waist. "I was in the shower."

"I'm sorry," she repeated, still appearing disoriented.

He cleared his throat. "Uh, how about some dinner? I was going to make some tomato soup and grilled cheese sandwiches."

Lightning flashed, and Alaina closed her eyes, as if steeling herself for the thunder that would follow. When it did, it was sharp, but she didn't flinch this time.

"Want to talk about it?" Mitch asked.

Looking at him, she wet her lips with the tip of her tongue. "Tomato soup happens to be one of my favorites."

He smiled, ashamed at himself for being relieved that she didn't want to talk. He knew it was selfish, but he was beginning to fear that once he knew her demons, they would stalk him as much as they did her. "I'll get dressed, then put together dinner."

* * * * *

Alone, Alaina covered her face with her hands and took several deep breaths. This was the fourth time she'd awakened screaming since arriving at the cabin. The last time such nightmares had invaded her sleep, the diagnosis had been post-traumatic stress. That would certainly apply here, she thought. But this time was different. Then, she had begun relaxing, enjoying her life, "letting down her guard," as her therapist had put it. Now, though, it was all falling apart. And so, it appeared, was she.

She'd managed to hold it together for seven days now. Her bruises had faded, along with most of the physical pain. But each day that went by without Jonah made it ever more difficult to hang on, to remain calm, in control. It was as if every second that ticked by chipped away at her chances of getting her son back. It took every ounce of strength she could muster not to dissolve into a distraught, incoherent mess.

And now the nightmares had begun again.

She forced herself to think about something else, and Mitch's glistening, bare chest came to mind. It was easy to focus on how good he'd looked just now, standing there wearing nothing but a worried expression, his hair wet and spikey, water streaming down his muscled thighs. As her cheeks heated, she steered her brain away from that territory, too. Such thoughts were futile and unlike her. The only reason she was having them was because she was such a wreck that any unbidden feeling could sneak past her defenses.

Plus, she was grateful to him. He had given her the space she sought, accepting her distance and going about the daily chores of chopping wood, cooking meals, retrieving supplies and conversing regularly on his cell phone with his partner. He'd tried to draw Alaina into casual conversation, but she hadn't had the emotional fortitude even for that. She was simply biding her time until she had Jonah back. Nothing else mattered.

She must have drifted back to sleep for a few minutes, because she woke when Mitch called out from the kitchen: "Soup's on."

Pushing herself off the sofa, she followed the scent of tomato soup into the kitchen, where she was greeted by another delicious scent: coffee.

Mitch was wearing jeans and a long-sleeved, navy T-shirt identical to hers, clothing that he had picked up for them both at Wal-Mart. As he set a cup on the counter and filled it from a thermos, he said, "We're running low on fuel for the generator. I'll have to make a run in the next few days to get some more."

She sipped the hot coffee. "Damn, this is good."

"You're not going to start talking to a log, are you?"

She gave him a baffled glance. "Huh?"

"Guess you never watched that TV show *Twin Peaks*. The guy was always raving about the coffee and the pie. And there was a lady who talked to a log."

Her brain had stalled on the sentence before the last. "There's pie?"

Chuckling, he gestured behind her at the table outside the kitchen door. "Go have a seat. I'll bring dinner to you."

She didn't move, holding the coffee cup just under her chin so the steam and its heavenly scent wafted right up into her face. She remembered how busy he had been in the kitchen earlier in the day, had determined from the cooking smells that he was making something tasty, but she had been too lethargic to investigate. Now, however, her interest was piqued. "Please tell me there's pie," she said.

He grinned. "That's a surprise."

Feeling fortified by the coffee and the banter, she went to

the table and settled onto a chair, noting for the first time how cozy the cabin was with only the light from the fire, thunder rumbling occasionally in the distance. If not for their circumstances, the ambience could have been considered romantic.

Mitch walked in with two bowls of soup, one of which he set before her with a flourish, along with the roll of crackers he'd tucked under his arm. "First up, tomato soup a la Progresso."

Picking up her spoon, she asked, "Did you talk to your partner today?"

"Yes. She said Grant Maxwell left the hospital today. He's doing well."

Her relief was profound. "That's excellent news."

"She's going to drop in tomorrow to give us an update on her progress."

"Where's she coming from?"

"The District. It's about a two-hour drive."

She studied him, struck once again by confusion. The man had seemed to hate her guts a week ago, and now he and his partner were putting themselves at risk to help her. He'd just spent seven days of his life cooped up with her in the woods, working his butt off to keep them warm and fed. He had killed a man to save her life.

Her stomach rolled as she remembered being splattered with the hit man's blood, and suddenly, tomato soup was not the least bit appealing.

"Are you okay?" Mitch asked.

Looking at him, she was struck by the concern on his face and fumbled for something to say. "I don't understand why you're doing this."

He took a sip of coffee, seeming to think carefully about his answer. "I made a mistake."

"You make it sound so simple."

His laugh was low, humorless. "It's not. It's complicated as hell. I don't even understand most of it. All I know is that Layton Keller is not the man I thought he was, and you're not the woman I thought you were."

"What changed your mind?"

"I met you."

"I doubt that did it. It was shortly after you met me that you handcuffed me to a bed."

Reaching out, he ran his thumb lightly over her left wrist, where the bruises had faded. "And I've been meaning to tell you how sorry I am about that. And several other things."

She dropped her hand into her lap, startled by the tingling that raced across her skin at his caress, even more unnerved by the breath that lodged in her throat. At a simple touch. She didn't trust herself to respond, and besides, what could she say? It's okay that you manhandled me, let's do it again sometime?

He studied her face, his gaze sober, and she wondered what he was looking for. Resisting the need to shift, she turned her attention to the bowl of soup before her. It was still unappetizing as hell. Life in general had become unappetizing, she thought. Even if she managed to get Jonah back, would she be able to make him understand why she had done the things she'd done? Would he hate her? Would he pull away, distance himself?

Mitch cleared his throat, and she glanced up at him in question.

"Lost you for a sec," he said.

"I'm sorry. What were you saying?"

"I was telling you what changed my mind about you."

"Right. You met me." She sat back, unconvinced and wondering why it mattered.

He rested his elbows on the table. "Let me put it in clichéd terms: Actions speak louder than words, and your actions did not support the picture that Keller painted of you."

"You said you've known him for two years. You've known me a week."

"Ten days, actually," he said. "In two years, I never saw Keller risk his own life to protect someone else."

"When did I do that?"

"At Rachel's. You threw yourself on top of her when we were being shot at."

"Oh."

"And in Chicago, when I was about to walk into the hotel room into a loaded gun, you warned me. You could have let me come. That hit man would have taken care of me for you."

"Maybe I thought you were the lesser of two evils."

"Either way, you saved my life." He smiled. "Now, are you going to eat that soup or am I going to have to pour it down your throat? Because we both know I can take you."

His eyes, as dark as coffee with just a splash of milk, gleamed, sending her pulse tripping. Rattled. That's how she felt with that glittering gaze on her. That and suddenly too warm.

Thankful for the distraction, she picked up her spoon and tested the soup, determining that it tasted good after all. And she was starving. She reached for the crackers.

They ate in silence, as they had the entire week. It wasn't a tense silence or a particularly comfortable one. It was simply the silence of two people who had too much to say and had gotten used to not saying it.

Mitch cleared his throat. "I have a question for you."

She mentally braced herself. "All right."

"What's your favorite Arnold movie?"

She blinked at him. "What?"

"Schwarzenegger. Everybody's got a favorite."

It was an odd question, but it also seemed safe to answer. "*Kindergarten Cop.*"

He grinned as he pushed his empty bowl back. "You didn't hesitate."

"It's a toss-up between that and *Terminator*, but I'm partial to the kids in *Kindergarten Cop.*"

He cradled his head in mock agony. "It's not a tumah," he said, parroting the famous Arnold accent.

She laughed, relaxed some.

"My son loved it when I did that," he said.

That surprised her. "You have a son?"

He nodded, his humor fading. "Tyler. He lives with his mother."

"How old?"

"Seven."

She saw by the way he fixed his gaze on the table that it was painful for him to talk about it, so she stayed silent, letting him determine the course of the conversation.

"I haven't seen him in three years," he said with a note of sad wonder, as if he were speaking to himself rather than to her.

"Why so long?" she asked.

"Because I was an idiot." He gave her a tight smile. "I imagine that surprises you."

"That you have a son?"

"No, that I messed up with my own kid."

She registered the self-loathing in his gaze. Whatever had happened to separate him from his child, he had punished himself about it for a long time. "It's not too late to make it up to him."

"You make it sound easy."

"I'm sure it won't be, but that doesn't mean you shouldn't try."

He considered her for a moment, then smiled. "Perhaps when this is over, I'll give it a shot." Rising, he collected their empty bowls. "Next course coming right up."

He disappeared into the kitchen, and she heard the clatter of dishes on the counter and the scrape of a spatula against a skillet. When he returned, he had two plates with grilled cheese sandwiches. Sitting down, he resumed their earlier conversation as if they hadn't taken a detour into his personal life. "It's interesting that you'd pick those two Arnold movies."

As she sank her teeth into the grilled cheese, Alaina tried to see the connection, but an unexpected flavor distracted her. Garlic. He must have sprinkled it on before grilling the bread.

"In one," Mitch was saying, "you've got a woman who has started a new life for herself and her son after escaping from the child's brutal father. In the other, the woman is on the run from a ruthless, unstoppable killer."

She didn't know whether to be amused or annoyed that he'd related her screwed-up life to action movies that had relatively happy endings. That he'd put that much thought into what her life was like unnerved her. "Is this some kind of Arnold-movie psychoanalysis?"

"Maybe. I have a theory that you can tell a lot about a person based on their favorite Arnold movie."

Seeing the laughter in his eyes, she relaxed a little more. "Then what's your favorite?"

"*Conan the Barbarian.*"

A smile tugged at her lips. "This theory has merit."

"What would Jonah pick?"

"Probably *Terminator 2.*"

"That's what I would have guessed."

"Why?" she asked.

"Kid on the run from something he doesn't really understand." He slid a finger down his nose, as if to remind her of how she'd bloodied it. "The kid's mom kicks butt."

She set down the second half of her sandwich as her newfound appetite and humor fled. "The kid's mom was pretty much nuts."

"Well, you're not nuts."

"How do you know?" she asked.

"Most of the time, I have good instincts."

"If they're so good, why didn't they tell you to get as far away from me as possible?"

"They did," he said.

"Then why didn't you?"

"I already told you. I made a mistake."

"And you're willing to die to correct it?"

"I'm not willing to die at all," he said. "It bothers me that you seem to be."

"Don't tell me you wouldn't die to protect your child."

"I would. In a heartbeat." He paused, as if debating the wisdom of saying what he was thinking. When he spoke, an edge replaced his earlier playfulness. "But I can't help but wonder how you reconcile that with the reality that you wouldn't be in the position you're in now if you hadn't kidnapped him to begin with."

The rising defensiveness irritated her. It hardly mattered what he thought. But maybe it did. "I didn't have a choice."

"Why not?"

She pushed away from the table, unable to sit there another second with his intense gaze on her, challenging her. Retreating to the fire, she sought its heat to chase away a sudden chill. This was dangerous territory that she was unwilling to tread. It was one reason she had kept him at a distance all week. "I don't want to talk about this," she said.

"I think we should."

"It doesn't matter. None of it matters."

"I think it does."

He seemed determined to hammer at her until she admitted . . . what? That everything that had happened was her fault?

Emma dead. Her mother murdered. Grant Maxwell shot. And why?

Because she had coveted her sister's fiancé. There was no question that she had been attracted to Layton. She had flirted with him on more than one occasion. He was a good-looking, intelligent man who'd paid attention to her when others had brushed her off. He'd laughed at her jokes. He'd seemed to respect her refusal to kowtow to her controlling father.

It had frustrated her that he was with Addison when it had seemed so obvious that Alaina was the one he'd wanted. She'd seen it in his electric blue gaze every time he'd looked at her. Maybe he had seen something in hers, too. She had certainly done nothing to discourage him when he'd looked at her that way.

Alaina listened to the snap-pop of the wood, felt its heat on her skin, though it failed to warm the chill inside her that had its origins in guilt. She'd learned to live with the chill. Jonah had taken the edge off, had very nearly banished it. Without him, she imagined her heart would have been a block of ice by now. Maybe one day it still would be. Maybe some day soon.

She felt Mitch behind her, waiting for her to respond, and sensed he would wait all night. She drew in a slow breath. "When he took my son away, Layton didn't even want him. Nobody wanted Jonah but me, and I was the only one who was told I couldn't have him."

"So the obvious choice was to run away."

She told herself his sarcasm didn't hurt, but it did. It really did. "It was absolutely the right thing to do. I made a choice. A hard choice."

"And when you slept with your sister's boyfriend? What kind of choice was that?"

Mitch held his breath. He expected her to be angry. At least, that's what he wanted. Fury, resentment, hostility. Any reaction would do. As long as there was emotion. Ten days ago, she'd been fiery with rage and frustration. Fierce with maternal defensiveness. She'd been mad as hell and fighting for her own life and the life of her child. Even the first morning here at the cabin, she'd been determined to beat Keller, to get her son back.

Since then, the fire had died out of her eyes. He didn't think she had given up, but hope seemed fleeting. She conversed. She even laughed. But she was going through the motions. It was as if she'd shut herself down because she didn't know how to deal with what she would feel if she didn't. Instinct told him that to jump-start her emotions, he had to tear down her defenses, and the angrier he made her, the faster that would happen.

When she finally faced him, though, he saw that his attempt had failed. Her features, though pale and drawn, were carefully blank, her eyes as expressionless. "Did you say earlier that there's pie?" she asked.

His plan had backfired. Instead of snapping her out of whatever torpor she'd slipped into, she seemed to have retreated even further. Frustrated but fearing she might be too fragile for him to push any harder, Mitch scooted his chair back and stood. "I'll get it."

After gathering their dirty dishes, he carried them into the kitchen and set them in the sink. His hands shook as he sliced into the fresh apple pie and served two pieces on clean plates.

He blew it, he thought. She'd been relaxing with him, and he'd pushed too hard. But, God, he wanted her to look at him just once without that damn wariness in her eyes. He wanted her to trust him. He just plain wanted her. It surprised him how much. Even as he'd kept his distance from her all week, his need had grown. And if she never trusted him . . .

When he returned with the pie, he saw that she hadn't moved from where she stood in front of the fire. She had her arms curved around herself as if she were cold.

"Do you want a refill on coffee?" he asked as he set the plates on the table.

She didn't move, and he thought she hadn't heard him. "Alaina?"

"He raped me."

She turned from the fire, and Mitch stared at her, wanting desperately to have not heard her correctly. But, on some subconscious level, he'd already known that she'd been assaulted. He'd suspected it after she had freaked out when he'd straddled her on the bed to subdue her. Hearing her confirm his fear—and that it had been Keller—didn't make the rage any less powerful. It rolled over him, heavy as a cement truck.

That bastard. That fucking bastard.

Alaina's gaze dropped from his, and she rubbed her arms. "He came up with his own version of what happened, of course."

Mitch didn't move, didn't breathe, as he grappled with the fury that threatened to aim his fist at the nearest wall.

She blew out a shaky breath, glanced at him, then away again. When she spoke, he had to strain to hear her. "They all bought it," she said. "My father. My sister. My mother . . .

though I think she didn't at first, until my father did his usual bullying. I suppose I can't really blame them. My behavior had never been . . . ideal." Her laugh was humorless as she gazed into the flames. "I didn't even tell them at first, because I was terrified that that's how they would react. They would think it was somehow my fault. I mean, I couldn't really expect them to think it wasn't my fault when even I didn't think that." Her voice cut out, and she paused, chewing her bottom lip.

Jesus, Mitch thought. She'd been eighteen, a kid, with no one to turn to. Pity simmered just below the rapid boil of his rage. But he said nothing. After waiting seven days for her to start talking, he wasn't about to interrupt her.

She sniffed, cleared her throat. "So I kept it to myself, tried to get over it. I made sure I was never alone with him again, never vulnerable. Locked my bedroom door at night, even shoved my desk chair under the knob in case he figured out how to pick the lock. Then I found out I was pregnant." She dropped her head back, as if looking toward the heavens for an explanation. "God, I wished so much that I'd fooled around with my boyfriend. Then there would have been a chance that the baby wasn't Layton's. It would have been so much easier. I even considered letting everyone think that, but I couldn't do that to Michael. And as time went by, I began to realize that I had to tell them. Especially Addison. She'd married him by then, and I let her, knowing what he was. That ate at me." She took a breath, held it in. "So I told them." She gave him a sad, tremulous smile. "It wasn't pretty."

Mitch's heart squeezed in his chest so hard it hurt, and his hands shook with the need to destroy something, to vent this terrible, impotent rage. He didn't know what to say, what he could say. Then it hit him why she hadn't told Jonah about his father. How could she tell her son that he'd been given life because a vile act of violence had been committed against her?

"Please don't look at me like that," she said softly.

He tried to force himself to relax, to school his expression. He didn't know how he had been looking at her, but surely the ferocity of his thoughts had been clear.

Perhaps too clear, because she had her arms wrapped around herself, as if for protection. Her gaze, watchful, steady, was on his, her gray-green eyes guarded as ever. He realized slowly that she was waiting for something. What? What did she need from him? What could he possibly give her that would make any of it okay?

"I'm sorry," he said, furious at the inadequacy of it. He'd never felt more like an inept jerk.

Her lips compressed as if to hold back a rush of emotion. Her chin trembled, and he could see she was struggling to hold it in. She started rubbing her arms again, as if she were freezing.

God, he wanted to scream, to beat the wall. If Keller had been standing there, he would have gladly ripped his heart out. What kind of monster did what he'd done? The son of a bitch had actually painted himself as the victim when he'd asked Mitch to find his son. *"My sister-in-law is a shrewd, ruthless woman."*

Suddenly, Mitch could understand how a man could be overwhelmed by the need for vengeance. The hate he felt was grinding, animal, as he clenched his fists at his sides. "He's going to pay, Alaina," he said in a low voice. "He's going to pay for what he did."

She went still. "You believe me?"

He gazed at her, baffled. "Of course, I believe you. Why wouldn't I?"

She moved jerkily to the sofa and sat, curving one arm around her middle and pressing the tips of her fingers to her lips. Tears began to fall, and her breath hitched once before she leaned forward to bury her face in her hands.

Perplexed and shaken, Mitch forced his anger aside and sat beside her. He didn't know what to do or say as she wept, so he rubbed a gentle hand over her back. As comfort went, it seemed insufficient, but he felt her lean against him ever so slightly.

Putting his arms around her, he cradled her against him, absurdly relieved when she burrowed in and held on.

Chapter 28

The phone rang, and Addison leapt up from Layton's desk chair, her hand covering her heart as if she'd been caught.

But, no, it was just the phone.

She debated answering it. Under normal circumstances, she wouldn't. It was Layton's office phone—and she rarely was in his office. The last time had been to swipe copies of the detective reports on the search for Alaina that she had given to the feds. Certainly she didn't belong there now, looking through his desk drawers for evidence of his affair.

That cheating son of a bitch.

She'd known for a week, and her anger was still strong. She'd been watching him for clues but had observed nothing. Oh, he was good, she thought. He was so good at deception. She hadn't thought she could despise him any more than she already had, but she did.

The phone rang a third time, and she snatched it up. "Layton Keller's office."

"May I speak to Mr. Keller, please?"

Addison didn't recognize the singsong female voice, and suspicion turned her vision red. "He's unavailable at the moment. May I take a message?"

"This is Dr. Ellison's office. Please tell Mr. Keller the blood test results were negative."

"What blood test?"

"He'll understand. Thank you."

The woman hung up, and Addison lowered the phone.

"The blood test results were negative."

She remembered the tiny bruise in the crook of Jonah's arm. "They took blood," he'd said. What kind of blood test would Layton want run on Jonah?

And then she knew.

Head spinning, she sank onto Layton's chair. Disbelief made her ears ring.

Alaina opened eyes that felt gritty and swollen. Morning sun was streaming through the windows of the cabin. The hair on her nape stirred, and she realized that Mitch's warm body was pressed against her back, his arms wrapped securely around her, his chin resting in the juncture where her neck and shoulder met. The fire had died down, and his heat felt good. So, she noticed, did his proximity. A man had never held her like this, and it surprised her how comfortable it was. It also surprised her that she was in no hurry to shift away.

Even though she was embarrassed by her crying jag, she couldn't deny that she felt better, lighter. Sleep had helped, too, but mostly Mitch had. She'd seen the rage in his eyes. She didn't doubt that if Layton had been standing there, Mitch would have torn him in two. Seeing his rage—anyone's rage—on her behalf . . . it was a foreign experience. Mitch believed what she'd told him without question. He barely knew her, and yet he appeared to have no doubt. It was as if that moment when his hands had curled into fists had somehow eased the feelings of betrayal she had lugged around for fifteen years.

It still surprised her that she'd told him. Did that mean she was growing to trust him? Was that possible in so short a time?

He shifted, and she smiled, sliding her fingers over the

back of the hand he had splayed over her belly, as if holding her in place against him.

"Hmm?" he murmured, his breath warm and moist near her ear. He wasn't completely awake, because he snuggled closer, and leisurely, as if they were lovers cuddling on a Sunday afternoon, one of his hands edged up to gently cup her breast.

Alaina stiffened, startled at the unexpected caress but even more shocked by her body's reaction to it. Her breath jammed in her throat, and every nerve ending seemed to leap to life.

Before she could do much more than gasp, Mitch jerked his hand away and sat up. She would have ended up in a heap on the floor if he hadn't caught her arm. Then, pushing himself up, he vaulted over the back of the sofa and started to pace.

"I'm sorry," he said, tunneling all ten fingers back through his hair. "I'm sorry. I was half-asleep. I didn't realize what I was doing."

Sitting up, Alaina watched him pace the floor in agitation . . . and laughed. "So you copped a feel. Big deal."

He stopped pacing to stare at her. Then he began to smile. "You're not going to bloody my nose again?"

"Not this time." She watched his face carefully, liking the light beard that darkened his jaw. His eyes twinkled, and she relaxed, relieved that he didn't seem to be looking at her any differently now that he knew. She'd heard that some men were uneasy after they knew a woman had been raped. But she saw no such wariness in Mitch's gaze.

"Good," he said, and idly slipped a hand under his shirt to scratch his abdomen. The action revealed a strip of lean flesh that rippled with muscle.

She looked away, astonished by the quickening pace of her

pulse. "What time is it?" she asked, further amazed by the huskiness of her own voice.

He didn't seem to notice as he checked his watch. "Wow. Almost ten." He headed for the kitchen. "I need coffee."

He disappeared into the other room, and she sat there a moment, faintly disappointed. But then, what was she expecting? She had no idea.

Realizing the room was chilly, she got up to tend to the fire. She'd just lowered a fresh log onto the pile of smoldering coals when Mitch came up behind her. "Let me do that," he said.

Straightening, she stepped back, content to admire the way his muscles moved under his T-shirt as he piled another log on and got the flames going with kindling.

When he rose and turned, she started to step back, but in one smooth motion, he snagged her arm and drew her into him. His palm brushed her cheek as he slid his fingers into her hair and claimed her lips with his.

The kiss, gentle but firm, stunned her. Her breath lodged in her throat, and her heart took off at a sprint as his mouth slanted against hers, warm and seeking. When her lips trembled open, in shock, in invitation, he took it deeper, his hand at her cheek their only other contact.

Time spun away as every nerve ending, every heartbeat, zeroed in on what he was doing to her mouth with his lips, his tongue.

Wanted. He made her feel wanted. And it took her breath away.

When he drew back, she stared up at his face, her body humming, her brain stalled. For God's sake, don't stop, she thought.

Laughing softly, he brushed hair back from her forehead,

his fingertips just grazing her skin. "I've been wanting to kiss you for a long time. Hope you don't mind."

"Mind?" she managed. "Why would I mind?"

Smiling, he tucked stray hair behind her ear and ran a knuckle down her cheek, his dark eyes lingering on her mouth. It was as if he couldn't stop touching her.

"You're an amazing woman, Alaina," he murmured. "You blow me away."

Dazzled, she felt her pulse stumble. No one had ever said such a thing to her. The words—and feelings—were so alien she didn't know how to respond.

His smile widened. "Take your time." He kissed her again, this time just a quick brush of his lips over hers, before pivoting to return to the kitchen.

Alone, Alaina stared after him, the tips of her fingers pressed to her still-vibrating lips, where the taste of him lingered. *He* was blown away?

In the kitchen, Mitch poured coffee into two cups and thought about what he'd just done. It was unlike him to be so impulsive. But seeing her standing there, her hair a mess, her eyes puffy and sleepy . . . he hadn't been able to stop himself.

His heart ached for everything she had been through, the depth of the betrayal she had endured—from Layton and from her family. He'd known betrayal in his life, too. His wife and his best friend/partner had delivered it, two for the price of one. The hurt had been shattering, and he'd decided then that women were far more trouble than they were worth. But not this woman. This woman . . . her strength, her resilience, her determination . . . she was worth every instant of trouble.

His cell phone started to ring in the other room, and he left the kitchen to answer it. Alaina was still sitting on the sofa, staring into the fire. It pleased him that she seemed as thunderstruck as he was by what had happened . . . by what was happening between them.

He flipped open the phone. "Yeah."

"It's Julia. I'm on my way."

He forced his brain away from the woman on the couch. "You remember how to get here?"

"If I get lost, I'll call you."

"You've made sure you're not being followed?"

"What do you take me for? An amateur?"

"You know the alpha male in me requires me to ask."

"You sound funny. What's up?"

His gaze sought Alaina, and his lips curved. "Everything's fine. See you when you get here." Closing the phone, he said, "Julia's on her way."

Alaina turned her head toward him. She looked as if she hadn't even heard the phone ring. "Julia?"

"My partner."

"Oh." The fire reclaimed her attention.

Amused, he went to the kitchen to retrieve the coffee he'd poured and brought it to her. She accepted it but didn't sip as he sat beside her. "Should we talk about it?" he asked.

She didn't speak for a moment, as if thinking carefully about what she was about to say. "I don't think it's a good idea," she said finally.

He hadn't anticipated anything different. He expected her to run. That was what she'd trained herself—what fate had trained her—to do the moment someone started getting too close. But he wasn't about to let her off the hook easily. Smoothing his palm over her back, he felt her stiffen but kept his hand in place, gentle, soothing. "Why isn't it a good idea?"

"I've never been a good bet." As she sipped coffee, her hands shook.

Seeing the tremors, feeling them under his palm, tugged at him, as did the sad comprehension of all that she'd been denied over the years. The joy of love, of discovery. The contentment of curling up in front of the TV, a roaring fire or in bed with a lover. "How often has someone bet on you?" he asked.

She shifted her gaze to his, her brow creasing. "Not very often."

She said it so softly that his heart rolled over in his chest. She deserved so much more. Probably more than he could ever give. He slid his fingers beneath the dark hair at her nape, lightly massaging. She was beginning to relax under his touch. That felt like progress. "Then how would you know what your odds are?"

She closed her eyes, dropping her head forward, as if to allow him better access. Her breathing had grown shallow. "It's just not a good idea."

"Maybe I'm willing to take my chances."

"Why?"

"Why not?" He smiled, cupping the back of her neck and drawing her toward him. Her lips were an inch from his before she resisted. Their breaths mingling, he met her troubled gaze.

"It's too soon," she said. "We don't know each other."

He held on when she would have pulled away. Irritation flared in her eyes before she focused on his mouth. The annoyance eased over to desire, sending his pulse scrambling. She wanted him, too. "It's too soon for what?" he asked. "A kiss?"

She swallowed. "Sex isn't casual for me. It can't be."

"I'm not looking for casual sex, Alaina."

"You think what we're doing here is going to lead to something more meaningful?"

"I think what we're doing here has snapped some things in perspective."

She pulled back so that he had no choice but to let her go. "If you're experiencing some need to celebrate the fact that your heart is still beating, I'm not interested."

He grasped her hand before she could rise, knowing he'd somehow lost precious ground and wanting to get it back. "Maybe you're right. Maybe I have a heightened sense of desire because we've been shot at more than once. Hell, I killed a man. My need to celebrate life is only normal. But it's more than that, and you know it."

"I don't know anything." She gave her hand a hard tug, freeing herself, then retreated to a place by the fire, several feet away from him, where she glared into the crackling flames.

She was scared, and he couldn't blame her. He was, too. He'd made a deal with himself never to let another woman anywhere near his heart. Yet here he was, willing to break that deal for a woman who should have been a virtual stranger to him, who had more emotional baggage than he knew what to do with.

"There's something you don't know about me," he said.

She arched a brow. "You mean everything?"

He smiled. At least she hadn't retreated so far she couldn't joke. "I don't usually experience . . . emotions . . . in extremes," he said.

"Lucky you."

His knees cracked as he rose and crossed to her. For an instant, her gaze flickered up to his, then flitted away. It was enough for him to see the uncertainty, the fear. He found himself wanting to say things he never would have said to anyone before he met her.

He stopped short of entering her personal space, waited

for her to look him in the eye. "You make me feel . . . things I can't explain," he said. "When I first met you . . . it was anger. I anticipated making you pay for the things you'd done to hurt your son, to hurt Keller."

She dropped her gaze, biting into her lower lip.

He waited for her to reestablish the connection, wanting to touch her but knowing he couldn't until he'd said what he had to say. "My rage," he went on, "was consuming. And unlike me. I'm the objective detective. I do the job, and I don't get involved because getting involved is dangerous. But when it came to you, I didn't seem to have a choice."

She dragged both hands through her hair. "I don't think I want to hear this."

He continued as if she hadn't spoken. "My objectivity was out of whack from the start. Then, as I realized that I had it wrong, that Keller had lied to me, everything shifted. Technically, I should have been able to walk away. It wasn't my fault he lied to me. And I didn't do anything illegal. He wanted you found, and I did that. As far as I knew, the feds were taking you somewhere safe, end of story. It should have been easy for me to cop the 'it's someone else's problem' attitude and leave it at that. So why couldn't I?"

Her features had gone taut with stress. "You tell me."

He gave her a grim smile. "I've managed to walk away my whole life. I did it when I found out my partner and wife were having an affair. I was pissed about it, pissed as hell, but I didn't fight back. When Shirley decided to take my kid to live in another state, I let her. I could have dragged her into court to stop her. But I didn't. You know what that says about me?"

She studied him, silent, emotions warring in her gaze. Anxiety. Sympathy. Desire.

Stepping closer, Mitch gently stroked the back of his hand over her cheek, noting that she braced against the caress. But she didn't draw back. Progress, definitely.

"I've never fought for what I want," he said, skimming his hand over the top of her shoulder and down her arm, the contact fleeting, aware that she held her breath. "Maybe I didn't know how," he said. "Maybe I was a coward. Maybe I didn't comprehend what I was letting go. But I get it now." He cupped her face, pleased when she didn't pull away. "I look at you, into your eyes, and I get it. You can hold me at bay all you want, Alaina, but there's no way in hell I'm walking away without a fight. Not this time."

Alaina's chest swelled with emotion, his words bringing a lump to her throat that she couldn't swallow. She drank in his razor-stubbled jaw, his dark, expectant gaze. It stunned her that this was the same man who'd looked at her in fury and mistrust more than a week ago. It stunned her further that they were having this conversation.

And he made it sound easy, as if all she had to do was say yes and fall into his arms and all would be okay. But how could any of it be that easy? They'd known each other less than two weeks under extreme circumstances. That didn't form the foundation of a lasting relationship.

And who knew if she could even tolerate an intimate relationship? She had never made love. She was, in essence, a thirty-two-year-old virgin. Would he still be so adamant about not walking away if it turned out that sex was too traumatic for her or that she hated it?

Yet . . . he made her feel things she had long ago decided she would never feel. Anticipation. Longing. She wondered what it would be like to have his hands on her, caressing, demanding. It took all of her willpower not to lean toward him, to invite him to touch, to take. What if she disappointed him? Or he disappointed her?

Which was why it couldn't happen. Too much was at stake, and their circumstances made everything all that much more unclear.

Mitch moved closer, and his body heat seemed to lick at her like flames.

She eased back. "I don't know what you want me to say."

"You don't have to say anything," he said, his voice low, hoarse, as if he had desire on a tight leash and all she had to do was say the word, and he would let it loose.

She moistened her lips, struggled to keep track of reason. "There's too much going on right now. I'm not thinking clearly."

"You don't have to think, Alaina. All you have to do is feel."

"I have a lot of emotional baggage."

"And I have a strong back. Let me carry some of it for you."

"You don't know what you're getting yourself into."

"It doesn't matter. I've already settled in."

He had an answer for everything, she thought, shutting her eyes as his thumb grazed her jawline. Thinking was impossible with him touching her so tenderly, so lovingly. It made her burn with want.

His lips brushed her forehead, her temple, her cheekbone, and she turned her head slightly, rewarded when his mouth sank onto hers. Heat flashed between them, and her pulse stuttered, then began to race. Apprehension fled and, diving in, she slid her palms over his shoulders and hung on.

His muscles bunched under her fingers as his hands moved up into her hair. With a groan, he deepened the kiss, his mouth slanting across hers, urging her lips open so his tongue could explore. Tastes and textures mingled, tangling emotions, short-circuiting her brain. Don't think. Just feel. That's what he'd said. All you have to do is feel.

She let it happen, let herself begin to drown in him. He felt good. So good.

His hand skimmed over the front of her shirt, gently cupped her breast, his thumb massaging the center. Her breath caught, then shuddered out against his mouth, as her nipple hardened. She felt his lips curve in a smile, and then that same hand slipped under the cotton fabric of her shirt, under her silky bra, to caress naked flesh. She went still, held captive by his mouth and his hand, her senses whirling, her head light.

Touch me.

"Breathe," he murmured, trailing kisses along her jaw, down her throat.

She dropped her head back, hitching in breath that she hadn't realized she'd been holding. The air seemed too thick, too heavy, as his tongue tasted the hollow at the base of her throat, as his lips trailed up the side of her neck, lingered under her ear. She couldn't focus, didn't want to. Her heartbeat seemed to thrum inside her head as he pressed a hand against her lower back, angling her hips into him. She felt the hard heat of him against her hip, felt a wild, answering ache within herself. She moaned with it, and the involuntary sound startled her.

She broke away, alarmed at how easy it would be to lose control with him.

He reached for her, but she backed into the wall, a hand on his chest to hold him off. Panting, shaking, trapped, she met his confused, desire-darkened eyes and felt like crying, screaming. "I can't do this," she gasped. "I'm sorry."

His breathing harsh, he touched his tongue to his top lip,

as if savoring the lingering taste of her. His face was flushed, but as his eyes cleared, he took a step back, raising his hands in submission. "It's okay."

"I'm sorry," she repeated, and her voice broke. "I . . . just . . . I can't."

Regret came into his eyes, accompanied by anger. "Don't apologize," he said.

"Please don't be angry. I should have realized sooner that I wouldn't be able—"

"I'm not angry at you," he cut in, his brow creasing.

Unable to look at him, she covered her face. "It's not you. It's me."

He put his hands, gentle and soothing, on her arms. "Alaina." When she didn't raise her head, he said, "Sweetheart."

Sweetheart. She squeezed her eyes shut as a whole new wave of emotion threatened to buckle her knees. None of this was real. This was never supposed to happen for her. She'd resigned herself to it long ago.

"Please, look at me."

She did, her eyes swimming.

He gave her a comforting albeit strained smile. "I'll admit I'm frustrated as hell. But I'm not angry. Not at you. We're going to get through this, but nothing's going to happen until you're ready." He kissed her on the forehead, the contact quick and chaste. "I'm going to take a cold shower now."

As soon as he was gone, she sagged against the wall, her knees as insubstantial as water. Her heart was still sprinting, and she pressed trembling hands to her too-warm cheeks. She thought of him in the bathroom, stripping out of his clothes, and her mouth went dry as she pictured the hard muscles of his stomach. Hearing the water come on, she imagined how easy it would be to join him, to slide her hands over his naked skin and—

A knock at the door snapped her head around, her heated blood running cold. Mitch had said his partner was coming. What was her name?

She glanced toward the bathroom door, debated interrupting him. Then she spotted his holster hanging from the back of a chair.

She had his gun in her hand when she opened the door.

The woman standing on the other side—long, wavy red hair in a ponytail, sky-blue eyes, freckles, almost-pointed nose—showed no surprise that Alaina was armed. She wore jeans, a backpack and leather jacket. A plastic grocery bag dangled from one hand.

"Well, hello," the woman said easily, her affable gaze staying direct on Alaina's. "Julia Rafferty. You must be Alaina."

Alaina kept the gun on her, not taking any chances without Mitch to confirm that this woman was indeed his partner. For all she knew, Julia had been replaced by another Layton assassin. She knew she was being paranoid, but she had learned over the years it was better to play it safe. "Are you armed?" she asked.

Julia smiled, unperturbed. "Of course."

"Where?"

"Holster under my left arm."

Alaina plunged her hand inside Julia's jacket, where she flicked the snap on the leather strap and drew the gun out. Squatting, she shoved it under the sofa, then, keeping her gaze and Mitch's gun trained on Julia, she felt for—and found—a second weapon strapped to her ankle.

"I was going to tell you about that," Julia said.

"Just waiting for me to ask?"

She gave a shrug. "Figured I'd wait to see how savvy you are."

Alaina set Mitch's gun on the floor and toed it under the couch, keeping Julia's ankle piece, which was smaller and more suited to her hand. "What's in the bag?" Alaina asked, gesturing for Julia to enter the cabin.

"Sandwiches from Mitch's favorite deli. He's partial to pastrami on rye. Where is he, by the way?"

"Shower."

Julia's gaze focused on Alaina's mouth for an instant. "I see."

Self-conscious, Alaina wet her lips, imagined they were swollen from Mitch's kisses. Shoving aside that very distracting memory, she indicated the sofa. "You can sit. He probably won't be long."

Julia moved to the couch. "The place hasn't changed since we were here last," she said.

Alaina wondered about Mitch's relationship with his partner. Had they been lovers? Before she could analyze the pang of jealousy, the shower shut off in the other room. She imagined him stepping out of the tub, water streaming over his smooth, tanned skin. She swallowed, and her mouth was so dry her tongue seemed to stick to the back of her teeth.

Julia cleared her throat. "I've seen your son."

The statement jerked Alaina's attention away from Mitch, and she focused on his partner, all senses sharpened. "When?"

"Yesterday. He and Keller were playing basketball. He's got a hell of a jump shot."

Alaina thought of Jonah's grace and energy on the court. A natural athlete, the high school basketball coach had said while trying to recruit him for the freshman team. But Jonah had said he was more interested in playing soccer. She'd loved that he'd been able to look beyond the flattery and focus on what he wanted.

Oh, how she missed him. It was an ache in her soul. "How is he?"

"He looks well," Julia said. "Healthy."

The growing tension in Alaina's throat made it dangerous to respond, but Julia didn't seem to notice. "He kicked the bastard's ass on the court," Julia said, as if relishing that fact.

Alaina relished it, too, and wished she could have seen Layton's face. His competitiveness was well-documented, and being bested by a teenager—her son, no less—must have chafed big time.

Mitch entered, rubbing his hair with a towel. He was barefoot, his shirt hanging open, his jeans zipped but unbuttoned. "It's all yours—" He broke off when he saw the gun in Alaina's hand and Julia on the sofa. "Hey, Jules," he said, smiling. "I see you've met Alaina."

Julia grinned. "We were just getting to know each other."

Alaina, tearing her gaze from Mitch's naked chest, lowered the gun. She gave Julia a chagrined look. "Please forgive me," she said.

"No problem. Better safe than sorry, I always say." Rising, Julia shrugged off her backpack and jacket, dropped them on the sofa, then crossed to Mitch, grocery bag in hand. "Stopped by the deli on the way," she said.

He snatched the bag from her, dropping a quick kiss on her cheek. "You're the best."

Alaina had not seen Mitch interact with a close friend, and she admired their easy camaraderie. Another door to his personality opened to her, and she liked what she saw.

Warmed, Alaina watched him retreat to the kitchen with the bag. Then, feeling Julia's expectant gaze on her, she forced herself to focus on why Julia was there.

"Mitch said you've been watching Layton's," she said.

Julia, seeming to suppress a smile, nodded. "For several days now." She gestured at the sofa. "Do you mind if I retrieve my weapons?"

Shaking her head in embarrassment, Alaina handed over the one that had been strapped to Julia's ankle. "I'm sorry. I've been paranoid so long I don't know when to quit."

"Don't worry about it. I'd be paranoid if I were you, too." Julia dropped to her knees, reached under the couch. "You're not the only one. Keller's place is like a fortress."

"You got close enough to see Jonah."

"With a high-powered telephoto lens." She holstered her gun, then dug around for Mitch's. "I brought pictures. They're in my backpack. Help yourself."

Alaina, annoyed that her hands trembled, sat on the couch and opened the backpack. An envelope of photos was on top, and the pictures inside stole her breath.

Jonah, his feet not touching the ground, the basketball just leaving his fingertips.

Jonah, grim determination on his face as he blocked a shot by Layton.

Jonah, his face set in tense angles that told her he was not happy.

"He's lost weight," she whispered.

"He's a good-looking kid."

Alaina raised her head, surprised that Julia had settled beside her. At the empathy in her blue eyes, Alaina groped for something to say to head off her growing emotion. "Mitch said you were going to get blueprints."

Julia nodded. "I'm still working on that. It'd help if we had some inside help."

"I don't know anyone."

"Mitch said your sister might be able to—"

"Like I told him, she's not an option."

Mitch returned, his shirt buttoned. "Come eat," he said, distributing plates, chips and soft drinks around the table. As Julia pulled out a chair, he tossed a wrapped sandwich to her. "Your Reuben, madam."

She caught it with a flourish. "Excellent throw, but you didn't put the usual spin on it."

He grinned. "Didn't want to show off."

"That's so unlike you," she replied, unwrapping her lunch and digging in.

Smiling at their banter, Alaina sat next to Julia as Mitch leaned over to hand her a sandwich, his eyes twinkling. "Turkey club?" he asked.

Her favorite. How had he known? Then she remembered that he'd shadowed her for three weeks. He knew far more about her than she did about him. She wasn't sure how to feel about that, but she was certain that once she figured it out, it wouldn't alter her sudden craving for that turkey club. "Thanks," she said.

"Aren't you lucky?" Julia said around a mouthful of sloppy corned beef and rye bread. "I've been trying to get him to stop throwing food at me for years."

"Maybe you need to work on your damsel-in-distress act," Alaina said. "He's obviously a sucker for it."

Julia shot Mitch a surprised glance, laughing. "She's got your number, bud."

Mitch waggled his eyebrows as he popped the top on a can of Coke. "Call me anytime."

Alaina might have blushed, but she was too busy falling in love with the turkey club that was easily the best she'd ever tasted.

No one spoke again until Mitch, who'd already wolfed

down half his sandwich, ripped into a single-serve bag of potato chips. "So what's the progress report, Jules?"

Julia took a moment to wipe Thousand Island dressing off her mouth. "I was telling Alaina earlier that Keller's is locked down like a fortress. He's got an electrified fence and guards patrolling the grounds. Looks to me like he's expecting someone to try something."

"How long do you think it'll take to get the lowdown on how to disable his security?" Mitch asked, reaching over to dump half the bag of chips onto Julia's plate.

"Could be two weeks or more," Julia said, snagging a chip.

Alaina, roused from her heavenly sandwich, swallowed hard. "Did you say two weeks?"

"At least," Julia said. "There's a ton of firepower. It's like a maximum security prison without the razor wire."

"How do the Kellers come and go?" Mitch asked, crunching on chips.

"Security cards open an electric gate."

"What about house staff?" Alaina asked.

"There isn't much of one. No kitchen staff at all—Mrs. Keller is known for her insistence that they cook for themselves. Landscape and cleaning crews come once a week. Pool people, too."

"How do they get groceries? Are they delivered?" Alaina asked.

"I don't know. I haven't observed any deliveries yet."

Impatience chased away Alaina's hunger, and she set down her sandwich. "There's got to be a way in."

Mitch covered her hand on the table, and the gesture drew her gaze first to their hands, then to his face. "We'll figure it out," he said. "But Julia is just getting started."

Easing away from the contact, she dropped her curled fist into her lap. "Two weeks is too long," she said evenly.

"We have to be careful, Alaina," he said. "Rushing could get someone hurt, including Jonah."

Frustration nearly broke through her composure. Two weeks. What kind of damage could Layton do to Jonah's psyche in another two weeks? How could she survive that long without having her son safe at her side?

She scooted her chair back. "I'm going to take a walk."

Chapter 29

The few remaining drops of wine dribbled into Addison's glass as she held the bottle suspended above it. For the first time in weeks, she felt calm. Deadly so. The two tranquilizers she'd popped before starting on the wine had been a tremendous help.

As she sipped the wine, she let her gaze wander the kitchen. She loved this room, with its stainless steel appliances, shiny black Italian marble floor and white countertops. A full set of the most expensive cookware you could buy dangled from hooks above a gourmet island in the center of the room. She'd spent many hours at that island, whipping up fancy meals for Layton, his top lieutenants and their wives. Her cooking abilities had often been the talk of her standing Wednesday lunch with several other PCware corporate wives. Apparently, Layton had even bragged about her. What would those people think if they ever found out about the secrets the perfect couple kept locked away? Actually, they would find out, she realized. At some point, either the FBI would conclude its investigation and take her husband away in handcuffs, or he would leave her. Not only would she be alone, but everyone would know why, her golden image tarnished beyond repair.

As if her thoughts had summoned him, Layton ambled into the kitchen, breaking stride when he saw the empty bottle sitting on the island counter. His face instantly hardened. "Isn't it early for that?" he asked. "Where's Joe?"

"In his room," she said, impressed that she sounded so normal despite the combination of drugs and alcohol working on her system. "He hates it that you call him that."

"Well, it's time he got used to it." At the refrigerator, he took out a pitcher of iced tea and poured himself a glass. "Did he meet with the tutor today?"

"Yes. I don't think he's too thrilled about the home-schooling thing."

"He'll just have to get used to that, too. In the meantime, he's spending too much time up there by himself."

"I didn't know you wanted me to keep him entertained."

"You know this is a crucial time, Addy. The more we let him sulk by himself, the longer it will take for him to get over it." He put the tea away.

"I know about her."

He paused, his hand still on the fridge handle. Everything about him was expressionless, but she sensed his tension.

"Who?" he asked.

"Winnifred Ellison."

He didn't even flinch. "What about her?"

"Do you love her?"

He folded his arms. "How do you know about her?"

"Does it matter?"

"Yes, it does. I've been extraordinarily discreet."

"Not discreet enough, apparently."

"Did you follow me?"

"Maybe I did," she said.

"Did you have me followed?"

"Maybe I did that, too."

He went to her, took the wineglass from her hand and set it on the counter. "You've been drinking too much lately."

"As if you care."

He cupped her face in his warm, dry hands, gazed deep

into her eyes. His were concerned, caring, and her stomach lurched. Suddenly, he was the old Layton, the man she'd fallen in love with so many years ago. Had she misjudged him?

"I knew something was troubling you, Addy," he said. "I wish you'd talked to me. I could have explained."

She drew back, blinking furiously to stop the tears before they started. "You can't explain this away, Layton. I know you're leaving me."

He stepped back. "What are you talking about?"

"I know about Belize. You're leaving me, and you're taking Jonah with you. Well, you should have waited for the results of his blood test before spending all that cash on his ticket."

He grasped her arm before she could push past him. "What test results?"

She glared at him, her vision blurring with emotion. Dammit, she didn't want to cry, didn't want him to see how much it hurt. After everything, it still hurt that he'd sought the embrace of another woman. "He's not your son, Layton. The test was negative."

He dropped her arm, looking as if he'd been struck, and turned away. "Dammit," he muttered hoarsely.

His reaction surprised her. She'd expected him to be relieved. "Isn't that what you wanted? Vindication? Alaina lied about everything. There's no question now."

He faced her, his features relaxing into a cool mask. "You're right, Addy. I'm leaving you."

She pressed her lips together. Why should it feel like he had just ripped out her heart? He was a monster. She'd heard him order her sister's murder, for God's sake. Even if he hadn't raped and impregnated Alaina, he still wanted her dead.

But maybe Addison could understand that. Alaina had accused him of horrible things, had very nearly destroyed their lives together. Her accusations had certainly haunted them for fifteen years. It made Addison feel murderous, too.

"I don't understand," she whispered. "I've stood by you through everything."

"I'm not leaving you for another woman. Winnifred Ellison isn't my mistress. I'm leaving you because I never loved you, Addy. I used you."

She sank onto a kitchen stool, feeling weak, as tears spilled down her cheeks. "Please don't do this."

"You had the life I wanted. A good father. A family. Money. I wanted a key role in your father's business, and I got it through you. I made it what it is today, you know."

She covered her face with badly shaking hands. "Please stop."

"But for some reason, no matter what I did, I could never entirely please your father. Always, just beneath the surface, he seemed disappointed in me, like there was something he wanted from me that I failed to give him."

She raised her head, not caring that her eyes streamed and her nose ran. All she knew was that she was about to lose everything. If he left her, there would be no pretending that everything in their lives was perfect. Everyone would know what a failure she was. She couldn't bear it, couldn't bear the thought of the other corporate wives gossiping about her, speculating about what had destroyed her marriage. Couldn't bear the thought of being alone, of starting over again, disgraced. She would have no one. No one.

"We'll see a counselor, Layton," she said. "We can try again to have a baby. I'll see the doctors, go through the procedures again, whatever you want."

Shaking his head in disgust, he strode to the double

swinging doors that led out of the kitchen. But instead of pushing through them, he paused. "You're not barren."

"What?"

"You've never been able to get pregnant because I had a vasectomy before we got married."

She dropped her hands onto her thighs, her jaw going slack. "But the doctor said your tests were fine."

He shrugged. "We made a deal."

Her stomach felt as if the roller coaster had topped its first peak and was plunging. "Why would you do that?"

"The last thing I wanted from you was a bratty kid."

"Why didn't you just say that? Why did you put me through—"

"Your father never would have understood why I didn't want kids. He would have hammered at me about it, trying to wear me down, trying to force me to do what he wanted. But if it was your fault we couldn't conceive, then there wasn't much I could do about it, was there?"

Clamping her hands over her mouth to hold in a sob, she shook her head in disbelief. Something was breaking inside her. She could feel it ripping away from its mooring, buffeted by an inner storm that was only just beginning.

Smiling slightly, he said, "Don't look so devastated, Addy. Later, when you really start to think about it, you might be glad we never had kids. Chances are, they would have grown up to be just like me." He pushed through the doors and was gone.

Broken, Addison put her head down on the counter and wept.

Mitch paused by the front window of the cabin, nudging aside the curtains to peer outside.

"She wasn't out there a minute ago when you did that."

He glanced over his shoulder at Julia, who was finishing up her Reuben. "I'm being a worrywart, I know," he said.

"I'm sure she's fine. There's no one out there for miles, and she's too smart to get lost."

Returning to the table, he sat. "I don't know how to help her, Jules. It's driving me nuts."

Julia licked Thousand Island dressing from her finger as she studied him. Then, her eyes narrowing, she slowly lowered her hand. "I'll be damned. Are you in love with her?"

He scrubbed his hands over his face. "I thought I was just feeling guilty, but I've felt guilty before and it wasn't like this."

"Like what?"

"There's a knot in my gut that won't go away, and when I'm around her, I feel like a stupid teenager." He gave her a grim look. "I want to tear that fucker Keller in two."

Julia grinned. "My hero."

"I'm serious, Jules. If I get my hands on him, someone's going to have to stop me from ripping his head off."

Her humor faded. "You *are* serious. In fact, I've never seen you like this." She sat back in the chair, folding her arms. "Maybe you need to back off this one."

He shook his head. "No way."

"I'll stay here with Alaina. You go back to D.C. and handle the security details."

"No."

She leaned forward. "Mitch, emotional involvement screws with our judgment. It's human. Don't put Alaina at risk because you're too stubborn to admit you've gotten too close."

"I won't walk away. I've done that my entire life."

"This isn't your life. It's hers. You're making it too personal."

"It is personal. Keller used me to terrorize a woman he brutalized fifteen years ago. He made me a part of her nightmare, and that pisses me off big time. But what he did to her . . . that's what I'm going to kill him for."

"I need you to back up and explain what you mean by that."

Chapter 30

Alaina shivered as she sat on the cabin's front porch steps. She couldn't bring herself to go inside. Not yet. Not when she still felt so close to losing control. It wasn't Mitch's or Julia's fault that Layton had stowed Jonah away behind impenetrable, prison-like walls. She was surprised his estate wasn't surrounded by a moat stocked with starving alligators.

Two weeks.

She and Jonah had never been separated for more than a weekend. Now, it had been eleven days. Who knew how many lies Layton had told him? Who knew what Jonah was thinking or feeling as he lay in an unfamiliar bed at night? Betrayal. Abandonment. Anger. Disappointment.

His wounds would form scars, even after he found out the truth, that would never go away. And once he did find out the truth . . . what kind of scars would that leave? How could she protect him from that? How would she ever be able to convince him that how he was conceived didn't affect how much she loved him?

"Hey."

Alaina started, glancing up to see Julia standing beside her, Mitch's leather jacket dangling from one hand, a cup of steaming coffee in the other. "I thought you might be cold," she said, handing down the coffee, then draping the jacket over Alaina's shoulders.

"Thanks." The jacket's instant warmth felt good, and Alaina drew its edges close with one hand, focusing on how it smelled like Mitch, like pine and wood and leather. Like shelter.

Julia sat beside her, hunching her thin shoulders in her own jacket. "It's brisk out here."

"I'm okay," Alaina said, wrapping her chilled fingers around the warm coffee mug. "You don't have to make small talk."

Julia's lips curved. "I don't know you, but you don't seem okay."

"It's been a rough week," Alaina admitted.

Julia laughed softly. "Now that's an understatement."

"I'm sorry I was rude before. I'm having a hard time being patient."

"I can understand that," Julia said. "Being away from your kid like this . . . I can't even imagine what it's like."

Alaina buried her chin in the jacket's collar, breathed in Mitch's scent. Somehow, it made her feel stronger. "Thank you for the pictures. They help."

"It's not much, but it's something." Julia clasped her hands in front of her face, blew on them. "Has Mitch told you why he left the Bureau?"

Alaina glanced at her without responding.

"This isn't small talk," Julia said. She obviously had something important to say.

"No, he hasn't. I know Chuck—I don't remember his last name—was his partner."

"Reiser. He had an affair with Mitch's wife."

Alaina, about to sip coffee, paused. "Oh."

"I don't know all the details, but it all started after he and Mitch worked a kidnap case. A woman grabbed a neighbor's toddler and took off to—"

"North Carolina. He told me about that."

Julia looked surprised. "He did?"

"He said he had to kill the kidnapper to keep her from hurting the child. It was very difficult for him."

"To put it mildly. As soon as he got out of the hospital, he quit the Bureau—"

"Hospital?" Alaina cut in, as much alarmed by what Julia had said as the way her stomach flip-flopped at the thought of him injured. "Why was he in the hospital?"

"Ah," Julia said, nodding. "He didn't tell you the whole story."

"Apparently not."

"When the woman started shooting at them, Mitch threw himself in front of Chuck and took a bullet in the shoulder."

Alaina remembered the puckered scar, and her insides clenched. He'd been hit in the shoulder, but he so easily could have been shot in the heart.

"In the ER," Julia went on, "Chuck 'fessed up about the affair. I guess the guilt was too much for him after Mitch saved his life. As soon as Mitch was released, he filed for divorce and turned in his resignation. He lost his wife, his best friend and his job all at the same time. He also had to deal with the fact that he'd taken the life of another human being. A couple years after the divorce—Shirley and Chuck didn't make it—Shirley married another guy and moved to another state with Mitch's son. You bet it was very difficult for him. It nearly killed him."

Alaina ached for what he had gone through, wished she could have been there to help him. But why Julia thought she needed to know eluded her. "Why are you telling me this?"

"Mitch doesn't allow himself to feel very much. He considers it too emotionally dangerous. To him, it's easier to close himself off and be alone than deal with the aftermath of a messy relationship."

As what Julia said sank in, Alaina remembered something Mitch had said to her: "You can hold me at bay all you want, but there's no way in hell I'm walking away without a fight."

That from a man who found it easier to shut himself down and be alone? It struck her how difficult saying such a thing had been for him. Yet he had seemed so fearless and strong and confident.

"We've known each other less than two weeks," she said quietly, still trying to wrap her brain around how something so serious could develop in so little time.

Julia sighed. "I've known him a couple years, and I've never seen him look at a woman the way he was looking at you in there."

Alaina's stomach did another nervous roll. "Oh."

"In fact," Julia said with a shrug, "seeing the way he looked at you made me really want to kick your ass."

Alaina laughed. "But you're not going to, I hope."

"Depends on whether you break his heart."

Alaina heard the subtle threat under the joke, but instead of being offended, she was glad Mitch had someone like Julia to watch his back.

Sobering, Julia said, "He's going to get your son back, Alaina. If it's the last thing he does."

Alaina's breath caught. Julia was not speaking casually. She meant it as a warning.

"You sure you don't want to stay over?" Mitch asked as Julia shrugged into her jacket and pulled on gloves. "We're having s'mores later."

Julia chuckled. "If only I had known, I would have arranged for someone to let the dog out for me. Rain check?"

"Sorry," Mitch said. "You know me and s'mores. There won't be any leftovers."

Julia winked at Alaina. "Don't turn your back on him. When it comes to chocolate and marshmallows, he's ruthless."

"Thanks for the warning," Alaina said with a laugh, struck by how easy she felt with them, as if they were old friends saying good-bye after an afternoon visit, rather than three relative strangers plotting a kidnapping.

Mitch followed Julia out onto the porch, pulling the door closed, either for privacy or to retain the warmth in the cabin. Alaina, filled with nervous energy after the conversation with Julia, kept herself busy by cleaning up the remnants of their lunch. She was in the kitchen, washing coffee mugs, when Mitch ambled in.

"You don't have to do that," he said, coming up behind her.

"I don't mind."

She set the last cup in the drainer and turned, surprised to find him standing so close. Rather than step sideways, away from him, she stayed where she was. He watched her curiously, as if trying to read her mind.

"What did you and Jules talk about on the porch earlier?" he asked.

"You tell me first," she replied.

He smiled. "She likes you."

"She told me she wanted to kick my ass."

The light in his eyes danced. "Then she really likes you."

She felt a pull in her chest, almost resisted leaning into him, then didn't. His chuckle died away when she placed a hand on the front of his T-shirt, felt the hard muscle underneath, the rise and fall of his breath. Her pulse raced, then stumbled as she met his darkening gaze. He didn't move. She thought of how he had taken a bullet for his friend and partner, a bullet that could have killed him.

She thought of the many times since she'd met him that a bullet could have easily taken his life. Because of her. Yet he was still risking his life to help her, to protect her.

She thought of how brave he'd been to open himself to her after shutting himself away for so long. And she thought of how foolish she would be if she let these moments with him slip away, when he was the only man she had ever wanted.

She stepped into him, curving her hand around the back of his neck and drawing him down. Their lips met, and heat exploded between them.

His hands came up her arms, and he backed her against the sink as he sank his fingers into her hair, his mouth and tongue desperately seeking. Her head spun with how much she wanted this. With him. The sharp edge of the need surprised and liberated as the joy of discovery, the joy of relief, tumbled through her.

Now that she had taken the plunge, impatience took over. She tried to deepen the embrace, tried to steer him toward the front room and the sofa or the floor or the bedroom or wherever. Now, please, now, was all she could think.

But he gentled the kiss, slowed it, and refused to budge, taking his time scattering feather kisses over her face to her ear, where he toyed with the lobe, his breath soft and deep, unhurried. His hands, God, his hands were on her shoulders, and she wanted them on her breasts, on her naked skin. She wanted to feel everything at once.

She released a low moan as he lowered his head to the hollow of her throat, his tongue tasting, testing, sending shivers down her spine. If he didn't put his hands on her soon, she thought she would burst.

But he didn't. He simply kept trailing slow, drugging kisses over her face and throat and down the side of her neck.

She worked her hands under his shirt, reveled in the feel of muscle and smooth skin, pleased at his intake of breath when her nails scraped a nipple.

His hands slid down her back and pressed her against him until she felt the heat of him through his jeans. He wanted her. The knowledge made her feel strong and powerful. And she wanted the barrier of denim gone.

Her fingers trembled as they went to the button on his jeans, but he grasped her hands, stilled them. "Not yet," he whispered.

Frustration began to worm its way through her but was forgotten the instant he closed his mouth over the tip of her breast, T-shirt and all. She gasped, stiffening as pleasure arrowed into her. Her knees went liquid, and Mitch laughed low in his chest as he lifted her into his arms and carried her into the back bedroom.

Finally.

But when he set her on the bed, his pace was anything but hurried. Giving her a languid look, he slowly drew the T-shirt over her head and tossed it aside. His fingers unhooked the clasp of her bra and let it fall open, lust darkening his gaze as his fingers stroked the curve of her breast, lingered.

"Perfect," he murmured. Warmth spread through her. He made her feel adored, cherished, like she'd never felt before.

"Now you," she said, her voice breathy.

Smiling, he doffed his T-shirt, baring that fabulous chest and rippling muscles that contracted when she grazed them with her fingertips. She drank him in, swallowing the urge to dive in and devour. His body was full of power. Looking at it, touching it, made her head light with yearning.

Joining her on the bed, he eased her back, kissing her softly at the same time, his mouth gentle, leisurely. When her head hit the pillow, he cupped her breast in one hand, teasing it to a peak, his lips curving against her mouth when she moaned. He replaced his hand with his mouth, and she arched against him, releasing a surprised gasp at the clench of his teeth. Her pulse went wild.

Then his hand was sliding down her torso, his lips following behind, placing light kisses along her ribs. His fingers slid under the waistband of her jeans, teasing, tickling, and she opened her eyes, surprised to realize that she'd had them closed. His dark eyes were watching her as he lowered the zipper on her jeans, and he pressed wet kisses against her belly as he exposed skin inch by inch.

Her breath shuddered out, and she lifted her hips so he could tug the jeans down her legs. He did it so slowly she wanted to scream. "You're killing me here," she said on an uneasy laugh.

He grinned. "That's the idea."

He slid her panties off as slowly, then stretched out beside her, gathering her close. She liked the rough rasp of his jeans against her bare legs, lost herself in the headiness of lazy kisses and gentle caresses that required all of her willpower to keep from squirming.

By the time he slid a hand between them and touched her, she stepped off the ledge with barely a nudge and fell through layers of quiet, unexpected pleasure.

As she floated down, he left her for an instant.

"Where are you going?" she protested.

"I'll just be a second," he said, gone long enough to retrieve his backpack from the other room. He fumbled around in it for a moment, then dropped it on the floor before settling back on the bed. His mouth returned to hers, and his tongue set a new pace, an insistent one that ratcheted her pulse rate up a couple of notches.

He quickly shed his jeans, breaking the embrace for only a moment. She heard the rip of a little foil packet before he was stretched out beside her again, skin against skin.

She skimmed her hand over his hip, her head whirling as his fingers stroked the back of her knee, the inside of her elbow, the small of her back. Every part of her seemed sensitized to the slightest touch, and he took his time rebuilding her need with his hands, his fingers, his mouth. She wanted to do the same for him, but she was so distracted by what he was doing to her that she couldn't focus.

She toppled easily over another peak, burying her head against his shoulder to stifle a ragged moan. She felt his lips curve on her throat. He was enjoying torturing her. And he was damn good at it.

When he shifted subtly, easing her onto her back, she moved with him, smiling. Yes, she thought. Yes.

He braced over her, his elbows locked to support his weight, his breathing unsteady. "Open your eyes," he whispered. "See me."

She did. His dark gaze locked on hers as he slowly filled her, and she arched up, eager to take him in, her breath hitching at the intensity of the sensation. "Oh, Mitch."

He closed his eyes, releasing his held breath. She heard him swallow. "If you move, it's over," he said. "I want you too damn much."

She held still, wanting this moment to last, conscious of his heart slamming against his ribs and her heart's answering, driving beat. She watched a drop of sweat trickle down his temple and stopped its descent with a kiss.

When he moved, she gasped and arched back, succumbing to another wave of shudders.

He held her tight against him through the quake. "You're not making me work very hard," he murmured.

She fought for air, her hands flattened against his lower back to hold him firmly in place. "Making up for lost time."

His chuckle dissolved into a groan. "Just so you know: If you do that again, I won't be able to keep from following."

"I'll try to control myself."

"I'd prefer you didn't."

Before she could respond, he resumed the onslaught, slow and easy. Tender. So tender. Then he shifted, taking her fast and hard but careful not to let her peak so easily again. Each time he sensed she danced on the edge, he slowed the pace, sometimes stopping altogether and leisurely kissing away her pleas.

Her breath was sobbing, her nails digging into his back, by the time he let her soar. He covered her mouth with his when she screamed, and she felt his body buck against her.

Damp and breathless, she savored the aftershocks that jolted through her, fairly certain she saw stars that time. This is it, she thought. This is what it's supposed to be like. And she'd been afraid she wouldn't like it.

Mitch kissed her nose, her lips, then paused, his eyes widening in alarm. "Are you crying?"

She swiped at the tear that had rolled back into her hair. "No."

"Oh, God, did I hurt you?" He started to roll away.

She caught his shoulders and, rearing up, kissed him. "You were incredible."

He relaxed, grinned. "Then you're up for another round?"

She smiled, thrilled to be there with him, naked and satisfied and knowing that her sexual appetite was indeed strong and healthy. "Bring it on."

"What kind of music do you like?"

Alaina smiled, enjoying the play of firelight across Mitch's bare chest as he sat cross-legged before her. Only moments ago, he'd brought two plates from the kitchen piled with grilled steak, mashed potatoes and green beans. A second trip had delivered two glasses and a bottle of red wine—compliments of one of his treks for supplies. It touched her that he'd cooked while she'd slept in front of the fire, exhausted from their lovemaking.

"You're not going to psychoanalyze me again, are you?" she asked as she cut into the steak. It was pink in the center, just the way she liked it.

"Only if you say Springsteen."

Her mind went blank when she sank her teeth into the first bite. "Oh my God. Where did you learn to cook?"

"My mama taught me, of course."

"Your mama rocks."

He grinned, digging into his own steak. "If you're really nice to me, I might be able to talk her into giving you some lessons."

She cocked her head as she chewed, savoring the teasing glint in his eyes. "Are you saying you don't think I'd be a good cook?"

He exaggerated a surprised expression. "You cook? In three weeks, I saw you and your kid eat pizza, mac and cheese, pasta out of a box, sandwiches and what else? Oh, yeah, more pizza. There are other food groups, you know."

"Tell that to a teenage boy. The only way I can get any vegetables into him is if they're smothered with cheese and tomato sauce on a crust." Her eyes widened as she sampled the mashed potatoes. "Oh my. These are real."

"Potato flakes just don't do it for me."

"You know how to live, Mr. Kane."

"I think I'm remembering how."

As they ate in silence, Alaina's thoughts turned to Jonah.

She wondered what he was doing, how he was doing, what he was thinking. Missing him was a pain that clamped around her heart like a fist. Helplessness squeezed it tight.

"He'll be fine, Alaina," Mitch said, as if reading her mind. "There are two people we trust—Chuck and Julia—keeping an eye on him. They won't let anything happen to him."

She met his eyes, felt a flutter inside. "How can you trust Chuck after what he did to you?"

"I trust him as an agent of the FBI, but I don't imagine we'll ever be friends again." He paused, studying her. Gradually, his eyes warmed, as if what he saw pleased him immensely. Then he held up the nearly empty wine bottle. "More merlot, darling?"

Her laugh was a bit breathless, and she imagined that was the response he was looking for. He enjoyed throwing her off guard, and the endearment did it big time. *Darling.* It was all so new and unreal. She, Alaina Chancellor, was sitting in front of a fire with a half-naked man, mellowed by wine and lovemaking . . .

Mitch's lips curved. "Want me to pinch you?"

"Try it while I'm eating, and you might lose a thumb." She said it with a sweet smile.

"Fiery," he said, snagging a green bean off her plate.

"Hey!"

He shrugged as he chomped on it. "Mine are all gone."

"You should have paced yourself."

"I'll save that for later."

Flushing with anticipation, she flashed a wicked grin. "Good food. Good sex. You're going to spoil me."

"Actually, that's the idea," he said.

Setting aside her empty plate, she said, "I might start having expectations."

"Maybe I'll even meet those expectations."

"I think you've already surpassed them by far," she said.

Male pride broadened his smile. "Yeah?"

She nodded, draining the last of her wine. "But then, they were pretty low."

Growling, he reached out and dragged her laughing across his lap. "That sounded like a challenge."

"Are you up for it?" She trailed a fingertip up the center of his chest, enjoying the way his flesh quivered. Because of her caress. It made her feel powerful, in control. Wanted.

"Oh, yeah," he said, his voice a rough rasp. "I'm up for it."

Chapter 31

"These are the best scrambled eggs ever."

Mitch chuckled, taking in Alaina's rosy cheeks and smiling gray-green eyes. She was propped against pillows, breathtaking in his T-shirt as she dug into the breakfast he'd whipped up while she'd dozed. They'd slept little during the night, yet this morning he felt more invigorated, more awake, than he had in years.

"I noticed you're adamant about constantly feeding me," she said. "If you're not careful, I'm going to expect a snack every time I wake up."

Chuckling, he leaned forward, cupping her cheek as he kissed her, pleased when she returned the embrace, her mouth hungry, sliding effortlessly into demanding. Her easy, heated response sent his pulse tripping. "You floor me," he said.

She gave a soft, self-conscious laugh as a faint blush colored her cheeks. "You mean you weren't just faking it all night?"

He shrugged. "I might have faked it one or two times, but mostly I enjoyed myself thoroughly."

Grinning, she swallowed a forkful of eggs. "What did you put in these to make them so tasty?"

"Hot sauce."

"Another cooking lesson from your mama?"

"Nope. My idea." He studied her, the way her hair fell into her eyes, the way she blew it away with a huff of air. The way the slim column of her throat flexed as she ate. The way her eerie green eyes glittered and darkened as they roamed his bare chest. He was pretty damn sure he'd fallen in love with her. In record time.

It took him a few moments to realize that Alaina had stopped eating and was watching him, her forehead creased.

He hated the wariness that crept into her eyes, hated the circumstances—life's cruel twists and turns—that had ensured its everlasting presence. He figured it would never go away, that she would always be braced for the next blow. He thought about what it would take to banish the wariness, imagined how satisfying it would be to slay her dragon, to be her hero.

"What are you thinking so hard about?" she asked.

Faking a leer, he snagged her hand on the bed and tangled his fingers with hers. "I'm thinking about what I'm going to do to you when you're finished with breakfast."

She dropped her fork and shoved the plate aside. "All done."

He shifted, drawing her down on top of him until her breasts under his T-shirt were flattened against his chest. Burying his hands in her hair, he kissed her, reveling in how her tongue sought his first. He tasted passion and hot sauce, the serrated edge of desire.

It shocked him that he could still want her so desperately. The feeling appeared to be mutual as her hands raced over him, greedy in their quest for his flesh. When she rose over him, he tensed, gritting his teeth. "Wait," he gasped, his fingers gripping her hips.

She paused, her gaze, dark with heat, focused on his. He gestured weakly at the bedside table. Understanding, she reached for a condom. When he started to take it from her, she brushed his fingers away. "Let me," she said.

He clenched his eyes shut, concentrating on not blasting off in her hands.

Finally, she sank down, taking him in, and moaned low in her throat, almost a purr. Then she pulled his shirt over her head, tossed it aside and shook her hair back, her eyes closed. The graceful, uninhibited motion turned his blood molten. He had to force himself to hold still, to let her set the pace. When she did, it was so slow, so languid, it was all he could do not to roll her under him and ravage.

She smiled down at him, catlike. "Come on," she murmured. "You can take it slow, can't you?"

He gulped at air that seemed too thick. "I can take whatever you've got," he replied, his voice strained, one hand gripping the edge of the mattress.

She laughed deep in her throat, then her breath caught, and she dropped her head back. He felt the tension coil in her muscles, felt her thighs flex against his. "Oh."

That one word, expelled on a hitch of strangled breath, very nearly sent him to the moon. Watching the wonder that spread over her features as her body rocked above him was sweet torment. And he couldn't take it anymore.

Grasping her hips, he surged up, changing their positions so fast that she blinked up at him in shock. "Your turn to squirm," he growled, and buried his mouth on hers.

The pace he set was hard, fast, and he noted with immense satisfaction that her hands clutched at the sheets, then his shoulders, then simply slid down his arms as if she didn't have the strength or presence of mind to hold on.

When she reared up with a sharp cry, he caught her close against him and pressed his forehead against hers as they exploded together.

After the tension drained out of her limbs, and she was limp in his arms, her breath still ragged, he kissed her damp temple. The silence was deafening after all the rockets that had just gone off in his head.

Sighing, she pressed a feather kiss against the scar that marred the skin of his left shoulder. The sweet gesture sent his heart soaring, and he didn't want to let her go. Ever. "Will you freak out if I tell you I think I love you?"

Alaina tensed in his arms, but before she could respond, his cell phone began to chirp in the other room. She started to shift, but he held her in place, reluctant to break their connection, or give her a chance to not respond to what he'd just said. "Ignore it," he said.

"It might be important."

Reluctantly, he acquiesced. "You're probably right." He eased away, smiling as she arched on an intake of breath. "Hold that thought," he said, brushing her forehead with a kiss.

In the other room, he flipped open the phone. "This better be good."

"It's Chuck. I need to meet with you and Alaina. It's urgent."

Mitch's sated mood vanished, and dread knotted his stomach. "What's going on?"

"I can't get into it over the phone. Let's meet—"

"I don't think it's safe," Mitch cut in, alarmed at Chuck's urgent tone but more concerned about keeping Alaina out of Keller's strike zone.

"I'll make it safe. Remember that place where we baby-sat the witness to that mob hit?"

"Sure."

"We'll meet you there. Twelve-fifteen."

The call cut off.

Lowering the phone, Mitch glanced at Alaina, who stood in the bedroom doorway, a sheet wrapped around her body.

Her mouth was swollen, her eyes glazed with the aftermath of passion. As he watched, anxiety drew her features taut, chased the color from her cheeks.

"What is it? Is it Jonah?" she asked, so softly it was as if she feared giving voice to her fear would provide a higher power with ideas.

He shook his head. "He's fine. Chuck would have said so otherwise."

"Then what's going on?"

"I don't know."

"We'll meet you there."

Who was "we"?

As Mitch steered the rental car into the parking lot of the Hyatt in the Fair Oaks area of Fairfax, Virginia, Alaina gazed up at the tall, glass building. It had seemed to rise up out of the tops of budding trees as they'd approached, the lone high-rise in a D.C. suburb dominated by foliage, restaurants, apartment complexes and big-box stores.

"You baby-sat witnesses in style in the old days," she said. "All I got was a broken-down safe house in Manassas." She'd tried to sound light, but the nerves were evident in her voice.

Mitch turned off the car, then slid his hand over hers resting on her thigh and squeezed. "This guy was a trip. The Bureau treated him like royalty because all he had to do was clam up and their case was fried."

She turned her hand so their fingers could tangle. Her heart hadn't stopped racing since they'd left the cabin, and it wasn't just because of Chuck's mysterious summons. Mitch had said that he loved her. No, he'd said, "I think I love you." So that meant he wasn't entirely sure. And, of course, he'd said it right after a powerful climax, and she figured that could probably skew a man's thinking. It certainly had scrambled hers, perhaps was still scrambling it.

Love.

The thought of it gave her chills. A man in love with her. And not just any man. Mitch Kane. The hunkiest guy by far that she had ever met. Kind, too. Considerate. Thoughtful. Honest. If circumstances were different, she would have been doing somersaults. Yet, if circumstances were different, they never would have met.

And, really, what kind of relationship could they possibly develop? Once he helped her get Jonah back, it would have to end. She and Jonah would be back on the run, and she couldn't expect Mitch to give up his identity, his detective business, his plans to reconnect with his son. And he'd have to, because Layton would never stop hunting. He'd use everything he could against them, including Mitch's son.

Plus, it would be far easier to track down three people than it was to track two. She and Jonah alone stood a much better chance of disappearing again, but adding to the equation . . . that would make it tougher. Tougher for them, easier for Layton.

So love wasn't an option. Not for them.

Not for her.

She had accepted that once. It shouldn't be that difficult to accept it again. Except now she would know what she was missing . . .

Mitch squeezed her hand. "Ready to go in?"

She glanced at him, her lungs constricting at the concern in his beautiful dark eyes. She wanted to touch his face, press her palm to his lightly bearded cheek, memorize his features. We still have time, she told herself. It's not over yet.

Slowly, she nodded. "I'm ready."

★ ★ ★ ★ ★

They walked, hands linked, into the lobby. At the concierge desk, Mitch greeted an impeccably dressed middle-aged man with slicked-back hair and a black bow tie. Alaina thought he looked ready to attend a ball.

"You have an envelope for Jack Palatine?" Mitch asked.

The man handed over a legal-size envelope with the name "Jack Palatine" scrawled across the front. On the elevator, Alaina watched Mitch tear it open.

"How'd you know what name to use?" she asked.

"Jack Palatine was the name we used when we baby-sat the witness," he replied as a key card slid into his hand.

As the elevator stopped at the twelfth floor, she noticed the card had no identifying numbers or markings on it. "And the room number?"

"Chuck told me on the phone." He guided her out into the hall with a hand at her elbow, as if ready to jerk her behind him if all hell broke loose.

"On the phone? Isn't that unsafe?"

"He didn't mention a hotel or a room, or at least what would have sounded like a room. He told me twelve-fifteen, which anyone listening should have assumed meant the time." He paused before a door. "This is it."

Before he could use the key card, though, the door opened, and Chuck waved them in. "Thanks for coming so fast," the agent said.

The room contained a Mission-style queen-size bed, desk, comforting muted yellow walls and a hunter green sofa. Large windows looked out over trees and a busy highway. Next to them, a minibar stood against the wall, its door hanging open, tiny, empty, wine bottles scattered across the top.

Tensing, Alaina turned, and sure enough, her sister came walking out of the bathroom.

Addison's appearance shocked her—her eyes were swollen and red-rimmed, dark circles underscoring them. She wore no makeup, and her hair was in desperate need of a brush. Her teal wrap dress looked like she'd slept in it.

Addison fixed Alaina with a burning glare. "You," she said, taking a jerky step toward her. Venom dripped from the one word. "Did you think no one would ever find out?"

Alaina smelled the alcohol on her sister's breath, heard the slight slurring of her words. She glanced at Chuck, hoping to get some background on Addison's mood. "What's going on?"

"Don't talk to him," Addison snapped. "Talk to me."

Mitch cleared his throat. "Perhaps you should tell us what this is about."

Alaina felt him behind her, close enough that his heat seemed to envelop her, reminding her that she wasn't alone. Not anymore. At least for now.

Chuck said to Mitch, "We've got the room next door, too. Let's let them talk."

"I'm not going anywhere just yet," Mitch replied mildly.

"I'll wait for you over there then," Chuck said, and made a hasty exit.

Addison walked up to Alaina, trembling, eyes spitting rage. "Jonah isn't Layton's kid."

Alaina didn't flinch, having learned long ago how to withstand Addison's attacks. The skill had not grown rusty. Besides, this wasn't the first time, or even fifth, that she'd heard those words come out of her sister's mouth. It disappointed her, though, that it appeared that whatever insight Addison had gained before their earlier meeting had vanished. Denial. Addison had it down to an art.

At Alaina's lack of immediate response, Addison's face reddened. "Don't just stand there and look at me."

Alaina kept her expression bland. "What do you want me to say?"

"You lying bitch!" Addison struck out, lightning quick.

Alaina staggered back a step, stunned by the stinging attack.

As if the slap had broken loose an avalanche of violent rage, Addison surged forward, her fingers like claws hooking into the front of Alaina's shirt. Before Alaina could do anything more than recoil, Mitch lunged between them. Hauling Addison off, he backed her against the wall and held her there by the arms. "Don't you ever touch her like that again," he said in a low, menacing voice. "She's too civil to make you regret it, but I'm not."

Alaina watched in shock, her hand pressed to her burning cheek. He was terrifying, she thought. Absolutely terrifying.

Addison gaped up at him, her face a livid red. She tried to break his restraint to no avail. "Who the hell are you?"

He held her calmly, almost gently. "Someone you really don't want to mess with," he said. "Do we have an understanding?"

Again, she yanked against his grasp. "Let me go."

"Not until we have an understanding."

"Fine."

He released her, then turned to Alaina, and the fury burning in his coffee-colored eyes died away. Calmly, as if he hadn't just threatened her sister, he stroked his knuckles down her arm. "You okay?"

She nodded, her stomach flipping as it sank in that what Addison had said hadn't fazed him in the least. He had defended her without hesitation. And, oh, how he had defended her. If Addison had been a man, Alaina was certain her sister would be flat on her back with her eyes rolled back in her head. Alaina took a moment to savor this new and unfamiliar sensation.

Until Addison, her back still against the wall, began to sneer. "You can hide behind your hero all you want, but you can't ignore me, Alaina. There's a blood test."

Alaina shifted her gaze over Mitch's shoulder to her sister. This was also something new. "What are you talking about?"

Addison gave her a nasty smile, pushing away from the wall but bringing herself up short when Mitch angled his body as if to intercept her if she made a threatening move toward her sister. Skirting Mitch, Addison said, "Layton took Jonah for a blood test. They're not a match. Plus, Layton told me he had a vasectomy before we were married."

Alaina put a hand on Mitch's arm. "Maybe you should wait with Chuck."

He didn't budge. "Are you sure?"

She nodded. He kissed her before he left the room, a casual gesture that might have been automatic for him but caught Alaina by surprise. Showing affection was so easy for him, so natural. Just knowing he cared, that he believed in her, made her feel stronger than she ever had.

But then he was gone, and she was alone with her sister, who didn't bother to hide her contempt.

"What's the matter?" Addison asked. "Don't want him to find out what a liar you are?"

Alaina leveled a cool stare at her. "Actually, I wanted to spare him the sight of you making an ass of yourself again."

Addison quivered, and her hands clenched into fists at her sides. "Do you have any idea what my life has been like? Always wondering, always worrying about what really happened that night?"

A years-old rage began to writhe to life in the pit of Alaina's stomach, but she drew the reins of control taut before the fury could leap away from her. "I told you what happened, Addison. You didn't have to wonder."

"Didn't you hear what I just said? Jonah isn't his kid."

"Have you seen Jonah?"

Addison blinked, her brows knitting in bafflement. "Of course."

"He has his father's eyes," Alaina said. "Their blood may be incompatible in some way, but it's not because they're not father and son."

"But the vasectomy—"

"Obviously, he had it after he attacked me, if he had one at all and isn't just adding to his already impressive pile of lies." She paused. "You keep trying to make it fit. You keep making excuses for him, for yourself. He's not who you thought he was, Addison. He never has been."

Addison glared at her, emotions warring on her face. "You'll say anything to—" She broke off, seemed to hunt for words.

"To what?" Alaina asked. "Try to turn you against him? I thought hearing him tell someone to kill me had already done that."

Addison stiffened, as if the words were painful blows against her chest. Then, shoulders sagging as if the weight of the world—or the weight of comprehension—had just crashed down on her, she lowered herself to the green sofa. "My entire life has been a lie," she said.

The pathos in her voice did nothing to soothe the anger simmering inside Alaina. Her sister had indeed lived a lie. A lie that she had helped perpetuate at Alaina's expense. Alaina kept silent, certain that if she responded, she would lose the slippery grip she had on control.

Addison dragged a wine-colored decorative pillow onto her lap and clutched it to her chest. Her chin began to wobble, and she buried her face in the pillow. A muffled sob escaped. "He's leaving me," she said. "I'm going to be alone. That should make you happy."

There was only one thing that would make Alaina happy, only one thing she wanted from her sister. "I want my son back."

Addison raised her head, and her eyes were red and streaming. "You don't even care."

"You made a choice fifteen years ago, Addison. I'm sorry it didn't work out for you, but it's not my problem."

"How can you be so cold?"

The reins on Alaina's fury snapped tight and held. "Where is Jonah now? Is he at your house?"

Addison's gray eyes narrowed. "Why don't you say it?"

"Say what?"

"What you're thinking, what you're feeling. You hate me."

Control slipped another dangerous notch. "Yes, my entire life has revolved around how I feel about you. Now tell me where my son is."

Tears began to flow again. "There's nothing I can do to change any of it," Addison said. "Don't you think I would if I could?"

Alaina concentrated on taking a deep, calming breath. "What do you want me to say, Addison? What is it you want so desperately to hear?"

"I know I screwed up, Ali. I know that what I did cost you. But you did okay, didn't you? You've had a good life."

"Is that what would appease you? Hearing how hunky-dory my life has been?" Rage boiled over, and Alaina struggled to turn down the heat. But it was too late. She'd held it in for too long. "I suppose it has been pretty hunky-dory, when you really look at it. I mean, being eighteen and the mother of a newborn and working my ass off as a waitress was pretty similar to what I had planned for my life." She held up one hand, as if weighing something in her palm. "Waitress." Then held up the other. "Concert violinist in the Boston Pops. Hell, they're practically one and the same."

The color washed out of Addison's cheeks.

"And letting people I didn't know watch Jonah wasn't so bad," Alaina went on. "Even losing my fourth job because the day-care center wouldn't take him when he was sick and there was no one I could leave him with . . . that was okay. I had plenty of money, after all. Enough to feed him, buy him medicine. Oh, wait, there was rent. And utility bills. And food. We had to have food. Well, Jonah did anyway. I didn't need that much. Once, I went three days without eating. Have you ever done that?" She plunged ahead without waiting for a response. "I don't recommend it. I ended up passing out on the street."

When Addison's mouth went slack with horror, Alaina whirled away, pacing behind a chair, her body trembling, her lungs constricting so tight she couldn't breathe. "And that wasn't even the best of it." She gripped the back of the chair, her fingers curling into the soft cushion. "The best of it was when one of your husband's thugs tracked me down. Things were going pretty well by then. This kind, generous woman had taken Jonah and me in. She showed me what it was like to be loved unconditionally. She got me thinking that things would finally be okay, that the worst of it was over. And then your husband's hired hand cornered me in her kitchen, and right after I slid a knife between his ribs, she—" Her voice choked off, and she clamped a hand over her mouth before a broken sob could escape.

Letting go had been a mistake. She fought for control, but her breath was coming too hard, too fast. She hadn't meant to let it go so far, hadn't meant to say so much. And now grief joined the anger, grief she had never dared allow herself to feel. It was as crushing, as blinding, as she'd feared it would be. Her knees felt weak, and she held on to the chair, suddenly terrified her legs wouldn't continue to support her.

"What did she do?" Addison asked quietly.

Alaina forced herself to say it, forced herself to acknowledge out loud what had haunted her since Emma had fallen to the floor and expelled her last breath. "She saw what I did to that man, and it gave her a heart attack." She swallowed hard against the unbearable tightness in her throat. "I killed her."

"My God."

Addison's stricken words jolted Alaina, and she looked at her sister, saw that her gray eyes were sober and that sorrow had etched lines into her forehead. Alaina's vision blurred with tears, and she focused on the one thing that had always gotten her through. "Where is Jonah?"

Addison closed her eyes, swallowed. When she opened them again, tears swam in them. "He's at the house with Layton."

Releasing the chair, Alaina slid into it as the shakes took hold. She willed them away, struggled to form a plan. "What's the nearest mall accessible by Metro?"

"Pentagon City. Why?"

"Would Layton let you take Jonah to buy new clothes?"

"Maybe. I don't know."

"I want you to bring him to me at the Metro stop at Pentagon City." Stronger now, determined, Alaina grabbed Addison's wrist and glanced at her watch. It was just after one P.M. Assuming Washington's rush hour was as crazy as Chicago's, she figured the crowds of commuters on the Metro would make it difficult for Layton to make a move if he found them.

"Bring him at six."

Chapter 32

"She's losing it," Chuck said.

Mitch was only half-listening, his attention focused on the voices on the other side of the adjoining room door. He'd heard Alaina's outburst, and his chest still burned from the hammer-like impact of what she'd said. Everything that she had been through. How had she endured it? But he knew. She was strong, determined. A survivor. It was one of the many reasons he had fallen in love with her so swiftly.

But now the women had begun speaking in lowered voices, and no matter how hard he strained, he couldn't make out one word.

"Did you hear what I said?" Chuck asked. "We're losing our chief witness."

Mitch faced him, annoyed. "Your chief witness isn't my concern."

"She should be. It's because of her that the Bureau is protecting Alaina."

"The Bureau isn't protecting Alaina. I am. Which raises the question of why you dragged us out of hiding. You said it was urgent."

Chuck rubbed at the middle of his forehead as if he had a headache. "Keller has made arrangements to take Jonah to Belize with him. And he's moved up the date. Their plane tickets are for the day after tomorrow."

"Damn." Mitch glanced back at the adjoining door, imagining what it would do to Alaina if Keller succeeded. Would it be the final blow? He swallowed the lump that formed in his throat, looked at Chuck. "You could have told me this over the phone."

"Addison demanded to see Alaina. She's coming unglued, Mitch, and she's all we've got. If we lose her, we've got nothing, and I mean nothing, on Keller."

"How can that be?"

Chuck looked like he hadn't slept in days. Even the usually perfect creases in his dark suit had wilted. "He knew about the bugs."

"Knew?"

"The listening devices—every one of them—have been disabled in the past twenty-four hours."

"Then Addison could be at risk."

"Her role as a witness has been classified information."

"Don't you think Keller's wondering how the bugs got planted?" Mitch asked.

"Our guys seem to think that if he knew it was her, he would have done something about it by now."

"What do you think?"

"I think the investigation's been tainted from the beginning."

"By whoever Keller's got in the Bureau."

Chuck nodded. "We're thinking now that it might be someone in A.D. Potter's office, if not Potter himself. I've got agents checking out him and all his people, but it's a moot point now." Turning away, he massaged the back of his neck. "Something has to break in the next two days or the window of opportunity slams shut."

"What kind of break are you looking for?"

"Dammit, Mitch—"

"Just tell me, Chuck, and then you can kill me. Maybe I can help."

Shoulders sagging, Chuck leaned back against the desk and sighed. He didn't speak for a moment, and Mitch knew from his own experience that he was weighing the fallout of telling a civilian federal secrets. Then, as if he decided that Mitch could be trusted, he cleared his throat. "The Justice Department got a tip about six months ago that a high-tech security firm had successfully hacked PCware's most popular accounting software—it's used by probably ten percent of businesses across the nation, and the number is growing every day. The firm notified PCware about the glitch, and PCware put out a press release and a patch.

"Couple months later, the high-tech security firm took another whack at the same software, and bingo, they get in through a glitch that appears to have been created by the patch. Except the security firm staffers notice that the bug looks deliberate. No software engineer in his right mind would have written the code that way. At least, not anyone wanting secure software. The firm tipped off Justice, Justice got the Bureau involved, and we launched an investigation."

"What are you looking for?"

"We've been looking for evidence that someone has been exploiting the glitch."

"To do what?"

"The opportunities with this type of security flaw are immense. Essentially, there's a technological back door into any company that uses the software. Anything on the company's network would be accessible to anybody who knows how to get in."

"And Keller's using the glitch to do what?"

"We don't know. Maybe nothing yet. But two months ago, Keller met with a known D.C. mob boss."

"I'd imagine payment for access to such a glitch would be hefty."

"Oh, yeah," Chuck said. "The money-laundering capabilities alone would be worth millions. Add in the access to sensitive information, possible blackmail material, financial information. The list goes on."

"But the scam gets exposed, PCware and Keller go down hard. Why would he risk everything when he's already got money coming out his ears?"

"Hell if I know. He's been wanting to sell PCware and can't."

Mitch nodded. "Because of Paul Chancellor's will."

"He takes the payoff from the mob and skates on out of the country. By the time anyone's on to the scam, he's long gone and couldn't care less what happens to PCware."

"But he's taking Jonah with him. Why would he do that?"

"That's another mystery. It doesn't figure from any angle, unless he plans to off the kid in Belize, where it might not get as much attention from the cops as it would here."

The thought of it sent jitters through Mitch's stomach. "In that scenario, he'd need Alaina dead so she can't raise a fuss about it over here and get something done."

"Right."

"How much evidence have you got to back all this up?" he asked.

"We've got the security firm that uncovered the glitches and Keller's meeting with the mob guy."

"That's it?"

"These guys know they're being watched, Mitch. By the time we realized the Bureau had a leak, it was too late."

Mitch turned his attention to the silence on the other side of the adjoining door. What was going on over there? "Have you tried to get his wife to plant a bug on him? He's got to talk to somebody at some point about what's going down."

Chuck sighed. "She won't do it. She's terrified he's on to

her. We haven't even been able to get her to give us access to his computer at home. And, honestly, I can't say I trust her anymore. She's obviously got a growing problem with alcohol."

Mitch glanced at him. "Maybe I can do it."

Chuck's eyebrows shot up. "You've still got an in with him?"

"Last time we chatted, he seemed to write me off as a loose cannon. But I might be able to push the right buttons to get a meeting if he's desperate to take care of Alaina before he leaves the country." He drew out his cell phone. "Let me give it a shot."

Chapter 33

Alaina dried her hands on the fluffy, white towel and studied her face in the mirror. She looked like hell. Dark circles of stress underscored her eyes. The control she had on her emotions was shaky at best.

She tried to focus on Jonah. If all went as planned, she would have him with her again in only a few hours. She imagined what it would be like to put her arms around him and hug him close. Safe. He would be safe. He would be hers.

But before that happened, she would have to betray the man she had fallen in love with.

Bracing her hands on the vanity, she closed her eyes as her stomach churned violently. Oh, how her betrayal would hurt him. And he'd already been hurt so much.

Yet no matter how much she cared for Mitch, her duty as a mother was to seize the first chance she had to whisk her child to safety. Once she did that, there was no other choice but to run. If she told Mitch her plan, she would place him and everyone he cared about squarely in the sights of Layton's hired guns.

She would rather betray him than get him killed.

Mitch stood on the other side of the bathroom door of the hotel room he and Alaina had checked into after the meeting with Chuck and Addison, debating whether he should disturb her. But she had been in there so long, and he was beginning to worry that perhaps she was ill. He rapped his knuckles against the door. "You okay?"

A moment of silence, then she swung open the door, a smile pasted on. "I'm fine."

He narrowed his eyes as he studied her face. She didn't look fine. She looked wan and stressed, her eyes shadowed. The showdown with Addison had taken its toll. Which was why he had yet to tell her that he had scheduled a meeting with Layton Keller that evening—to deliver her. Except that the Alaina he showed up with would be an FBI decoy agent who would be carefully shielded from Keller while Mitch, wearing a wire, tried to get him to spill his guts.

It was a desperate, risky ploy, one that didn't ensure Jonah's freedom or Mitch's safety. So he kept it to himself for now, waiting until Alaina seemed less fragile. Maybe he wouldn't even tell her. He'd just go do it and apologize profusely later. If all went well, he would return with her son. He was certain all would be forgiven then.

He cleared his throat. "Are you hungry?" They hadn't eaten since breakfast, and it was already mid-afternoon.

"Not really." She seemed to dodge him to go to the windows, where she peered out at the gray day as if it were the most interesting thing she had ever seen.

Distance. He was disappointed by it, but it didn't surprise him. She'd had a tough day. The exchange with her sister had no doubt ripped open old wounds.

Yet, there was something more. She'd avoided his gaze when she'd come out of the bathroom, and that was unlike her. Crossing to her, he slipped his arms around her from behind and drew her against him. Her resistance alarmed him. "Talk to me, Alaina. Please."

She turned into his arms, ran her hands under his shirt. "I don't want to talk."

* * * * *

Addison tossed her purse and keys onto the counter and lowered herself to a kitchen stool. Her head ached from all the wine she had consumed. Her heart ached from what Alaina had told her. And for the first time, Addison saw the past clearly.

It struck her how thoroughly their lives had contradicted expectations. Addison had been considered the smart sister with loads of potential. She had married well and had an impressive home and philanthropic career. She had been the golden child, the one considered most likely to succeed. The strong one.

Alaina had been the rebel with creative aspirations that were not only considered unrealistic but defied her father's wishes. She had lived for fun, her behavior, though not a harm to anyone except perhaps herself, occasionally causing the family embarrassment.

Addison had looked down on her at the same time that she had admired her ability to cut loose and have a good time. Addison never would have dreamed of staying out past curfew or borrowing their mother's car without asking. She certainly never would have dared to strew streamers of toilet paper through the trees of a friend's house. But Alaina had done it, gotten caught and spent the night in juvenile detention because of it.

Her rebellion had only burgeoned after their father refused to let her attend an audition at Juilliard. Alaina had been crushed, and looking back now, Addison began to understand why her sister had become ever more defiant, skipping school, staying out all night, coming home with alcohol on her breath. She'd been angry, frustrated, and perhaps those were the only times she felt able to exert some control over her own life.

Things got much worse a month after Addison and Layton were married, when Alaina told them that Layton had raped her and she was pregnant with his child. Paul hadn't believed her story about the attack for an instant. He'd accused Alaina of making it up to cover for her no-good boyfriend. What else could they have been doing together into the wee hours of the morning besides boozing it up and having unprotected sex?

Addison hadn't believed her, either, and she'd been livid at the lie, accusing Alaina of coveting Layton from the start. It was obvious in the way she flirted with him at every opportunity. Alaina's crush on Layton was no secret. It was also no secret, Addison charged, that Alaina was insanely jealous of Addison. Addison had the gorgeous fiancé and their father's adoring attention. Paul had often told Alaina she needed to be more like Addison.

Then, shockingly, Layton had confessed that he and Alaina had indeed had intercourse, that he had been drunk and unable to turn away when Alaina had aggressively seduced him.

Looking back, Addison saw how shrewd that move had been. He'd seen "the big picture," as her father had often put it when he talked about Layton's excellent management skills. Assuming that eventually a paternity test would show that the child was his, Layton had used their weaknesses against them. He'd exploited Alaina's lack of credibility with Paul brought on by her constant rebellion. Paul adored him, considered him the son he'd never had, so when it came down to "he said, she said," Paul chose to believe the one he trusted: Layton. After all, he had reasoned, Layton didn't have to confess to anything. He could have simply denied that anything ever happened between him and Alaina. Plus, there was the matter of why Alaina had waited until after she'd discovered she was pregnant to say anything about the alleged attack. Her response that she'd known her father would never take her word over Layton's had sent him into a spitting rage.

With Addison, Layton had played perfectly to her conviction that Alaina was jealous of their relationship and had conspired to steal him away. While babbling out apologies and self-recriminations, he had reluctantly (so it seemed) revealed that Alaina had laughed about their encounter afterward, saying she couldn't wait to see the look on Addison's face when she found out. He'd pleaded with Alaina not to say anything because he knew Addison would be devastated, and the last thing he wanted to do was hurt the only woman he'd ever loved. He told Addison that once it became clear Alaina was pregnant, he knew he had to come clean about his lapse and beg for forgiveness.

Addison remembered being almost eager to forgive him. He—the handsome, charming and very coveted Layton Keller—was her husband. Everyone loved him. Alaina was the only one who had anything bad to say about him. That made it very clear to Addison that Alaina was the liar and that Layton had merely stumbled unwittingly into her trap.

Only Eve—Alaina's and Addison's mother—had questioned Layton's claims of drunken and weak male resistance, Addison recalled. Only Eve had been horrified at what had transpired between her youngest daughter and her oldest daughter's fiancé. She had tried to insist that Alaina's claims be investigated, perhaps even by the police. But Paul had shot her down in a thundering tone that had brooked no argument. The publicity alone would be devastating, both to the reputation of an innocent man and the image of a well-respected family already made shaky by Alaina's earlier transgressions. Eve, having been cowed by him for nearly twenty-five years by then, had meekly shut up.

The depth of betrayal staggered Addison. That she and

her parents had been so cleverly manipulated by a man they trusted . . . she still couldn't quite grasp it. And she didn't think she would ever be able to comprehend what it had been like for Alaina.

"There you are."

She turned, surprised to see Layton in his trademark position, one shoulder leaning casually against the door frame, hands in his pockets. "Where have you been?" he asked. He acted casual, curious.

"I had an appointment," she said.

"I see. Were you driving?"

The question threw her. "Of course. Why?"

"You're drunk. In fact, you've been spending entirely too much time drunk. Perhaps it's time for you to seek help."

"Why? So you can get me declared incompetent and screw me over in the divorce?"

He smiled, and there was no humor in the expression. "You're too quick for me, Addy."

"You won't get away with it, Layton. I won't let you."

"What, exactly, are you not going to let me get away with?" he asked. "Because you've let me get away with a lot over the years."

"I didn't know then—"

"Sure you did," he cut in with a smirk. "On some level, you knew all along what I was doing. And you let me because it got you what you wanted."

"I didn't want you to rape my sister."

"No, that was just a bonus."

"You bastard!" She launched herself at him, fingers hooked and aimed at his eyes.

Catching her by the wrists, he shoved her back against the counter. And chuckled. "Gee, Addy, it took you only fifteen years to work up that indignant rage."

Shame erupted inside her, and she tried to jerk away, but he held fast to her wrists. "I believed you," she said through her teeth. "I loved you."

"No, you didn't. You loved that your father loved me. You loved what I looked like and what you looked like next to me. You loved the image we presented of the perfect couple with the perfect marriage who lived in the perfect house and hosted perfect parties. We both got what we wanted from each other, Addy, but it wasn't love. It was never about love. And face it, if you truly loved me, you never would have ratted me out to the feds."

She gaped at him.

He began to laugh. "You're so cute when you're shocked. Yeah, I know what you've been up to. In fact, I knew every move you made before that new guy took over."

"Agent Potter told you?"

"Someone in his office, actually. I knew about the listening devices, the deal you made to protect Alaina, everything."

"But why didn't you—"

His icy eyes danced with smug satisfaction. "Because, Addy honey, if I'd let on that I knew what you were doing, someone would have figured out that I had sources in the FBI. And, at the time, finding Alaina and her brat was more important to me than punishing you for betraying me." He paused, pursed his lips. "Though I am curious about what tipped you off."

She gave him a smug smile of her own. "I overheard you on the phone. You said, 'Kill the bitch and bring the kid to me.' I may be an expert at denial, but there was no plausible explanation for that one. So tell me, Layton, what do you want with the son you never wanted in the first place?"

He made an impatient gesture. "I don't have time for this.

I have preparations to make. Your sister is paying us a visit tonight."

That startled her, and she blurted, "I wouldn't count on it."

His gaze sharpened. "Why would you say that?"

Realizing her blunder, she tried to shrug it off. "Forget it." Grabbing her purse and keys off the counter, she turned to walk out of the kitchen, only to surge back when he came at her. The counter at her back stopped her retreat, and he cornered her against it, a hand braced on either side of her.

"What did you mean by that?" he asked.

She saw in his eyes a feral determination to tear apart anything or anyone who stood in his way, and she couldn't help it. He scared the living crap out of her. "Nothing," she said. "I misspoke."

"No, you didn't. Have you had contact with her?"

"Of course not."

"I know when you're lying, Addison. You suck at it, just like she does. Now tell me what's going on."

She swallowed against the fear constricting her lungs. "I'm not going to tell you anything."

He bracketed her throat with one hand. "Yes, you are."

Chapter 34

Alaina's body hummed with satisfaction, every nerve alive and screaming. She was conscious of her heart thumping in time with Mitch's as she lay sprawled on top of him, their bodies slick with perspiration.

"You alive?" he asked.

She smiled, her damp cheek pressed to his sweat-slick shoulder. "Barely."

"Me, either." His palms brushed over her back, ever in motion, as if he couldn't stop touching her, caressing her. "Will you talk to me now?"

Raising her head, she gazed down into his fathomless, dark brown eyes. She couldn't believe he had happened to her. In a matter of days. It didn't make sense any way she looked at it. She also couldn't imagine what life would be like without him.

He sifted his fingers through her hair, smoothed damp strands back from her forehead. "Do you trust me?" he asked.

A lump formed in her throat, and she closed her eyes.

"Please don't do that," he murmured.

She looked at him, taken aback by the raw emotion in his gaze. "Yes, I trust you."

"Then tell me why you just made love to me like it was the last time."

"It's nothing." She tried to draw away, but he held on, almost desperately.

"You're pulling away from me, distancing yourself," he said. "Why?"

"I love you." She said it without thinking, then immediately regretted it. What was the point of saying it? In a matter of hours, it wouldn't matter.

He looked stunned, then slowly smiled. "Really?"

She curled her fingers around his wrists, drew his hands from her. "Yes, really. And I don't know what to do about it."

He sat up as she shifted away from him. Sitting on the edge of the bed, she reached for the T-shirt he'd pulled off of her an hour ago. She felt less vulnerable with it on, her back to him.

"If there's anything to be done about it," he drawled, "I'd say we just did it."

She glanced at him over her shoulder, noted the satisfaction that curved his lips. She remembered what his mouth, his tongue, had done to her body minutes before, and her pulse stammered. For a moment, she couldn't think.

Grinning, Mitch shifted so that he was behind her. He ran his warm hands over her shoulders, down her back, around to the front of the T-shirt and under the hem, then filled them with her breasts. She shuddered, her breath catching. "We can do it again, if you'd like," he whispered near her ear, his teeth catching her earlobe.

She turned into him, fusing her mouth with his, diving her fingers into his hair. He chuckled, his body vibrating against hers, when she pushed him back and straddled him. He rolled her under him and pinned her with his hips. "I get to be on top this time," he growled.

She answered by dragging his head down to her, where she kissed him deeply, her tongue tangling with his.

Did she trust him? Yes. Yes yes yes.

His hands seemed to be everywhere, already knowing what she liked and giving it to her. She reveled in the sensations, committing every caress, every indrawn breath to memory. Because this really would be the last time.

She heard the rip of the telltale foil packet, then he was braced above her. "Open your eyes, Alaina."

She did.

His gaze delved into hers, seeking, seeking . . . what?

He sank into her slowly, with a long groan. She took him in, catching her bottom lip between her teeth. He felt so good . . . he made her feel everything.

When he began to move, she crested almost immediately, and he paused as the shudders rippled through her, his body tense, his muscles seeming to strain against the need to take. "You do that so easily," he said, kissing her eyelids, her nose.

She tried to catch her breath, intensely aware of their link, of how her body throbbed around his. Holding still had to be killing him. "Why don't you join me?"

"It's too soon," he said. "It's only been five minutes."

"Who's got the stopwatch?"

"I'm not a damn teenager. I have far more restraint."

"It's okay. I don't mind."

He answered by lowering his head to take a nipple into his mouth, rolling it with his tongue. The tug nearly sent her over again, but then he started moving, slowly, leisurely, building the ache until it blossomed and spread.

She held on to his shoulders, her face buried against his neck. His arms were wrapped tightly around her as he rocked into her, as if he couldn't hold her close enough.

When her body went rigid, her breath sobbing out, her head dropping back, he held her against him, waited for the quake to ease, then began again.

"I can't," she panted. "No more . . . I can't . . ."

He silenced her, burying his mouth on hers as he eased her

back, flattening her hands against the bed and sinking his fingers between hers, linking them.

He began pumping his hips, fast now, grinding, demanding, driving. Colored lights exploded in her head. Rainbows and kaleidoscopes and fireworks. She couldn't breathe, couldn't think. When her body began to buck again, he let himself go and joined her.

Afterward, Alaina couldn't lift her arms. She wanted to hug him, hold him. But she couldn't move. He must have felt the same, because he lay limp on top of her, his breathing harsh, sweat trickling down his temple. She marveled at the satisfying weight of him, reveled in the sensation of their still-linked bodies.

Raising his head, he kissed her. "Told you I had more restraint."

"That was restraint?"

He laughed, still breathing hard. "You have no idea."

The idea of living without him physically hurt.

His gaze grew serious, as if he sensed her growing despair. "What is it?"

When she shook her head, he gently withdrew and lay beside her, drawing her against him. "Please tell me. Whatever it is, we'll figure it out."

As she lay in his arms, feeling the heat of his body against her, she realized that she couldn't live without him. She wasn't strong enough to walk away, to spare him. She was selfish and in love. Human. She pulled in a breath, let it slowly out. And prayed she wasn't about to sign his death warrant. "Addison is taking Jonah to Pentagon City at six. To meet me."

Sitting up, Mitch glanced at the clock. "We have an hour and a half."

"I was going to ditch you."

He looked at her, his eyes at once hurt, then shadowed. "I see."

"I couldn't stand it if something happened to you because of—" She choked as the memory of Emma dead on the floor filled her head.

He leaned toward her, took her face into his hands and kissed her. When he eased back, the hurt in his gaze had been replaced by an understanding that she couldn't comprehend. "I heard what you told Addison about the kind woman who took you and Jonah in. What happened to her wasn't your fault, Alaina."

She hid her face against his throat as hot tears began to fall. He knew her so well already, knew how she thought. "I exposed her to danger when I let her get close to me," she said. "I never warned her that she was vulnerable."

He held her close, soothing her with a warm hand stroking her bare back. "When you ran away with Jonah, did it ever occur to you that Keller would kill to get him back?"

As his words, spoken in a low voice near her ear, sank in, her racing heartbeat calmed. She remembered being frightened of Layton, of worrying about being forever separated from Jonah, of going to prison. But Mitch was right. Even after Emma had died, Alaina hadn't feared that Layton would try to kill her or anyone she cared about. The man who'd tried to blackmail her hadn't been sent by Layton and had at first seemed to have no intention of harming her. After that, her determination to keep her distance from others had been just as much about protecting herself as protecting them.

Not until Grant Maxwell had been shot and Lucas hurt had the realization struck her that Layton's intentions had turned deadly. So while knowing her had most certainly placed Emma and the Maxwells in peril, she had put them there unwittingly.

She started to cry again, for what knowing her had cost them. And Mitch's arms never left her, nor did his hand ever stop its soothing caress against her back.

Sniffling, she tilted her head back to meet his worried gaze. "I've cried on you more than anyone I've ever known. If it keeps up, you might need to invest in flippers and nose plugs."

Smiling, he pressed his lips to her temple. "You can cry on me anytime."

"Just so you know, I don't make it a habit."

"Maybe you should," he said. "Holding all those feelings inside isn't good for you."

Stroking a hand over his chest, she said, "Emma would have liked you."

"Emma?"

"The woman I told Addison about. She would have approved."

"Thank God."

Sobering, she savored the scrape of stubble on his jaw against her fingertips. "He might go after your son," she said.

"He doesn't know anything about Tyler."

"He'll find out."

"You're not going to frighten me away, Alaina. So give it a rest." With that, he placed a quick, hard kiss on her lips. "Do you want to shower first or shall I?"

Dressed in jeans, T-shirt and one of Mitch's flannel shirts, Alaina was sitting on the bed, brushing out her wet hair, listening to the shower running in the other room, when Mitch's cell phone rang. Picking it up, she flipped it open. "Hello?"

Silence answered her.

"Hello?" she said again. "Is someone there?"

"Alaina."

She flinched, the brush slipping out of her fingers and landing with a hollow thunk on the floor. She'd know that voice anywhere.

"I know it's you, Alaina. I hear you breathing."

"What do you want?" she asked.

"So Mitch was telling the truth. He really does have you in his possession."

"What are you talking about?"

"Ah, this is rich. You really have no idea, do you?"

"Make your point, Layton."

He chuckled. "So tough. So unsuspecting. He said he's been pretending to protect you until he could bring you to me. Tonight, in fact. Did he tell you about our meeting later?"

She didn't believe him for an instant. "You're lying."

"That was always your problem, wasn't it? You trusted too easily. You always believed in the good in people. But some people have only as much good in them as you pay them to have."

"Good-bye, Layton."

Quickly, he said, "Addison won't be showing up with Jonah like the two of you agreed."

Her heart dropped as if he'd just kicked it off the roof of a skyscraper.

"Are you still there?" The bastard sounded playful.

"Yes."

"I'm taking him away, Ali. Out of the country. You'll never see him again."

Pain knifed into her. "No."

"Perhaps you'd like to come say good-bye."

Shaking, she gripped the phone so tight her wrist ached. "Where?"

He gave her an address. "Take a cab. I'll buzz you in at the gate. And Ali?"

She held her breath.

"Come alone. Anyone who shows up with you I'll consider a threat and I might take it out on the kid. Got it?"

She bit into her bottom lip. "Yes."

Mitch strode out of the bathroom, a towel wrapped around his waist, his hair dripping. He wondered if there was time to make love to Alaina once more before they left. He couldn't seem to get enough of her.

Near the bed, though, he paused, confusion giving way to alarm as he realized that she was not in the room. He started to turn when something on top of the sheets caught his attention. His cell phone.

He snatched it up, opened it. Caller ID told him the name of the last person to call his number, and his blood went icy.

Throwing off the towel, he pulled on his clothes with shaking hands.

What was she doing? Had she gone after Keller? Why would she do that without telling him?

Oh, Jesus, Keller would kill her.

He reached for his holster and froze.

His gun was gone.

Chapter 35

Alaina sat in the cab, trying to be patient with the traffic jam, but her pulse was racing.

Layton's words haunted her: "Some people have only as much good in them as you pay them to have."

Did that mean he had paid Mitch to set her up?

"He's been pretending to protect you until he could bring you to me."

"That was always your problem, wasn't it? You trusted too easily."

Her heart told her Layton was lying, but her head told her she couldn't afford to take a chance. Her head was also telling her that she was being foolish for going to Layton like this when she knew he wanted her dead. But she couldn't not go. Not when Jonah's well-being—his life—was at stake.

She looked down at Mitch's backpack on her lap. His gun was inside, so she wouldn't be confronting Layton unarmed. She only hoped she would be able to pull the trigger this time.

"Chuck, we've got a problem."

"Slow down. What is it?"

"Alaina has gone to confront Keller."

"How the hell did she get away from you?"

"It doesn't matter. You've got agents watching Keller's house?"

"Yes."

"Tell them to intercept her." Seeing the traffic jam ahead,

he slammed the palm of his hand against the steering wheel. Fuck.

"How do you know she's gone to his house?" Chuck asked.

"Keller wants to be in control, and the only place he can be completely in control is on his own turf." He thought of his missing gun, and his insides lurched. While he had seen first-hand Alaina's inability to shoot someone to protect herself, he didn't doubt for a second that she wouldn't hesitate to take out anyone who stood between her and Jonah.

"Dammit, Chuck, tell them she's armed."

The cab dropped Alaina in front of Layton Keller's palatial home in an old neighborhood that overlooked a golf course and the Potomac River. The area was quiet and regal, the houses few and far between, odd for the D.C. suburbs, where such acreage was rare and so expensive that only the truly rich could afford it.

She approached the gate, noting the camera positioned at the top of the gate, aimed at an intercom where visitors could announce their arrival. Before she could approach the device, a black sedan rolled into the short driveway in front of the gate. Two men were in the car, but only one got out and walked toward her. He looked like an FBI agent, dressed in a dark suit, white dress shirt, tie with diagonal, alternating red and navy stripes, and shiny black shoes. He struck her as a little gawky, so thin and youthful that he might have been a teen without the pimples.

"Ms. Chancellor?" he called.

Alaina shifted her weight from one foot to the other, telling herself to be patient even though every cell in her body was screaming at her to get to Jonah. She was so close. "Yes?"

Holding the inside of his wrist near his lips, he spoke softly into what she assumed was a microphone. A white, curly cord dangled behind one ear. Pausing before her, he flashed a badge. "Special Agent Bristol, FBI. Will you come with me, ma'am?"

She hesitated, casting a glance at the camera above the gate. If she went with the agent, she would blow her one and only chance of seeing Jonah, of getting him away from Layton. Casually, she slipped her hand into Mitch's backpack and closed her fingers around the cool butt of his gun. She had no intention of firing it, of course. All she had to do was point it at the guy and force him to back off until Layton buzzed her in. But the thought of pointing a gun at this man, this federal agent who looked not much older than her own son, made her shudder. What if he pulled his own weapon?

"Ma'am?"

She didn't move. If she walked away with him, her chance would be gone. Jonah would be gone. It would all be over, and Layton would win.

She let the backpack drop to the ground.

The agent focused on the pistol in her hand, but his expression didn't change. "You don't need that, Ms. Chancellor."

"I'm going to go in to see Mr. Keller," she said. "All you have to do is let me go."

He nodded. "All right."

"I'm going to—"

He attacked so fast, he had her on the ground and pinned on her back, the air gone from her lungs, before she could blink. He easily plucked Mitch's gun away from her.

A car door slammed, followed by running feet. "What the hell's going on?"

Agent Bristol got up. "Bitch pulled a gun on me."

"You're kidding! You oughta make her pay for that."

"I like the sound of that."

The tone of the exchange set off alarms in Alaina's head as she wheezed in her first breath since he'd taken her down. Would FBI agents speak that way? Then she remembered Mitch's fear that Layton might have a source inside the Bureau. Apparently, he had two.

"Go get us buzzed in while I take care of her," Bristol said.

"Okay. Oh, and after you got out of the car, he called to say one of us should stay and watch the gate. Guess he's expecting some uninvited guests."

"You stay. I want to play delivery man."

"You got it."

As his partner jogged back toward the car, Bristol nudged Alaina with his foot, Mitch's gun still in his hand. "Get up."

"Give me a minute," she gasped, exaggerating distress that had already eased. She glanced toward the car, saw the other man was on the other side of it, a good twenty feet away. She might have just enough time—

Bristol hooked a hand under her arm. "We don't have all fucking day, lady."

She launched herself up at him, hitting him at the waist with desperate force that tumbled the slight man backward. She landed on top of him, nailing him in the gut with her elbow before scrambling up his body as if it were a jungle gym. Her fingers had just clamped over Mitch's gun when someone grabbed her from behind and lifted her up.

Twisting violently in strong arms, she drove her heel into her captor's shin, heard him grunt. His grip loosened, and she squirmed, thinking she was almost free, almost—

He pivoted, swinging her around, and she glimpsed Bristol's face before something hard and warm smashed into her jaw.

★ ★ ★ ★ ★

Addison sat on the floor of the bathroom, a bottle of tranquilizers clutched in her hand. She wondered how many it would take. Ten? Twenty?

She held up the bottle, studied the label. It had originally held thirty. She was sure she'd taken no more than five in the few days since she'd had the prescription filled.

Her cheek throbbed where Layton had struck her. But it was difficult to tell which pain was more intense—where he had hit her or shame at how she had spilled her guts after only one blow. Such weakness shouldn't have been a surprise, she thought. She had been weak her entire life. Weak and stupid.

The guilt seemed to thrum in the bruise on her face. She had betrayed Alaina, forcing her only sister into a life of unimaginable hardship and fear. What kind of person could blindly let Layton do what he'd done? She had failed in every way possible. As a sister, a daughter, an aunt, a human being. Perhaps it was best that Layton had denied her the chance to be a mother, because she no doubt would have screwed that up, too.

Plus, once the feds exposed Layton's transgressions with PCware, whatever they were, their image as the perfect couple with the perfect life would be shattered. Everyone would know, and if their friends didn't shun her, they would pity her. She couldn't bear the thought of it.

Her only consolation at this point was that once someone found her body, her bruised face would raise questions, as would the lengthy letter she had written, stuffed in an envelope and slid under the mattress she had shared with her sister's rapist for more than a decade.

Rising up to her knees, her hands shaking, she filled a glass with water.

★ ★ ★ ★ ★

Mitch pulled into Layton Keller's driveway and stared at the tall front gate. Alaina should have been here by now. Where were the federal agents Chuck had summoned to intercept her?

He'd just flipped out his phone to call Chuck when he saw a man he pegged as a fed walking toward him. He looked familiar, and Mitch remembered him from the ER waiting room right after the shoot-out at Rachel's. He was one-half of the two-member newbie brigade. Itchy and Scratchy, he'd nicknamed them. As young and inexperienced as this guy was, Mitch was still glad to see him and got out of the car.

"Where is she?" he asked, too anxious to see Alaina to bother with a greeting or even an introduction.

The newbie agent responded by going for his gun. His first shot slammed into the driver's side door of Mitch's rental car.

Mitch dropped to one knee and, in an instant, had in his hand the gun he kept strapped to his ankle. He nailed the rookie in the shoulder with the first bullet, but not before the guy got off another shot.

Mitch's head snapped back as a searing pain flashed along the side of his head, and the day went black.

Chapter 36

The throb of the pulse in her jaw brought Alaina awake, and she lay still, disoriented, taking in white and black furnishings, a high ceiling, marble floors. Glass and chrome accents gave everything a sterile gleam.

"She joins us at last."

She turned her head, wincing at the answering ache, and saw Layton sitting across from her on a plush, black overstuffed chair, a complement to the white sofa beneath her.

His legs were crossed, his posture relaxed, maybe even amused. He wore an impeccable black suit with a yellow silk shirt and blue tie. He had changed little in fourteen years, his blond hair curly and thick, his waist lean, his clothes corporate, if a good bit more expensive. He was still a very attractive man. On the outside.

Pushing herself up, she put her feet on the floor. Her head spun, but she shoved the weakness away. "Where's Jonah?"

Layton waved an elegant hand, a subtle ring of gold and diamonds winking on his left ring finger. "We'll get to that in a minute."

"I want to see him now."

He sat forward, bracing his elbows on his knees. "I may be way off on this, Alaina, but it appears to me that I am the one holding the cards here."

Taking a moment to get oriented, she glanced around the large living room, seeking possible escape routes and potential weapons. She ordered herself to remain calm. Jonah was depending on her to keep her cool.

A set of double doors was to her right, probably leading to a kitchen or perhaps a library. Behind the sofa where she sat, a wide, arched doorway looked like it might lead to a front entryway. To the left, a bar stocked with liquor, a large mirror behind it. As for potential weapons, a hefty-looking crystal vase on the glass-and-chrome coffee table before the sofa looked promising.

"Don't even think about it," Layton said. "You bean me with that, and you'll never find out where he is, let alone ever see him again."

She focused on him, her eyes narrowing. Her muscles twitched with the need to lunge at him. "Is that how this is going to go? You're going to taunt me to death?"

Amusement quirked at the corners of his mouth. "Ah, here's the bravado. As usual, it's stunning on you."

Unable to sit still and let him goad her, she shoved to her feet. Only to sway.

Layton rose, too, reaching out to steady her. "Perhaps you should stay seated."

She slapped his hand away. "You got me here. Now what do you want?"

His eyes glittered like blue diamonds. "There's only been one thing I've ever wanted from you, Alaina."

A noise above them, as if someone had thrown a heavy object at a wall or a door, brought Alaina's head up. But then Layton stepped around the table between them. Startled by his sudden move, she jerked back. The backs of her knees hit the edge of the sofa, and off balance, she toppled backward onto the cushions. Before she could scramble away, Layton came down on top of her. In one smooth motion, he trapped her hands above her head and clamped her thighs between his. Then he started to chuckle.

"Getting you under me again wasn't nearly as difficult as I thought it'd be," he said, nuzzling his nose just under her ear.

Alaina struggled to think above the fear that rammed into high gear. She couldn't breathe, his weight crushing on her chest as memories erupted, nearly stalling her brain. "Why are you doing this?" she asked, annoyed at the strangled sound of her voice.

"Isn't simple revenge enough? You took my son away from me."

She held off the fierce need to thrash, to try to squirm away from him. Doing so would only enflame him, and as far as she could tell, he was already enflamed. She concentrated on being still, on breathing shallowly, focused on surviving. It was the only way she would be able to walk out of there with Jonah. "How can you want revenge for that when you didn't even want him?" she asked.

"You're right," he said with a sigh. "I didn't want some snot-nosed kid anywhere near me. You see, your father was crazy about me. That kid would have been deadly competition for everything I wanted. I was glad when you took off with him. That solved lots of my problems. The daily reminder of my transgression with you would have eventually eroded my relationships with your sister and father. They couldn't have stayed mad at you forever, and they no doubt would have fallen in love with an adorable helpless little baby. Their allegiances might have shifted to you and the kid, and I would have been left in the dirt. I couldn't afford for that to happen." He eased back some, clamping one hand around both her wrists, then leisurely trailing his free hand down her torso. His fingertips glided over a breast, taunting, teasing. "Ah, Alaina, every time I see you, you're more lovely."

Panic threatened to make the breath hitch in her chest.

Keep him talking. Jesus, keep him talking. "But you hired detectives to find us."

"I hired them to write reports, tons of reports, about all the dead ends they encountered while looking for you."

"Two of them found me."

"The one in Colorado wasn't mine. Your mother—God rest her soul—hired her own detective. She didn't trust mine, she said. So she got one of her own, and when her detective found you, my detective was right behind him and tipped me off. That was a close call. Everything would have changed if she'd managed to bring you home. By then, your father was wishing like hell that he had a grandson."

Fury swelled at his flip tone. "You killed my mother," she said.

Layton hummed low in his throat, his tongue wetting his lips as if recalling what he'd done to Eve heightened his desire. "I had to make her pay for the skillet over the head. Plus, she'd seen me at my worst. I'm afraid I was terribly careless that day, but you see, I was very excited to see you, Ali, very eager to revisit what I considered an extremely good time."

She fought to school her breathing, fought to hold herself rigid.

Layton ground his hips against her. "God, I can feel the tension coiling in you, the rage. It's really turning me on."

She closed her eyes, closed her mind to the memory of him on top of her fifteen years ago. *Keep him talking.* "Why now? What do you want with Jonah now, after so many years?"

His smile turned grim. "That's where the story gets annoying." Suddenly, as if his passion had flagged, he released her hands and pushed off her. "If you try anything, I'll flatten you," he warned as he straightened his clothes. Then he crossed to the black-lacquered bar and started fixing himself a drink.

Sitting up slowly, Alaina rubbed her bruised wrists and watched him warily, wondering why the hell he'd let her go. She considered making a run for it but figured that would be foolish when he was still physically able to chase her down.

He faced her, a glass a third full of amber liquid grasped in one hand. "I've got leukemia," he said.

She gaped at him, too stunned to do anything else.

"I was diagnosed a little more than two months ago," he said. "Right before your father's mugging, which I was not responsible for, by the way. Just plain old luck, that. Then his damn will muddied everything up even more. Not only did I not inherit the majority of PCware, like I should have, but suddenly my life had an expiration date." He paused to drink, his throat working as he took a liberal swallow. "My doctor found it during a routine physical. So far, I've just been tired. My only hope was a bone marrow transplant, and the donor had to be a relative—a sibling, a parent. My son."

He drank again, draining the glass. "But Jonah's not a match," he said. "Apparently, that's not that unusual, my doctor tells me. She says siblings are more likely to be a match, but I don't have any of those. Jonah was my only shot."

For an instant, hope soared. "Then you have no need for him."

"You're right." He glanced at her, tilted his head as if with affection. "Ah, Alaina, always the optimist. You don't think I'm going to let him go, do you?"

"What more could you want of him?"

"He has something else I want. You both own a third of PCware."

"You can have it."

"You can't give away his piece of the company, Alaina. And neither can he. Not until he's twenty-one, according to your dad's will. But I can't wait seven years. I might have only three to five years to live, perhaps longer if the disease goes into remission. I need all the pieces of PCware now so I can sell it and live extremely comfortably on the proceeds before I die."

"Don't you already have enough for that?" she asked. "You're a millionaire."

"It's not just about the money, Alaina. You can't imagine how hard I worked. How many hours, how many years I devoted to making PCware the company it is. And for what? Your father gave me a fraction of what I deserve, what I earned. He gave the same fraction to you and your kid. He never even knew your kid, and you . . . you he couldn't stand. It's a slap in the face, and I'll be damned if I'll spend what's left of my life baby-sitting the company—and the whiny, alcoholic daughter—of the man who betrayed me."

"He betrayed *you?*"

"He was like a father to me. I thought I was like a son to him. But he obviously didn't feel that way or he wouldn't have cheated me out of what's rightfully mine. Can you imagine how infuriating that is?"

"It's probably as infuriating as having a sociopath turn your entire family against you." She couldn't hide her contempt. The man was like a bratty kid who didn't get what he wanted and was taking it out on everyone around him.

Layton nodded, smiled. "See? You get it. You know where I'm coming from. I had goals. I had dreams. And he took them away."

"Yeah, I can see how you've really been left out in the cold, Layton."

Grinning now, he set aside his empty glass and crossed to her. "You know, I felt pretty lousy when I decided you had to die. Not at first, of course. At first, I was so angry at your son of a bitch father that anyone who came near me risked getting hurt. Then, when I realized that our kid had no idea who I was . . . well, that angered me, too, because of how difficult that was going to make it to win him over. I mean, there was no telling how long I was going to have to keep him around to help me beat this disease.

"But deep down, I felt bad about having you killed. I felt bad that I had to have you out of the way so I could do whatever I needed to with the company and the kid without you raising a big stink about it."

"What about the innocent people who got hurt?" she asked. "Do you feel bad about that?"

"You're speaking of the Maxwells," he said, frowning. "Yes, that was unfortunate. No one was supposed to get hurt in that altercation. Except you, of course. You were late, and my men didn't feel comfortable waiting any longer. And Mr. Maxwell . . . well, according to my employees, Mr. Maxwell was very adamant about defending his home and your son. The situation escalated beyond their control, and they had no choice but to protect themselves."

"By shooting an unarmed man and pistol-whipping a young boy."

"It's my understanding that Mr. Maxwell and his son were well aware that my people were armed."

She fought down her rising rage. The man had no remorse whatsoever for involving innocent people. "And how were you going to explain Jonah being with you after all that?"

"That's an easy one," he said with a grin. "I was going to tell the authorities that I hired a detective to find you and my son, but that detective wasn't the most upstanding citizen, because instead of informing me when he found you, he and a cohort kidnapped Jonah and demanded a ransom from me.

Naturally, I paid it. The plan, however, was for them to kill you when they grabbed Jonah at the home of the Maxwells."

"You thought of everything, Layton," she said in mock admiration. "Every last detail."

His grin blossomed anew. "That's why I always liked you, Ali. You have fire. Your sister doesn't have fire. Never has. And, lately, she's too busy feeling sorry for herself. It really is a drain. But you, you've been fiery all along. You kicked your dad's ass every time he tried to tear you down." Stepping to her, he rubbed his thumb over her bottom lip, his eyes meeting hers in approval when she didn't flinch away. "I enjoyed watching your spirit grow ever more unbreakable. But mostly I enjoyed being the one to tame the wild child inside you."

"Don't flatter yourself," she said, holding his gaze defiantly. "You hardly tamed me."

"Sure, I did. I changed your life. You were headed down the wrong road. Ditching school. Flunking out. Staying out all night with those shady friends of yours." He sifted his fingers through hair that fell to her shoulder, and she had to brace to keep from grabbing his hand and wrenching it up between his shoulder blades.

"I made you a mother," he said, his gaze fond. "When I did that, I forced you to choose another path. You had to grow up to survive, to help your kid survive. Frankly, on top of being relieved, I was impressed when you took off with him. That surprised me. It surprised me even more when I saw you in Colorado, how you had your act together, especially after that gruesome scene in Madison with my detective and the kitchen knife. You bounced back from that admirably, Ali. I can't help but feel a certain pride that something I did turned you into such a strong, resilient woman."

If he hadn't been standing so close, taunting her with constant physical contact, she might have laughed in his face. The man was clearly off his rocker. "You know, you're right," she said. "I really should thank you for raping me."

His chuckle vibrated the air between them. "See? Unbreakable. It's a shame that I have to kill you." Then he turned conspiratorial. "Want to know how I'm going to do it, how I'm going to get it all and live happily ever after, high on the hog, without having to explain three dead bodies?"

This time, surprise did make her jolt. "Three?"

Pocketing his hands, he rocked back on his heels, his eyes dancing with glee. "I'm afraid your sister has finally caught on to what a rat I am. That didn't take long, did it?" His grin broadened at his joke. "Plus, she's become far too high-maintenance. I just don't have the energy to deal with her anymore. So I've arranged a trip for three to Belize. The clever thing is the airline uses PCware software, which means I can go into its system and do all sorts of neat little tricks. Such as change the names on the tickets and alter the record to indicate that all three tickets were used. Can you guess which three names will be on those tickets?"

He didn't give her a chance to respond, too caught up in his ingenuity. "Yours, Addison's and Jonah's. You see, I'm treating the three of you to a vacation to celebrate your reunion. Unfortunately, you're all going to vanish on your way from the airport to the hotel in Belize. It will be very puzzling and sad. A tragedy. No one will blame me when I sell PCware because I can't bear to be the sole survivor of a once-great family. Then I'll be free."

He caressed her cheek, the gesture tender, wistful. "Don't worry, Ali. I'm not going to make you watch me kill the kid. It's never been my intention to make you suffer."

She'd heard enough and, with his hand so close to her face, she saw a chance and snatched it. Seizing his thumb, she yanked it back hard. He yelped, jerking back from her, and as he bent forward, cradling his injured thumb against his belly, she scooped the crystal vase off the coffee table and smashed it against the back of his skull.

He dropped like a stone at her feet.

She didn't waste time checking on him. Scrambling over the back of the sofa, she raced for the wide, arched doorway, the soles of her sneakers squeaking as she tore across the marble floor. In the entryway, she had a choice: right, to the front door, or left, to a marble staircase that curved up to the next level. She remembered the thump she'd heard earlier, how Layton had immediately tried to distract her from it. Someone was upstairs.

"Jonah!" She screamed her son's name as she swerved for the stairs, taking them two at a time. "Jonah!"

She'd nearly made it to the top when something big and heavy crashed into her legs from behind. She went down hard on the marble steps, gasping as the unyielding edge of one cracked against her still-tender ribs. Then Layton flipped her over, straddled her. She fought blindly, twisting, kicking, punching, shoving. She smelled blood, didn't know if it was his or hers, thought maybe she was starting to gain some ground before he managed to grab a handful of her hair and slam her head back against marble.

Her world spun, and she arched under him at the exploding pain, locking her hands around his wrist to keep him from doing it again. She felt his muscles flex, felt him lift her head again. This is it, she thought wildly. He's killing me.

Then, miraculously, he was dragging her up to her feet. The instant her soles made contact with a marble step, she grabbed hold of the handrail for an anchor and heaved herself against his chest.

Layton's arms pinwheeled, and then he fell.

Chapter 37

Mitch groaned as he came to. His head was on fire.

He put a hand to his temple, felt the blood there. It was sticky, coagulating.

What the hell had happened?

Then he remembered. Half of the duo Itchy and Scratchy had pulled a gun on him. Luckily, the rookie had lousy aim.

Grimacing, he sat up in the dirt. Probing the wound at his temple, he was relieved to feel no splinters or shards of bone that would indicate something more serious than a concussion and a deep groove where the bullet had grazed his head. Aside from the loss of blood and a monster headache, he appeared to be okay.

Looking around, he took stock of his surroundings. Itchy, or possibly Scratchy, was on his back several feet away, writhing and swearing.

Mitch forced himself to his feet, hanging on to the car until the worst of the dizziness passed. Then he walked in a drunken line to where the rookie agent squirmed, blood oozing through the fingers of the hand clamped to his shoulder. His face was pale and sweaty. He couldn't have been more than twenty-five.

The guy lifted his head, the cords in his neck standing out. "Help me. I'm dying," he groaned through clenched teeth.

He couldn't have been dying, Mitch surmised, not from a shoulder wound. The worst damage would involve muscle and bone. If the bullet had nicked any important arteries, he would have bled out by now. But Mitch wasn't about to tell him that when he needed information. After kicking the renegade agent's gun away, Mitch dropped clumsily to his knees beside him. "Where is she?"

"Jesus, man, I'm fucking dying. Call 911."

Mitch braced a hand on the ground as his head whirled. Chances were, someone already had. Gunshots in a neighborhood like this were sure to bring the cops running. "Not until you tell me where she is."

"Oh, God," the guy said, letting his head fall back.

Curling his fingers into the man's lapels, Mitch tugged him back up. "Tell me where she is, and I'll make the call. You don't have much time."

"She's in the house."

At the top of Layton's marble staircase, Alaina sank to her knees, bracing both hands on the cool surface of the floor as she fought down the violent need to be sick. The taste of blood filled her mouth, and her lip stung where she'd either bitten it or Layton had split it.

At the bottom of the stairs, Layton lay on his back, unmoving, eyes closed. The repeated thuds his body had made as it crashed down the steps echoed in her pounding head.

Get up get up get up.

She chanted it in her head, forcing her wobbly legs under her and pulling herself up by the railing. The hallway went in both directions, flanked on both sides by several closed doors. Which way?

"Jonah!" Her voice echoed back at her. He didn't answer. She looked down the steps at Layton, couldn't tell if he was breathing. Was he dead or just unconscious? If he was unconscious, how much time did she have?

She ran to the right first, shoving open door after door, finding bedrooms and bathrooms, a library, an office, none of them locked, all of them empty of human life.

"Jonah!"

She sprinted back past the stairs, glancing to make sure Layton was where she had left him. He was, eyes still closed.

Again, she flung open doors, growing more desperate. What if Jonah wasn't up here? Where could he be? Where would Layton keep him? Maybe he wasn't even in the house. She shoved that thought away.

"Jonah!" Her lungs and leg muscles burned for air, but she didn't dare slow down. "Answer me. Please, answer me."

She was babbling out loud, her breath hitching with fear. Then she opened the last door and stopped. Pieces of something that had been ceramic and black were scattered across the white carpet, as if someone had thrown a lamp at the door. Remembering the thump, she stumbled into the room, hope rocketing. "Jonah?"

The bedroom—it looked like a master suite—contained a four-poster bed, armoire and dresser. A door stood open along one wall, a light shining from inside revealing a bathroom.

A sound, like clothing rustling as someone shifted, drew her farther into the room, and she froze. At the foot of the bed on the floor, Addison, still wearing the teal wrap dress, was sprawled on her back.

As if sensing her there, she turned her head toward Alaina and opened her eyes. "Ali?"

Alaina hesitated, frantic to find Jonah before Layton regained consciousness. Every instinct screamed at her to run, to keep searching, to get her son and get out. There was no time to spare.

But then she saw that Addison had something clenched in her fist. An empty pill bottle.

"Oh God," Alaina moaned, dropping to her knees beside her sister. "Addy, what did you do?"

She pried the bottle from Addison's fingers and scanned the label. Valium. The prescription had been filled only a few days before. Alaina checked her sister's pupils, found them fixed and dilated. A nasty bruise darkened her cheekbone.

Addison smiled. "I feel better already."

Alaina glanced toward the door as indecision slashed at her. Time was running out. She had to find Jonah and escape before Layton came around. But she couldn't just leave her sister to die.

Could she?

Scrambling over the bed to the phone on the bedside table, Alaina snatched it up. No dial tone. Layton must have cut service.

Spotting Addison's purse on the dresser, Alaina grabbed it, dumped it upside down on the floor and pawed through the contents. No cell phone. "Dammit!"

"Ali?"

She went back to Addison but hesitated to kneel beside her again. She didn't have time for this. If Layton came to, he would go to wherever he had Jonah hidden and kill him. He might already have regained consciousness. He might already have a gun pointed at Jonah's head.

She had to save him. She had to save her child . . .

"Ali."

She looked down at her sister, her chest feeling as if someone had tried to split it in two with an ax. Addison's gray eyes were surprisingly clear. "Go," she said. "Go to Jonah."

Alaina's frantic desperation shifted, and she went to her knees beside her sister. "Do you know where he is?"

"He's in the house. . . ." Addison's lids drifted closed, and a soft sigh escaped her lips.

Alaina grasped her by the shoulders. "Where?"

Addison didn't respond, sinking so far under the control of the drugs that Alaina realized getting any information out of her would be impossible unless she did something. "How much did you take?" she demanded.

"It doesn't matter."

Alaina shook her, impatient and terrified. For Jonah. For herself. For the sister who'd never been there for her. "How much, dammit?"

Addison's fingers curled around Alaina's wrists, gripped. "Three at first . . . because I was afraid. And then . . . later . . . I took the rest."

Oh Jesus. Oh God. No time. "How long ago?"

Addison's head lolled back. "I'm sorry," she whispered. "So sorry. I was an awful sister. An awful person."

She was still relatively coherent, so Alaina determined that she couldn't have swallowed the pills that long ago. Either way, they had to be expelled.

Tugging her into a sitting position, Alaina pushed Addison forward until she was bent at the waist. Leaning against Addison's spine to keep her from flopping back, Alaina reached around her and gripped her sister's jaw. "Open your mouth."

Addison resisted, shaking her head like a toddler rejecting a spoonful of strained peas.

"Damn you, don't fight me," Alaina snapped. Every second that ticked by eroded her chances of getting to Jonah before Layton did. With strength born of determination and desperation, she pried Addison's teeth apart and shoved her finger down her sister's throat.

While Addison vomited on the pristine white carpet,

Alaina supported her trembling shoulders to keep her from slipping backward, where she might asphyxiate on her own vomit. "That's good," she said, rubbing Addison's back. "That's good."

Addison threw up a second time, then gulped in air as if she'd been held underwater for several minutes. Her head sagged on her shoulder, and Alaina could see that her eyes kept trying to roll back in her head.

Alaina jostled her, slapped her cheeks. "Come on, Addy, come on. Stay with me. Tell me where Jonah is."

"I don't know," Addison rasped, the words slurred.

"Yes, you do. You said he's in the house. I've checked this floor, and he's not here. Where could he be? What's on the lower level?"

Addison was fighting to stay conscious, her face deathly pale. "Why didn't you just let me die?"

Alaina seized her sister by the front of her dress. "Dammit, Addy, I need you to help me. Please. Layton might have put Jonah somewhere that he could lock from the outside."

Addison focused on her, or tried to, her eyes red and bleary. "The wine cellar. I thought he put the lock on the door to keep me out."

Hope expanded in Alaina's chest. "Where is it?"

"The basement."

"Yes, yes, but how do I get there from here?"

"Double doors into the kitchen. Door to the right of the back door—"

Alaina didn't wait for the rest as she tore for the stairs.

Chapter 38

Mitch, his head swimming, leaned against the side of his rental car. His coordination was off as he fumbled with the cell phone he'd managed to retrieve from the catch-all bin between the seats. Dammit. He didn't have time to be a klutz. Alaina didn't have time.

Chuck answered on the first ring.

"It's me," Mitch said. "He's got Alaina."

"Where are you?"

"I'm outside the gate at Keller's. Son of a bitch rookie shot me."

"What?"

"One of Potter's rookies. He's not on our side. I thought Potter's people were out."

"They were. Look, the agents I sent to intercept Alaina haven't checked in. I've been trying to get them on the phone for the past fifteen minutes. Hold on a minute."

Mitch dropped his head into his hand, willed it to stop spinning, forced back the nausea that swirled into his throat. It seemed an eternity before Chuck's voice returned. "I've got more backup coming, and I'm on my way. Mitch, how bad is it?"

"It's bad. He's going to kill her."

"No. You said you were shot. How bad is it?"

"Oh. Think I'm going to live. But the rookie needs an ambulance."

"Got it. We're on our way."

Mitch crawled back to the fallen rookie agent's side, staying conscious a constant battle. On his knees beside the wounded man, as sirens began to scream in the distance, Mitch cocked his gun and aimed it at the guy's head. "I need your security access."

At the top of the staircase, Alaina skidded to a halt.

Layton was gone. Only a thin smear of blood across the marble showed that he'd been there.

Dammit!

Praying he was looking for her and not Jonah, she raced down the steps. Her sneakers squeaked on the marble floor, and she paused for an instant to toe them off. In her stockinged feet, she ran silently to the swinging doors that led to the kitchen. Pausing outside them, she listened for movement on the other side, heard only the sound of her own harsh breathing. Slowly, she eased one door inward and peered into a kitchen that had very shiny black floors, white countertops, stainless steel appliances and an island with pots and pans hanging above it. No people.

"Looking for me?"

She whirled, off guard, unable to deflect or duck the fist he aimed at her head.

The blow hurtled her back through the doors, and she landed flat on her back, lights bursting behind her eyes. She clung to the black threads of consciousness, her jaw in flames as the coppery taste of blood gushed into her mouth.

Layton loomed over her, his fake, amiable smile gone. He kicked her viciously in the ribs, and she cried out, curling blindly around the pain.

Sinking his fingers into the front of her shirt, he jerked her to her feet. "Actually, you're not looking for me, are you?"

Her senses whirled, and she grasped his wrists for support,

unable to do much more than try to remain standing. Pain sawed through her chest, stole her breath.

"Let's see. Who could you be looking for?" he asked.

He shoved her toward the door near the back exit that Addison had told her about. She stumbled, caught herself against a kitchen stool with a gasp, fought to get strength into her legs even as the room tilted. She felt her eyes start to roll back.

Layton grasped her arm, kept her on her feet. "Don't do that." He pulled her over to the sink, where he flipped on the water and pushed her head under the cold spray.

Full consciousness returned with a vengeance.

She stomped his instep, and he let her go with a grunt.

Pivoting toward him, she landed a punch on his square jaw, ignoring the pain that sang up her arm and down into her injured ribs. When he staggered back, probably shocked more than hurt, she grabbed the first thing that was handy, a heavy pot hanging from the rack above the island, and slammed it up under his chin, the way she'd seen Mitch nail the hit man with the desk chair in the hotel room in Chicago.

Layton went down on his back with a thud, eyes closed.

Wheezing, a hand pressed to the searing pain in her side, Alaina limped to the door that Addison said led to the wine cellar. She opened it to darkness that was as black as night. Sliding her hand over the wall, she found a switch and flipped it. Light flooded the stairwell. At the bottom was a door.

She stumbled down the wooden steps, clinging to the railing as her legs threatened to buckle, gray closing in on the edges of her vision. Pure determination kept her from giving in to it. Not until she saw her son.

"Jonah?"

There was no strength in her voice, no volume.

A padlock hung from the door's latch. Defeat almost drove her to her knees, but she locked them and searched the area around the door for the key. Nothing.

Layton must have it.

Frantic, terrified, certain that Layton would regain consciousness at any second, Alaina scrambled as best she could back up the steps and over to where he lay, unmoving. Shoving her fingers into his left front pocket, she felt the cold metal of a small key. *Yes!*

Again, she made her way down the steps, clutching the safety railing, the key clasped so hard in her hand it dug into her flesh. At the door, praying under her breath, crying, she slid the key into its hole, felt the lock give.

When the door swung open, she peered inside the dark room, blinking as she strained to see into the dark. "Jonah?"

"Mom?"

Her son emerged from the night, his face white, his eyes squinting against the light.

He was unhurt. And he was rushing toward her.

She opened her arms to him.

"You really should be on your way to the hospital."

Mitch ignored Chuck, leaning on him as they made their way through the house that seemed to be swarming with agents. "Where is she? Why haven't they found her?"

"We just got here," Chuck said, his voice tense. "The place isn't even secure yet, which is why I shouldn't be wasting my damn time hauling your ass around."

The radio clipped to Chuck's collar crackled. "Living room's clear."

Another voice said urgently, "We've got a woman on the second level. Looks like an overdose." A pause. "She's breathing."

Mitch tensed, his muscles itching to run up the stairs to see if the woman was Alaina.

Chuck, as if sensing his thoughts, said, "I'll check it out. You stay down here."

"No—"

"You're going to slow me down, Mitch. Stay here, in the living room. You're in no shape to be a hero. Hear me?"

Mitch nodded, frustrated at his impotence.

Leaning weakly against the wall, he stayed put for about half a minute. Until he heard what he thought were agents moving around beyond a pair of swinging double doors.

He pushed through them, found an empty kitchen.

A smear of red on a door that appeared to lead to the basement drew his gaze. Blood.

Drawing his gun from where it nestled against his lower back, he wobbled toward the open door.

Alaina clasped Jonah against her, any pain caused by the embrace numbed by the joy of feeling him hug her back as fiercely. "God, I've missed you," she said. "I've missed you so much."

"You're not going to cry all over me now, are you?" he asked, his words muffled against her shoulder.

She heard the break in his voice, knew if he wasn't crying, he was damn close. Laughing, she buried her face against his neck, inhaled his Jonah scent, reveled in feeling his hands against her back, patting as if to soothe her. "Yeah, I'm going to cry all over you now," she said. "Deal with it."

His answering laugh was the sweetest sound she'd ever heard.

The cocking gun was the most frightening.

Thrusting Jonah behind her, she whirled to see Layton at the foot of the stairs, a pistol braced in both hands. Blood trickled down his temple and from the corner of his mouth. His eyes burned like blue flames as he smiled crookedly, showing bloodied and broken teeth.

"Remember when I said I wasn't going to make you watch me kill the kid?" he asked. "I changed my mind."

Alaina lunged at him.

Mitch, at the top of the stairs where he could do nothing but watch in horror, saw Alaina's desperate move.

Saw Keller's finger squeeze the trigger.

Saw Alaina stagger back against Jonah.

Saw Jonah fall backward with her in his arms.

Saw blood blossom like a deadly flower on the front of her white T-shirt.

"No!"

Keller whirled at Mitch's hoarse roar and brought his gun up.

Mitch, his vision blurring, pulled his shot at the last instant, fearing that if the slug went through Keller, it might hit Jonah or Alaina directly behind him.

"Drop it," Mitch said. He forced himself to focus on Keller, forced his brain away from the image of Alaina, broken and bleeding on the floor, Jonah bent over her, frantically trying to revive her. If Keller would take only one step to the side, Mitch was certain he could drop the son of a bitch without the risk of the bullet hitting Alaina or Jonah.

Keller gave a nasty, snaggle-toothed grin. "Oh, good. I was hoping I'd get to—"

With a snarl, Jonah jumped Keller from behind, hooking his arm around his father's neck. Jonah's pure, adrenaline-fueled rage jerked the bigger man off his feet and landed him on his back.

As the teen pumped his fist into Keller's face, and more

blood spurted, Mitch skidded down the stairs, first on his heels, then on his butt, his head spinning as the jarring impact of his tailbone on each step reverberated through his bruised brain.

Keller's gun. Where the hell did Keller's gun go?

Mitch heard shouts in the next room, knew federal agents would storm the kitchen, then the wine cellar, at any second. Ordinarily, he would have thrown himself into the melee, somehow gotten between Keller and the kid. But he knew he would have been worthless in a fight in the shape he was in.

So instead, he braced his weapon and aimed it at the tangle of limbs that was Jonah and his father as they rolled across the floor, grappling for the upper hand. Keller rammed an elbow up under the teen's chin, slamming his head back, but Jonah came right back at him, nailing him with a right hook.

Mitch narrowed his eyes, his focus deadly, waiting for the precise moment when Keller was in his sights and he could—

"Jonah, get down."

Mitch flinched at the sound of Alaina's voice, so calm, so steady.

Jonah dropped to his knees and covered his head.

Keller tottered, surprised at the swift move, then clamped his hands together and raised them, preparing to drive them down with deadly force on Jonah's bent head.

Mitch pulled the trigger.

Keller's body jerked. Shock froze his mouth in a bloody O before he crumpled to the floor and lay still.

In the silence that followed, Mitch stared down the length of his weapon at Alaina. She was holding Keller's gun firmly in both hands. A curlicue of smoke wafted from its barrel. They had fired at the same instant.

Her brow furrowed as her gaze roamed Mitch's face,

alarm growing in her eyes. "What happened to you?" she asked faintly, just as federal agents appeared at the top of the stairs.

When her knees buckled, Mitch lurched up off the step to catch her.

Chapter 39

Alaina woke fast, instantly aware that she was in the hospital, instantly aware that she was alone. Fear for both Jonah and Mitch—who'd been covered with blood when she'd seen him last—had her pushing herself up, wincing at the dull throb of pain in her ribs and shoulder.

She was sitting on the edge of the bed, dizzy, working at the tape that secured the needle in the back of her hand, when the door opened. She glanced up as Jonah walked in.

When he saw her, he paused in mid-step, a grin spreading across his face. "Hey, Mom."

She fought the simultaneous urge to laugh and cry at the sight of him and instead held out her uninjured arm. As he hugged her, she saw over his shoulder that he wasn't alone. Mitch stood just inside the door, his head bandaged, face colorless, dark circles rimming his eyes. The sick horror she'd felt when she'd seen him last, his head unbelievably bloody, rolled through her again.

But then he smiled, and his eyes shimmered. "Hi," he said.

She smiled back. "Hi."

Pulling back from her, Jonah asked, "Where were you going just now?"

She eased back against the pillows, exhausted but ecstatic that both her men were safe. "Nowhere."

"Don't let her fool you, kid," Mitch said. "She was coming after you."

Perching on the side of the bed, Jonah held up the nurse's call button. "Next time, use this. I'll even show you how it works." He made an exaggerated display of pushing the button.

Smiling at his antics, Alaina blinked wearily. "How long have I been here?"

"Couple hours," Jonah said with a shrug, then jerked a thumb over his shoulder at Mitch. "He's actually hurt worse than you, the doctor said. All you took was a hit in the shoulder, but he got it in the head. He wouldn't let them drug him up or anything. He's been acting like you did that time I fell out of the tree and broke my arm. All blustery and impatient."

He chattered when he was nervous, and she clasped his hand, feeling the tremor in his fingers before he fell silent and gripped back.

A nurse pushed through the door. "Ah, she's awake."

"We caught her trying to escape," Jonah said.

The nurse smiled at the teenager, charmed, then cast a critical glance at Mitch. "Perhaps it's time for you to sit down, Mr. Kane."

Mitch sank onto the chair in the corner of the room. "Yes, I think it is."

The nurse turned her attention to Alaina. "And you—"

"I'm not going anywhere," Alaina said. "I found what I was looking for."

Epilogue

"Hey, Al," Rachel said. "Where's your hunk? I was hoping to cop a feel when he hugs me hello."

Grinning at her best friend, Alaina set a stack of plates and napkins on the dining room table as Rachel plunked a pile of DVDs from the video store next to it.

"He and Jonah are picking up the food," Alaina said. "What movies did you get?"

"You asked for Arnold movies, and you got them. *Kindergarten Cop*, *Terminator* one and two, and my personal favorite, *True Lies*."

Alaina's grin broadened before she turned to go into the kitchen. "Interesting."

Rachel followed close behind. "What?"

"Mitch has a theory that you can tell a lot about a person based on their favorite Arnold movie," Alaina said as she lined up glasses on the counter and dropped ice cubes into them. "What do you want to drink?"

"Iced tea. I'll get it." When Rachel returned from the fridge with the tea pitcher, she gave her friend a dubious look. "What could *True Lies* possibly say about me?"

"It's just funny that you'd gravitate toward a movie about people who aren't who they appear to be."

Rachel laughed as she filled the glasses with tea. "Right. I like that guy." Picking one up, she sipped, her gaze on Alaina's face, assessing. "Is it okay if I ask how you're doing since . . . everything?"

Alaina smiled as she gathered silverware. "You can ask anytime. And I'm doing just fine," she said. In the dining room, she started to set the table as Rachel distributed the glasses of tea then began to fold napkins for her.

It had been three months since Mitch had shot Layton—at least he insisted that his was the bullet that had killed the man, though Alaina wondered whether he was simply sparing her. Nightmares still haunted her in which Layton pointed a gun at Jonah and Mitch, and she was helpless to get to them in time. But she and Jonah were in counseling, together and separately, and she was pleased with how that was going.

"Jonah seems to have weathered the storm, considering," Rachel said, handing over the last folded napkin.

Alaina agreed. Of the two of them, Jonah was bouncing back the fastest, though she worried about post-traumatic stress in the future. For now, he seemed to relish the idea of his mother taking on a bad guy and kicking butt. It helped tremendously that he and Mitch had become fast buddies. Jonah had even bonded with Mitch's seven-year-old son, Tyler, who had begun spending an occasional weekend with them at Mitch's, where she and Jonah had been living the past three months. Jonah had hinted several times already that having a second little brother or sister around would be okay with him.

The idea of having a child with Mitch made her stomach flutter. But they hadn't discussed where their relationship was going. There was no question that she loved him. Distance from the intensity of their first days together had done nothing to dull her feelings for him. If anything, they had sharpened, because now there were no distractions and no reasons for her to feel the need to distance herself. The danger, the running, the fear . . . all were gone. Every day, she felt lighter, almost giddy with how suddenly uncomplicated everything seemed.

There were still complications, of course. It would probably take years to sort out the PCware issues, but she was leaving it to the lawyers and accountants her father had trusted over the years. Addison certainly wasn't in any shape to help figure it out, but at least she was improving. She was scheduled to be released in a few days from the private clinic she had checked herself into after spending a week in the hospital. Alaina had visited her often, knowing that her sister desperately needed a support network. While things were tense between them and Alaina didn't see them ever becoming the best of friends, she was satisfied with the progress they were making.

"Does he know?" Rachel asked.

Alaina focused on her friend. "I'm sorry?"

"Does Jonah know what his father did to you?"

Alaina shook her head. "Not yet. I'll tell him eventually, when he's older. But for now he needs time to adjust to other things."

"Such as the man in your life," Rachel said with a grin. "Have I mentioned how much I like that guy?"

Alaina laughed. "I think you mentioned it earlier."

"Well, I can't say it enough." Rachel checked her watch. "Where are they with the food, anyway? I'm starving."

As if on cue, the front door opened, and Jonah bounded in, laden with sacks of Thai food that he dropped onto the table before launching himself at Rachel. "Hey, Aunt Ray."

Rachel laughed, grabbing on to him when he picked her up in a bear hug and spun her around. "Stop! You know I'm afraid of heights."

He set her down. "I'm not that much taller. Geez."

She ruffled his hair. "Are you kidding? What are you? Seven-five? Seven-six?"

Rolling his eyes, he plopped down on a chair, reached for a bag and tore it open. "Five-eight and counting. We have to start with the spring rolls."

"Hey, I thought your buddy Lucas was going to be here tonight," Rachel said.

Jonah shrugged. "We're doing a movie later." He lifted a spring roll out of the box. "This one's for Mom."

Alaina left them bantering and met Mitch as he came through the door Jonah had left hanging open. As usual, seeing him took her breath away. He looked especially good tonight in jeans shorts and a white T-shirt that hugged his muscles. His dark chocolate eyes told her he thought she looked pretty damn good, too, as he caught her against him and planted a warm kiss on her mouth.

"Hi, you," he said. "Miss me?"

"You were gone only twenty minutes, but yeah, I missed you." Beneath the palm she rested on his chest, she felt his heart beating fast and hard.

He kissed her again, then set her away from him. "Let's eat," he said, and made a beeline for the table. "Hey, Ray," he said.

Rachel beamed at him in absolute adoration. "Hey, yourself."

Bemused by Mitch's abruptness, thinking he must really be hungry, Alaina followed him and sat in the chair he pulled out for her.

Jonah had already passed around spring rolls and was munching on his. Alaina thought he seemed unusually intent on it and exchanged a questioning glance with Rachel, who shrugged and went to work on dousing hers with sweet and sour sauce.

"These are so good," Rachel said, licking sauce from her finger. "Where's this place again?"

Alaina looked at Mitch, expecting he would answer, but his attention was focused on the spring roll she had halfway to her mouth. A glance at Jonah confirmed that he was, too. Her pulse tripped, then began to race, and suddenly she knew what they were up to. Humoring them, playing it cool, she bit into the crunchy Thai appetizer.

"This is the best spring roll I've ever had," she said, rolling her eyes in mock ecstasy.

Rachel arched an amused brow. "Geez, Al, you want us to leave the room so you can be alone with it?"

Alaina feigned a gasp, though she wasn't faking the tremor in her fingers when she plucked the glittering diamond out of what was left of the spring roll. "What's this?"

Rachel sat back on a laugh. "I'll be damned."

Alaina met Mitch's gaze, and smiled as emotion swelled in her chest.

Reaching across the table, he slid his hand over hers. "So, will you?" he asked.

She felt the dampness of his palm, and her heart went out to him. The poor guy was nervous. She decided to put him out of his misery quickly. Not that there was any question. "Yes. I will."

He turned his hand, gripped her fingers hard, and she saw his eyes shimmer.

"Excellent," Jonah said, beaming.

"Ditto," Rachel said, tears in her eyes.

"It was my idea to put the ring in your spring roll," Jonah said.

Alaina grinned. "You two plotted together." They were her men, she thought. Her beautiful, amazing men.

Jonah nodded. "He wanted to do something mushy and

romantic, but I told him you weren't into crap like that."

Alaina's laugh faded when Mitch tugged her out of her chair and onto his lap. Taking the ring from her, he wiped it clean on his napkin, then slid it onto her finger, where it shot off sparks of color. "We'll do mushy and romantic later," he said, and kissed her.

Alaina closed her eyes, sinking easily into his embrace, finding there, in his arms, everything she'd ever wanted.

About the Author

Joyce Lamb, born and raised in Rockford, Illinois, is an editor at *USA Today* in suburban Washington, D.C. *Found Wanting* is her third novel. *Booklist* called her first, *Relative Strangers*, "a rollicking ride full of blazing passion, nonstop suspense and heart-pounding action," which is very much like Joyce's real life. For her second novel, *Caught in the Act* (a RITA Award Finalist), which *Booklist* called "riveting," Joyce drew extensively from her experience as a journalist . . . except for the parts about murder and mayhem . . . well, except for the parts about murder. Joyce is busily working on her next novel. For more information about her books or to send her an E-mail, visit www.joycewrites.com.